I0772359

the DEMON CROWN

USA TODAY BESTSELLING AUTHOR

EMMA HAMM

ALSO BY EMMA HAMM

The Otherworld
Heart of the Fae
Veins of Magic
The Faceless Woman
The Raven's Ballad
Bride of the Sea
Curse of the Troll

Of Goblin Kings
Of Goblins and Gold
Of Shadows and Elves
Of Pixies and Spells
Of Werewolves and Curses
Of Fairytales and Magic

Dragon of Umbra
Fire Heart
Bright Heart
Brave Heart
Torn Heart
Taloned Heart

and many more...

For everyone who's had a tough year, multiple years, lifetime, I hope you can find a little escape between these pages.

emma hamm

PRIDE
GREED
LUST
GLUTTONY

ENVY
SLOTH
WRATH

Chapter 1

A sledgehammer to the face wasn't how Greed expected to be welcomed back to his kingdom.

But it had certainly done the job his attackers had wanted.

His thoughts filtered back in as he tried to think past the pounding in his skull. It was hard to take down one of the demon kings. Apparently a sledgehammer would do it. He hadn't expected that.

In any other circumstance, he might have allowed himself to feel surprised. Proud, even. His people were warriors first and foremost. They took what they wanted, and they let nothing stop them. Someone had been brave enough to attack him. It wasn't the first time, but it was one of the few where he'd felt pain.

He'd like to meet the person who'd done it. Maybe clap them

on the back and then crack their nose with his forehead. A little blood never hurt anyone, and he deserved a little retribution.

Grinding his teeth so he didn't moan, he rolled over onto his side and set his palm down on the earth. No, not earth. Metal. Bad sign. He should have been flat on his back in the dirt, waking up moments after the blinding pain that he remembered. Not somewhere else entirely.

"Ach," he muttered, groaning as he opened his eyes. Light flickered beyond where he could see and it burned behind his gaze, a headache suddenly blooming at the back of his skull.

He frowned, brows drawn down so tightly they almost hurt as he forced himself upright. His head throbbed. Worse than he'd thought it would. And he tenderly touched the knot on the back of his head while he looked around for any clues as to where he was.

What he found made his blood turn ice cold.

He was in a cage. A metal cage crudely made of iron and what looked like steel. The bars were all uneven distances apart, as though someone hadn't had enough time to throw this together.

There was a bump on his skull that was the size of a chicken egg, and already he felt rage simmering underneath his skin. Greed could not lose it here. He would not lose control when his people were doing what he'd taught them to do.

Looking down at his body, he tried to assess the damage but was mostly surprised to see there wasn't really much damage to see. He wasn't wearing a shirt anymore. All his rings were gone, the necklaces he'd worn, not a scrap of wealth left behind. His pants were still on him, thank goodness, but even they looked dirty. Like he'd been dragged through the mud.

How had he gotten here?

Nerves churned in his belly as he looked around. They were in a cave, it appeared. Nowhere near where they had first attacked him, and unnervingly, his guards were not with him either. Greed had trained his people himself. They were impressive fighters who would stop at nothing to keep him safe, and yet, they were nowhere to be found.

The cave itself was dirty and old, not his attacker's home base if he had to guess. And his new enemies were all sitting around a fire that burned through his eyes and set fire to the headache that was hard to think around.

They must have heard him sit up. Greed had groaned the moment he'd been upright, but none of them moved. It gave him a moment to look them over.

Dirty.

Musty.

Dirt streaked on their clothing and through their hair. But they were large, at the very least. Tall and broad and muscular. He might have hired them in his own castle if they had approached him for a job.

Unfortunately, they'd tried to kill him, and now he had to kill them.

The biggest of them looked up and yellow eyes met his glare. Yellow, just like Greed's. Unusual for a human. The man stood up, his height making him seem even more massive than the wide set of his shoulders and broad chest. A scraggly beard covered his face, probably to make him more unrecognizable. His belly stuck out, but not only with weight. There was a natural power to this man, and Greed could see why others would follow him.

He wore leather armor over his chest, molded into the shape of pectorals and abs that he certainly didn't have. And then the man leaned down, flashing a grin full of gold teeth through the largest gap in the bars.

"Look at you," he said, his voice low and guttural. "The legendary

Greed, all locked up. Right where we want you."

Greed would not bare his teeth at this criminal like an animal. He was more than that. He was a demon king, and he'd taken this kingdom for his own and held it for almost a thousand years now. Just like his brothers, he could be the politician when the situation called for it.

So he reclined back on his palm and tilted his head to the side, even though it made the world spin. "I'm glad you know who I am. Now, who are you?"

The man laughed. His beard shook with mirth, although it moved slightly too much, like there was something living in the messy tangles. "Wouldn't you like to know?"

What was this? Some kind of kidnapping attempt?

Greed could bend these bars in half if he wanted to. He could destroy the entire cage that they'd built him and then rip out their hearts with his bare hand! They had seen him do this. Everyone in the kingdom knew the rumors or knew someone who had died, impaled on Greed's claws. Were they so willing to risk their lives?

Apparently they were. Because they all turned to look at him now, their eyes alight with something fierce and dark.

Curious. So curious.

Greed wanted to see where this went. He wanted to know their deepest desire, because they wouldn't be in his kingdom of thieves if they were good or righteous. If they wanted something from him, they would have to take it. And he wouldn't make it easy on them.

A few of the others stood from the fire, all their attention focused on him and their leader. The man tilted his head back and laughed. The sound boomed through the cave like thunder.

And Greed might have focused on him if not for a small shadow slipping across the rocks behind them all. He blinked, thinking perhaps the sledgehammer had done more damage than he'd thought, but the shadow kept moving no matter how many times he fluttered his lashes.

A little thief, he realized. A creature who had seen the opportune moment to slip into these villains' camp. Unaware, they all continued to watch him and their leader without ever noticing the movement at their backs.

The thief was using his capture to their advantage.

He almost felt dirty knowing that. He was a decoy in whatever this person's plan was. They slid over the rocks, as silent as Greed himself might have been. But then the light illuminated the padding around their shoes and he realized this had likely been the plan for some time. This thief hadn't wandered across this camp. They knew exactly where these people were going to be and how to steal from them without getting caught.

"You are going to feel pain," the man in front of him snarled. "For all that you have done. And then you are going to tell us exactly where the Beastmaster's Horn is."

That got his attention.

Greed snorted and looked their leader in the eyes again. The man really should notice that Greed hadn't been paying attention until this moment, but he obviously didn't. "Absolutely not."

"You will tell us after the pain I cause you."

Arching a brow, he replied, "That would require more pain than you are capable of."

The Beastmaster's Horn was legendary. It had taken Greed almost three hundred years to track it down. The stories about it claimed that it could control even magical creatures. It summoned them, the sound wriggling through their minds until they were completely under the control of the summoner.

It was not an artifact that needed to be in the hands of a warlord idiot who thought he could trap a demon for long. Still, it was an interesting request and Greed was curious to see how much pain the man thought he could cause.

Greed had spent his entire life fighting. He'd been in this form for a thousand years, and the first memory he had was pain. When he and his brothers had taken on their mortal forms, turning spirit into flesh, he'd been the first to fight off those who tried to stop them.

The taste of metal had never quite left his mouth since.

The shadow moved again. It snuck closer to the fire as the remaining few dirty scoundrels stood up and approached his cage with the others.

He almost growled at them to move. He couldn't see behind them and watch what was happening with the little thief. Clearly, they were all idiots who were about to lose something important and he wanted to watch.

Then the firelight cast its glow upon golden hair that slipped out from underneath a hood, and all the breath in his lungs caught. Bright blue eyes flicked up, staring at him with wide shock from across the fire. Her face was covered with a strip of dark green fabric and her body was encased in matching leather, hugging her perfect, curvy form.

By all the seven kingdoms, he'd found a goddess in a cave. Maybe he was already dead.

She moved lithe and cat-like over one of the stones the bandits had sat upon. And then, to his surprise, she sat down and pulled one of their bags in front of her. Dismissing him like he was nothing interesting at all.

Even if he hadn't been Greed himself, he still was a man in a cage. And she wasn't even going to look at him for more than a brief flick of her eyes?

He should tell them she was there.

But the moment he had the thought, she looked at him again. A pale face with glowing chips of sapphire that widened for a moment and then narrowed as if threatening him. As if saying that she would kill him herself if he let them know she was here.

And so his attention returned to the leader of these bandits, and for the first time in his life, Greed distracted someone so another person could steal.

"I don't know why you're laughing," Greed snarled. "I'm not joking."

"Neither am I, Greed." He held out a hand and one of his cronies placed a knife with a silver hilt on his palm. "Do you know what this is?"

"No." He didn't have to try to sound bored. He was.

"This blade is known as Bonescraper." The man held it over his head and drew it out of the scabbard. The light gleamed on the faint yellow edge. "I think you know it well."

Damn it.

How the hell had a bandit gotten his hands on the Bonescraper? That blade had been lost to the desert centuries ago, for the last time it had carved its way through Greed's back. The damned knife deserved to be locked up in his castle, where no one would ever put their hands on it again.

Bonescraper. These bandits were lucky, and they didn't even know how lucky they were.

Wincing, he leaned to the side to get a glimpse of the beautiful woman rifling through their bags. She had three of them around her knees now. Elbow deep in the third, she noticed him looking at her again.

Rolling her eyes, she widened them forcefully and then nodded at the bandits. As if telling him to keep his attention on the problem at hand.

But something in him said that she was the problem here. He knew how to handle bandits, and Bonescraper wouldn't kill him. It would just hurt like a bitch until he lost all control and likely tore himself out of this cage. The wave of blood afterward would be so wondrous to see.

His eyes flicked to the blade before he bared his teeth in what he hoped resembled a smile. "That blade is familiar to me, yes."

"Then you know it will make you scream."

He knew nothing of the sort. Leaning back on his hand one last time, he noticed the little thief had tugged out a roll of parchment from one of the bags and stuffed it into her pants.

If it was that important, she shouldn't shove it against skin and fabric. The damned woman would ruin whatever it was that she was risking her life for. And she was risking her life.

These men were ready to kill him. What did she think they'd do to her?

Greed had never once wondered about the repercussions of another person's wellbeing. Clearly he had been affected by his time with Lust and that rather pretty sorceress his brother had captured. And he'd spent far too much time watching them go all moon-eyed for each other before he'd left.

He didn't care if she got caught. He didn't care if she stole that scroll that she'd risked her life for. None of it mattered to him because… because…

One of the bandits was turning around. He was going to see that woman, sitting at their fire like she belonged there, and he would have to show them how powerful he really was because he damn well wasn't going to let her die.

Greed let out a snarl of rage that had everyone in the cave freezing. All the bandits watched him with wary eyes, but the woman bolted upright, immediately looking for her exit. Good girl. She knew how to run when she had to, and that's all that mattered.

He launched himself at the bars, ensuring all the bandits saw him move. They would fear him. They would soon writhe underneath his claws while they begged for mercy.

The moment his hands touched the metal, his palms burned. He released the bars, hissing in anger and backing away from them. Not a metal he was used to, apparently.

"Did you think we haven't spent time learning about you? Hm?" The bandit leader bent, tilting his head to the side and brandishing the blade. "We've been hunting you for a very long time, Greed. We will not waste all that effort on a single night where I just cut you up a little and then give you a chance to escape. You're going to tell us everything you know, and I'm going to break you by the end of it."

Unease bubbled in his stomach. "Who exactly are you?"

The man raised his arms from his sides, stretching them out wide. "We're the Horde."

"That doesn't answer my question."

"No, I suppose it doesn't. But it's the only answer you're going to get."

One bandit tossed something into his cage. Smoke erupted between his feet and Greed wondered just how much trouble he was actually in. His guards didn't know where he was. No one would come for him any time soon. The bars were untouchable, and the people here wanted him dead.

The mist hit his nose and rage went wild through his body. He hadn't been in his battle form for centuries, and yet he could feel it writhing underneath his skin. Claws piercing through his nails, teeth lengthening into fangs while his tail whipped wildly behind him. He'd never lost control. Never...

His eyes sought the little thief. She'd used the distraction to scramble back on top of the rocks at the mouth of the cave, slipping into the shadows. All three bags were placed exactly where they had been before, not a single thread out of place.

As a roar built in his chest, he had a single moment of pride. She'd stolen it. She'd succumbed to her own greed, and that was... good.

The roar ripped out of his chest and Greed lost himself in the anger, rage, and torture that would soon come.

Chapter 2

Varya wasn't insane, she just had very little self preservation. That was precisely why she'd taken this job, stealing from the fucking Horde, and getting a map that would lead them to more of the magical artifacts hidden throughout the sands in this kingdom. The map was important. She would use it for the betterment of others, rather than what the Horde was likely planning. It wasn't like she was trying to find some mystical blade or an orb that could see the future. Yet.

She'd known it would be difficult. The Horde was notoriously hard to find unless they were attacking some poor settlement, and it had taken her three months following in their tracks before they made a big mistake.

They settled here for the night. A cave with a wide open mouth where anyone could see their campfire flickering in the distance.

The Horde was crazy. They didn't recruit anyone who had a lick of sense to them, and they'd kill a child if one stood in their way. But she hadn't realized just how insane they really were.

Until she walked into the cave and saw who was in that cage.

Greed himself. The demon king who ruled their kingdom with idiocy and lies, sitting in the middle of a makeshift cage with his eyes seeing everything. Seeing her.

And then she'd been stuck locking eyes with the most dangerous man who ruled their kingdom, and hiding behind the most dangerous men who ruled its underbelly.

She had a death wish. Probably. Everyone knew Varya didn't take care of herself at all. She would throw her body into the most insane situations because she didn't care if she lived or died. Taking care of others? She was good at that. Taking care of herself?

Less so.

Still, she'd completed her mission. Somehow she had shoved that scroll deep between her thighs so it definitely wouldn't move and then snuck to the exit of the cave. She'd tilted her head back, taken a deep breath of the chilly desert air, and then...

He screamed.

Greed roared like a lion, and her mind flickered back to those gold coin eyes staring at her. He'd definitely distracted the wall of man meat that would have torn her head off her shoulders if they saw her. And then he let her steal the scroll. He'd let her go.

Why?

That fit nothing she knew about him. And that roar? She knew the sound of pain when she heard it.

Swallowing hard, Varya told herself to keep moving. This scroll would save so many people. There were artifacts out there that could grow food, create an oasis out of nothing, draw water out of the desert until all her people could drink clean, fresh water whenever they wanted. All she had to do was run.

But her feet turned back toward the cave, and she could hear them talking. The Horde taunted the demon king.

"This is the great Greed? When we're done with you, you'll be little more than an animal."

Maybe she would have left it at that if she didn't hear Greed reply, "I still don't know who any of you are. At least I'll be remembered."

And her heart twisted in her chest. Because he didn't know who they were. He didn't know that the Horde had been plaguing his kingdom for centuries now. They lived in the sands. They moved throughout the kingdom without fear of anyone harming them. They were the problem. And he was meant to be the solution.

She turned her gaze up to the stars and glared at them as though the gods themselves were playing a trick on her. They knew she wouldn't leave someone in pain or torment. They knew she couldn't take another step when someone needed her help.

Even if that meant risking her own neck. Again.

Swearing under her breath, she spun on her heel and ducked into the shadows of the stones one more time. The Horde was still invested in their torture. They traded a knife between hands, each one reaching through the bars of the cave with a sharp jab at Greed's sides.

And he didn't look like himself. She'd gotten a good look sitting at the fire, risking everything to stay quiet. He was a handsome man with sharp features and a close-cropped beard. His red hair billowed around his head like flames, unruly and clearly meant to be tied back so the shaved sides were visible. But his long, lean body was like a lion.

The muscles bunched underneath him, as though tensing even when he was sitting.

Right now, his eyes were entirely gold. No whites, no black, just gold. His bared fangs and claws slashed at anyone who tried to touch him. That tail whipped behind him until one of the Horde grabbed it and yanked hard.

She winced at the sound of a crack and the answering scream of an enraged demon who was well and truly trapped.

Think, Varya, she told herself. Think.

Her eyes wildly scanned the cave, and there they were. The jugs that the Horde were so well known for, because their whiskey would burn through your stomach in a second.

And they always drank after they won.

Biting her lip, she looked back to the cage and knew she had very little time. They were enjoying harassing their new pet, but they would not kill him tonight. Which meant soon they would drink.

She tried to remember which bag she'd seen the dust in. She had no idea what it was, but it had no smell and she knew the Horde well enough to assume the pale lavender powder was a drug. Enough of any drug would make people sleep.

If they died, ah well. It wasn't her fault. They didn't have to drink.

She dove for the bag, ripped it open, and tugged the powder out. Funneling it into the jugs as quickly as possible, she gave each of them a tiny shake for good measure. At least the Horde was making so much noise that they weren't likely to hear the swish of liquid.

And then she sank back into the shadows, like the good thief she was.

Varya stayed there for what felt like hours. They toyed with Greed like cats with a mouse, circling him, stabbing, splashing blood on the walls. And the sound the demon king made... She'd never forget the horrible noise as they sliced and diced to their hearts' content. He healed too quickly for them to stop their play any time soon, even though she knew he had to be weak from the loss of blood.

She watched the first one go back to the alcohol and her heartbeat kicked up a notch. If only one of them drank, then that would be a problem. One would pass out, the others would realize the alcohol was spiked, and...

Fuck.

She skittered down from her place on the stones and counted to ten. The Horde member near her drank deeply, closing his eyes as he swallowed mouthfuls, and she rolled another one of the jugs toward the others. Gently, but hard enough to bump against one of their ankles.

The man glanced back suspiciously, and she froze, hoping that she was still hidden enough behind the rock.

"Garm, you fool!" another shouted, then laughed and picked up the jug she'd rolled. "You'll waste it all on yourself!"

If she wasn't worried about being caught, Varya would have sighed in relief. She pressed the back of her head to the rock and counted again, to twenty this time, just to be sure. Then she bolted for her shadows between the rock crevices and watched her plan unfold. The Horde members all seemed to realize that they hadn't been drinking. They tucked into the jugs with more gusto than she'd expected, draining them quickly, like it was a race to see who finished first.

And then it really was.

They all started dropping to the ground, one after the other. The Horde leader was the last of them to remain standing, but she'd known he would be. The man had survived more poisoning attempts than any other person alive. But even he eventually slumped against a rock, the jug falling from his hand and thudding hard in the sand.

Good? Good. She thought they were all passed out by now.

Varya took a few light steps into the fire light, waiting for one of them to groan or make a noise. None of them did, though.

"Keys," she muttered. "Which one of you bastards has keys?"

Because surely they hadn't welded the demon king into that cage. They weren't going to carry him out of here. They'd all be far too close to his claws.

She didn't even look at the demon king as she rummaged through the Horde members' pockets. As long as it wasn't the big one, she didn't care who had the keys.

Thankfully, she found them rather quickly in the fourth bandit's pants. Making a face at the smell of the man, she darted over to the cage and started running her hands over the bars. One of them had to be the opening, but damn it, this was so crudely made. She was impressed they'd even installed a keyhole.

"There," she muttered before unlocking the door and yanking it open. The damn thing creaked like it wanted her to be caught. She flinched, glancing over her shoulder at the piles of bodies before counting to twenty again. No one moved.

Good enough.

She stepped into the cage with a deep, brave breath, and then turned her gaze back to Greed.

He laid out on the floor like an ancient god, as though he'd been waiting for her. Blood streaked all over his body, long slices decorating his skin where apparently his healing capabilities had failed. His tail was kinked in three places, making it look more like a lightning bolt than a smooth line. There were bruises all over him, but his gold eyes still flashed when he saw her looking.

Did he... Flex? He lifted his arm over his head and she swore his bicep twitched like he was flexing.

How was she supposed to focus when all that golden skin was bared before her? He still wore pants, of course, but they weren't exactly made to hide anything. She could see every twitch and flex of his muscle.

"The thief in the night," he said, his voice far too loud. "You've finally come for me."

"Shh," she muttered, kneeling on her knees at his side to look him over. "I need you to move."

He did, but not to get up. Instead, he reached out and wrapped a strand of her hair around his finger. "Gold," he muttered. "You are so golden. Why can I not see your face?"

Varya slapped his hand away. "Get up."

"What did you steal, my thief?"

"I'll tell you later." She pressed her lips into a thin line, then slapped his hand away again when he tried to touch her mask. "Get up."

"What if I wish to bask in your beauty?"

"Then I will tell you to shut up and then get up. They're not going to stay like that forever." Varya pointed at the Horde, as if that would explain why she was rushing. And it should.

Except he sat up on his elbow, looked them over, and then returned a wide-eyed gaze to hers. "Did you kill them?"

Why did he sound so impressed by that? "No," she snarled, then wedged her shoulder underneath his at the opportunity. If she had to haul him to his feet, then so be it. "I did not kill them. They are asleep. And if you keep insisting on booming like that, then they will wake up and we will both die."

He tried to lie down again, nearly dragging her with him. "The cage is open. I will kill them all when they are awake enough to see me coming."

Varya grunted and pulled him upright again. He looked surprised, perhaps at her strength, before she wrapped her hands around his wrists and tugged even harder. "I will pull your arms out of their sockets. Get up."

His gaze narrowed on her, but at least he started moving. He stood and for a second, she thought he would be all right. But then he listed to the side, and she had to shove herself back underneath his arm.

At least he looked frustrated about how weak he was. Frowning, he stared down at his flexing hand and watched it for a little too long.

"We have to go," she hissed.

"Yes, little thief, we do." He was still staring at that clawed hand, though.

Why? Why was he taking... so...

Ah.

His claws slid back into his hands as though he'd retracted them. That wasn't entirely right, she didn't think, because there were still nails on his hands that now looked very human. But...

No, she would not look too much into it. She was getting him out of here, dropping him off where he needed to go, and that was it. Good deed done. Her soul saved from all the stealing and lying and general thievery.

"Come on," she grunted, shouldering far more of his weight than she wanted as they moved through the cave.

They had to pause a few times so Greed could step over the bodies lying about. She swore she saw a flash of gold in his eyes as he looked down at the Horde leader, and she really thought he was going to ruin everything by kicking the man.

Not that she wouldn't like to give a good swift kick to his ribs herself, but a woman had to know when to pick her battles. And right now? The battle was getting outside and running like a demon king was on her heels.

Too bad she was holding the demon king upright. Otherwise, that thought might have had a little more punch to it.

They passed by the last Horde member, the one who still held that horrible knife in his hands, and she felt a shudder go through Greed. He straightened and then pulled away from her.

Before she could stop him, he'd snapped the man's neck. So easily. Just a quick flick of his wrists and a dead man laid on the floor with his head at a wrong angle.

She flinched. Varya was embarrassed to admit it. She'd seen countless dead bodies in her time, had even killed people to stay alive. But… she'd never killed a sleeping man.

Greed picked up the blood stained blade. His own blood dripped from the metal, and he wiped it on his pant leg before sticking the naked blade into the belt loop at his waist.

"What did you do that for?" she hissed, grabbing onto him when he almost fell on top of the dead body.

"I wanted to leave a message."

"What does that say?" She was dead. If the Horde knew she'd been here, she was so dead.

"That I survived," he grumbled, then hooked his arm over her shoulders again. "And that I won't forget."

They stumbled out onto the sands together and she dragged him up over the nearest dune before they both slid down the other side on their butts. Varya helped him stand, made sure he was stable, and then wiped her hands off on her hips.

"All right," she said, trying to catch her breath. "You're welcome."

"Ah, yes. Thank you, beautiful thief. When we return to my castle, you will be rewarded." He nodded, his eyes going slightly cross-eyed and unfocused, before he found her again. "Whatever you wish, I will let you take."

"I'm not bringing you anywhere. I saved your ass. Now you're on your own." And that was that. She wouldn't help him any further. He was Greed! The man could probably whistle and have a thousand guards descend across the sands. "Good luck."

"You're... what?"

She didn't stop to look at the disappointment or whatever else was on his face. She turned and started off. The journey ahead of her was long, tiresome, and if she didn't get started, she'd be walking in the heat of the day and that was never a good idea. Never.

But the sun was already coming up on the horizon, the hazy waves of heat wriggling in the distance, and she knew traveling was a terrible idea.

She needed shelter. She needed... A cave.

Damn it.

Grinding her teeth, she turned to look back at Greed who was still standing in the same spot. His crinkly tail barely waved behind him, his hands limp at his sides as he stared at her as though he couldn't understand what she was doing. Or why she was doing it.

Stomping back to him, she shoved her finger in his face. "You're the king of this kingdom, right? So you better damn well know where there is a hidden oasis or something similar where we can wait out the day. Yes?"

He blinked at her, focusing far too much on her finger and going cross-eyed again. "Yes."

"Are you just saying that?"

"No. I know everywhere in this kingdom."

"And you know where we are now?" For some reason, she highly doubted that he did.

A snarl ripped out of his chest and he looked like an actual demon king for a moment. "I know where we are, thief. And I can get us somewhere safe."

"Good," she hissed. "I didn't save your sorry ass for nothing, then."

He turned and stomped away from her, giving her a rather impressive view of his tail. There was a small hole in the back of his pants for it, and she wondered if all his pants were like that.

Why was she thinking about his tail? She had a map in her pants, a three week walk ahead of her, and the demon king was now her reluctant companion!

Varya glanced up at the clear sky and glared at the gods. They were laughing at her predicament, she just knew it.

"I don't find this funny," she hissed at them before stomping after the demon, who looked like he was about to fall over.

Chapter 3

He didn't feel so good.

Greed hated to admit when he felt weak, but right now? Bonescraper had done service to its name. That blade cut through not just flesh and sinew, but magic as well. It had taken all his power away, leaving him feeling limp and shaky.

He couldn't remember the last time he'd felt so wobbly. Even his first memories in this body were of power, strength, and certainty with every step. Now the sands tugged at his feet, making him slip this way and that, and it frightened him.

How was he so weak? Why couldn't he stand on his own, and instead, felt certain one wrong step would send him tumbling down the nearest dune?

A small body tucked itself under his arm, and the surprisingly strong thief grunted as he leaned his weight against her. It was her duty, of course, to take care of her king. An honor, if he was being honest. No one else was given the opportunity to be this close to him. She should be thankful.

Her expression made him wonder if she was also injured. She looked rather ill.

He hadn't been lying when he said he knew a cave close by, though. It was an old one. Likely the stuff of legends to her and her people, and it was a shame to reveal its location to an average thief.

Greed told himself that she'd proven her value and worth in stealing from the people who had captured him. That was why it was acceptable for him to tell her, and share this scared place.

But he also knew that without her, he would fall flat on his face in a spectacularly terrible fashion.

Leaning on her a little more, he let her carry most of his body weight toward the cave system that he'd seen hundreds of years ago. Except, once they reached the place, he was certain that the sand had swallowed it up.

"Fuck," he muttered before taking his arm off her shoulders and falling onto his knees. "This needs to..."

She groaned. The sun was already up much higher on the horizon than he'd wanted it to be, and they were both sweating. Dark splotches coated the green leather armor she wore, and he hadn't even realized that leather could stain like that. For the first time, the little thief removed the mask from her face and sucked in a gasp of air.

And by all the seven kingdoms, she was more beautiful than he'd imagined.

Greed had imagined a lot, letting his mind play over the possibilities of her looks as she carried him over the sands. He'd seen the coiled tangle of her blonde hair, like strands of gold escaping from her hood.

He'd thought maybe she would be stoic and hard, a lean thief who had spent most of her years stealing to keep herself alive. Or perhaps she'd startle him and be much younger than he thought. The strength she had in carrying him this far suggested that she might be younger.

He hadn't expected an angel to stand before him. Smooth, pale skin, her cheeks flushed red from exertion and heat. Pretty pink, plush lips and sharp brows that were already drawn down in anger. Her golden waves were weighed nearly straight with sweat, just brushing past her collarbones, but she was the prettiest thing he'd ever seen.

He had to have her.

The greed in him, that emotion that he'd lived his entire life with, flared harder than it ever had before. He knew this feeling. It was the same one that he always got when he saw an object that no one else had. Something unique. Something specific that no other person would touch again. He had to take it. He needed it to be his, and that fierce flame roared through him the moment he saw her face.

She cut him a scathing glance. "What?"

He shook his head, trying to clear what he was certain was a dumbfounded expression off of his face. "We need to dig."

"We need to what?"

He gestured at the sand, the world suddenly spinning. "The caves are down there."

She looked at the ground, clearly not believing him one bit. And when was the last time someone hadn't believed him? "Are you sure?"

"Yes, I'm sure."

"How long has it been since you've last been inside?"

"A while," he grumbled. Honestly, he didn't know. Greed hadn't been on this side of his kingdom in the better part of a hundred years, and he couldn't remember if he'd visited these caves the last time or the time before that.

Of course, they didn't have much time. He felt the rumblings underneath their feet long before he sensed their presence. The Horde had woken from their slumber, likely much quicker than this little thief had anticipated.

"We need to hurry," he added, then glanced over his shoulder at the hazy horizon. The sun was already well above their heads. Sweat turned into a river between his shoulder blades and he wasn't exaggerating how difficult it had become to stand. "Your friends are awake."

"Friends," she snorted. "What friends do I have that you're aware of?"

"The ones you stole from." He hooked his thumb over his shoulder as he met her gaze. "They're coming."

All the blood drained from her features, leaving her bone pale. He hadn't expected that. Most people had that expression when they looked at him, not someone else.

He was almost insulted.

"Fuck," she hissed before dropping to her knees and scooping the sands with more vigor than he'd thought she would still have after trudging all this way. "Are you helping or not?"

"Not." He scanned the horizon before putting his hands on his hips and glaring at her. "You're not afraid of me, are you?"

"You wouldn't be either if you could see yourself right now, big guy." She huffed out a breath and turned in the opposite direction. Crouched over the sands, using both her hands to scoop it all between her legs, she rather looked like a dog.

That shouldn't be as attractive as it was.

"But you're afraid of them?"

"I absolutely am."

"Why?" He crouched, wincing as the wounds all along his back and sides stretched, splitting open again.

"You would be too if you knew anything about them." Her fingers hit stone, so it wasn't exactly the right place to dig. Still, she scrabbled over it like it would have some secret button to press before starting over at another spot.

"They are weak and small." Greed moved, so he was in her line of sight again. "You watched me kill one of them, and you still do not fear me more than them?"

A little growl rumbled in her throat and she glared at him with all the anger of a lioness. He'd never seen something more pretty, nor anything he'd wanted to claim more. When they were done with this, when the night had fallen and they'd returned to this home, he would keep her. He would dress her in all the rare gems and clothing that he'd gathered over the years. And she would be his greatest prize.

She wrinkled her nose. "Would you stop looking at me like that?"

"Like what?"

"Like you want to eat me," she muttered, then let out a little sound of victory as she found the opening to the cave.

"Maybe I do wish to eat you," he replied wickedly. And when she flicked her gaze up to his, he licked his lips slowly.

Most women would have at least blushed. He'd made many women flustered with a look like that, especially considering he knew what they said about being in his bed. Greed had a reputation in this kingdom, and he'd worked very hard on that.

Greed was not necessarily a good emotion to have with a partner, but he was greedy in the best of ways. He took everything they could give him and then insisted on more. More, until they were shaking in his arms and incapable of walking.

What woman didn't want that? And he was certain she'd heard the stories. He'd paid a lot of people good money to take that truth far and wide.

So why...

"Greed," she hissed. "I sure could use a big strong man who could push some of this sand aside before the Horde comes and removes our heads from our shoulders."

"They'd be hard pressed to do that."

"I am but a small woman with only a few weapons on me. You are hardly at your best and they have already captured you once. Forgive me for not putting my life in your hands." She gestured at the small hole she'd made in the sand that disappeared into darkness. "You're sure about this?"

"Positive."

She gave him one more look before sucking in a deep breath and staring up at the sky. "If you have tricked me, Greed, I will haunt you for the rest of your life."

"That would be a very long life." He felt the ripples through the air. The anger and the rage and the greed that rolled through the approaching Horde. It almost rocked him back onto his ass in this weakened state.

The spirit he'd always been wanted to feast. It wanted to turn toward all those raging emotions and feast upon them. He wanted to feed the Horde more, to give them even more greed, just to see what they would do. Would they take it and run? Would they turn toward the nearest town and unleash their rage?

No, that was not who he was anymore. He'd tried that when he had first taken this kingdom and it had not gone well. He knew what it was to watch this kingdom burn. It had been his first and greatest mistake.

He would not make it again.

Greed grabbed the woman's wrist, turning it slightly in his own so his claws pressed against the sensitive skin where blood rushed underneath. "I will not betray you, thief. Slide through and I will make the hole bigger for myself."

"Why does it seem like we've run out of time?" she asked, her eyes searching his.

"Because we have."

And then he shoved her through the sands. Her feet slipped easily into the hole and she slid with her hands crossed over her chest, as though she knew the safest way to get to the bottom.

Damn it, he'd never met a woman so reckless. She had no idea what was down there waiting for them. It had been a long time, so he didn't either. But...

Sighing, he started digging. His wounds screamed at the movement and he could feel blood dripping down his sides in earnest now. But all he could think about was getting away from the Horde so that he could cozy up with this beautiful treasure in a hidden oasis.

The thoughts spurred him on. The desire to lick his way up her throat, cherishing the sounds she made for his ears only. She would whisper what she wanted. He was certain of that. A woman like this would only know how to give orders and he would take them all. Until he didn't.

Greed could hear their footsteps by the time the hole in the sand was big enough. He released his claws, dragging them behind him as he slid into the darkness. The sand followed him. It would seal them in the cave system, hidden from the Horde's gaze, but it also dragged a waterfall of gold behind him as he fell what felt like forever.

The ground hit him hard. Or maybe he hit the ground. Whoever hit first, it hurt. His legs went out beneath him and he sprawled out in the sand while another horse sized amount hit him on the chest. He might have groaned. Or maybe he took the beating without making a sound.

All he knew was that one minute, he was drowning in sand and the next, he was yanked out by the wrists from underneath it until a grumbling woman sat on top of him.

He stared up at her with perhaps delirious happiness until she dropped his arms with a sigh and dusted her sand covered hands off on her hips. And then, when she glared down at him with those lovely, lovely eyes, he let out a little sigh.

"Stop it," she snapped, pointing at him with a finger. "Enough of that. What did they give you in that cage? There must be something in that smoke that makes you lose your senses."

"Maybe," he said. Was his voice a little thin? He wasn't sure. All that dragging had scraped his back even more raw than it already was. "Could be the pain."

She frowned and looked him over. He swore he felt fire wherever her eyes lingered on his body. "You are bleeding again."

"All for you."

"That's a stupid thing to say." She hissed out a breath between her teeth, then made a tsking sound. "Can't be avoided. I'll see if there's anything in here that I can use for the time being to help the bleeding, but we're not exactly near a healer."

"Ach, don't pretend you don't like a little blood. Pretty thief." He reached out a hand toward her ankle, only to have it fall in the sand as she stood and moved away from him.

"Don't touch me, I will kick sand in your face." But her words were softened by how carefully she looked over the interior of the cave system. As though she were desperate to heal him.

Maybe she did like him, after all. He wouldn't mind it if she did.

The thief crouched next to his head, and Greed couldn't quite take his eyes off those lovely thighs as they flexed in her leather pants. She pressed her hand to his forehead, and he arched into her touch. Any touch. This was all getting worse, and he didn't understand why.

She hissed another breath out. "You're burning up. Have you ever had a fever before?"

"I don't know what that is."

"A fever. It's when you're injured or sick and your body raises its temperature to heal." She stared down at him, tiny wrinkles between her eyes that made him want to smooth them out. "Do you ever get sick?"

"I am a demon king," he muttered. "I do not fall ill."

"Well, apparently you do and I don't know if you have specific things you are allergic to or cannot eat. Is there anything like that you can think of?"

He just wanted her to touch his forehead again. He wanted her to touch him. But there were things that he shouldn't eat or consume, but she couldn't know that. Could she?

Suddenly, he was feeling very hot. And not in the way he was used to, where he wanted to rip off his clothing. He felt like he needed to shiver, but he wasn't cold at all.

No, maybe he was. He was definitely cold now.

Shaking, he tried to sit up, only to be shoved back down by a stern hand on his shoulder. "Lotus flower," he muttered. "No palm or persea either."

She sat back on her heels. "Nothing symbolic to the dead, then?"

"Precisely."

"Why?"

He couldn't answer that question. No matter how many times she asked.

All Greed wanted to do was sleep. The sand was comfortable enough, and surely this woman hadn't saved him to leave him on his own to die.

"Don't fall asleep," he heard her say. "Oh, by all the seven kingdoms, you ass! Stay awake!"

He'd never been very good at following directions.

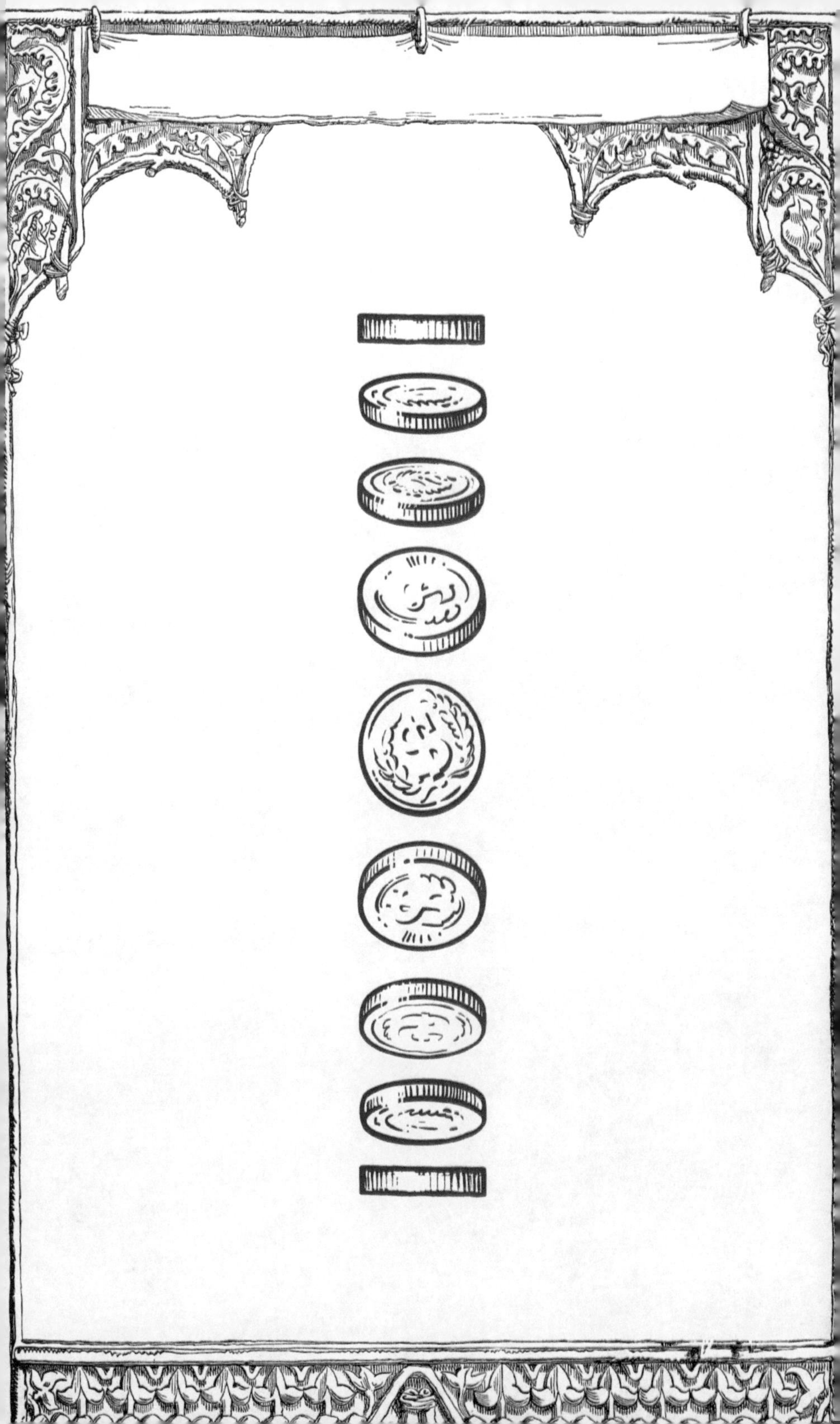

Chapter 4

This damned demon.

Varya should have left days ago. She had the map. She had the key to her people's salvation and here she was, sitting in a fucking oasis in the middle of a cave system, waiting for the demon king to wake up.

Three days. He'd been asleep for three days and she'd been packing his wounds with yarrow that she'd found beside the small stream that led into a pool. She'd been trying her best to keep him alive, and he hadn't so much as twitched.

If he died, she knew they would kill her. Who? Oh, there were lists of people who would kill her if they found out she'd been with the demon king when he died. His own guards, for one. Half the people in this kingdom who somehow liked the man. His brothers, no doubt, would hunt her in whatever kingdom she tried to flee to.

Varya would have to live the rest of her life on the run, and she wasn't so good at that. She'd escaped the Horde this long only because she'd learned from other people. But she had a mouth that ran off without her permission and a rather memorable face.

Although, she supposed if she had to be anywhere right now, this wasn't a terrible place to be.

The demon king had pointed her in the right direction of a cave that was safe for them. He'd forgotten to tell her it was a literal oasis. The stones above their head trapped moisture and kept it a cool, consistent temperature even at night. Holes in the ceiling rained sand with the breeze, but let the light in during the day so there were countless numbers of plants growing inside this cavern with a ceiling that was easily five men high.

A stream of water that snaked out from underneath more rocks gathered up in a pool at the center, crystal clear and drinkable. The food was a little scarce, but she'd found enough prickly pear and some rats to keep herself well fed. The demon king wasn't likely to eat while he was asleep, so she did her best to stay alive.

And wait.

She'd waited too long, really. The man had to wake up at some point, but she didn't know if she could just leave or not.

Staring up at the spears of light above her head, she took a deep breath and counted to fifty. When that didn't seem to help, she did it again. She'd started counting when she was little and anxious and the habit hadn't ever left. She liked counting. It calmed her nerves with repetition that was even and familiar.

Varya had to go back to where she'd stowed his body. She'd put her jacket over him, leaving her arms and shoulders bare. Her leather chest plate was only so good for heat, though.

At least Greed put off a lot of heat on his own. She'd huddled up next to him for the past three nights, fully expecting to wake up with his arm around her waist and his nose in her hair.

He never did.

She tried not to feel too disappointed with that fact. After all, it had been a long time since she'd entertained the touch of another person. She wasn't about to do it again any time soon.

Huffing, she rolled onto her feet and started back toward the safety of the entrance they'd come in through. At least she knew there was an exit there, even if she didn't know how to get back to it. Maybe she'd clamber up those rocks today, but she was afraid the Horde was still there. She could only assume they weren't. They'd have tunneled in here by now if they knew where Greed and Varya were hiding. So she should be able to... to...

She stopped, hands curling into fists at her sides.

Greed was gone.

She'd left his body right there, the same place he always was because she didn't know what else to do with him. But her jacket was still there. No giant body bleeding all over the sands for her to take care of, though.

"Damn it," she hissed. "Where are you, you colossal idiot?"

She followed the sound of splashing to the pool of water that was icy at best. She'd tried to bathe herself yesterday, but the water was so bitterly cold that she'd thought her nipples would crack right off. The best she could do was splash herself a few times and then wait until her leathers dried out.

The last thing she needed was some idiot demon thinking he could get into a pool of ice water and somehow cool himself off when it was just going to make everything worse. She had to leave this cave. Wasn't he worried about the kingdom or saving... whatever it was demon kings did?

Stomping toward the water, she crossed her arms over her chest and stood there, staring down into the pool.

And there he was. Pants on the ground next to her feet and all that muscle laid out in front of her to stare at. His bright red hair was slicked to his skull, giving her the opportunity to really look at the sharp edge of his cheekbones and the way the water played on those broad shoulders. There was the faintest dusting of freckles on the caps of his shoulders, but nothing else other than warm, bronze skin. He was built like a god, like what an artist would imagine the perfect man to look like, and she shouldn't be having those thoughts.

Not when he turned around and there wasn't even a faint dusting of hair on his chest to distract from those broad planes that dipped toward his waist. Sharp abs flexed under her eyes, shifting her gaze to the narrow strips of muscle that ran over each of his hips and drew her gaze to more red hair, and...

Damn it.

She snapped her gaze up to his grinning expression and refused to look down again. "What are you doing?"

"That fever of mine is still hot," he said, his voice guttural and low. She could feel him looking at her body, almost like a physical touch. "But maybe I'm hot for another reason. Come in the water, little thief. Let's find out together."

"That's enough from you." She had to force herself to not press her thighs together at the thought.

She'd heard of this king. Women whispered of his talents in the market as they glossed over how their husband had been disappointing the night before. The demon king Greed was a myth among women. A man who pushed and pushed until there was nothing left but a quivering mess beneath him.

What would it be like to touch a god like that? Just how much could she push him when all she wanted was to bite into that strong column of muscle at his throat and ride him?

No, she would not have these thoughts about a living myth. He was a man standing right in front of her, shivering, even though he was trying not to let her see it. And though his words were brave, his face was slowly turning grey, and he'd widened his stance as if he didn't trust his balance.

She kept her arms crossed and narrowed her eyes. "You can't get out, can you?"

"I am fine. I'm a demon king. My healing is much faster than yours."

"All right. Take two steps to your right, then."

He eyed her with no small amount of suspicion. "Why?"

"Because I want to see that you can put weight on that right hip when I saw the blade they'd used slice right through to the muscle. If you can balance on that foot alone, I'll leave you to your bathing."

His eyes flashed gold, reflecting the sudden beam of sunlight that illuminated his form. The water around him seemed to glow. Glistening droplets clung to his shoulders as if even they didn't want to let go.

A muscle in his jaw jumped, but he didn't move.

She rolled her gaze up to the ceiling. "How long have you been stuck in there?"

"Long enough."

The last thing she wanted to do was get her leathers wet. Again. She'd already washed them, but they were terrible to dry out when the cave was already rather humid. She'd have to find a safe place to dry them and for her to wait while she lacked her clothes. He'd look if he got the chance, and she didn't want him to look.

But she also refused to let him sit in a pool of ice cold water longer than he needed to. So Varya waded into the water, gritting her teeth against the cold.

"Why are you so set on helping me?" he asked as she slotted herself underneath his arm. "You don't seem like one of my subjects who likes me."

"I don't have to like you to help you," she grunted.

"I'd think that's a requirement for helping people, actually." He didn't lean as much weight on her as last time, at least. Maybe the water was helping.

She grunted again, heaving him up to sit on the edge of the pool. And then froze between his legs as he stared at her, face pale and eyes sunken. He looked... tired. Or perhaps resigned. Not at all what she'd thought a demon king would look like.

Varya braced her hands on either side of his bare hips and admitted, "I like helping people. Even people I don't like."

She could see the confusion on his face. He didn't understand. But how could he? This entire kingdom ran on foolishness and greed and...

The question popped out of her mouth before she could stop herself. "Is it true that you can only feel greed?"

He sighed, leaning back on his hands as though he had to put space between them to answer her question. "In a sense. I can feel happy or sad or angry, but none of them are as powerful as greed. It is who I am, and what I was born to be."

"You were born?"

"In a sense." His lips twisted as though he'd said some kind of strange joke. "Now, I've been dying to ask. What is it that you desire?"

She felt it. His magic. People had always claimed that if they were close to him, that they felt the greed that he spread. They could feel it flowing through their veins and into their lungs, tangling in their blood. He made people do terrible things, but right now, he wasn't asking her to do anything. He was asking for an answer and she couldn't deny him that.

"I want my people to be safe," she found herself saying. "Even if that means I have to steal from the Horde themselves."

He frowned. "That wasn't what I was expecting."

"And what were you expecting?" she asked as his power flowed off her shoulders like water.

With an arched brow, he looked down between his legs. Then he flicked his eyes back to hers, and something warm sparked between them.

Suddenly she realized she was still standing in the pool of water, halfway up to her waist and she'd gone numb from the knees down. He was leaning back on his hands. All that lovely muscle flexed and bared before her. And she knew that if she just looked an inch lower, she would be treated to a sight of a half hard cock that bobbed for her attention.

She couldn't do this. Not with the king of their kingdom, and certainly not with a demon who had used his magic against her to get her to fuck him!

Yanking herself out of the water, she shook off the frozen droplets and snarled. "Enough, demon king. You have made yourself very clear."

"Have I?"

"Yes!" she shouted, her words echoing through the cave. "I am only here so I'm not hung after someone finds your dead body in this cavern and then realizes I was here with you. I will not have you die on my watch and the rest of my family die because I did not get back to them in time. You will heal. Faster than you say you are trying and then we will leave. That is what is going to happen here. Nothing else."

He poked at a cut over his ribs and seemed to mull over her words. But then he tilted his head back, and that grin stole over his features again. "What if I want to add something to that list?"

"You will not." Varya bared her teeth at him. "There is nothing you could possibly wish to add to that list. I have not, will not, entertain any more of your foolishness. I don't know what your game is, demon king, but I have no interest in playing it with you."

"Ah, I think you have more than a little interest in playing it." He leaned back on his hands, looking far too comfortable and making her want to smack that grin off his face. "Do you want to know a secret about me? I haven't told anyone about it before, little thief."

"Stop calling me that."

"Is it not what you are?"

"I'm not a thief," she ground between her teeth. "I do not steal from the living very often, and I try to replace what I steal when I do."

He arched a brow. "What did you take from the Horde, then?"

He had her there, and he knew it. She'd stolen not only the map, but would steal countless artifacts that were listed on it. And then she'd stolen him. If Varya got any more tense, she feared her muscles would start spasming. He had no right, no right at all, and would it be such a bad thing if she delivered him with a few additional bruises? No one would know which ones she'd caused.

The infuriating man snorted. His eyes flashed that bright yellow again. "Every demon king is different. You've heard the rumors, I'm sure. Lust has his horns. Gluttony, his claws. I have a tail. All of us are a bit... different, yes?"

She should walk away. But her curiosity had always gotten the better of her. So instead, she stood there like a moron, dripping water out of the creaking leathers that were likely ruined. "I know the rumors."

"Then I'll admit to you, and I have never admitted this to anyone, that the rumors are true. Lust can use those horns as he wishes, but he also has another form. Gluttony can no more retract those claws than a leopard can its spots. And me?" He grinned, his teeth a little too sharp. "I'm more animal than you'd ever think. Tread carefully, little treasure, or I'll gobble you up."

Her face heated. The hairs on her arms raised, and she didn't know if she was turned on or terrified.

"What?" she hissed. "Gobble you up? What are you, a children's story? Ridiculous!"

She stomped away from him, muttering about foolish men and their attempts at being anything other than idiots. And she swore she heard him laugh at her.

It would serve him right if his fever came back. He could get back to his makeshift bed on his own.

He didn't like admitting the little mortal might be right, but... she was right. He'd thought bathing would help the fever. The water in that pool was certainly cold enough to ease the heat in his body. But then all of that had backfired.

His fever was worse. The night time chills and sweats made it difficult to sleep, and throughout all of it, the worry battered through his skull.

Why wasn't he healing?

He and his brothers had always healed faster than the mortals. He could suffer through a sword wound and continue fighting. By the end of the battle, he'd be covered in blood, but never with a scratch on him.

Damned Bonescraper. The knife was somewhere. He'd forgotten what he'd done with it, but he needed to throw it off the edge of his kingdom. Let it sink into the darkness where the monsters lived. At least then it couldn't hurt anyone else like this again.

Or any of his brothers. The last thing he needed was to unleash a weapon like that upon his own kind.

If only he could heal a little quicker. He'd felt a bit better in the stream, but then he'd gotten worse. How did one heal when they were in a mortal body? This body had always given him trouble, but never like this. Greed knew he and his brothers were closer to mortal than spirit these days, but this was ridiculous.

Rolling over again, he heaved a sigh and tried to curl up tighter. If he dragged his knees in toward his chest, maybe he could contain the heat he was losing. And if he wrapped his arms around his chest, then that felt a little better. Of course, it made his heart do some strange beat and race, but maybe that was just the side he was lying on. If he rolled...

"Would you stop?" a voice hissed.

Right. He wasn't alone. He had a very unwilling partner in all of this, who was insistent that she would stay on the far side of the cave. She was so far away, he could only see the faint glow of her foot in the moonlight.

"Stop what?" he asked, his teeth chattering. "If there was a warmer part of this cave, then I would find it, woman."

"Don't call me woman."

"It is what you are."

"I am more than just my sex," she snarled. And then he swore he heard her mutter something about heartless demons, thinking the world revolved around them.

Ah, but arguing did warm him up a little. A shiver shuddered through his spine, but he found his lips curling into a smile. "I'm sure you are. A woman who steals from dangerous men, then carries her king to safety, and now... I'm not sure what you're doing in the shadows over there, but I do hope you're having fun."

"I swear to all the gods, I will walk over there and step on your throat until you stop breathing."

A zing of pleasure arched up from the base of his tail, so powerful he wasn't certain if it was pain or desire. He groaned, low and deep in the back of his throat, "I wish you would."

The rustling sound of leaves moving made him wonder if she'd rolled away from him. Maybe he'd pushed their argument too far. He wouldn't be surprised at all. She didn't seem to enjoy talking about sex or anything of the sort.

Except then he heard the rustling from right behind his head and froze when he felt the touch of a hand around his neck. Eyes blinking open, he stared up into her angry expression. Not her foot, but her hand, wrapped around his neck like a collar.

"Don't test me, demon," she ground through her teeth. "There is nothing I would like more than to leave you here on your own. No one would find you. And if they did, then I would be long gone."

"Perhaps." He placed his hand over hers and squeezed a little harder. "Move your fingers like this though, darling, or you'll cut off my blood flow. You want to limit air, not blood."

Her eyes widened as she realized what he was suggesting. The thief released her hold on him quickly, shaking off his hand as he chuckled.

She shook her head at him, displeased with the direction their conversation had taken. Again.

"How can you even think like this when your lips are blue?" she muttered.

Then he realized she was sitting in nothing other than her underclothes. Her leathers had gotten wet. Of course, he'd forgotten that she wouldn't be able to sleep in those.

He hadn't thought she would be beside him in nothing more than her underwear and a wrap around her breasts, though. She was… tiny. Muscular. Her sinewy body flexed with every tiny movement, and she shivered often. She was more athletic than most women he'd entertained, and he hadn't realized just how much he liked that. The woman was…

Freezing. Just like him.

He'd been with Lust and Selene for far too long. Those two lovebirds had turned his attention away from the pleasures of the flesh and more toward what a woman might actually want. The sorceress had ruined him, damned woman.

Or maybe she'd just made him realize he didn't mind helping others if he got something in return.

Uncurling his legs felt a bit like he was trying to force ice to bend. But he somehow managed as he rolled himself toward her and opened his arms.

"What are you doing?" she asked.

"We're both freezing. Desert nights can get dangerously cold, and both of us are wet."

"Who's fault is that?"

"Mine, little viper." He shook his head at her spitting acid, before gesturing again with his hands. "Now come here."

"I don't think that's a good idea." She looked uneasy. Far more than he'd expected.

But she had to know that this was entirely about heat. He wouldn't put her in a situation where she felt he would take advantage of her. He'd let her stick her hands down his pants and feel how much he'd receded into his body in cold if that made her feel better.

She bit her lip and as he stared at that plush pillow between the flashing white bite of her teeth, he had second thoughts. Maybe he wasn't as cold as he'd thought.

"Fine," she muttered. "But this is only to get through the night. Don't take this for anything other than what it is, demon."

"I won't," he replied with a snort.

She turned her back to him and scooted closer. She snuggled in hard, slamming her back to his front, her arms wrapped firmly around her chest. But that also meant that her rather impressively hard ass was right up against his cock and he'd be damned if it didn't twitch for her. Because, by the gods, all this woman was in his arms and he wanted to curl her up even tighter.

Through gritted teeth, he asked, "Fine?"

"Fine."

But he felt another shiver shake through her body and couldn't take it anymore. Greed snaked his arm around her waist and tugged her even tighter against his chest. He curled his legs up against hers and then sighed as her warmth sank into him.

She was stiff for a few moments before relaxing in his grip. She even wiggled her shoulders a little closer to his chest, her own sigh echoing through his mind as he wondered what sound she would make if he did something else. Like tug her a little closer, just a bit lower. She was so small, he'd have to move her underneath his chin, but then he could slide between those hard thighs and...

"You're thinking out loud," she muttered. "Stop doing that."

"Doing what?"

"Talking about sliding between my hard thighs. They aren't that hard, you know."

Oh, she wasn't going to say something like that without him taking advantage. Greed slid his palm down her waist, over her hip, and down to one of the thighs in question. He grabbed onto it, his palm holding onto the meat of her muscle. "Feels pretty hard to me."

She sniffed, but he thought it might be with a little pride. She wasn't ashamed of her body, no. But her words made him feel as though she'd almost goaded him into touching her.

Did she want him to touch her?

He suddenly leaned up on an arm, looming over her and staring down at her face in the darkness. "Are you giving in?"

"Giving in to what?"

His next words were little more than a growl. "Me."

She rolled too, looking up at him with all that golden hair spilling around her head. "The only thing I'm giving in to is your body heat. You're taking this in the wrong way, Greed. I should go back to my shadows."

But she wasn't moving. She was staring at him with a look in her eyes that he was oh so familiar with. Hunger.

And his breath caught in his chest at the sight of it because it was so infinitely beautiful, even if she wanted to deny herself. He licked his lips, then looked down at his hand still on her thigh.

"Greed isn't always a bad thing," he mumbled. He tracked the movement of his hand as he slid it back up her hip to her flat belly that flexed underneath his fingers. "Sometimes greed is giving in to what we really want. To what we really desire."

His hand moved again, sliding in between her breasts and up to her throat. She swallowed hard against his palm, and he looked back into those lovely blue eyes that were filled with so much hunger it sparked his own.

He leaned a little closer, her breath fanning over his lips. "So what do you want, little thief?"

Oh, he hoped he knew what she wanted. He hoped it was that she wanted to warm herself on him more than they were now. To send their hearts racing together as they beat the cold and the darkness away for a few moments.

And gods, he was right.

She grabbed the back of his neck with a surprisingly firm hand and slammed her mouth into his. They tangled together, lips and teeth and tongue. He tasted her, all bitter and acidic as she was sweet. She nipped at his bottom lip with her teeth, and he gladly opened for her.

This first time, he'd let her think she was in control. He'd let her take what she wanted, and the woman took with all the ferocity of the lioness he'd once compared her to. This thief devoured him whole.

She kissed with her entire body. Her hand holding him in place, her other trailing down the bare planes of his chest. One of her legs came up and coiled around his thigh. Not enough for him to rub against her as he desperately wanted, but still enough to connect them even further. As though she couldn't stand to be so far from him.

And through it all, he held himself still and careful above her. Letting her take. Letting her touch. Letting her learn his body in whatever way she wished.

Until she pulled back, her cheeks darkening in the silver moonlight. Doubt warred on her features, and it seemed as though the world slammed down upon her.

"I shouldn't," she whispered, but then she licked her lips and stared at his. "We shouldn't do this."

"Ach, my turn now," he growled.

Greed lunged for her. He'd given her time to learn him, to take what she wanted, and now she owed him the rest.

He scooped the back of her neck with his palm, not caring that she let out a hiss of pain as he pulled her hair. He dug his other hand into her waist, yanking her up against his chest as he hovered over her like the animal he was.

And she met him. By all the seven kingdoms, she met him in the middle and unleashed all his dreams upon him. Her legs curled around his hips, giving him the perfect opportunity to place himself between her thighs where he wanted to be. He ground into her, spiking pleasure nearly into pain as he bit at her lips.

At some point he'd pinched her jaw between his fingers, too hard, but she didn't seem to mind in the slightest. Her hands gripped him back, her nails digging into his back, and it was perfection.

She was exactly what he'd been waiting for. This wondrous, impossible woman who would fit into his collection better than he'd ever thought possible.

Heat consumed him. Desire burned through his body and he couldn't think. Couldn't be anything other than the animal who bit at her, devoured, and needed to slide down her body and eat until they both were satisfied.

But the moment he shifted, he felt all those wounds on his back and ribs opening up once more. Warm blood slid down his torso and dripped over her hands, onto her skin, and he hoped she would ignore it.

It wasn't the first time he'd wanted to fuck covered in blood. He hoped that maybe, just maybe, she was as messed up as he was. But she wasn't. She stopped him, her hand holding onto his ribs and forcing him to freeze.

He stared down at her swollen lips, her eyes that searched his features, even though she had to know what was there. He wanted her.

Gods, she could feel him pressed up against her inner thigh if she just focused.

How could he not want her? How could anyone not want her?

She slid a hand up between them and held her fingers up to the moonlight. Her hand was coated in blood, slick and thick, dripping from her palm and down her wrists.

"We have to stop," she whispered, still staring at the blood.

"I'll heal," he growled. Greed bent low to capture her lips again, but she turned her face away from him and all he kissed was her jaw.

"You won't, though." She shook her head and then shoved his chest with her palm. Surprisingly strong, she almost forced him onto his back with just that little movement. "You're not healing like normal, Greed. Remember? We have to stop."

"And if I don't want to?"

"Then dream about it." Still, she was a little more gentle as she arranged herself. She laid her head on his chest, her arms wrapped around his torso and her leg thrown over his. "I refuse to hurt you any more than you've already been hurt, you stubborn demon."

He had the sudden fear she might hurt him, anyway. His thief was a person, not some treasure that he'd found lost deep in the sands of time. She was a living, breathing person who could deny him if she wished. She could leave his castle and never join his collection of beautiful things. Time would tarnish her. Other people would touch her, bruise her, leave blemishes he wouldn't be able to heal.

Wrapping an arm over her shoulders, he tugged her a little closer and pressed a kiss to the top of her hair. "What is your name, little thief?"

He felt her smile against his chest, her lips pressed to his bloody skin. "You can call me whatever you want, Greed."

"What if I call you treasure?"

"It's better than thief."

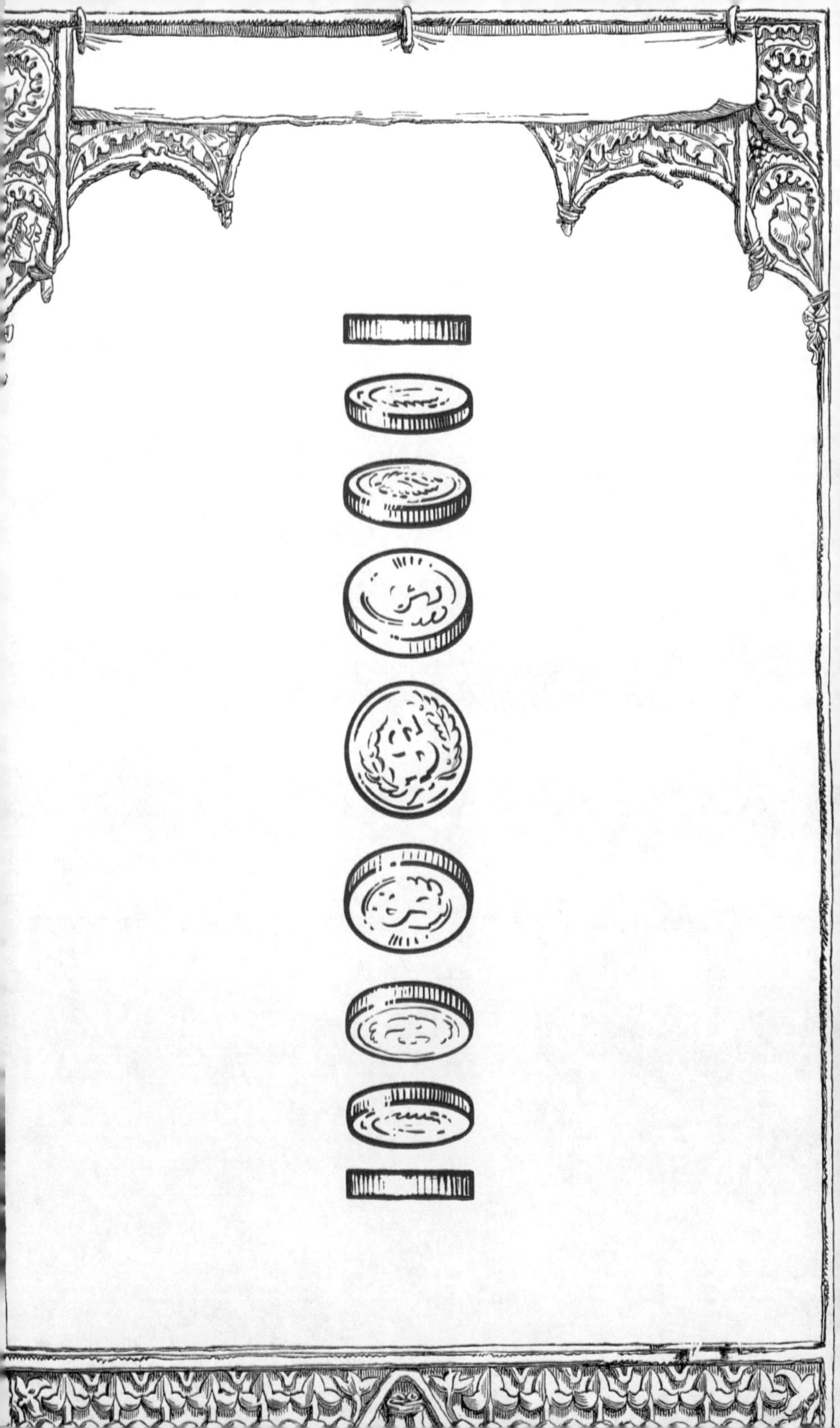

Chapter 6

She was a horny idiot and needed to get rid of him immediately. Kissing him? What had she been thinking? There was no excuse for kissing the king of their kingdom, the one who she should fear. It didn't matter that he was a spectacular example of his sex. She should have had better self control.

And she had better self control. That was the most frustrating part about all of this.

Varya had spent a very long part of her life making sure that everything was in its neat little place. She was alone; she had no attachments, she only cared about her friends and they were wonderful people who might even miss her when she was gone. But her adventuring nature disturbed no one. They all had their own lives that she was barely part of. Sure, things would be a little more difficult for them if she wasn't bringing in treasure to sell. But would they mourn her?

Maybe.

Maybe they would for a few days or a few weeks. But what would be different for them? If she was gone, it changed nothing about their day-to-day life. This was how she kept people at bay and how she kept her heart safe.

And then this big idiot had lumbered into her life, expecting someone would save him, and she felt like she had to, because he was a king, and now she was rambling in her own head while staring at him sleep.

Varya had woken when the very first rays of the sun had broken through the sand above their head. Spears of light came with the wind spraying sand down upon them as though they were in an hourglass.

His arm had been wrapped around her waist when she woke. His face buried in her hair, and he'd worn a soft expression that made her question her sanity. He clearly wanted to be wrapped around her. He enjoyed lying by her side, if the way he'd tangled his legs through hers revealed anything.

She'd taken a very long time making sure he didn't wake up while she maneuvered herself out of that situation. She would not, could not, get involved with anyone at all.

And she had to get out of this cave.

The only reason she'd succumbed to the madness last night was because he'd surrounded her. He'd been everywhere with that spicy, warm scent that whispered of safety and quiet. She'd almost been able to imagine the warm mugs of ale, flickering firelight, and soft furs that likely cushioned his privileged head every single night.

She'd wanted that life. For an absolutely insane moment, she'd wanted him to take her back with him. Maybe she'd fit right in with his castle life. Maybe she would see what it was like to have all that luxury at her beck and call?

But that was insanity. She had a life, and it was one that she liked. She'd worked very hard to make sure that everything was exactly the way it was supposed to be. No demon king would ruin that for her.

The moment he'd asked for her name was the moment she knew she had to run. He was getting too close. Sinking in too deep. She'd seen the look in his eyes and she'd known that he was too interested in keeping her.

He wouldn't be the first. He wouldn't be the last. None of these men seemed to understand that she would not lose herself for any of them. Even one this magnificent.

Greed groaned as he rolled over in his sleep, his hands automatically searching for her.

Varya didn't even try to hide her flinch. He wanted to touch her, sought her out as the first thought in his head after waking, and she was saying no?

She had bigger problems than she'd even realized if that was the case, but she would not bend. Not for him. Not for anyone.

Greed sat up, his red hair wild around his head as his eyes narrowed. He peered through the shadows, right toward her, as though he knew where she was. He shouldn't be able to see her at all, and yet, this man constantly surprised her.

"Why are you up already?" he grumbled.

"Because you're not healing," she replied, her heart catching in her throat. "And we've run out of time."

"If this is about last night—"

"You're real arrogant. Has anyone ever told you that?" She stood, her leather armor already strapped onto her body and her coat over her arm. "There's no more food, Greed. A woman can only survive on rats for so long and I'm not waiting any longer. You need a healer. I need to eat. I made the decision long before I woke up."

His expression screwed up in confusion. "Rats? You've been eating rats?"

"What do you think I've been eating?"

Greed held out his arms and gestured around them, as though there was plenty to eat.

She took a deep, steadying breath and told herself not to argue. She didn't need him to dig in his heels. She needed him to be a good little boy and stand up. "There is nothing edible in this cave, Greed. I don't know what you need to eat or if you even do. But I need food. If you want me to bring you back to your castle, then you have to stand. I can't carry you the entire way there."

"You know the way?" he asked, and then pushed himself onto his feet. The movement was labored and new, bright streaks of blood splattered across his back.

She'd done that, Varya thought with a wince. She'd hurt him even more.

Greed knew where her attention was. He glanced down at a particularly red, now open cut on his chest and then grinned at her. "Ach, don't beat yourself up about it, treasure. I might even let that one scar to remember who gave it to me."

No, no, she would not listen to this nonsense. She couldn't.

Varya narrowed her eyes at him and frowned even harder. "I see no reason why you'd want to keep a scar from a woman you knew for only a few days."

"But I know you're going to be with me for a lot longer than that, treasure. If you insist we move, then we move." He glanced up at the holes in the ceiling. "What time of day is it?"

"After mid day. You slept for most of the time the sun was in the sky." It would still be hot traveling, but at least they would be trudging through the sands toward colder weather.

She could only hope they were close to the castle. The man was not dressed for travel, and being shirtless without even a blanket would make the journey difficult for him.

And she shouldn't be worried about him.

Damn it, again.

"You're worried about our travel speed?" he asked as he strode up to her, looking like a man who had no cares at all. "Are you going to be excited to get rid of me?"

"Yes," she replied instantly.

She would be very glad to get him out of her hair. She needed to figure out what she was thinking. Why she was so tempted by him? She needed to get home and bring the map back to them so they could all move forward into a brighter future. A future he should have provided them without Varya needing to steal and...

The map.

Where was the map?

She'd put it down when she changed her clothing, and she'd forgotten this morning to put it back into her pants. It had already been horribly sodden by her stupid decision to leap into the water after him. She had hoped that drying it out on a rock nearby would be enough so that it was back to legible, and it was this morning, but she'd meant to put it back into her pants and... and...

Greed had it in his hands. He was tilting it back and forth, trying to catch a sunbeam on the parchment as he stared down at it.

Oh no. If he realized what it was, would he try to take it back?

Varya eyed the pool behind him. If he tried, she could kick him hard on his bad hip, and that would send him careening into the water. If she didn't grab the paper then, which she was fast enough to do, then she could always follow him into the pool.

He was weak, and she was much stronger than he thought she would be. Surely that would give her the advantage enough to retrieve the map and run.

Where? She had no idea. The exit to these caves seemed as ephemeral as their entrance.

Greed tilted his head and the map at the same time before flicking his gaze up to her. "Where did you get this?"

"The Horde. You saw me steal it."

"Where did they get it?"

Varya shrugged. "I have no idea. The Horde has their contacts, and they gather items from all over the kingdom. They could have stolen it from your very castle for all I know."

"Oh, they didn't do that," he muttered. "I haven't had this in years. Someone took it from me three centuries ago."

She choked on her own tongue. "Centuries?"

"Did you not know? My brothers and I are all ancient." He flashed her a wicked grin. "It has its uses. For example, I spent nearly ten years deep between the legs of a very talented—"

She held up her hand and stared at the ceiling. "I don't need to hear about that."

"Why?" He was suddenly much closer, and she could feel his breath against her shoulder. "Are you… jealous?"

Varya grabbed the map out of his hand and rolled it once more. She stared at the ground as she replied, "No, I am not. I just want to get going and if you don't stop dawdling, we'll be walking while it's freezing out and I won't lend you my jacket."

"Ah, but last night we already realized how much easier it is to warm each other."

He leaned a little too close for comfort, so Varya took three very large steps back. It was only a little satisfying that Greed stumbled before she turned and started toward the pool.

"Drink up, demon king. There will be little water on the way, I suspect."

"We're not that far from my castle," he grumbled, but she had a feeling he was only saying that to make it sound better. They were very far from the castle, at least four hours of walking, and he wasn't at his best.

What should have been a quick journey was sure to turn into a very long one.

She took her own advice and drank as much water as her belly could hold before turning back to him. He gestured behind her at a rock wall.

"Go on then," he muttered. "If you're so insistent that we need to start this moment, you can feel the heat first."

She approached the rock wall, but there was no opening or sliver for her to slide through. There wasn't even light coming through the stones. What did he expect her to do with this?

Greed grumbled behind her the whole way. Unsurprisingly, he still wasn't feeling like himself, and he expected this to be a very trying day. If she didn't want to acknowledge that, it was fine, but he refused to be shuffled around like a child. Or at least, that sounded like what he was mumbling. A lot of the deep guttural tones were difficult to understand.

Then he paused behind her and grunted. "Well? What are you

waiting for?"

If she could punch him, this would all feel so much better.

Varya faced him and gestured toward the wall, trying her best not to look ridiculously put out. "There are rocks in front of me, Greed. What do you want me to do?"

"Go through them."

"How?" she snarled through her teeth. Varya had to mutter to herself not to clench the map in her hand and completely shred it because of the stupid, moronic, asshole of a demon in front of her.

He flashed her a bright grin, as if he knew how much he was getting under her skin. "Just walk through it."

"Not all of us have magic."

"I don't have magic." He shrugged and started toward the wall of stone. "Demons aren't real, anyway. You mortals are the ones who insist on calling us that, and it's rather ridiculous. We aren't monsters who were summoned out of the deep."

He turned and waggled his fingers at her, backing toward the stone. He continued to make hand movements like he was casting a spell and then... disappeared through the rock.

"Rat bastard," she hissed. Had he trapped her in here? Was that the plan all along?

When she saw him next, she would wring his stupid, fat neck.

But then Greed's head appeared through the stones again, grinning like an absolute lunatic covered in dried blood. "Are you coming or not? I told you, no magic required."

Completely and utterly confused, Varya stepped closer to the rocks and held her hand up to them. Her hand disappeared as she touched the stones and then reappeared when she moved it closer. There was no sensation of magic or even a spell, but obviously there was one here.

She was braver than this, she reminded herself. And so she stepped through the stones.

Out onto the sand beyond.

The sun warmed her chilled skin, and she pulled on her jacket and drew up the hood. Her mask was attached to the interior of it, so that was easy to pull up and cover her mouth. The wind had already kicked up, sending sand swirling around their feet and soon enough into their faces.

"You see?" Greed said, holding his hands at his sides. "Innocent and easy. No magic."

"Good enough." The mask muffled her voice. "Are you ready, or do I have to carry you?"

"You couldn't..." He paused, then looked her over. "Actually, maybe you could. And I'm almost ready. There's just one last thing."

She rolled her eyes. What else could this ridiculously frustrating man have to do?

He stepped closer and gently took hold of the edges of her mask. Carefully, ever so carefully, he moved the mask around and tucked the loose strands of her hair more comfortably behind it. He took his time, making sure there wasn't a single thread of gold revealed before he ghosted his fingers over the peaks of her cheekbones.

"You're blushing," he murmured.

"No, I'm not."

Greed frowned, his brows drawing down in that expression she'd come to recognize so well. "No, you aren't. That is rather strange, don't you think?"

"Not really," she muttered as she tucked the map into her waistband again. "Come on, we're wasting time."

But as she stalked off into the sands, she couldn't help but feel like she'd fled his touch. It made her a little too warm, a little too comfortable, and... a little too close to blushing.

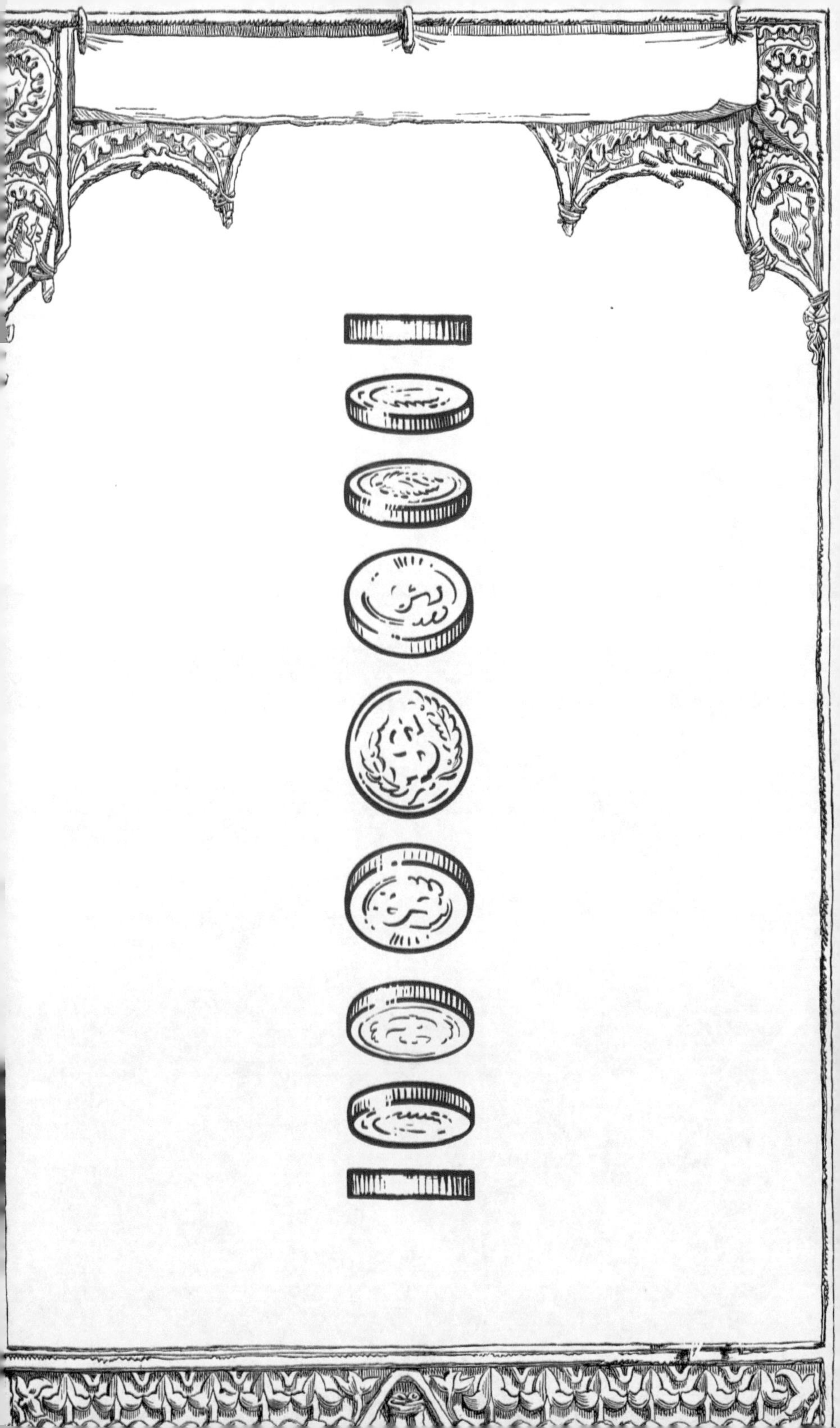

Chapter 7

He barely made it to the castle on his own two feet, and Greed felt rage simmering the harder it got. He was a god, damn it, a demon king! He should be able to walk across the sands for a few hours.

Instead, he was the slow one. He made the mortal stop more times than he could count, so he could catch his breath. She was quiet about it at least, but her pinched expression and unimpressed gaze rankled.

He wanted to keep moving. It wasn't like he was trying to stall getting back to his home, where he could gather up all the energy he needed from the countless greedy subjects who lived there. All that energy would transfer into power and he would be back to himself in no time.

Back to the man who could sweep her over his shoulder and then show her what she'd been missing by ending that kiss. The memory still burned through him, giving him all the fight that he needed so he could keep trudging through the never-ending dunes.

"We should stop again," she said, her eyes skating over his body before looking up at the moon. "And maybe try to make a fire."

"With that?" He gestured around them. "There's nothing here but sand and dust, treasure."

She rolled her eyes at his antics. "Why are you calling me that now? I almost prefer thief."

"That's not what you said last night."

"I said a lot of things last night that I shouldn't have." Her eyes were cutting and barbed like a cactus as she glared at him over the mouth of her mask.

He'd thought it was a silly addition to her outfit. What need did she have to wear a mask? They were out in the desert without another person around them for miles. Who was going to see her face?

But then sand blasted him in the face as the wind picked up. And again. And again. So many times that even his cheeks had reddened as his natural healing abilities failed him. Like the magic inside him was tired of healing the same damned abrasions over and over again.

It was a rare moment for him to hate the kingdom that he'd taken. Greed enjoyed this place, and he'd spent most of his days watching as the greenery had faded into the desert, as the relentless sun killed anything that tried to live. He admired the people who were still here for their hardiness and stalwart desire to stay alive no matter the costs.

But right now? Right now, he hated this kingdom with every fiber of his being.

"We're not stopping," he grumbled. "We'll reach the castle soon enough."

And not quickly enough for his liking. But he knew it was just over two more ridges. That's all it would take.

Greed staggered, falling to one knee in the sands before hauling himself back upright. He could keep going. He would. Nothing would stop him from getting home and having a warm cup of mead in one hand, and the tiny waist of his woman in the other. They'd fall back on the furs together, bellies finally full and alcohol warming their blood. She'd trail her hand down his chest, her palm soon meeting—

Said woman wedged her shoulder underneath his and gave him something solid to lean against. Teeth grinding, the muscles of her jaw flexing, she started them forward at a much quicker pace.

"Why didn't you say the castle was right here?" she grumbled.

"Because you should have been able to see it."

He could. The glittering lights of his home had been in the distance for some time now. But perhaps her mortal eyes could not see as far as his. Or maybe she just didn't see as well in the dark.

Ah, that was it. She wrinkled her nose and looked up at him, her eyes tracking his in the moonlight. "Your pupils are so wide I cannot see any color."

"The benefits of being a demon, I suppose." Greed wanted to admit the whole truth. He wanted to let it spew out of his lips so she would be the only person who understood that he wasn't really a demon at all.

He was a spirit. A wispy creature of emotion and light that fed off humans, and somehow had taken flesh with his brothers. He'd been given a chance at power and he'd taken it over and over again until he had finally been awarded this form. This kingdom. And everything that lived within it.

Greed squeezed her tighter against him. That included her. She was also in his kingdom and he had been gifted her as sure as if she'd been wrapped in a bow. And now he would keep her.

Even she was breathing hard as they crested the first hill. And he felt her sharp gasp as she caught sight of his home. The oasis he'd built it in was massive, larger than any other in the kingdom. His home stretched even higher above it, with tall spires and bulbous circles at the peaks where he fit so many of his favorite rooms. The castle looked for all intents and purposes like it had grown out of the sand itself. It glowed bright golden in the sunlight, and even at night was an impressive building.

The grounds flooded out from the castle like a jungle. The tall trees and endless water sources were all sprawled around his home as if the castle itself fed them. Usually he could hear the bright sound of many-colored birds that flew over the treetops, but they were all silent now in sleep.

Somewhere in all that green were the stables that held his most prized possessions. The nuckelavee were stolen from Gluttony's empire, but they bred very well in his kingdom. Many feared the skeletal horses, their hide stretched over their bones like leather. But if treated right, they were the fastest mounts in all the kingdoms.

A huffed breath from his companion interrupted his thoughts. She shifted him higher, wedging herself more firmly beneath him before asking, "So what do you miss most about all that… that."

She repeated the last word like it explained her thoughts about his home. How could she not see the beauty in it? He'd been nomadic, like many of his people, for years before casting aside his warlord mantle to live here.

"Bathing," he muttered. "With warm water rather than icy runoff, that would flay the skin off anyone else who tried to linger there."

She snorted. "Bathing? Of all the luxuries you have in that castle, the warm water is what you miss most? Even I have that in my home.

That's very little to be proud of."

"Ah, you mistake me. You asked what I missed most, not what I'm most proud of." He could almost feel the heat in his eyes flashing at the thought of his collection. "I have items in that castle that would make you gasp in awe, treasure. Soon you'll see them all."

And he would have her wear them. Diamonds, rubies, and emeralds, all dripping from her form as she wore nothing else. He'd dress her in the finest of silks if he wanted her clothed. But he didn't. He thought she'd be better bare for a while yet.

After all, he enjoyed looking at his collection with nothing standing in his way. For the first few weeks, she'd have to endure. And then he would let her dress as she wished. Even if that meant putting this horrible leather armor back on.

"What's gotten you all riled up?" she muttered as they crested the last dune.

"Thoughts and dreams." Greed paused at the peak, breathing hard and knowing that they were about to walk into a hornet's nest. "Listen, the guards can be a little much with new people. I need you to stay close to my side while I deal with them."

"I'm not going to do that," she said with a snort. "I can handle myself."

"I know you can. But this is my castle and my rules." He turned, keeping his arm around her shoulders so she was drawn in tight against him. Greed skated his fingers down her ribs and, oh, he enjoyed the little shiver that traveled down her spine. "I think you're going to enjoy those rules, though. There's a heat in you that you haven't fully explored yet, treasure, and we'll both enjoy figuring out what it is that you desire."

She was so distracted by his mildly unwelcome touch and the heat that flared in her body that Greed stole the map back without her noticing. She didn't sway in his arms as he had hoped, obviously under his spell. But of course she didn't. His little thief kept her spine straight and her hands braced against his chest. Holding him away from her, or trying, at the very least.

But he'd gotten his powers back enough to be more formidable than her. Tucking the map into the waistband of his pants, ensuring it was flat against his skin and hidden from her eyes, he turned them back toward their new home.

"Come," he murmured. "You are going to love this place. I'm certain of it."

What woman wouldn't? She'd see every beautiful inch of his home, fall under its spell, and then she would never want to leave. Why would she return to whatever squalor she lived in? This place was so much better and had so much more to offer her than anywhere else.

The thief marched him all the way to the front door of his castle, her arm around his waist and her breathing ragged. He worried perhaps the amount of armed guards would frighten her as they waited on the other side of that door.

Greed turned, something twisting in his chest that felt suspiciously like he cared that she might be afraid. He cupped her cheeks, forcing her to look at him. "You are with me, and that means you are safe. Yes?"

A shadow flickered in her gaze. "Of course. I know."

And, oh, how he relished that feeling. She trusted him. She'd put her life in his hands by saying that, knowing that he would keep her safe. That felt... good? Better than good. It felt like he was feeding off her trust in the same way that he fed off her greed.

Though he felt no more powerful, nor did he feel like he was healing any faster, he still felt his chest puff up with pride.

"I will," he repeated. "I will keep you safe."

The doors opened to reveal the armed guards on the other side. There were plenty of them. He hadn't been exaggerating when he warned her about the manner in which she would be greeted. At least thirty men and women stood in front of them, all armed to the teeth and wearing matching feral expressions of hatred.

And at the front were his two most prized guards. Twins, almost as tall as he was, easily six and a half feet tall. They towered over the others, their hands on the swords at their hips and their eyes missing nothing.

"My lord?" The man on the right asked. He was Ivo, and his twin sister was Morag. They were deadly beings who had more secrets than he could count. And yet, he trusted them with his life without question.

"I am fine," he replied, pulling his arm from the thief's shoulders. He needed to stand on his own two feet in front of his people.

Greed refused to be seen as weak. Not in front of them, and certainly not in front of anyone else.

Other than the thief, apparently. He had been weak in front of her and... safe to do so.

The thought blistered in his mind, festering as it grew into something he was uncomfortable and unfamiliar with. Was he safe with her, too? In the same way she was safe with him?

Impossible. A woman didn't offer safety. A new collection piece did nothing other than exist on the shelf where he put it and gather dust once he was bored with the item. That was how he lived his life.

Morag stepped forward, her eyes flinty and her mouth pressed into a thin line. "We have words to speak with you, Greed. Those people who attacked us were unlike any other we've met before."

"I know. I have seen them." He started forward into his home, running a hand through his hair in frustration. "I do not know who they are, but my companion here has information. Perhaps if we start asking about, we might find more. Send out scouts, if you have them to spare, and inquire about a group calling themselves the Horde."

"What companion?" Ivo asked. And Greed watched his guard's eyes skate around him before a frown furrowed his brows. "Are you feeling well?"

"What do you mean, what companion? She's right here." But he turned and she... wasn't.

The thief was nowhere to be found. Turning on his heel, he marched back to the front doors that surrounded his keep and found her footprints still lingering in the sand. Footprints that led back to the dune they'd just clambered down.

Wicked creature. She thought she could drop him off to safety and then disappear? He'd never let her go that easily.

A grin on his lips, he turned back to Morag and Ivo. "Ready my mount. We're going hunting."

"Are you so sure that's appropriate?" Morag gestured up and down his body. "You look..."

Worse for wear, he knew. Greed had never felt so weak in his life, but he was not about to let this woman get away with his heart dangling from her fists as she laughed into the wind. That thief was staying here. Right where he wanted her.

"Get the nuckelavee ready," he snarled. "I will not let her get away."

"Can you even ride?" Ivo circled him and then grabbed the base of his tail.

The pain that lanced up through Greed's spine made him hiss and spin, grabbing his own tail out of his guard's hands. "Don't touch that."

"It's very broken."

"I'm aware!" Greed snapped. He also knew that riding would be more painful than anything he'd ever endured in his life. Even Bonescraper hadn't hurt so badly, and damn it. Had he lost that blade again? He'd forgotten that it had existed while he stared into eyes the color of sapphires.

He was such a moron around items he wanted to keep. Greed saw something shiny and new and the entire world fell away in those moments.

"Damn it," he hissed, stalking back into the oasis of his home. "She's gotten away, and it's all your fault!"

Ivo and Morag shared a look before they made their way after him. Neither of them said a word as he marched up the massive front stairwell that led toward his castle, only to pause and pat down the back of his pants.

No crinkle.

No paper at all.

"That little thief," he hissed. Greed turned to stare out at the dunes that surrounded his home, not even his eyes catching a glimpse of a figure in the distance.

She'd not only escaped his grasp, but she'd stolen her damn map back.

Chapter 8

Escaping Greed had been a little too easy, but she wasn't about to look a gift horse in the mouth. Varya had stayed buried underneath the sands for a full hour before she crawled back out.

For a man who had lived a thousand years in a desert kingdom, he sure did forget that sand wasn't stone. She'd tunneled underneath it until there wouldn't be a person shaped mound and then had herself a little cat nap. Just an hour or so, preparing herself for the long journey ahead.

And when the coast was clear, and it was definitely clear, she'd emerged out of the sands in a burst of energy and raced away from his home. Her legs carried her long and far before she stopped running.

She never quite got over the feeling of being watched, though. Maybe that was just her old habits dying real hard. Varya always felt a bit like she was being watched. The life of a thief had certainly dug its claws deep into her psyche.

Three days of lonely travel passed quickly enough. She'd long ago perfected the best way to keep herself alive. And being lonely wasn't all that bad. At least she was alive and no one was hunting her this time.

The Horde had no idea she'd left with their bounty. Greed likely knew that she'd stolen his map back, but really, did he think he could nick something like that from a thief? She'd felt him take it out of her pants. The man wasn't sneaky in the slightest.

He probably thought he'd pulled the wool over her eyes. That she was so captivated by his seduction she wouldn't notice he'd slipped his fingers against her skin. But she knew everywhere that he touched her, and she damn well knew where that map was at all times.

She wasn't an idiot. And she wasn't some swooning fool who would let a demon get the better of her.

She even enjoyed being alone a bit. No one was prattling on at her or trying to ease her. No demon was whispering in her ear about all the naughty, seductive things he wanted to do her. Even better? The only sound around her was silence. Complete, utter, boring silence.

So it was no surprise that her heart skipped in her chest the moment she saw the Shambles.

It was one of the few cities in the sands that was actually built out of stone. Though it had long ago been a thriving city, the Shambles was more buildings battling back the sands than anything else now. Rumor had it that there were at least four levels underneath where they lived. If someone dug into their sand floor, they'd eventually find more entrances into even greater buildings. But now, there were only about four sand filled levels where people could live.

And most people who lived there were a little hard around the edges. Being a stationary city had its flaws. The Shambles were real easy to rob. Anyone who had put down roots in this place was bound to have a few family heirlooms, but those were all lost a long time ago. Now it was just a city of thieves, pilfering and stealing from each other whenever they got the chance.

Such was the reason she didn't stay long. Still, she did think it was filled with good folks. Just the kind who couldn't keep their sticky fingers to themselves.

They all had their vices, after all. She couldn't say much, Varya made her living stealing.

She walked down the family center street, her gaze up on the colorful red flags above her head that fluttered in the wind. Red, that meant it was... what? The dry season already?

Twenty people milled about, their heads covered with brightly colored scarves and their clothing the same color as the sands below their feet. There were four venders set up already, a little early for the rest of them to be so prepared. Of course, that meant she got a good look at what they were selling.

They knew the risk. If they showed off their wares too early, then they were likely to get thieves' attention. But if they were lucky enough, and most of them were, then they'd find someone who actually had a bit of coin to spare.

Varya sidled up to the nearest one, eyeing the fresh slice of watermelon with hungry eyes. "How much?"

"Three coins."

She didn't have any coin on her, but that didn't matter. If she stared hard enough, she swore she could taste the sweet juice on her tongue. "You know I don't have anything to pay you with. Just came back from a job."

"Then finish the job and come back." The man behind the stall was weathered and leathery from the sun. His dark hair and dark eyes were oily as they looked her up and down, and then he smiled a grin that was missing at least three teeth. "Or you can find another way to pay."

"You like losing teeth? Is that what this is?"

Varya readied herself to punch the man straight in the throat when another voice interrupted her. "Always resorting to violence, this one. Or you could ask to borrow a few coins from a friend."

A gasp echoing in her throat, Varya spun around to see the man standing behind her. In three months she swore he'd gotten more handsome. It wasn't possible, every woman in the Shambles would agree with her. But Altan was the blinding sun on a warm summer's day. So handsome that it was sometimes hard to look at him.

His dark skin always seemed well oiled and shining in the light. His broad form, wide shoulders, and trim waist had many women wondering how it was possible he looked like that. But Varya had always noticed the kind wrinkles around his eyes, the wide smile that easily broke out whenever someone mentioned his name, and the kindness that radiated through his very being.

She launched herself into his waiting arms. The big man wrapped her up in his grip, chuckling as he spun her around, legs dangling in the open air.

"Varya! Look at you, our lucky gold coin. I didn't think you'd be back for another month at least!"

"I found them faster than I'd thought." She ripped her mask off so her dearest and oldest friend could see her grin. "I got it, Altan. I got it."

He stilled, his arms spasming around her as he slowly set her back down on her feet. "You did?"

"I did. I didn't think it was possible, but... They had it. It took me three months to find the right group, and the bastards didn't make it easy. They wanted no one to see where they ended up but they made a mistake and I... I..." She shouldn't be talking about this out in the open. Anyone this excited made themselves a target for unwanted attention.

Still. She grinned up at him, relief and hope blossoming in her chest for the first time in ages.

And she saw that same expression in Altan's features as well.

He wrapped a hand around her wrist and tugged her away from the vender. "I'll get you food back at the house. Then you're going to tell me everything that happened."

"Absolutely."

She let him drag her through the streets, giving half hearted waves to the people who knew her as they both raced across the sandy dunes. All the houses were covered in the sand, sinking deeper and deeper into it. Even his house, the one at the very far end of the Shambles, had a sand dune making its way through his front window. At least his doorway was clear as he shoved it open and then pushed her through.

His eyes narrowed as he searched the streets behind them, clearly looking for anyone who might have dared to follow them before he ducked inside the cool darkness beyond with her.

There were four other people in the house. His home was usually a revolving door of some type. There were people who were friends, though, and those who were merely passing through and needed help.

These were all friends.

"Varya!" A cheer went up and she was rushed. Four people

throwing arms around her, kissing her cheeks, pressing ale into her hands and shoving her toward the table where there were comfortable seats waiting for her.

"It's been too long," she said with a laugh. They all looked healthier than the last time she'd seen them. No more shadows underneath their exhausted eyes or clothing hanging from knobby bones.

Altan had made good on his promise. She'd said she would leave on this foolish adventure only if he promised to take care of everyone else. Usually she was the one on supply runs, making sure that everyone had something to eat and that they weren't starving.

Apparently, Altan was just as capable as she was. Even better, if the looks on their faces were any proof of it.

And there was the normal sting she felt at someone doing her job and doing it better. She hated knowing that she wasn't necessary anymore to these people. All she did was seek out impossible treasure. Sometimes she brought it back, other times, she failed. But still, her work was meaningful. If she brought back the magical artifacts, then that meant they all had a better life.

Even if it was a little more far-fetched than just bringing back food to those who needed it.

"She said she found the map," Altan declared, slapping his hand on her shoulder firmly. "Our lucky gold coin has found yet another way to help us all."

Another cheer went up, although a little quieter than the last so they didn't raise any suspicion outside of these walls.

She looked around the comfortable room and sighed with happiness. All the furniture had been carved out of the same stone as the house years ago, worn down by hundreds of hands that had passed comfortably over the surfaces. She had sat on this stone bench next to the stone table a hundred times. The windows were covered with stretched leathers, beautiful tapestries woven on the walls, and a room filled with all the people she loved.

Two of them sat on the floor nearby, brightly colored cushions protecting them from the sands beneath them. Four lanterns hung over her head, the metal guards forged to look like stars that sparkled all across the room.

Altan's hookah was in the corner, suspiciously quiet and unlit. Usually he'd be well into smoking by this time of the morning, but she didn't have any time to wonder if he'd finally quit.

Instead, she pulled the map out of her pants and laid it out on the stone table. Unfurling it, she pointed to all the markers that mentioned different artifacts.

"This one denotes the last known place where the Spear of Water was found. Three dots here mention that the Staff of Meadows was last seen in all of these locations. But this one..." She tapped the paper hard over a single marker deep in the desert. "The Eternity Goblet."

Even Altan hissed out a breath while the rest of the people in the room hummed out impressed sounds. "So the rumors are true?"

"One of the last sultans before Greed hid it away in a cave system. Apparently there are countless objects there, so many of them are marked on this map. I can't be sure that the Horde hasn't already taken what they wanted from the loot." Varya met his gaze with a wild grin. "But there still might be something left."

Altan sat heavily on the opposite side of the table, his big body splayed out in shock. "And you think we can find all of it?"

"I do."

"That's impossible."

"Only if we don't try." She ripped off her coat, letting it fall to the floor behind her. The leather was too warm and too sticky. She refused to let it ruin her excitement over this moment. "I just need a week to prepare. All it will take is a few days to rest up, then I need to get everything ready for the journey. It's a long way to go, and unsurprising that I'll need a mount. I don't think there's any venders with horses at the ready, but I might be able to barter one of our previous treasures with someone in a nearby town. Otherwise it'll take me at least three weeks to get there..."

She let her words trail off as she noticed Altan wasn't really looking at her anymore. No. He was staring at her shoulders.

"What?" she asked, looking down at her shoulder.

And son of a bitch.

That bastard.

That thieving, lying, moron had left his fucking handprints on her shoulders.

At some point while making out with him two nights ago, he must have squeezed hard enough to leave his fucking handprints on her skin. Varya bruised easily, but she could count his fingers. When had he done that? She didn't remember him grabbing onto her that hard but maybe he had.

"Where did you get those?" Altan asked, his voice quiet and dangerously low. "I thought you said you didn't get caught by the Horde?"

"I didn't." She snatched her jacket up from the floor, already angry at herself. "I ran into a little trouble along the way, but this has nothing to do with the Horde."

"Then what happened?"

She shouldn't tell them. She shouldn't tell anyone. It was a risk and she was stupid and...

Varya sighed. Rounding her shoulders in on herself like she was expecting a blow, she muttered, "Greed."

"Yeah we're all greedy, I get that's the problem. We live in this kingdom for a reason. Now how did you get those bruises?"

"Greed," she repeated. For good measure, Varya tilted her head and widened her eyes. "As in the Greed."

He blew out a long breath, eyes widening. "How'd you meet the king?"

"It's a long story."

"And I assume he knows you have the map."

Varya sat down, her jacket abandoned in her lap as she braced her elbows on the table. "Oh yeah. He knows."

"So we all need to run then." He shook his head, ankles crossing as he stared at her with disappointment. "You're always so careful! How did the king himself catch you?"

"He didn't. I sort of caught him." She tucked a strand of hair behind her ear and launched into the story. Conveniently forgetting that she'd kissed him, or shown any kind of interest in the demon, of course. And she didn't mention a word about how he was ridiculously tempting or that he'd made it very clear that he wanted her.

By the end of her rambles, Altan was looking at her with a very suspicious expression but also a resigned one. "All right. So you don't think he'll find you here."

"He doesn't know my name, had no idea the Horde existed, and I'd guess he doesn't even know the Shambles exist." She shrugged. "He's not exactly very aware of his own kingdom. Not in the slightest."

She omitted that the Horde might know who had stolen from them, though. They were more wily than any of them gave them credit for and... Well. She wasn't all that certain they weren't going to hunt her down for the rest of her days.

Better to leave town sooner rather than later.

Altan finally gave her a shrug. "Then if you think it's safe..."

"I do," she interrupted. "I'm ready for the next adventure."

But he still seemed a little hesitant. Not ready to risk her life. If that meant she had to play all her cards, then so be it. Varya was not going to stay here. She couldn't. Not when the warmth of a soft bed and friendship was already so tempting.

Sighing, she reached down and pulled out the knife that she'd strapped to her thigh. Laying it on the table between them, she pointed at it. "This is the blade they used to harm him. It cut through his flesh, and he couldn't heal."

"What is it?" Altan leaned slightly closer, his nose wrinkled as he stared at the green blade.

"They called it Bonescraper."

"Hm." He shook his head. "I don't know it."

"Niether did I, but now we have it." Varya took a swig of ale and then lifted her brow over the edge of the mug. "Well? What do you think? I have the only weapon that can harm him. I have a map to all our dreams. What reason do I have to stay here?"

Though he hesitated for another brief moment, he leaned forward and grabbed a free mug of ale, then lifted it up to her. Though his eyes were still filled with shadows and worry. "To treasure hunting."

She clinked her mug to his and then turned to the rest of them. "To treasure hunting!"

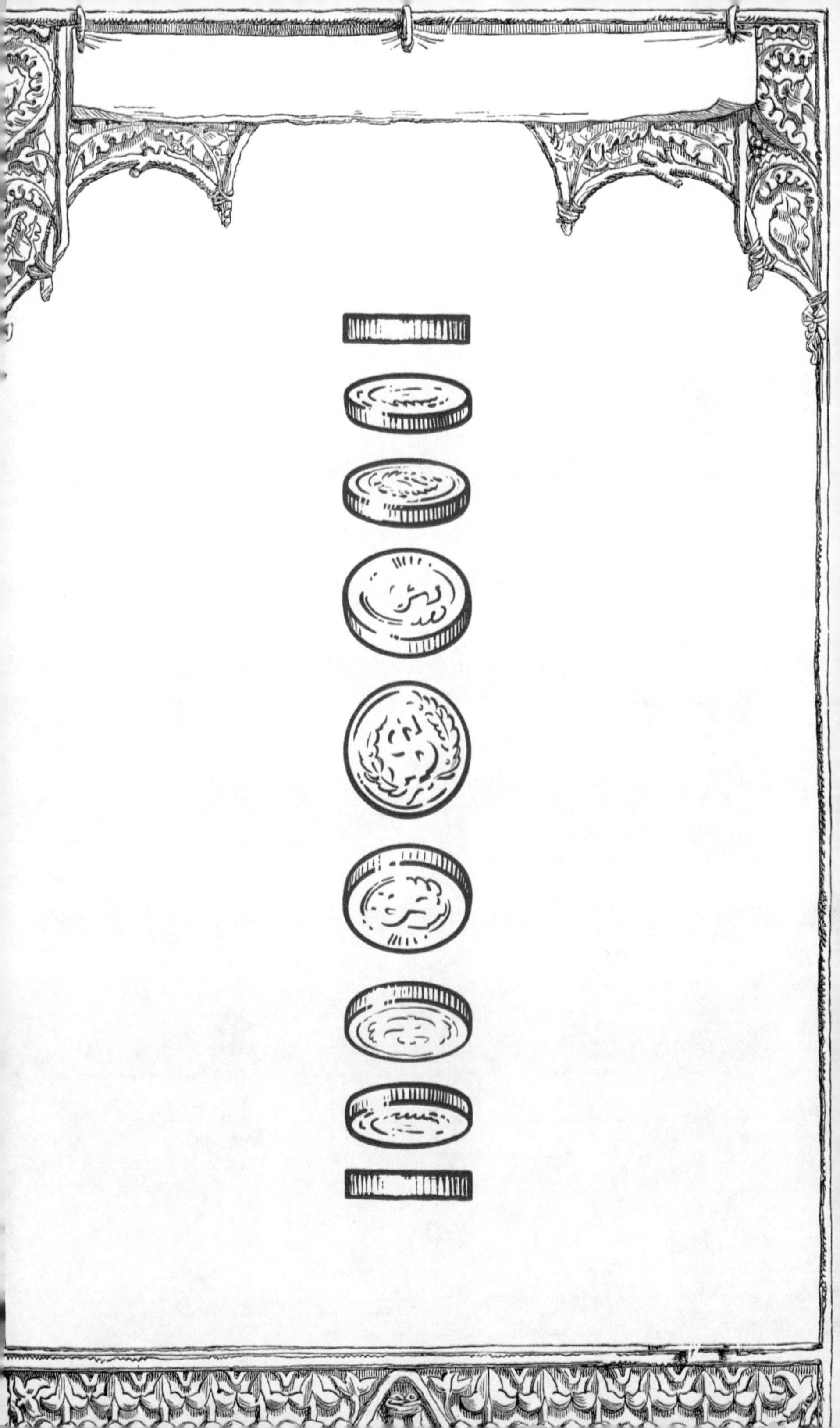

Chapter 9

W hat do you mean, you couldn't find her?" Greed snarled. He'd taken the advice of his two most trusted advisors, Ivo and Morag, and stayed in the castle. They had claimed it was far too dangerous for him to ride in his current state, and he hated to admit that they were correct. His skin hurt. His muscles ached. His tail was in a sorry state that he genuinely hoped could be fixed.

Riding his mount would have been a painful and arduous process toward what he knew would be a disappointing endeavor. And he knew the beast would fly over the sands.

In his mind, he'd already ridden toward the thief. He'd scooped her up underneath her arms and tossed her over his saddle. She'd scream, of course. The woman was a fighter and she wouldn't give up without drawing blood. But he'd have her at that point. Slung over his saddle and the back of his mount like a war prize he'd hunted down himself.

Ivo blinked at him. The tall guard at least had the understanding that he'd angered Greed. Of course, he had no idea what the reasoning behind the emotion was.

His sister, on the other hand, had a bit more sense to her. She frowned at Greed with a curious expression, trying to puzzle together why he was so upset over a little human.

Greed pinched the bridge of his nose and reclined back on the silk pillows strewn about his room. Bandages covered his entire body. Too many to count. The healers had seen to him well, but that didn't mean he wasn't ready to leap to his feet and hunt that woman down.

They'd popped him back into his private rooms, the luxurious silks covering the floor meant to make it easier on him to heal. He'd thrown countless pillows across the floor to lie upon, and a sunken bed in the corner was where he was meant to rest. Everything was painted in shades of green. The pillows, emerald. The sheets, olive. The walls were even a pale grassy color, although they were hard to see. Everywhere he looked were jungle plants, blooming in bright pinks and violets while covering the walls with their massive green leaves. Monstera plants grew tall over his head and moved in the slight wind from the floor to ceiling windows that were currently standing open.

Ivo shuffled his feet. "She disappeared across the sands. By the time we'd gotten enough of our warriors together—"

"Did I not train you myself?" Greed asked. He lowered his hand to glare into his guard's eyes. "Did I not give you all the abilities that you required? Hid you? Kept you safe? I have given you far more than any other of my brothers would have, and still you deny me this?"

"We deny you nothing," Morag replied. "We merely wish for you to understand that the thief is not as easy to find as you might think.

Greed, we will find her. We have never failed you before."

"No, you haven't," he grumbled. And there was a good reason for it.

Gesturing to the pillows in front of him, he watched as his two most trusted guards sank onto the cushions. Ivo didn't move quite like a mortal should. His body had an inherent grace that would give him away to anyone with a pair of working eyes. His movements were so fluid, so smooth, so unnatural.

"I thought I told you to work on that," Greed said, pointing at Ivo. "You look like a spirit."

"You move like this."

"I do. But people expect me to move like that. My brothers included. You are not supposed to exist." Greed leaned forward, the heat of his power rolling through his body as he said Ivo's true name. "Loyalty."

Immediately, Ivo bristled. He sat down hard on the pillows, almost tripping into them. "Is that better?"

"It is."

Morag hissed out a breath and settled on the pillow just the way a human would. Perfectly awkward and natural in her awareness of her body. "Leave him alone, Greed. You know it's not as easy for him as it is for you and I."

"I do, Passion." He eyed his two guards with a critical gaze before he let out another sigh. "I apologize for snapping. I find myself in a strange situation with this woman. I have never... Desired something so much."

"Desired?" Morag asked, her eyes seeing everything. "Or wanted?"

"Want, desire, need." He waved a hand in the air and sank back onto the pillows. Staring up at his emerald painted ceiling, he shook his head. "She would be the most impressive addition to my collection in years. You should have seen her, Passion. All fire and ice and hatred wrapped up in one lovely package."

"I saw her."

He sat back up at that, his hair flopping in front of his eyes before he shoved it all back. He stared at her, waiting for Morag to continue with her nonsense before angrily grumbling, "And?"

Morag shrugged. "She looked like any other little human. Her nose was crooked, so I assume she's broken it before. There was a scar above her right eyebrow and that's all I could see past the mask she was wearing. Pretty eyes, I suppose."

He hadn't noticed the broken nose. He'd thought her nose was rather charming when he'd looked at it.

Frowning, he flicked his gaze to Ivo. "And you?

"I didn't see her."

Ah, why had he wasted so much time bringing these two into existence?

Flopping back onto his back, perhaps a tad dramatic, he stared back up at the ceiling. "I will not rest until I have her back. You understand me?"

The two spirits remained staring at him, quiet and confident as always. He hadn't meant to bring them into this world, not really. The two of them had followed him since the beginning.

They were his friends, he supposed. Neither of them were like him or his brothers. Their emotions were not as complex, nor were they as powerful as Greed or any of the others had been. Likely, they shouldn't have been gifted bodies at all. But he'd seen them, trailing along behind him and never feeding—because when was he going to feel loyalty or passion—and he just... couldn't stop himself. He couldn't let them continue on like this when they had attached themselves to him for some stupid reason.

He already knew what his brothers would say. It wasn't his place to decide which spirits got bodies and which didn't. In fact, it should have been the entire group's decision. If they knew that Ivo and Morag were anything other than very strange twins, then they'd likely kill them.

And he didn't know what happened to spirits if they were killed in their mortal forms. He had a feeling it wasn't pleasant.

Still. He'd helped them find bodies. He'd poured them into the forms himself, and then he had trained them to be the perfect soldiers. The perfect guards who would never betray him, no matter how many mistakes he made.

Maybe he had been a little greedy in creating them but... well. It was in his nature.

"What do you want us to do?" Morag asked, her eyes flashing with the faintest pink. "I can hunt her down for you if you'd wish. She may fight me, but I doubt she could fight as hard as I."

"None of us will hurt her," he grumbled.

"Then I can send another battalion after her if you wish. They lost her tracks after the storm blew through the desert, but there are plenty of towns. We know what she looks like. Do you have her name? I could send the scouts."

No, he didn't have her name. That was part of the problem.

His mangled tail flicked. The pain that laced up through his spine helped to focus him on the moment at hand. If he knew her name, this would all be a little easier. Perhaps he could have sent out the scouts, asking for a very specific thief who had stolen from Greed himself. Anyone with half a brain wouldn't argue with them. They'd point fingers immediately.

But right now, all he knew was that there was a thief with blonde hair out there. A woman. That didn't narrow their search in the slightest, and any scout asking about her would be laughed out of every town and nomadic group in the kingdom.

There were plenty of blonde women here. Plenty of beauties. Plenty of thieves.

Morag's face appeared above his, her eyes seeing far too much. "You don't know her name, do you?"

"No," he growled.

Ivo grabbed onto his sister's shoulders and shoved her back. "Leave him alone."

"Ugh, brother. You are meant to be loyal, not blind! He does not know who she is, and has found himself stuck in obsession yet again that will lead us around the kingdom when we should do anything but!"

They argued like siblings, even if they weren't. Their spirits weren't even all that similar. Passion and Loyalty had no reason to be in the same room together, at least, Greed certainly didn't think so.

He sat up again, his tail aching and his ribs screaming in protest at the movement. His two guards squabbled over what was the right decision here, and he couldn't help but see the spirits inside them again.

This wasn't why he'd given them bodies. They weren't supposed to stay the spirits that were inside them. They were supposed to be mortals, people, learning and growing and changing. But he hadn't even known if that was possible when he'd poured them inside the two children that had died in the womb.

Lust had proven that spirits could change when they were in this form. That they could grow, just as they did outside of bodies like this. But being in a physical form gave them even greater opportunities and abilities to develop. They didn't have to just be spirits who were one thing or another. They could be many.

And though he thought himself too far gone for any of that, he'd like his guards to experience it.

Holding up his hand for silence, he waited until the two of them settled before looking at him. "I want you to feel this moment. Yes? Both of you are passionate about what you believe. Both of you are loyal to your desires. You are one and the same, with different opinions on how best to go about it."

They stared at him with blank expressions.

"What I mean to say is that you're both changing. Growing closer to regular humans every day. This pleases me."

And there were the blank stares for even longer. They clearly didn't care if they seemed like humans. They were still in the mindset that they were created for him to point at an enemy and fire. Strangely enough, he'd thought the same thing for a very long time.

Why the change of heart?

He had no idea.

That little woman had wriggled her way under his skin and he wondered if she might stay if he was a better version of himself. Still greedy and desirous of all the things she could give him, but perhaps a little softer around the edges.

Like Lust.

Lust had changed himself almost entirely for his woman and he looked... Happy. Greed hated that he'd seen the way they looked at each other. Now he couldn't get the sight out of his mind.

He wanted it, he realized. That's why he had pursued Selene at first, and that was why he'd let her go. Not because he wanted to help his brother, but because he had been so jealous it made his throat close up and his hands curl into fists. Greed didn't want Lust to have something he didn't have, and now his brother had the most stunning woman with power unlike anything the brothers had ever seen.

He wanted... that. He wanted his brothers to be jealous he'd found the better woman.

And now, he thought, perhaps he'd found someone who would give him that. He thought perhaps he would bring this woman to his brothers and display her in all his gems and jewels. They would gasp in awe over what she looked like and they would tell him for the first time that they were jealous.

Rubbing his chest, he tried very hard to keep the thoughts to himself. He didn't want anyone to know what his plan was. Not yet. Not even his most trusted guards.

"Greed?" Ivo asked, his voice hesitant. "Are you all right?"

"I'm fine." He waved a hand and then tried a pained smile. "This woman saved my life. You understand? They had Bonescraper, the blade which almost took my life centuries ago. They knew exactly how to hurt me and they would not stop until I was tortured and beaten. She didn't have to save my ass, but she did. And now I wish to repay her for that."

Ah, it was cruel the way he played Ivo. The spirit's loyalty had never once been in question, but loyalty like what the thief had proven? It was bound to ignite a fire in his guard's chest. Ivo respected one thing and one thing only. The proof that the person anywhere near Greed was just as loyal as he was, and that meant that he would suddenly be very interested in this thief as well.

Flicking his gaze to Morag, he played with the strings of his other guard's heart as well. "She was unlike any woman I've met before, Morag. Fierce and dangerous. She fought me every step of the way, corrected me when I stepped out of line, told me when she didn't like what I was doing. There was a fire in her unlike any I've seen before. She thieves, yes, but she does it for a reason I cannot understand. I think, perhaps, you could understand it."

And there it was. Passion. The pink hue in her eyes darkened, the only sign from his second guard that she wasn't quite what she seemed. The two of them were suddenly much more interested than before.

If he was anyone else, he might have felt a little guilty for manipulating them like this. But he had created them. Given them the breath in their lungs. He had the right to aim them, just as they wanted him to. If that brought them further away from being mortals who made their own decisions, who learned and grew, then so be it.

He would aim these weapons at that little thief and they would drag her kicking and screaming back to his side.

"You can find her," he told them. "My guards, my friends, who are so much more talented than any of my other scouts or soldiers. You will find her and then you will report back to me. Don't touch her. Not yet."

"She'll never know we're there," Morag said. She pressed a fist to her heart. "But we will find her for you, Greed. And then you will have your newest toy."

His newest toy.

Why did those words sting?

Instead of looking deeper at that, he turned his attention to Ivo, who nodded. "I'll find her, Greed. No matter the cost."

Chapter 10

The Sanctum of Exiles was a holy place. Well, sort of at least. Varya had heard about it when she was a little girl. This was where they sent all the people in the kingdom who had broken the law. The ones that weren't fixable. And in their kingdom, most laws were meant to be broken. Murder, thievery, all of that was fine. But there were a few laws that Greed himself did not abide by.

Did anyone else know what those laws were? No. Of course not. The idiot that she couldn't get out of her head was the only one who knew what those were. And she had a sneaky suspicion he could change them whenever he wanted.

Still. It wasn't a good idea to be here, of all places. And yet, here she was.

Tightening her fingers around the straps of her bag, she blew out a very long breath. Steeling herself for whatever she might find on the other side of the cave mouth opening.

Someone had carved it into the head of a lion. Long fangs hung down from the mouth and up from the opening. Stalactites and stalagmites had grown up further in, making it look like the throat of the lion was filled with even more teeth.

If she made it out alive this time, she would be surprised. But it was worth it. She'd take the risk for her friends that needed someone to do it. The gods knew she wouldn't send anyone else out here when they had children waiting for them back home.

A week had turned into ten days. She'd had a difficult time trying to get a mount, and even Altan had agreed that she needed one if she was going to go on this journey. He'd been a little weaselly about it, though. Insisting that he was the one to make the deal for her to get the mount, and then saying over and over that he couldn't find one. No one would barter with her either. They just kept saying Altan was handling it.

By day eight, she'd gone to the next town over, a half day's walk at that, and bartered for a donkey. The old beast wasn't happy to plod all over the sands, but it had managed faster than she'd have walked. And it carried food and water, which she would have had difficulty lugging around.

Altan hadn't been pleased. He'd worn that pinched expression on his face when she got back, and then argued that he'd been handling it. But he hadn't. And she'd had to take matters into her own hands.

Sometimes she wondered if he wanted to keep her around more. He certainly stood in the way of every adventure she headed out on, trying to keep her home more and more these days.

Stopping her from adventuring would be like killing her. Varya would never stand for it.

"One foot in front of the other," she muttered as she started up into the lion's mouth.

And there it was again. The faint prickling at the back of her neck which had started four days ago and never quite let up. Turning on her heel, she scanned the desert horizon but still saw nothing. No matter how many times she looked, there was never anyone there.

Still, she couldn't quite shake the feeling that someone was following her. It had started in the town, then trailed her across the desert to get here. She never saw any movement, though. Nothing. Not even a grain of sand out of place.

Squinting, she turned back to the entrance and headed inside. The Sanctum of Exiles had once been a thriving kingdom, or so the legends said. All the people who were banished here ended up building an empire. They'd lived for centuries underground, gathering all the magical artifacts they could until Greed led a battle to their doorstep.

They'd fought. They'd lost. The story was the same as all the others. Anyone who tried to stand up against the demon king always failed.

She didn't quite understand how, of course. He wasn't that impressive. But she had only seen the man when he was weak.

The mouth of the cave quickly descended into darkness. Varya pulled out a small torch from her bag and lit it on fire. The blaze illuminated the interior of a massive cave, one that was filled with bats above her head. At the light, they all shrieked and took off in the air, funneling up toward an opening at the very top of the cave that she hadn't noticed before. There wasn't any sunlight coming through it, though. Another exit?

Beside her feet, stairs disappeared into the darkness. There was no railing, only a steep drop off into what looked like nothing.

She nudged a rock with her foot and listened, counting the seconds until the rock suddenly clattered against the ground. A long way down.

"All right," she muttered, her voice echoing in the cavern. "Down we go."

She hated stairs. They were the worst part of raiding tombs like this. They always took forever, they were always spirals, and it always made her nauseous and dizzy by the time she got to the bottom. It didn't help that they were always wet, too. Algae covered the stone surface, making it hard for her to brace herself against the wall because her hand slipped in the sticky substance.

Not that she was in any rush. Varya already knew she'd be staying the night in the haunted remains of what had once been a rather bloodthirsty kingdom.

At the bottom of the stairwell, there were three pillars. Each one carved with a symbol of an element. Waves. Air currents. Flames. There should be earth too, she thought. Varya stepped closer, her light catching on one of the pillars that had fallen into ruin. Crumbled like dust.

"Damn," she muttered as she circled it. "This looks important."

Tombs like this were always part of some intricate puzzle. She was probably supposed to know what deities these people worshipped, turn the stones in the right pattern, and then press a stone button. The Sanctum had been very exclusive, she knew that. They were intelligent people as well.

Unfortunately, their puzzles didn't stand up to the test of time.

"Well, that solves it." Varya set her bag down on the ground, and dusted her hands off on her pants.

She'd taken to talking to herself on adventures like this. Varya so rarely saw other people, and when she did, she wasn't allowed to speak with them or they might steal from her. The sound of her own voice echoing in caverns like this was soothing.

Looking at the puzzle one last time, committing it to memory so that someone at least would remember it had once existed, she sprinted at the pillar with fire symbols. Her shoulder struck it hard, and it fell as she expected.

Wincing at the pain in her shoulder, she did it again. And again. Until all the pillars were on the ground and revealing the mechanisms underneath them. It was a shame to do it, but a girl had to keep moving. No one was stopping her.

Varya rummaged through her bag to get out her chisel and hammer, and then she spent the next hour chipping away at the metal underneath. It took a while for the first one to click into place, but then she'd gotten the hang of it. The only one that fought her was the damn earth symbol that had rusted so much in the century since this place had been abandoned that it almost didn't give.

But it did. They always did.

Grunting in approval, she stood and watched the floor beyond groan. There were circular markers on it that she'd thought were just indentations and carvings. Instead, they turned out to be a giant doorway that opened up and revealed running water about two stories down.

Deep running water.

"Oh, damn it." She muttered. She'd hoped she wouldn't get wet, but she also knew how these tombs went.

Back in the days when this was used, there were probably boats down there. There were stairs that meandered down into the darkness for people to walk down as they leapt into their boats and made their way to the real kingdom. Unfortunately, that was not the case for her.

Tightening the straps of her bag, she said a brief prayer and then toed the edge of the opening. One leap. She'd hold her breath and then the river would take her where she had to go. At least she didn't have to walk anymore.

Varya lifted her foot and then stepped forward into nothing.

Only to hang by her bag as the straps caught at her shoulders.

"What—" she hissed, wriggling until she was lifted higher in the air and then dangled in front of golden, gleaming eyes.

"Are you so quick to kill yourself when I'm not here?" Greed grinned. The man was all too pleased to be holding her like a cat who had caught a mouse.

Swearing, she tried to kick him in the thigh but couldn't quite reach. "Put me down, Greed."

"No, I don't think I will. You were insistent on leaping to your inevitable death without a single thought to what kind of place this is. You'd be dead if I didn't grab you."

Eyeing the floor, she made sure she wasn't hanging over the gap before freeing herself. She palmed the clasps at her shoulders and flicked them open. Falling into a crouch right at the edge, she punched him hard in the knee.

Hissing out a breath, he staggered away from her while hissing a few choice swears of his own. "Feral woman! What was that for?"

"I'm not a plaything," she muttered before walking up to him and kicking the back of his already weakened knee. He went down onto it, eyes wide, before he rolled away from her. "Now give me back my things."

"The things you stole from me." He turned in a crouch, her bag still in his clutches. "Don't start something you can't finish, treasure."

"Oh, I can finish it." She reached behind her and pulled out a knife. "I will not be so nice this time. You needed my help, I gave it.

Now you're trying to steal from me, and that's an entirely different situation."

He shouldn't look so tempting with that grin on his face. It shouldn't make a flash of desire heat her entire body as he reached for his own knife. "You won't win a fight against me."

"I'm a lot smaller and quicker than you. I think you'll be surprised."

He tilted his head to the side. "Come on then, little one. Let's see just how terrible a fighter you are."

Oh, she was going to kill him.

Varya launched at him, not waiting to see what he might do. He was bigger, but she was faster. She slid between his legs the moment he stood, her fingers already grasping onto her bag. But he used that handle to yank her back toward him.

Slithering out of his arms, she rolled over his back and lunged away from him. The stair, she could use the stairs.

But it was over before it started. He'd already caught up to her, using one of the straps from her bag to slide over her shoulders and yank her back to his front.

He ground himself against her hip, already hard and hot and far too tempting. "I think I like you, treasure. What do you say that I keep you?"

"Absolutely not." She struggled against the strap, but it was too tight around her shoulders and his muscular arm was a band of iron around her waist. "Let go of me."

"Absolutely not," he mimicked, before jerking her around.

Greed walked her toward the edge, the rushing water echoing in her ears as he dangled her above it again. Her feet no longer touched the ground. The only thing holding onto her was his arm and the very precarious hold of her bag.

His lips brushed her ear, his words stirring every ounce of desire in her body. "This way is a lie. Any who dared to touch the sacred waters ended up stuck in a wedge of stone where the water disappears in the earth. It is a slow way to die. You can gasp for air every minute or so, but only that. Eventually everyone drowns."

By the seven kingdoms, he'd saved her life.

Gasping, she tried not to show how pale her features had become. "Then what's the right way to go?"

He released his hold around her waist and she felt the strap give. Varya hated the little sound of shock and fear that came out of her mouth as she slipped, just a little. But he just waited until she looked at where he'd pointed, where a small opening had appeared on the opposite side of the wall. Not down, but across.

"We go that way," he murmured into her ear. "The door is the entrance into the rest of the kingdom. And depending on what you seek, I can bring you the rest of the way."

"What do you want in return?" Because nothing with this man was ever free.

His arm returned to her waist, dragging her away from certain death and pressing her against all that warm skin. The heat billowing off him warmed her to the core, but it was the feeling of his impressively large cock wedged against her ass that made her blush.

He moved, shifting against her, rubbing and teasing and she had to get control of this or they'd have a repeat of that stupid moment in the cave.

"Greed?" she asked, and hated how breathless her voice was. "What do you want in return?"

"You," he growled into her ear. "I only want you, little thief."

Oh.

Oh, that sounded so nice.

And that was exactly why she had to get out of here or she would make an idiotic mistake. She struck out with her foot, catching him on the thigh again. He made a lovely little grunt in her ear before letting her go.

"That's enough of that," she hissed, straightening her shirt and reaching for her bag. "Thank you for saving my life, but I think I'm fine on my own now."

"I'll go with you."

"No."

"I don't know how you found the Sanctum of the Exiles, anyway." He meandered away from her, eyeing the distance between them and the next ledge. "Few people know of this kingdom anymore."

"I don't know how you found me." Varya ignored him and surveyed the distance herself. "Neither of us knows everything, it seems."

He looked down at her with a much too amused expression. "I'm part animal, treasure. Didn't I make that clear?"

"That doesn't mean you can sniff me out whenever you want." He touched her back, and she didn't want him touching her. Angrily glaring, she looked over at him again to see his arms were crossed over his chest.

Was that...?

Letting out a choked sound, she slapped his tail away. "Stop that."

"Well? Did you want to investigate the rest of this tomb or not?" he asked.

"I do, but I have to find the right rock to connect my rope to and then I'll throw it over to the other side. I see nothing to attach it safely to, so I suppose I could start rock climbing." If only the ceiling was a little lower. This would be an entire day's worth of figuring if she was lucky.

Greed wrapped his massive hands around her waist and tugged her in close to him. On impulse, she held onto the top of his pants and then shrieked as he... leapt.

He jumped. From one edge to another that was easily fifteen feet wide and far too large a distance for anyone to just jump over.

But he landed in a crouch, his arm around her as he set her feet back on the ground. Chest puffed out, pride glowing out of his body. He shrugged at her horrified glance. "It's faster this way. I'd like to get back to the castle by dinner, wouldn't you?"

She watched him swagger away from her and had the thought to throw her knife into his back. The man just couldn't... he didn't have to...

Growling under her breath, she pinched her lips into a thin line and followed him. But if he thought for a second that she would let him take the treasure, she would steal it back from him in a heartbeat.

A quiet voice in her head whispered maybe he wanted her to.

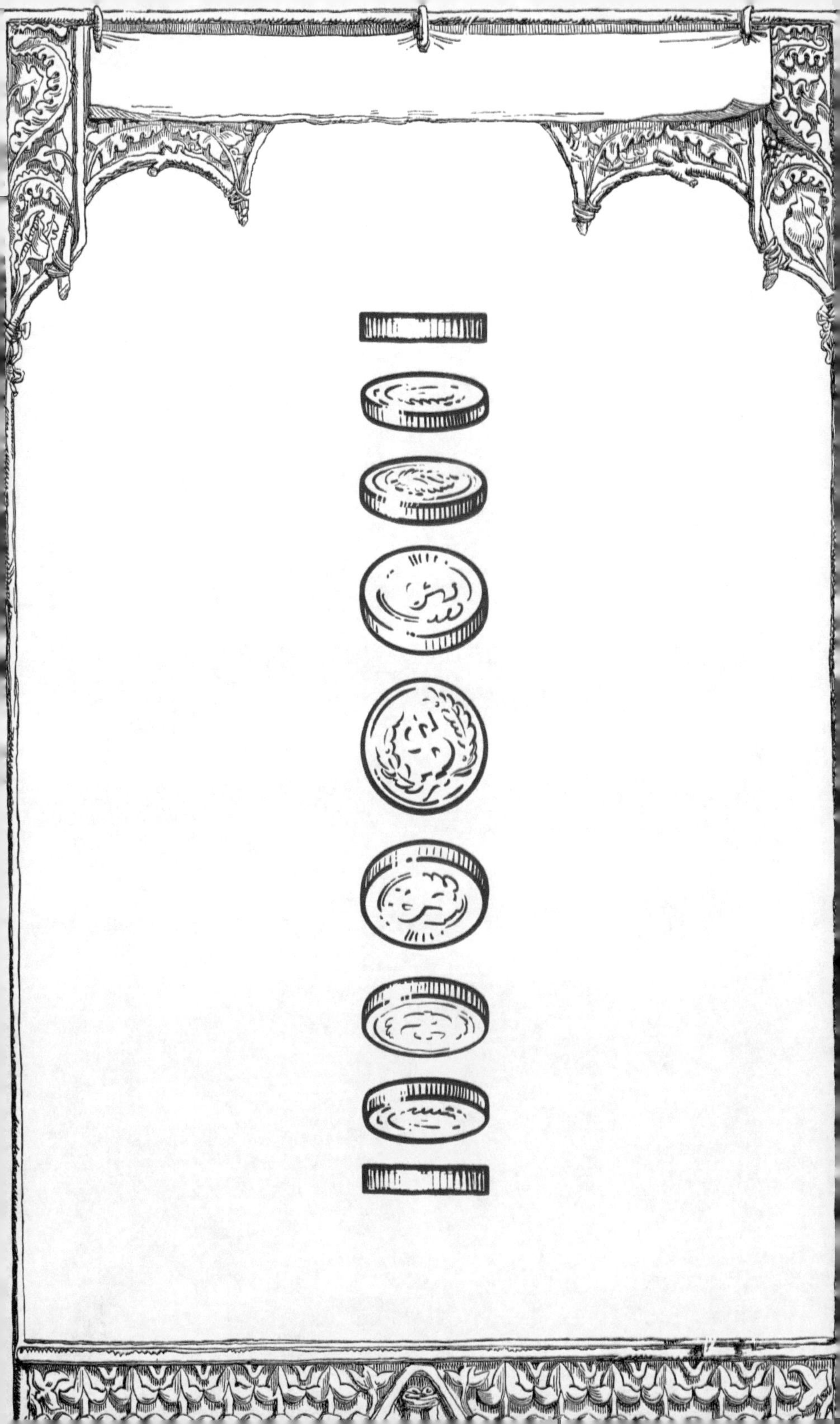

Chapter 11

It had taken him two weeks to find her. That was ridiculous and longer than it had ever taken for a single one of his hunters to find anything. And they'd hunted magical artifacts, sultans, even assassins that were sent to murder him. They found everyone they tried to find.

Except her.

And as he watched her stomp away from him, swinging that stupid leather backpack over her shoulders, he had to wonder if it was harder to find her because she was… nobody.

She was just a thief. No one knew who she was or where she'd come from. Even his scouts hadn't been able to get any information about her. Only that she flew with the wind, came home every three months or so for a few nights, and then disappeared again.

He didn't understand it. He didn't understand her.

The only thing he knew was that he was painfully hard the moment he touched her. He'd had her dangling over a cliff and she hadn't cried or begged for mercy. She'd kicked him in the knee so hard he'd felt the bones creak together and then she'd threatened to kill him.

What a thrill. What a woman to have no fear of the terrifying king of their kingdom. He'd never thought he'd find someone like her in his life, and he'd be damned if he didn't get to keep her.

A large archway had once been the grand entrance to this underground kingdom, but it had long fallen into rubble at their feet. The thin rays of sunlight from above didn't give them any light to move by, but she seemed to be fine, picking her way over the rocks. He watched her lithe body shift and move, the muscles underneath her clothing bunching with every flex of her legs and back.

Perhaps it was strange to think, but he preferred her in the green leather armor. She'd looked much more like herself rather than this strange ensemble.

"Why are you dressed like this?" he asked.

"Like what?"

He leapt over a fallen chunk of stone that had once been carved into a face to stand in front of her. "I prefer your armor."

"I don't care what you prefer," she muttered. She gave him a wide berth as she moved around him and then continued forward. "I didn't get up this morning, assuming I would see you and pick out my outfit accordingly."

He flashed her a grin. "So you would have dressed better if you'd known you would see me."

He didn't need to be able to see in the darkness for her glare to slice through him. "No."

"You would have."

"I definitely would not."

He felt his chest fill with a small sense of pride. She'd have wanted him to see her at her best. And these thin brown pants and white billowing shirt simply were not her best.

But she didn't look back at him for even a moment. Instead, she kept moving forward, picking through the rubble to the long bridge that led to the next set of puzzles.

Was she... ignoring him? He tried to lunge in front of her again, forcing her to look at him, but she kept side stepping. Repeatedly. Every time he tried to out maneuver her, she went around in the opposite way.

That wouldn't do. He had come all this way for her, after all, and this was a wonderful place to make a first impression.

"What are you looking for, anyway?" he asked, corralling her toward the edge of the bridge. The river continued underneath the stonework. And he'd already warned her why she shouldn't fall into those raging waters.

"I won't tell you that."

"Why not?"

"Because you don't need to know." She tried to go left, then right, then realized her heel was already over the edge of the crumbling bridge. Letting out a long sigh, she ground her teeth together and hissed, "What do you want, Greed?"

"I want you to pay attention to me."

"Well, unfortunately, not everything is about you and I have a job to complete. So unless you are going to help me with the next puzzle to get deeper into this kingdom, I'm afraid I need you to step aside." She even held out her arm for him to move, pointing to where she wanted him to go. "I don't have the time, energy, or desire to pay attention to you right now."

"Oh, I think you have the desire." He stepped closer to her, knowing there was nowhere for her to escape.

And ach, he was rewarded. Her pupils blew out and her mouth thinned into a firm line. Her eyes were set over his shoulder, but he could feel her wavering.

"You feel it too, don't you?" he whispered, ducking his head to inhale deeply at her neck. He ghosted his lips over the rapid pulse fluttering there, so tempting, so sweet.

"Feel what?"

"This connection between us." Her heart rate skipped against his lips, and he pressed a smile to her throat. "I haven't stopped thinking about you since I saw you outside my cage. You have consumed me, little thief."

She gasped, the sound echoing up in the cavern they stood in. And he knew he had her. She would not back away from him. She would not push. And if their first time was in a cave, ready to rob a tomb of its treasures, then so be it.

He'd find the safest place to lay her out. His thief wouldn't mind if a few rocks pressed against her spine or bit into that lovely, smooth skin. She'd slept on rocks beside him for hours on end. She didn't care about a little creature comfort and neither did he. Besides, once he started in on her, she wouldn't be able to think about anyone but him.

"Greed..." Her hand slid up his chest, fingers skimming his throat.

"Ask, little treasure, and I will give you the world."

Her hand tightened around his neck and shoved. He was so startled he actually stumbled back a few steps before she marched around him, her eyes spitting fire and her words venom. "Move, you big lunk."

Lunk?

No one had ever called him that in his life!

Frowning, he watched her move to the end of the bridge and then look back at him. She should be angry, but instead she looked... pleased with herself?

The damned woman was playing with him and he didn't know how to feel about that. She was all together not what he expected, and he wasn't sure if that was a good thing or not.

He stalked after her, his movements quiet and slow as he took in the situation. She wanted to play the game. That was fine. Greed knew how to toy with others in the same way she was toying with him. All she had to do was ask for him to give her the attention she so clearly wanted.

The next room was where most people had been greeted. He remembered the golden days of the Sanctum of Exiles. The days when there had been countless people here, all certain that they would never see him in the flesh.

"There used to be a podium over there," he said, pointing to a small crumbled section that was decorated with broken glass tiles. "The entire section had a mural of sun. Handmade with glass and more beautiful than anything you've ever seen in your life."

"I've seen a lot of beautiful things in my life."

"Not like this." He walked up to it and picked up a yellow shard the size of his hand. Holding it up, he watched the faint light flicker through it. "This was a kingdom of wealth, and oh, the art they created. I still have some of their pieces in my castle, but it's not the same without the artists themselves there to see the awe they inspire."

She paused in front of him. Her lovely blue eyes turned green through the lens of the glass. Those big eyes stared up at him with a soft expression he'd never seen on her face. "What?" he asked.

"You want me to believe you've been here before, when you were the one who sent them to this place? The exiles all wanted to go home."

He tsked. "Is that what they're saying these days? I never sent them here to rot. They all wanted to make their own place, and it's not like it's easy to build an entire city in the middle of the desert. These caves were safe. Cooler than the surface realm. They were easier to know who was coming in and who was going out."

"Is that why they made it so hard to get into the kingdom?" She rolled her eyes and turned away from him, and he swore she wiggled those hips a little more as she strode away from his side. "It sure seems like they were trying to keep you out."

He didn't follow. Maybe that was because he couldn't stop staring at her perky ass, or he'd heard her wrong. He had no idea. Greed had a hard time thinking about anything other than what he wanted to do to her when she gave him that look over her shoulder.

Still, maybe he needed to get himself a little more under control. "What do you mean, it seems like they were trying to keep me out?"

"Well, so far it's been all intricate puzzles." She glanced over her shoulder, a wicked grin on her face. "Clearly puzzles too difficult for you to figure out."

Oh, and now he was insulted.

Feigning anger, he pressed a hand to his chest. "You think I can't figure out these easy little traps that they tried to make difficult?"

"I think you'd find it harder than you expect."

He'd been here when these damned puzzles were made. But she didn't need to know that he was cheating a bit if he could remember where they were.

Crossing his arms over his chest, he feigned looking around them in detail. Long roots and vines hung down over their heads, the faintest hint of light spearing through the darkness. The remaining glass podium flickered in the light that touched it, but he remembered this place being much brighter in his day.

Ah, that was the puzzle, wasn't it? The light.

He snapped his fingers at the thief. "Give me flint."

"What makes you think I have flint?"

"You have everything ready for your travel here, do you not?" He tried very hard not to look down his nose at her, but was quite certain that he failed. "Flint, woman."

"Oh sure, now that I've challenged you all of a sudden I'm 'woman', not little thief or treasure." She swung her bag over her shoulder and rummaged around in it before handing him flint and steel.

As she dropped it in his hand, he curled his fingers around hers and tugged her closer. That soft gasp she made was music to his ears. "I'd call you by your name if you would tell it to me."

Her glassy eyes met his, so round and wide and startling. "I don't think I want you to know my name."

"Why's that?"

"Because I think you would use it to your advantage."

She knew him so well already. They were moving in the right direction.

Puffing up his chest a bit once again, he meandered over to the wall before spearing her with a pointed stare. "What do I get if I solve this portion of the tomb?"

"Nothing."

"Then I will not help you."

"I can figure it out on my own."

He scoffed. "No, you really can't. But that is fine. I will leave you here in the dark, by yourself, and I will wait until you come crawling out of it. I'll give you three days, and if you haven't come back out, I'll assume you died."

She almost seemed insulted that he would leave her here to die. He would never, of course. Greed knew how to treat one of his most prized possessions, and that did not include leaving them in a dank cave where they would rot.

But she didn't need to know that.

The thief crossed her arms over her chest and mimicked his pose, her hip cocked out to the side and her shoulders straight with aggression. "What do you want?"

"A trade."

"What do you want to solve this puzzle?" She emphasized each word.

"A kiss." No, that wasn't what he wanted. He wanted far more than that, but Greed would settle for a kiss if that's as far as he could get.

The thief tilted her head to the side and eyed him. "And if we find the artifact I'm looking for?"

"A woman who likes to bargain. I appreciate that." He stepped closer to the wall, fingering the flint and steel. "Then I expect your name, treasure. So I might scream your name when you bring me the utmost pleasure."

"That will never happen." But he could see the gooseflesh that had risen along her neck and shoulders at his words. She wasn't as unaffected as she wanted him to think.

He flashed her a smile.

"Then another kiss shall suffice for now."

Cracking the flint and steel together, he watched as the flames crawled up the walls. Ancient oil channels had been unaffected by age, apparently, and for that he was glad.

How embarrassing would it have been if he lit the oil and nothing happened? As it was, the fire roared to life and ran down the walls, circling them and stretching higher and higher until the entire room was illuminated.

Oh... Not all the glass had been destroyed by time.

The ceiling was still hand tiled with glass and marble and beautiful gemstones. All above their heads glass trees grew tall. Colorful birds were frozen mid flight, their wings outstretched and each feather so lovingly crafted that it almost looked like they could come to life at any moment. Rays of glass sunlight gleamed with fire burning behind them, almost as though the people here had once captured the sun.

He'd forgotten. How had he forgotten how wondrous this place was?

He had hated it when he had first come here. He'd hated how they could have something like this and he would never be able to recreate it. Greed couldn't even steal it away from them because it would only look so beautiful in this place, made by those hands.

And he hated them all over again right now. He hated them and loved them for their talent at the same time.

"It hasn't changed," he breathed, his voice echoing in the cavern. "Not one bit."

Then he turned his attention to her, to the awe that had her tipping her head back and looking up as well. And he realized that even with the greatest beauty above her head, he was still more enraptured by her than anything else. Her long, graceful neck. The coil of wavy hair that brushed against her cheeks. The wonder in her eyes. All of it called out to him and he wanted... needed...

The floor shuddered underneath his feet. He stretched out his arms to stay balanced and then saw in horror that another opening in the floor had appeared behind her. And she wasn't moving fast enough.

Fear flashed in his thief's eyes as she teetered on the edge, her arms pinwheeling, her mouth frozen in shock.

He'd never moved so fast in his life. Greed flew across the chamber, his arm outstretched, his heart thundering, and he just... barely...

Caught her.

His hand wrapped around her wrist. She leaned back over the chasm, all her weight supported by his grip alone. Her feet were still on the edge and her stomach and back must burn with the fight to keep herself from tumbling into the darkness.

They both had to wait until the rumbling stopped, and he felt his palm grow sweaty with nerves. But it did stop. It stopped, and he reeled her into his arms with a soft exhale of relief.

He tugged her into his chest, clutching her tightly against his heart as he bent to put his face in her hair. He could have lost her. She could have tumbled into the darkness and he'd never have seen that wonder on her face again.

And for some strange reason, that left him shaking.

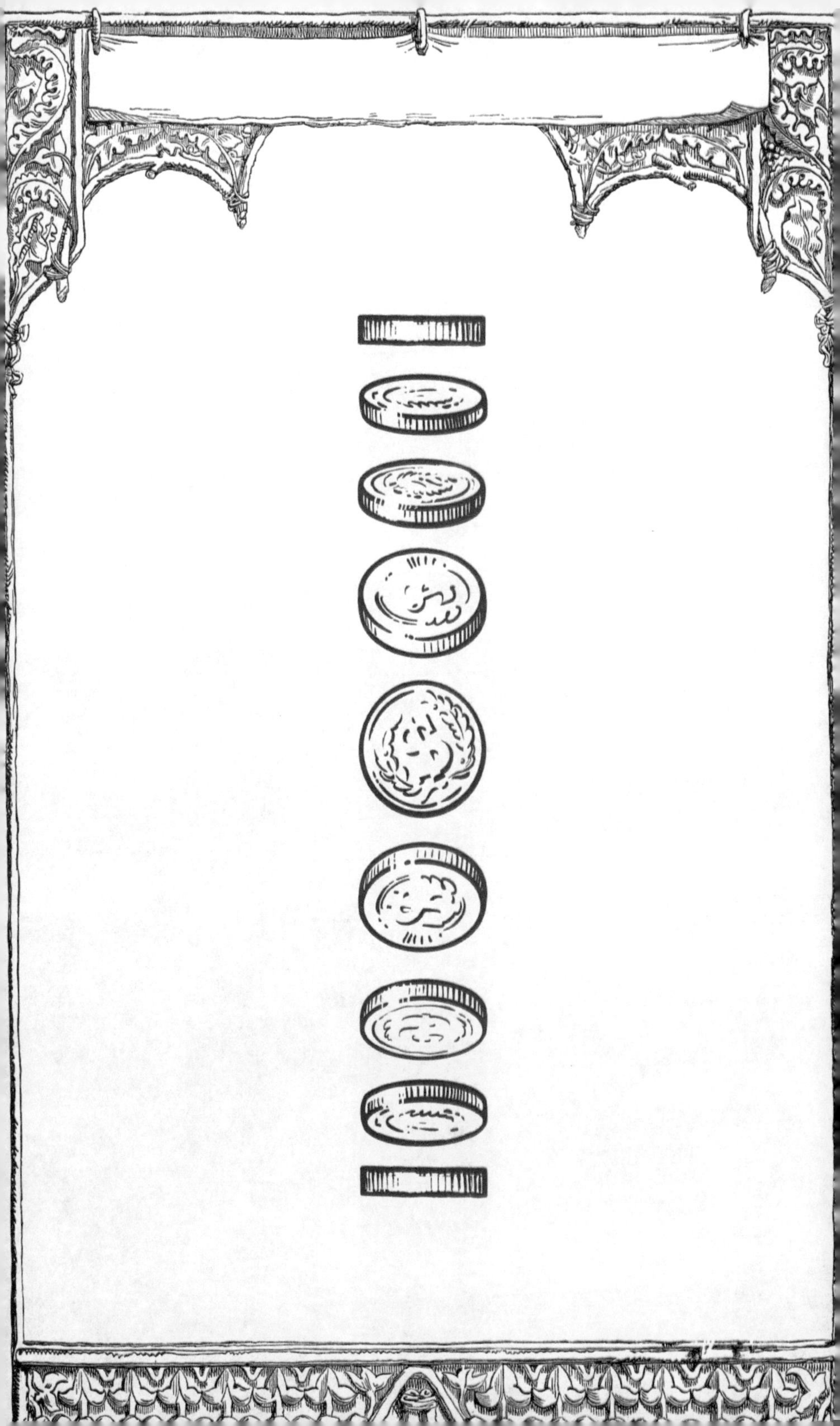

Chapter 12

Why did he have to show up and ruin everything?

She was trying her best to stay utterly avoidant. He didn't have to look that good. He didn't have to wear that smirk that made her entire body shiver every time he looked at her. And he didn't have to tease her with all those dirty words that kept echoing through her mind.

He was Greed. The king of this kingdom. A terrible demonic beast who had ruled these lands for a thousand years. The idea that he was interested in a thief like her? That was a ridiculous thought.

She'd thought he was bored in the cave. A man had to entertain himself somehow, and someone as old as him likely wanted to toy with whatever he could get his hands on. She'd admitted that it was all right. She'd kissed him back, and it had been the best kiss of her life and that was fine. Moving on would happen eventually.

And then he saved her life.

Not only that, he wrapped her up in his arms, breathing hard with his lips pressed against her head, and it felt like he cared. It felt like he would have been devastated if she fell into the water and he never saw her again.

What was that? How was she supposed to talk herself out of liking him at all when he seemed so genuinely concerned?

Cautiously, she wrapped her arms around his waist and hugged him back. Her heart wouldn't stop thudding in her chest and every time it tried to slow down, it thundered right back into that horrible drumming sound that echoed in her ears.

She almost died.

She didn't, though.

And now this man was holding her against his heart like she mattered and all those walls she'd built up around herself to stay safe came crumbling down. Just like the tomb they stood in.

"Varya," she whispered against his shoulder. "My name is Varya."

He repeated her name, savoring the sound of it on his tongue. "Varya. It's a lovely name."

"Is it? I have heard no one else with the name before."

"Because it is as rare as the woman who wields it." He leaned back, frowning down at her. "You are unharmed?"

"I'm fine."

"I didn't pull your shoulder too hard?"

"I'm tougher than I look." In fact, he'd been quite careful with her. Other than her stinging wrist that he had squeezed a bit too hard, she was fine. Alive. Whole.

And embarrassed to look him in the eye after all that. She tucked a strand of hair behind her ear and turned her attention to what had been revealed on the floor. "Is that another puzzle?"

"I think we've done enough puzzles for the day."

"And I think we're close, so we're going to keep going."

Greed hissed, his teeth bared and sharp in the flickering firelight. "You almost died."

Yeah, she had. Varya shrugged before replying, "Hazards of the job. It's not the first time."

She wanted to take advantage of the adrenaline flowing through her veins as well. If she didn't, then they'd be standing here for a while as she emptied her body of liquid through her eyes.

She wasn't a crier, and she certainly wouldn't cry in front of him.

Stepping out of the warm circle of his arms, she flexed her wrist once before continuing to the edge that had been revealed. There were stairs descending into the darkness, crumbling and old and missing whole portions. She hoped it was solid enough. The fire trailed down the outline of the stairs, sluggishly following the oil tracks that seemed much thicker than the others. Perhaps older, or affected more like the water on the walls.

Hopefully, that fire continued deep into the underbelly of this place. Otherwise, she'd have to find a makeshift torch since she'd left her other one behind.

Sighing, she picked her way down the stairs. One by one. Testing each step to make sure it would hold her weight. And the entire time she felt a massive shadow lurking behind her, watching her with troubled eyes and an expression that said he wasn't happy they were still moving.

But he didn't argue.

He didn't ask about all the other times she'd almost died.

Varya didn't know if that made her more nervous or less. His silence was almost worse than his endless chattering.

The bottom of the stairs came too quick, but at least now they faced only a wide circular door made of the same material as the trees in the other room. This one had a massive symbol on it, one that she didn't recognize. It looked a bit like a snake eating its own tail, with leaves woven all around it.

"Now what?" she muttered, trying to look closer into the design. "Is the snake a clue?"

"No." Greed pointed above them. "There's a pattern."

Ah. All along the walls were more tiled creatures. Butterflies, snakes, mice, cats, owls, so many creatures, it made her head hurt to look at them. "And what are we supposed to do with these?"

She had no idea. But it was a challenge, and she loved those. Varya set her bag on the ground by her feet and turned her attention to the creatures. "Is the pattern what eats what? The snake is eating its own tail, though, so that wouldn't make sense. What will happen if we touch things out of order?"

Greed rolled his eyes. "I am tired of this game. Do you want your treasure or not?"

"Of course I want the treasure, but I also want to keep this cave intact. What if they rigged this so the entire thing comes down on our heads if we get the wrong pattern?" Glaring at the demon, who clearly did not care about his life at all, she turned her attention back to the pattern. "We don't even know if this is the treasure room."

"It is."

"Oh, and you're so certain of that?"

"I was here, woman!" He threw his hands up in the air as if she frustrated him to no end. "I was here when this place was built and then countless times after. They would greet people at the front, where we came in. They tested to see the truth of people's ambitions in the second room. And then once they had passed those tests, they were brought here to leave all their valuable items before they entered the city. This is the treasure room, and the pattern is not that difficult. By all the seven kingdoms, I am tired of this."

She blinked and suddenly he had a fistful of knives. Where had he been keeping those? One moment he was just standing there and the next, those knives flew out of his hands. One hit the wall above the butterfly, the next the owl, a third over what looked like a toad, and then the snake.

The door behind her grumbled and groaned. Years of sand and rust made it difficult for the mechanism to open it, but there was more than enough room for the two of them to slip through.

Blinking in shock, she eyed him and asked, "What the hell was that?"

"The combination you were looking for."

"How did you know it?"

He gestured toward the floor, which was little more than chunks of earth and dirt. "There used to be a mural on the ground here. One for each of the four clans that lived inside the walls. Depending on the order you chose, that would be the room that was revealed. You wanted treasure. This is the treasure room."

"How is that possible?"

"Magic," he grinned. "And also there is a set of four rooms on top of each other. They all can be lifted and moved by a pulley system hidden on the outside of those rooms. I remember thinking it was rather genius at the time."

She agreed it was genius. And she hated how impressed she was because it made her want to see him in a different light, and she didn't want that.

"Come on then, I guess," she grumbled as she picked her way over fallen stones to the small gap in the door.

"I'm following your lead, treasure."

She shoved her bag through first and then slid through the opening, which wasn't all that tight for her. But the door was at least six feet thick and she thought it would be a tight squeeze for the massive man following her. He really did dwarf her entire body. Every time he touched her, it reminded Varya just how small she was compared to him.

Not that she'd ever met a person who wouldn't look small next to the redheaded giant that wouldn't leave her alone.

She might have even told him to wait outside the room if what was inside the treasure room hadn't made her breath catch. There was so much gold in this room. Beyond anything that she'd have ever guessed. It was...

Immaculate.

A kingdom's worth of treasure laid out in front of her and down a set of stairs into a second room. Piles of gold coins. Countless gemstones and necklaces and bracelets and rings and crowns, and was that even armor? Not to mention the heaps of magical artifacts that hummed with power just a few feet from where she was standing.

And there it was. The Eternity Goblet. It was already brimming with fresh water and she knew that even an entire city couldn't drink it dry.

They'd prepared for this. Altan had sent her with a slice of worn lamb skin and a rubbery thread that would wrap all around it. It should stay waterproof in her bag and not douse her in water for the rest of her trip. And hopefully that wouldn't empty it. No one had ever left the Eternity Goblet on its side, so she could only hope that... that...

The massive demon who followed her slid through and then chuckled when he saw what she was looking at. "That's what you risked your life for? That old thing?"

A flash of anger burned her cheeks and chest. She stomped over to it and started sealing the water inside. "This old thing can provide water for an entire village for the rest of their lives. It should be used."

"By whom?"

"By anyone who needs fresh water to drink." She turned in a flash, anger churning in her stomach as her palm itched to slap him. "No one should have to go to bed thirsty. No one should fear where they are going to get their next sip of water that wasn't gathered from a rainstorm or collected in a pit of mud. But you wouldn't know a thing about that, would you Greed?"

She hadn't meant to say so much. She'd just been so insulted that he would think it was all right to say that the goblet wasn't worth risking her life over. Like she was more valuable than something that would water an entire village, provide clean drinking water to children who were dying because there wasn't anything for them to drink.

It was just... Horrible to think about. Him saying something like that made it hard for her to even breathe.

"Hey," he whispered, approaching her like she was a wounded animal before he gently cupped her jaw. "I didn't say any of that. I didn't know."

"You are our king. You should know."

His jaw tightened, his eyes darkened, and she saw something pass between them like a shadow. But then he was back to his joking self. That flash of a grin suggested he'd already thought of something wicked to fill their time.

Greed reached over her shoulder and dangled a necklace in front of her face. "Did you see this?"

It was a beautiful necklace. A bright emerald at the center with a ring of gold and diamonds around it. It hung on a gold chain, swaying slightly in his grip. "It's a necklace."

"It's more than a necklace. It's an amulet." He winked. "Want to guess what it does?"

"Not really."

He slipped it over his head and disappeared.

Varya gasped, then got angry at herself for making the noise. Of course, he disappeared. The asshole knew every magical item in this room and would use them to his advantage.

His touch disappeared from her face and she felt a small shiver of fear travel down her spine. "Where are you going?"

"Find me."

"I will leave you in here." She crossed her arms over her chest and stepped away from the goblet. "I'm not playing this game with you, Greed."

A warm breath fanned over her ear and she felt it deep in her core. "Oh, come on, now. Play with me."

Her fingers itched to do that. She wanted to slap him, or maybe she wanted to kiss him. She didn't know, and that drove her insane. Her body didn't react to him the way it was supposed to. Instead, she was lost in this feeling. This need. This desire to indulge in her senses.

He made her lose her mind. And she wasn't sure how to feel about that.

Stepping further into the treasure, her eyes narrowed at the coins that skittered under his feet. "I see you, demon."

"Do you?" His fingers slipped over her belly, tugging her back against a warm, hot chest that felt suspiciously bare of his shirt. His fingers tickled up her ribs, ghosting underneath her soft breasts. "What do you think you see?"

Her breath caught. She shuddered, heat flooding through her entire body. She froze in his arms, suspended as though waiting for whatever he might do. Touch. Claim.

Damn it, she was better than this. Wrenching herself out of his arms, she backed down the stairs, watching the coins that should shift underneath his weight. They didn't.

Was he not following her? He must be. He wouldn't let her get away that easily.

She bumped into a warm body. Impossibly behind her, even though she'd been watching.

"So?" he growled in her ear. "Do you want to play with me?"

Damn her. Damn him. Damn this connection between them that he felt too, because she whispered, "Yes."

He lifted her by the waist, his big hands nearly touching as he lifted her up onto one of the platforms that was covered in gold and gemstones. She flattened out on them, not caring that she sent priceless stones tumbling onto the floor and plinking away from her. Because he'd ripped off the amulet and suddenly appeared, crouched above her like a lion who had run down its prey.

Eyes gleaming like the gold he'd laid her out on, he grinned. "I have yet to claim my kiss, treasure."

Oh, she would kiss him. If he wanted her to kiss him, then she would devour his lips just like she had last time. But he didn't kiss her. Instead, he leaned down, warm breath fanning over her throat as he slowly dragged his tongue along the vein that throbbed there.

"Can I kiss you?" he asked, and somehow it sounded like he was asking permission for something very different.

"What?"

"Can. I. Kiss. You?" Greed repeated, his lips sliding down her shoulder and hovering over her breast.

Oh.

Oh.

Yes.

No. No, definitely not. She hadn't said yes to this, and she couldn't. Her entire soul was on the line right now and if he did that then she would never...

"Please," she heard herself whimper.

The growl that came out of him was nothing short of animalistic. He latched onto her nipple through her shirt, his tongue flicking at the tip until electric shocks zinged between her legs. And then he bit hard. Hard enough that she arched up into him, and shouldn't she be arching away? She should not be trying to shove herself closer to that wickedly talented tongue that flicked and circled and made her wild with need.

His hands flexed on her sides, drawing down and over her hips, digging into her flesh in a way that made her see stars.

She wanted him. The same desire as before burned her up from the inside out, and she didn't think she would survive if they didn't continue. If he didn't touch her the way she needed. If he didn't plunge inside of her, as only a demon king could do.

She opened her mouth to beg him, only to feel a cold breeze on her chest. She sat up on her elbows, looking down to see... nothing. No one. Just the pale outline of her nipple through the wet cotton of her shirt and her legs spread obscenely wide.

She didn't have time to feel embarrassed. Her pants slid down to her thighs, just enough to expose the shaved mound there to the same breeze. And then warm breath.

He was still here.

Her breath caught, shocked as she stared at what couldn't possibly be an invisible demon king who leaned down and licked.

Varya's head fell back and her eyes fluttered closed. He did it again, wrenching a moan from her lips as that wicked, rough tongue licked between her folds. She felt how wet she was. How embarrassing that should be. But all she could think about was the friction of that wonderful tongue against her clit as she ground herself against him.

Over and over. He licked and sucked and flicked and she couldn't think.

Until she was right there. Right on the brink. Right where she desperately wanted him to bring her, and then he stopped.

She felt the rush of heat as he loomed over her again. Heard the wet sound of his tongue licking up her juices from his lips and if she focused hard, she could almost see it glistening on his beard.

"Come find me again, little thief," he snarled, his voice echoing in her chest. "That's just a taste of the hours I would give you. The pleasure you would find in my castle."

"I found no pleasure," she spat. How dare he stop now? And then to talk to her like he'd given her a gift when the man had done nothing.

He chuckled, and the sound turned her cold. "I know. You don't get to come unless it's on my tongue, Varya. You don't get to feel that rush unless you're wrapped around my cock. Do you hear me?"

"You don't tell me what to do."

"Oh, I do." He leaned down and nipped at her ear, hard enough to draw blood. Hard enough that she gasped and flinched away from him. "If you disobey me on this and touch yourself, I promise you that your punishment will be most severe."

And then he disappeared. For real this time. She felt the cold air rush into his wake, leaving her sprawled out on a massive mound of treasure. Alone.

Breathing hard, she stared up at the ceiling and wondered what the hell had just happened?

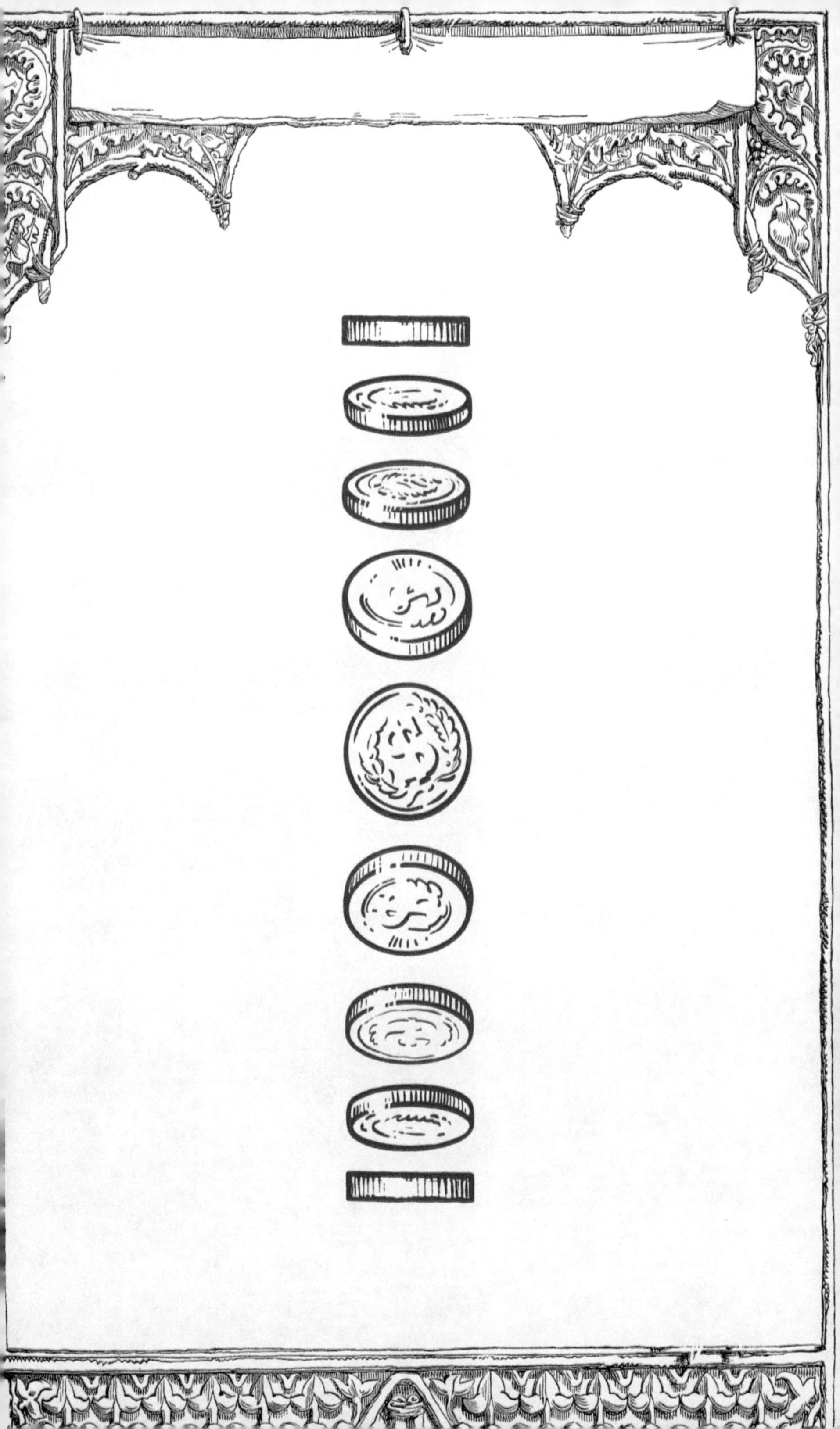

Chapter 13

Two weeks later and he could still taste her on his tongue.

A part of him had wanted to gather her up and drag her back to his castle. He'd lay her out on silk pillows and cushioned ground, decorate her body with the finest of jewels and stunning gold. He would drown her in wealth and comfort until she agreed to stay with him as long as he wanted her.

But he also heard her when she'd explained why she was there. Varya, his little thief, had been there because her people didn't have enough water to drink. And that was his fault.

She had yelled at him. Told him off. Done all the things that everyone in his life should have been doing. He had an entire panel of advisors. People who were from all around the kingdom who should have told him about the dire circumstances that had befallen his kingdom.

They had not.

There were countless towns and cities in his realm and none of them had deigned to tell him that their people lacked water. None of them had even hinted that they needed help and instead, he had been forced to stand in front of his newest treasure like a moron who didn't know how to run a kingdom.

He supposed he shouldn't have expected anything more from a kingdom of thieves. But a part of him had. He'd elected those advisors because of their capabilities in mathematics and their shrewd minds. They were the most prepared to run a city on their own, and he had given them all the tools to do so.

They had betrayed him. They'd betrayed their kingdom and their people, and he didn't know which was worse.

So he'd left her surrounded in priceless treasure and magical artifacts, her chest heaving while she was completely unaware of the vision she had been. Laid out on gold coins with long strands of gemstones and pearls tangled underneath her back. She'd glared at him, her legs still askew and all that pretty, pink, dripping flesh just waiting for him to return.

She'd been angry at him for leaving her like that, and he was angry at himself. He'd wanted to feel her clench around his tongue and fingers. He'd wanted to know the sound she made when she came apart just from his touch.

And yet... something in him had said "this is not the right time," and so he'd withdrawn.

It had taken him the better part of a week to understand why he'd stopped himself. And then, of course, he had felt foolish in not realizing why sooner.

He did not deserve to taste her on his lips until he could answer her questions. He refused to stand there like a dolt while she accused him of not knowing what was happening in his own kingdom. And he didn't know what was going on.

But he would damn well find out. Only then would he reward them both.

The sound of a fist clenching around reins drew Greed from his thoughts. Tilting his head slightly, he saw Ivo's hands shift back into a relaxed state. His sister had done the same thing on Greed's other side.

"What is it?" he asked, his eyes scanning the sands as they approached one of the nearest townships.

"I don't know." Ivo looked in the same direction. His brow wrinkled. The spirit turned flesh had a sixth sense for much of his mortal life. Greed had learned a long time ago to be nervous when Ivo was.

Frowning, he drew back on his own reins and paused on the highest dune, looking down on the town. He knew what they looked like. Three dark figures on the horizon, seated upon skeletal beasts that looked similar to horses. But their flesh was withered and wizened, leather hides creaking as they moved. And the three tall figures upon them were larger than life, bigger than most humans, and menacing, with their armor and blades strapped upon their backs.

No one in that town would look at the horizon and feel anything other than a shiver of fear down their spine. As they should.

This was the first advisor Greed discovered to have lied. The man's name was Oryx. He was perhaps the youngest on the advisor council and had proven himself to have a quick wit. He'd even kept up with Greed while he had spoken with the young man, and Greed had been more than a little impressed. Now he understood why.

He could not, would not, under no circumstances, allow one of his advisors to lie to him. Not while their own township or city needed his help.

This was a smaller town. Not a city by any means, and it was not one that had ever prospered well. He'd given it to Oryx in the hopes that the young man would prove himself. If he could bring a city like this out of the dust, then he would get a bigger one. And so on.

Looking down at it now, he could see just how wrong he'd been. The town was filled with dust and sand. There were no crops growing in raised beds, or even an attempt at farming. No cattle, no horses, not even a chicken wandered those streets. Essentially, nothing that Oryx had reported.

Laundry hung outside a few of the houses, but even that was threadbare and thin. These people were poor and likely hungry.

Greed didn't enjoy seeing his kingdom in this state. Not when he knew how much they paid out to his advisors, who then gave him money as well.

"Do you think he's pocketing some of the money?" Morag asked, shifting on top of her mount. The beast shuffled to the side, hungering for battle. Its sharp teeth would tear into the flesh of any who stood in their way.

"He's definitely pocketing a lot of it."

"How are you going to get him to admit to that?"

Greed flicked the reins, and his nuckelavee lunged forward toward the town. He could already feel its heaving breaths as long strings of drool landed on the sand. The beast knew this was a fight they were about to run headfirst into, and it was pleased.

"Let me deal with Oryx," he growled. "He'll confess to everything."

And if he didn't, then Greed would get his satisfaction one way or another. The advisor had no idea what monster he'd unleashed.

They thundered through the sand covered streets. People leapt out of their way, landing in pottery or even the few stalls where people were selling food and what looked like muddy water. He didn't care. Soon they would have enough food and water to last them a lifetime. He'd send it from his own personal stores if only to gather their trust once more.

He was just as greedy with the attention of those who lived in his kingdom as he was with everything else he owned. They would show him fealty and they would love him. Because he was their king and no one else would ever surpass him.

Not even their advisor, who thought that he was better than the very demon king who ran this kingdom.

They raced to the house at the very end of the city. The one that was larger than all the rest. And though Oryx did not decorate his home on the outside, nor had he left any plants, it was cleaner than all the others. It was clear his house had wealth and power.

The small courtyard out front even had a water fountain. Though it did not flow over the top and bubble down, there was clean water in the basin of it. Considering the blockades made of twisted metal that surrounded the property, Greed had a feeling that water was for the inhabitants of that house and no one else.

Sighing, he drew his steed to a halt outside the home and dismounted. A small crowd had already gathered in his wake, the people of this town watching him with shock and awe.

They knew what their king looked like. They knew who the monolith of a man with flaming red hair had to be.

"Is that Greed himself?" someone whispered.

Another person hushed them, but yet another voice lifted. "That is! It's the demon king!"

He turned toward them, a frown wrinkling his features as he

watched them. "Where is your water?"

No one replied.

He tucked his hands behind him and started toward them. A few of the villagers skittered back as they realized just how large he was the closer he got. "I won't ask again. My guards and I look for fresh water. You should have this. Where is your water?"

A few people in front of him flicked their gazes at each other. A man and woman, wearing matching red scarves over their heads that had faded into a dull rust color. Their skin was burnished by the sun, dark and leathery from years of burning in the desert heat. Neither of them would tell him anything.

But the little girl who clutched at her mother's dusty brown skirts? That was the one who would tell him everything.

He bent at the waist and held his hand out for her. Her wide, dark eyes took him in. He must appear even larger at her height, his bulk spreading out on the sands and his smile a little sharp as he tried to gesture her forward.

"Please," her mother whispered. "Please, no."

"I have no interest in your daughter other than for answers."

The woman shook and placed a hand on her daughter's chest, holding her child away from the demon before her. "I... She's not good eating, m'lord. All bones, this one."

He flinched and glared up at her. "You think I'll eat your child?"

"We've all heard what the demons do with children they get their hands on." She swallowed, but a hardness straightened her shoulders. "I'll not have my child subjected to that end."

"I'm not hungry," he snarled. "I want someone in this fucking cursed place to tell me where the water is."

His voice thundered and roared, too loud for anyone to be

convinced he didn't want to hurt them.

But it was the little girl who pointed at the house behind him. "It's in there."

Greed closed his eyes and took a deep, quieting breath. "Is it, now? Little one, how often do you get to drink that water?"

"It's for the lord of the town," she whispered, then hid those big dark eyes behind her mother's skirts. She still finished telling him, though. "We get our water from the rain."

From the rain?

Damn it, his little treasure had been right, and that made him burn from the inside out. Apparently, he'd made some noise or appeared even more frightening because the parents raced away from him. The mother scooped up her daughter in her arms and sprinted into the nearest alleyway.

It didn't matter. He would take their fear of him as much as he would take their love.

Turning his attention to Ivo and Morag, he jerked his chin at the house. "Bring him out."

Other villagers were arriving already. They were clearly interested in what their king was about to do, and he felt their greed scenting the air. Like whiskey and wine, all powerful and consuming. He could grow drunk on it. Feast upon their emotions and glut himself on the power that only he fed from.

Instead, he held himself still and quiet until he heard shouting behind him. Oryx stumbled out of his home, shoved out by Ivo, who stood behind him like a living shield. Morag stayed in the shadows behind them, her hands on her blades. Already, a thin line of blood marred Oryx's handsome face.

The man was what every woman dreamed of. Tall, thin, lean, more muscular than most of his counterparts. The man's skin was like warm caramel and his eyes were framed with long, dark lashes. He gathered himself and strode toward Greed, uncaring that he lacked a shirt and his trousers were still half buttoned.

"My king!" he called out. "I didn't know I should expect a visit from you. Please, come inside."

"I'm not coming inside."

A flash of fear in Oryx's eyes gave him away. One moment, the man was looking between him and the crowd of people standing behind him, and then he was running. Ach, they always tried to run.

Rolling his eyes, Greed paced beside the fountain as Morag launched into movement. Her quick feet were faster than any mortal. And in this moment, he didn't care that she failed to hide how different she actually was. Passion was agile, too fast for human eyes to even track. So fast even the wind couldn't catch her.

In moments, she had his advisor on his knees in front of him. Her hand on his shoulder, not even breathing hard, she stared back at Greed with an understanding.

This man died today. He had lied and so he would pay.

Greed leaned down, hands on his knees, and grinned into the face of the terrified man. "You've been lying to me, Oryx."

"I haven't. I would never."

He gestured to the crowd of people. "Then why did I hear your people were lacking water? When you have been given a water source to dole out to your entire town, making sure your people were cared for?"

"It was always implied that I could do whatever I wished with the water." Oryx swallowed, but then his gaze turned flinty. "You've never cared for your people or how our towns were run."

He hummed deep in his throat. "And I was always told that humans were kinder than demons."

Wasn't that what everyone always said about him and his brothers? Demons were monstrous beings that were unpredictable and evil to their core. Should he show them they were right?

He thought so.

Grabbing Oryx by the back of the neck, he dragged the man toward the fountain. Of course, his advisor fought against him. He had to know what Greed was going to do, but he carried the man by his head like a toy.

And when they reached the edge of the stone, Greed peered down into the three inches of still water there.

"You know, it's possible to drown in an inch of water." He sighed and then gave the man a little shake. "I've never believed that. Do you?"

Oryx spluttered something that he couldn't quite make out. That was all right, though. Greed didn't need to hear him speak. He already knew the man was guilty.

Lifting him up, Greed shook him one more time. "Let's find out if it's true together."

Oryx's eyes widened in fear before he tried to grab onto the edge of the fountain. But Morag held onto his arms and then Greed plunged the man's face into the water. Three inches ought to be more than enough. He held him down as the man struggled, already wasting precious bubbles of air as he screamed.

Ignoring the man in his grip, he turned his attention instead to the crowd. "Your water was always meant to be rationed between all of you. Your advisor was a fool. You will be appointed a new one."

They all stared at him with horrified expressions, but no one argued with him. They wouldn't put forth their own suggestion for an advisor either, but that was fine. He'd find a better one. One who wouldn't be such an idiot.

Already Oryx's fight had weakened. His hands didn't so much as push at the stone as he was grabbing onto it now. Trying his best to stay alive when his body knew the struggle was futile. Soon he would die and Greed would feel a margin better.

"Mercy!" a voice screamed across the crowd.

Frowning, he narrowed his eyes and tried to find the origin of the voice. But everyone in the crowd looked at each other as though surprised as well.

Who would dare interrupt him in this? He punished a man who deserved to be punished. A man who had no right to take from his people, and therefore to steal from Greed himself.

Then he saw a flash of deep green in the back of the crowd. A green he recognized.

As he peered through the crowd, Greed saw the glint of gold and a dark mask that covered her face.

Ah, but his treasure hadn't been able to stay away from him for very long, it seemed. Perhaps she'd even been following him.

"Say it again," he called out, his voice deep and gruff.

"Mercy!"

He knew that voice anywhere. How could he forget it?

The crowd took up the call as well, and just as he felt Oryx go limp in his hands, he dragged the man out of the water and slammed him down on the ground hard enough that his lungs spewed the fluid out. Rolling onto his side, Oryx coughed and curled into a ball as Greed looked at his guards and raised a brow.

"I'm going hunting," he snarled. "Clean up this mess."

"As you wish," Morag replied, already circling Oryx on the ground like a predator around its prey.

And then Greed took off through the crowd, following the flash of gold and green that disappeared between the sandy buildings.

Chapter 14

It shouldn't be so thrilling to run from him. Varya shouldn't feel a little zing of excitement as she raced down the alleyway and into the next. He was a demon hunting her. She'd heard the words he'd told his guards.

He would not let her go this time. She was certain of it. The desire to control her had been right there in his eyes the moment he'd realized who was standing in the crowd.

He was dangerous. A beast wearing the clothes of a man and she knew just how little equipped she was to handle him. He'd let her go the last time he'd seen her, but he wasn't likely to make that mistake a second time.

Feet slamming on the ground, she forced her thighs to work through the burn of running in sand. She had to get away from him, or maybe she just wanted to see how long he'd chase her.

Mere heartbeats later, she could hear him. His booted feet made quick work of the distance between them, as though he was made to run through sand like this. She'd thought he would be a lazy king, one who stayed in his castle and never once came out to see all those he ruled. She'd thought that she had gotten the better of him, shouting that he was a terrible ruler who had left his people to thirst and hunger.

But he'd... surprised her. Just as he surprised her now with his speed and agility as he raced through the buildings after her.

A low growl struck her spine, and she felt him reaching for her. Clawed hands already outstretched. But she was faster than this. She could prove herself a little more before he ever laid a hand on her.

She spun down the next alleyway, but she didn't really know where she was going. Varya wasn't even supposed to be here in this tiny town without a name. She'd been coming back from watching the Horde's movements, as the group had apparently gotten wind that she'd stolen the Goblet of Eternity.

Then she'd seen him. Greed and his two guards. Not nearly enough protection for a man who had already fallen once to the Horde. And something in her gut said to follow him. To make sure that his guards did their job this time, just in case. What if she had to help him again, because no one else would risk their neck for such a fool?

And now, here she was. Running away from him down alleyways that were growing tighter and tighter the more she ran.

Until she found herself staring at a dead end.

Breathing hard, she looked around, searching for whatever details she might use to her advantage. But there were no laundry lines, nothing other than three tall stone walls on either side of her. No crates. No windows. Nowhere for her to go.

He seemed to know that.

Another growl echoed from behind her as the predator stalked his prey. She stood still, her back to him. Varya flexed her hands at her sides, promising herself that she would not, under any circumstances, show fear. He didn't deserve to win her fear after chasing her through the streets like that.

It wasn't fear that made her chest feel hot and her cheeks burn. It was a flash of memory that nearly brought her to her knees.

A warm tongue between her thighs, strong hands holding her down as she wriggled against him, the sound of his groans as he'd tasted her for the first time. And then it was like she was right there again. His warm breath fanning down her neck, a heated palm touching her belly and pulling her against a muscular chest that was as still as the sand on a windless day.

He lowered his lips to her ear, and a shiver traveled down her spine. Gooseflesh rose all over her body, and she wanted to beg him to touch her again. Just as he had before.

This was all so stupid. He was a demon king and she shouldn't want him in the slightest, but she had been so lonely for such a long time. Would it be all that bad to let him touch her? She didn't have to go on all these adventures and dangerous supply runs and seek all the magical artifacts she could find when he was right here. Wanting to give.

And she wanted to take.

She leaned her head back until she could feel his chest against the back of her head. He inhaled, and she knew he was dragging her scent into his nose. Delicately, slowly, she turned her head to the side until the long length of her bare neck was available for his lips.

He did not disappoint. Greed trailed kisses up her throat until he growled in her ear, "So, treasure? How much do I need to punish you?"

Of course he would bring that up. Her cheeks flamed even darker red, and she didn't want to tell him anything, but found herself saying, "No need for punishment."

He froze, every muscle in his body seeming to seize against hers. Stiff and voice deeper than she'd ever heard it, he said, "Two whole weeks since I've seen you, and you tell me not at all?"

"You told me not to," Varya replied. And because she wanted to see how much power she had in this situation, she added, "I listened to my king's demands."

And oh, his entire body shuddered behind her. She felt it travel through him, how he shook beneath her with barely contained need.

She had more power here than she expected. If she was right, then she could put this demon king on his knees at any point, and he would do exactly what she said. Greed wanted to pretend like he was in control. He wanted to order her around and whisper filthy things in her ears, but that was because he wanted her to have all the power in this. He wanted her to command his attention so that when he desired to feast, he could.

Why did that tempt her so?

She wanted to turn around in his arms and wrap herself around him. She wanted to push his shoulders down and force him to finish what he'd started because he had left her in a state of near constant arousal since that damned tomb they'd raided. He had consumed her mind and body and all sense of reason because she wanted him.

Blowing out a breath, she tried to calm her mind and all the desire. Think, Varya, she thought to herself. Why was she even here in the first place?

"Were you looking for me?" he muttered against her neck.

She opened her mouth to answer, but all that came out was a groan as he dragged his tongue up her neck. His lips closed on her earlobe, gently biting and distracting her from whatever she might have said.

"I…"

His hands clenched around her waist, and she thought for a moment he might spin her around. Instead, he growled, "You what, treasure?"

Varya swallowed hard. What had she been thinking? Saying? She couldn't quite remember, but all she knew was that he was sliding his hands up her sides and it felt so wonderful.

His hands cupped her breasts, and even through her leather armor, she could feel the heat of his palms. He squeezed gently, and then growled again, "Varya, you're supposed to answer me when I ask you a question. Yes?"

"Yes." She nodded. "I was following the Horde when I saw you and your riders. I followed you because I wasn't sure why you were here when the Horde was here as well."

"Were you going to protect me again?" He walked her forward toward the wall. "What a feral woman you are."

"Well, no one else was going to do it," she snapped. Varya slammed her hands to the stone before he planted her face first into it. And though she had thought he was being careless, she realized with his groan of pleasure that he'd put her right where he wanted her.

Hands against the rock, slightly bent forward. Her breath skipped as he kicked her legs into a wider stance. Was that the sound of his belt? Surely not. He wouldn't take her right here where anyone could find them?

Or maybe he would. Maybe he would press himself inside her, plundering every part of her body and soul before the entire township that he had just saved. Because she asked him to. Because she had said they needed water.

Greed ground against her, but he'd kept his pants on. His stiff cock pressed between her thighs with all the impossible weight and bulk of a demon.

"I told you what I wanted," he said, leaning over her to nip again at her ear. "But, my treasure, you have to want it just as bad. I want to hear you say it. I want to hear you beg for me."

Biting her lip, she rocked back against him. The friction was incredible against the leather of her armor and whatever he was wearing. She didn't care. Right now she just needed him to move, to do something other than press himself against her and not move.

"You seem frustrated, treasure." He rocked again, his hips pressed flush against hers. Almost too hard. "You have to ask me for what you want, remember? Ask and I will give you the world at your feet."

She wanted that. Yes. She wanted the world at her feet.

Spinning around, she turned in his arms to face him. To force him to look into her eyes as he said these wonderful things because she didn't quite believe him. How could she?

Greed was a demon king. He had left this kingdom to rot on its own while he lived in the only oasis in the entire kingdom that still survived. He couldn't want her, a wandering adventurer who had never settled down with anyone. And he certainly didn't want a woman who could only give him a small amount of who she was.

He was Greed. If she gave him an inch, he would take a mile, because he would want everything she had to give him.

Varya slid her hand up between them, gently touching all those hard planes of muscle that were so tempting. He was a man made for sex. A sledgehammer of pleasure that took out any woman he wanted in front of him. All she had to do was let go.

Still, she touched his close cropped red beard, tangling her fingers in the surprisingly soft hair. Tugging hard, she pulled him closer to her.

Her lips ghosting over his, she whispered the words against his skin. "I will ask you for nothing, Greed. You are going to give it all to me of your own free will. I will take from you all that I desire, and you will not complain."

"I do not give anyone anything," he snarled against her lips. "I am Greed. I will have you as I wish, when I wish, and how I wish."

"Yes, you can have all that." Varya pressed her lips to his, hard enough to bruise, and then wrenched back. "But I will take as well, demon king. I will take from you just as much as you take from me."

He almost looked frightened at her words, but then something in him snapped.

His hands scooped down to her ass, lifting her up into the palms of his hands as he thrust her back against the wall. This high, he pressed against her core perfectly. Her face reached his where her legs had once been too short. Tunneling her hands into his fiery hair, she kissed him. Fierce and proud and giving no quarter when he tried to take from her.

All that passion, pain, and need coursed between them. Arcing back and forth like they'd both been struck by lightning.

He ground himself into her core until she felt herself slipping against the leather, soaking wet and needing him inside her.

"Aye, then," he growled into her lungs. "Take from me, treasure."

Hooking her ankles behind his back, she threw all her worries to the wind. It didn't matter who he was or who she was. All she wanted was to lick and bite and fuck him until neither of them remembered words.

Trapping his lower lip between her teeth, she bit at him while he reached between them. His big hand worked between her legs before he let out a hiss. "Why are these still on?"

"Are you really going to fuck me in an alley for the first time?"

He bit her neck, his teeth grazing hard against her skin. "I'll fuck you wherever I want, treasure. Against a stone wall and between cool silk sheets."

She melted at the words. Her head fell back as he laved at her neck, his fingers making quick work of the ties between her legs. He was almost frantic in his movements as she rolled her hips against his to urge him on.

She wanted this. Gods, she wanted to feel like someone other than who she really was for a few moments.

Neither of them heard the faint sound of smoke hissing from a magical canister. But she felt him sag against her, then stagger a bit. And even though he was weakened by whatever spell had been thrown at him, Greed never once released his grip on her. He let her legs go gently, easing her down until she could stand on her own.

"What trap did you lay for me?" he asked, his words slurred.

She hoped he was looking at her face when she looked up and saw shadows moving toward him. She hoped he realized that terror ran through her veins as she recognized the faces that grinned at her.

"Greed," she whispered. "Where are your guards?"

He shook his head like a massive lion, his hair a mane around his head as he struggled to stay upright. "Close."

"Good. That's good."

Because she'd come here knowing that the Horde would try to attack him again. She'd felt it deep in her bones that they were going to do something that would make her need to protect this man. Greed had done what she'd asked, even though she hadn't really asked for anything.

This was just one town. But now they had water, and that was because of him.

Tilting her head back, she let out a scream that they must have heard all the way at the other end of the town. Lunging around Greed, she ran right for the members of the Horde who had come here.

Perhaps they had already intended to steal from this town. Maybe they wanted to pick on people who couldn't defend themselves. Or maybe they'd been hunting her. She didn't care. Whatever it was they wanted, she would divert them from the demon king, who already fell onto his knees in the mist.

Whatever spell this was, she would destroy it soon enough. No one should have the ability to knock a man like him out.

Dodging underneath the arm of the first, she whirled around the second. Varya cast a single glance back toward Greed who had struggled to turn around and watch her go. And when one of the Horde members approached him, she let a knife fly. Embedded in the man's back, it did its job.

The Horde was distracted just enough for Greed's guards to meet her at the end of the alleyway. They didn't look at her at all. They raced toward their master and then stood over him, teeth bared and knives gleaming in the sunlight.

He looked up at her, his eyes unfocused and his face pale. But he still snarled and his voice rumbled as he said, "Touch her and die."

She sprinted toward another alley, but there were more Horde members there as well. The sands were up to her knees now. She must be close to the edge of the city that was soon to be swallowed up by the desert.

Nowhere to run.

Turning, she palmed her remaining knife and crouched low. Counting under her breath, she estimated there were at least six of them. Then more came out of another alley.

A smaller figure approached her and tugged its hood down. The woman was terrifying. Broad features covered in scarification patterns, some circles, some lines, all making her sand blasted skin look horribly wounded. Her vibrant blue eyes met Varya's and she spat on the ground.

"You ruined our hunt," the woman snarled. "Now you will pay for that."

"I'd like to see you try," Varya snarled.

She didn't hear the man approaching from behind her. And she only barely felt the pound of pain against the back of her skull before the world went dark.

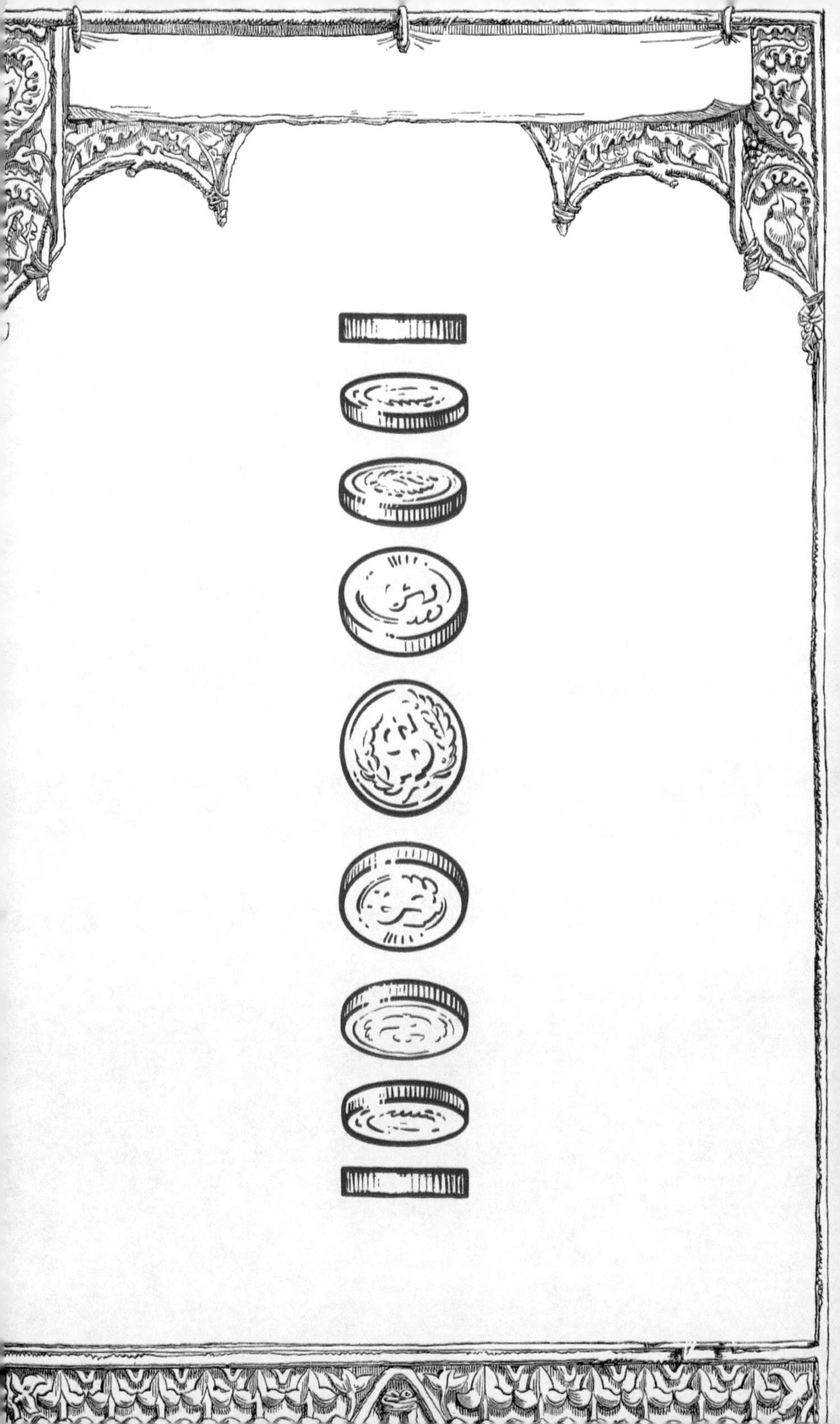

Chapter 15

Greed woke in his own castle. How he'd ended up here again, he had no idea. At least he wasn't in a cage in some cave far away from the safety of his home. However, this was almost worse.

Waking up on silks, alone, his head cushioned by such comfortable pillows that he woke up almost in better condition than when he'd passed out.

But then he remembered the position he'd been in before he had passed out. He remembered all that soft skin, those lovely lips, and words that set his entire body on fire.

Now he was alone.

Sitting up straight, his hair falling in front of his face before he shoved it back, Greed stared wildly around him. His bedroom was the same. All silk pillows and greenery that climbed up toward the walls.

There was no soft woman lying next to him, her golden hair spilling over his emerald pillows.

What had happened? Why was he here and where the hell was his treasure?

He staggered to his feet, still woozy. The ground seemed to shift and roll underneath his feet, like he was trying to walk on top of waves, but he would not be deterred. He'd find her. She must have come back with him. His guards would never have left the woman he desired on a street somewhere while others attacked her. They would have brought both of them back to the castle. They must.

"Where the hell are you?" he bellowed, reaching out a hand to grab onto something and then collapsing onto his side. Thank the gods there were more pillows here, or he'd have injured himself again.

The gold double doors leading into his room busted open. Ivo strode inside, lacking the usual presence of his terrifying sister. "Greed."

"Where is she?"

"She's out in the sands seeking to find the people who attacked you. I brought you back myself, but Morag refused to return with us." Ivo sank onto a knee, his bulk making it rather difficult to crouch in front of Greed. "I do not know the spell that has affected you, but we will discover its origin and destroy it."

Greed didn't care at all that he had been laid out by simple mist. What he cared about was where that little thief had gotten herself off to because his gut was twisting in his belly. Something was wrong. He could feel it right in his core. She had been taken from his side, and that had to mean something.

Had the Horde attacked them both? Were they trying to take him back and had they somehow found out that she was the one who had released him from that cage?

Greed wasn't certain he'd survive it if that was the case. He'd never felt guilty for anything in his life, but the curious emotion making him nauseous seemed very similar to what he'd always thought guilt would feel like.

He should have left that man alive. It would have been so easy to do so and yet, he had been the one who had to snap that Horde member's neck.

Ivo reached forward and wrapped his hand around Greed's arm. "Come on. Let's get you up and to a healer."

"I don't need a healer."

"You do." Ivo was too strong, and Greed was far too weak to fight the man.

He let Ivo drag him upright and then stood with locked knees as his guard steadied him. Ivo was too important of a man to be playing nursemaid, and yet... Well. Loyalty would do anything to ensure that Greed was well. Even if that meant debasing himself in the process.

Greed brushed his hands away. "Please. The last thing I need is another healer chattering in my ear. I've survived this before and I will again. What we need to do now is to find the woman."

"What woman?" Ivo's eyes squinted at him, as though he might peer inside Greed's skull to understand what he was asking for.

"The woman who was with me in the alley. The same woman who delivered me back to the castle." Greed wanted to tear out his hair. "Did you not see her again?"

Ivo's expression creased with discomfort and then obvious confusion. "There was a woman, yes, but she ran. She was running toward us when we found you, and then your attackers turned to chase her off. We assumed she was with them or a deserter."

Oh, someone please save him from the blind loyalty of the creature he'd created. One was wandering off in the desert thinking she could single-handedly find a group of people who had been impossible to find for anyone else, and the other was here with him, certain that they had done the right thing.

He couldn't scold Ivo for doing what he was born to do, however. Greed supposed in a way this was his punishment. He'd created two creatures who were not yet ready for mortal bodies. He and his brothers were the only ones who had ever reached this state of mind and by pushing these two in mortal forms, he had created his own monsters.

"Find her," he snarled. "That's all that matters. I don't care if the Horde is wandering around this kingdom. I will deal with them later. You have let the most exquisite piece of treasure that I have ever collected slip through your fingers, and I want her back. Do you understand?"

"The woman is treasure?" Ivo shook his head. "People can't be treasure, Greed."

"This one is."

And he was prepared to argue that point until the two of them were blue in the face. He'd have done just that if one of his servants hadn't knocked on the wall outside the still open doors.

She was a tiny little thing, all voluptuous curves and pretty smiles. Greed thought maybe he had hired her because of that beauty, but right now, her red hair wasn't nearly the color of gold that he wanted. Her pretty soft curves weren't angular enough, nor did she have muscles poured over her from head to toe. And she was far too giving with those smiles.

But he noticed Ivo's cheeks turn bright red. The spirit turned flesh looked everywhere but the young woman who was also suspiciously not looking at Ivo.

What was going on between the two of them? He almost didn't want to know, but he also was very curious if his guard had finally turned his attention toward the pleasures of the flesh.

He was getting distracted.

"What is it?" Greed snapped.

She bowed so low her face almost touched the floor. "Your brother is summoning you."

He hissed out a long breath. Of course, his brother was calling. Why not make this shit day even shittier?

The last thing he wanted right now was to have to sit through Lust, telling him more about Selene. And that's all Lust talked about these days. Selene did this. They went on a trip together and did that. Did you know Selene's favorite food is cherries and isn't that so difficult to find this time of year?

Groaning, he turned his gaze up to the ceiling covered in billowing green silks. "I don't want to talk with Lust. Tell him to fuck off and that I'll use the spell when I get a chance. I'm a busy demon king, and I don't have the energy for his incessant chatter today."

The servant bit her lip, obviously trying not to laugh or find humor in the situation. And she was pretty when she did that. Her cheeks rounded and her eyes sparkling with mirth. Maybe he could see what Ivo saw. Now it was easy to understand why his guard was so tongue-tied.

Then the girl had to ruin everything. She lost all the color in her face and then shook her head. "Actually it's... It's not Lust. I walked into your office to clean it for the day and I found him waiting for you."

"Him?"

"I don't recognize him." Again, that uncomfortable expression.

"He was tall, dark hair, red glowing eyes. And when he reached for me, I thought his fingers were... claws."

Damn it.

Damn it all to the monsters below.

He made eye contact with Ivo, who had straightened at the description of the man. That could only be one of Greed's brothers, and he didn't want to talk with that one.

"That's all there was?" Because Gluttony never called without someone to back him up.

The servant licked her lips and shook her head. "I thought there was another person in the room, but... I didn't see anyone. It felt like there were eyes on me, though. From the shadows."

Ah, shit. He was in a lot of trouble.

Sharing one last worried glance with Ivo, he stalked from the room. The stairwells were filled with servants hustling about. Most of them were headed to the kitchens, where they were likely getting their breakfast. Gilded and gleaming, the floors of his home were all exterior. There were pillars holding up a roof over their heads, but no walls in this oasis. He'd always wanted to feel like he was still outside in the jungle this place had once been.

Now, he felt as though there might be eyes hiding in every one of those massive monstera plants. Eyes that belonged to the only one of his brothers that he didn't want to see. Ever.

If he could avoid all of them, then he would. But he'd struck up a rather comfortable relationship with Lust, almost like they were actually brothers. The others, though? He didn't care for any of the others.

Grinding his teeth, he strode over to the small enclosed dome that was attached to a hundred stairs, all the floating stairwells connected to different rooms that were required to have roofs. All of them were glass circles, held up by magic and incredible craftsmanship of people who were long dead.

The closer he got to his office, the more his stomach twisted. He didn't have time for this. He needed to keep his focus on where Varya had been taken and how to find her again. If she'd even been taken. His wily little thief was too quick and too smart to get caught.

And this was what was on his mind as he strode into his office and saw the image of Gluttony waiting for him. His brother was as the little servant girl had described. Terrifying to look at and equally beautiful. Where Greed was made with blunt edges and broad strokes, the finest of artists had sketched Gluttony.

His eyebrows winged back in perfect arches. Smooth, alabaster skin that rarely saw the sun covered his form, easily visible with the open shirt he wore tucked into the tight leather leggings he called pants. Long claws tapped his sides as he stared at Greed with those all-knowing, terrifying eyes.

"Brother," Gluttony said, his voice almost musical in quality. "It's been a long time."

"Almost three hundred years." And not long enough away from this particular member of the family. "My servant said you summoned me?"

"Not just me. I wouldn't waste my time asking for your help." Gluttony pointed behind Greed as the door closed behind him. "You have company."

An ice cold chill slithered down his spine and Greed knew who stood behind him. But still, he turned around even though there was no more prickle of magic. He already knew what brother had visited him.

The man who stepped out of the shadows was nothing short of a monster. Dark, leathery wings hugged close to his body, scarred and faintly dragging on the floor because their tips were too long to keep upright. His dark hair was a wild tangle halfway down his back, and hung in front of his face so no one had to see the monstrous being underneath.

Greed had seen it before. Many times. He remembered what had happened to his brother and knew the scars that circled his mouth where it had been sewn shut for years. How one eye was blinded and milky. But worse than that, he knew the darkness in those orbs and the responsibility that weighed upon his brother's shoulders.

"Wrath," he rasped. "You haven't left your kingdom in centuries."

"That you know of." Wrath's voice was stone striking stone, thunder rumbling in the distance, and the terrifying sound of a predator growling in his ear. "I have left my kingdom before, and I will again. In this circumstance, I thought it best to convince you in person."

"Convince me of what? What would drag you away from the abyss and away from the monsters of the deep?"

Wrath lifted his head just slightly, dark hair sliding over his forehead as he glared at Gluttony's shimmering mirage. "Your brother is in trouble."

Gluttony scoffed. "I am no more in trouble than any of the others. There is no need for such theatrics."

If they were both in his office, this was very bad indeed.

Eyes wide, he watched Gluttony's twitching movements and strange stance. "What did you do?"

His brother had a penchant for causing trouble but also for feeding his rather unusual... desires. Whereas Greed wished to possess, Gluttony wished to consume. He had started with meager and simple pleasures such as alcohol and drugs. But from the rumors that swirled between kingdoms, Greed had heard his brother had turned toward much more specific tastes.

"Nothing," Gluttony hissed. "Nothing I am not permitted to do. It is my kingdom! I may do what I wish within it."

"Within reason," Wrath replied with a growl. He lurched forward, as though he intended to wrap his fingers around Gluttony's neck.

Greed swallowed as he saw the state of Wrath's hands. His brother did what it took to keep the monstrous creatures of the abyss far away from the other kingdoms. But those hands were so scarred now. The knuckles swollen beyond recognition and... By all the seven kingdoms, what was his brother doing?

Apparently, neither of his brothers noticed Greed's sharp intake of breath because they continued to glare at each other and not him.

"You were the one who said all our kingdoms were to be as we wished," Gluttony hissed, pointing at Wrath with more confidence than he should. After all, Wrath could easily travel to his kingdom as well. "You gifted it to me wrapped in a pretty little bow and if I wish to devour it—"

"You may devour your kingdom as you wish, but you may not devour your subjects!" Wrath interrupted with a howl of rage. "You're lucky you're dealing with me and not Pride!"

The silence between them all was deafening. Gluttony's eyes had widened in shock, flicking between his two brothers as his fingers started twitching on his thigh again. And Greed's stomach turned. They'd all been afraid of it, of course. Gluttony couldn't stop consuming whatever he wished, but they never had thought he'd... he'd...

"Ach, Gluttony," he muttered, rubbing his forehead. "You're not eating people now, are you?"

There was no response, and that was answer enough.

"What do you want me to do?" Greed asked, not of Gluttony, who now refused to even look at him for shame. He asked the monster who stood beside him. "You wish me to feed my own subjects to him?"

"This is bigger than you," Wrath replied. "This is bigger than all of us. The mortals cannot know that an uprising is very possible."

"It's not."

"It is." Finally Wrath lifted his head and straightened his back, standing a good head taller than Greed, who was already well over six feet. But Wrath was unlike the rest of his brothers entirely. He was more demon than man these days. "We are immortal, yes. But we can be imprisoned, tortured, and weakened. I think you know that more than any of us."

How did he know?

Greed felt his heart stop and then suddenly thud harder than ever in his chest. "So what do you want me to do about this, then?"

"Let him lie low here while I fix things. Don't let him touch anyone. And try to knock some sense into his head while you're at it."

"I'm not staying with Greed," Gluttony said, squawking at the idea. "That's ridiculous!"

Wrath turned on him again, every bit the embodiment of his name. "You will do exactly what I say, and you will shut up about it!"

"And if I don't?"

"Then I will drag you down to my kingdom and bury you in a hole until I know what to do with you. You won't die. Both of us know that. So unless you want your mouth filled with dirt for months on end, you will keep it closed."

That made Gluttony stop talking.

Wrath shook with anger as he rounded on Greed. "Any complaints from you?"

He held up his hands in peace. "Absolutely not. Keep an eye on Gluttony. I understand my place."

"Good," Wrath snarled. "At least one of you does."

Chapter 16

Her head hurt. Bad. The headache that seared behind her eyes and nose was one that came from blunt force trauma, not because she'd drank too much the night before.

Varya had broken her nose once. She'd hit the ground too hard as a child, fell off a building or something like that, she couldn't quite remember. But she'd hit her face on the dirt so hard that she'd snapped the fine bone and twisted it to the side. She'd never forgotten how her neighbor had come out of his yard and seen her. The old man had laughed, then grabbed onto the mangled bone and forced it back into place.

That kind of pain never left a person's memory. How could she ever forget the blinding ache?

Sighing, she tried to open her eyes, but they were stuck together. She wasn't sure how that had happened, but she was certain to find out soon enough.

Rolling onto her side also proved impossible. Her hands were tied behind her back and her legs bound. A bad sign, really. She was more concerned with how to get herself out of this situation than with figuring out where she was.

It didn't matter who had kidnapped her. There were plenty of people in this kingdom that wanted her dead. She'd stolen things her entire life from a lot of powerful people. And even if those items were used to make her own little town better, that still meant she had taken from another town who had been using it.

She'd had a bounty on her head most of her life. Varya was used to it by now.

Wiggling her fingers, trying to get some feeling back into the numb digits, she tried to pull her lashes apart by sheer grit and will. Unfortunately, that wasn't working at all. And her arms must have been tied behind her back for a while because even moving her fingers felt impossible.

"Ah, you're awake."

She stilled at the sound of the voice. Familiar in a way, although she couldn't quite place it. Tilting her head toward the sound, she tried to act like she was fine. "Thanks for welcoming me into your home."

"You won't be saying that for long."

Hands curled in her hair at the base of her head, dragging her face upward to look at what she expected was a man. The hand was big against the back of her head. Covered in callouses too, as his palm ripped her hair from her skull.

Who? Who was this? She should have been able to at least guess...

Then she smelled it.

Whiskey, rum, vodka, all the alcohols combined into a breath that made her nauseous. Only one group of people drank like that and it was the last group she wanted to catch her.

Memories filtered in. She'd been unlucky enough to be caught by the Horde. Greed had gotten away, though. She was certain of that. His guards wouldn't let anyone near him, and they'd all rushed after her, anyway.

Maybe she'd left a lasting impression on the demon. If she'd done that, at least, maybe she'd finally succeeded in making this place a little better for all those who lived in this cursed desert.

It didn't matter what they did to her.

She remembered the Horde were talented in the art of torture. This would be an endless battle between her and them. Soon enough, she would want to break. And she wouldn't be able to.

The hand in her hair tightened, twisting hard enough that tears burned in her eyes with nowhere to go.

"You're the one who stole from us," the deep voice snarled. "You will tell us where it is."

"I don't know what you're talking about."

"You do. How else would you have found that goblet?" The voice warped, as though he were looking in another direction before his attention returned to her. "Let's make sure you can see, yes? Then you will know exactly what torture comes for you."

She already had a good idea.

Icy water poured over her head from above. She spluttered, trying to draw in a breath through the running water, but she couldn't. Her lungs screamed, burning for a single breath, but all she could do was open her mouth and then try not to inhale the water that poured over her. Too long. Her stomach seized, coiling in on itself as vomit pressed against the back of her throat. She was going to drown. They had to stop! Didn't they know they had to stop? They must... They had to...

The water slowed to a trickle, and she gasped in a deep breath. Her lungs burned with the liquid that had inevitably sunk into them. Coughing made her entire body stiffen with the pain and opened up the scabs inside her nose.

Blood poured over her lips, but miraculously she could open her eyes. Dirt and grit scratched against the delicate orbs, but she could see.

They were in another cave. Shocking. The Horde loved to pour their massive bodies into tight spaces. She'd never understood it. Blinking again, her eyes watering and blood coating her tongue, she finally looked at the man who tortured her.

Damn it. The big bearded beast had been the leader of the men who had caged Greed, and she had a feeling he was the same man who led the entire Horde. She was seeing double of him, though, so it could be anyone.

He opened his hands at his sides, gesturing to her. "You stole from us. You know what you stole?"

"I am just a villager," she tried. "I lived in that town my whole life. You've got the wrong person."

"Do we? What's the name of the town?"

Fuck. He had her and he knew it. Because he also knew that she absolutely was not from that town. He remembered her, but she didn't know how he remembered her.

Baring her teeth at him, she hissed out a long breath. "I stole nothing from you."

"You think I have not spent my entire life being poisoned?" The leader of the Horde crouched in front of her. His big belly jutted so close that it touched her knees, but she saw the power in his form.

He could snap her neck in those powerful hands if he wanted to. "I watched you both. It was a neat trick, using good poison to make me immobile. But I watched you both as you walked over my body. I saw my treasure in the waistband of your leggings. So tell me one more time that you don't know what you stole, thief, and I will cut your throat and drink your blood as it pours out."

Swallowing hard, she wondered if she should spit in his face. Get it over with. They were going to kill her, no matter what.

Still, she didn't think she wanted to die watching him drink her blood. So she nodded, "Fine. I took a map."

"You took a map." He nodded and stood up, his knees creaking with the movement. "I know you did."

His fist flew out and caught her on the side of the head. She saw black and white stars in her vision as she rocked to the side. And then she was falling. Her head struck rocks and oh, there was the nausea again.

He leaned down and grabbed her tied arms. With a wrenching jerk, he dragged her across the sharp stones on the ground. They tore into her skin, leaving a bloody streak in her wake, but she didn't mind that. Instead, it was her arms that screamed. The sockets of her shoulders were bent too far. If he kept going they were going to...

Snap.

She screamed, her voice raw and aching as the pain ripped through her.

"My arms," she whimpered as the scream died out. "My arms, please... my arms..."

"I don't care about your arms!" The Horde leader threw her away from him, his anger sending her flying across the floor and sliding until her back slammed against something hard.

Moaning, she tried to inhale a shuddering breath as she looked up to see a man standing above her. No, not one. Three. Three other men, and more behind them as they glared down at her prone form.

The Horde leader crouched again. He looked like some kind of monster out of a children's book. Large and round and ridiculously powerful as he rested his limp wrists on his knees. "You are going to tell me where the map is."

"I don't know where the map is."

He continued as though she hadn't spoken. "You're going to tell me where you put it, or who you sold it to. And then you're going to be a welcome treat to my men, who haven't known the touch of a woman in a very long time."

For the first time in this ordeal, she felt fear.

"No," Varya whispered. "Why would I tell you anything if you're threatening me with that?"

"Because they can be kind or they can be rough." He shrugged. "Either way you choose, I'm going to get the information I want. You'll either tell me now, or you'll tell me after they break you."

"It sounds like they'll break me no matter how I choose."

He grinned, all teeth and gleaming dark eyes. "Probably. They're not known for being kind."

Her heart thudded hard in her chest as a cold sweat broke out over her body. She wouldn't let them do this. Of all things, of all nightmares to be trapped in, she'd never expected this of the Horde.

They were terrible people, everyone knew that. They didn't care about the state of the kingdom, only themselves. But that shouldn't have led to... this.

She couldn't even think the word in her mind. Couldn't put a name to what they were threatening even though her stomach clenched and her thighs sealed together in a bid to keep herself safe.

What was she supposed to do with arms that were popped out of their sockets and lungs that now were wheezing?

He saw the thoughts flickering over her features as though she had spoken them aloud. "You know what is happening, yes? You know there is no more fight for you. You will tell me where the map is, and I will do my best to see you through the night still alive."

"Is that even worth it?" she hissed. "Who wants to remain alive after that?"

He reached for her face, his fingers ghosting over the bruises on her cheeks. "You are strong. You'll want to stay alive for as long as possible. Giving up now is just letting us win. You will fight, and we will battle, and in the end, I will win."

She ground her teeth. "What makes you so sure you'll win?"

She saw his fist draw back. The movement was so fast it was almost like a cobra striking at her. But she felt it connect with the socket of her eye and she felt the earth shattering pain of bone on bone.

Had he broken her skull? Had he done irreparable damage? What if she couldn't see out of that eye anymore? How would she thieve?

But then she supposed that didn't matter. Because he was wrong. She wasn't that strong. She wasn't a fighter who wanted to live with the memories of these horrible men who had laid her out in the sands and then took their time with her.

Already the one whose leg she'd backed into was working on his pants. He struggled with the tie. The dolt had knotted it so tightly that he'd need a knife to get out of it.

Varya didn't feel like she was here. Her soul had whisked away from her body, leaving her to sit there on her own. Numb, icy cold, she muttered, "Why does he get to go first?"

"He doesn't have to." The Horde leader combed his fingers through her tangled hair, tugging too hard and ripping as he went. "You could tell me where the map is, and I'll go first."

That was supposed to be better?

This time, she spat in his face. Let him punch her again. Maybe she wouldn't be awake for any of it. Maybe she'd pass out for hours and only wake with an ache between her legs. But that was equally terrible. This was all terrible.

The Horde leader lunged to his feet, cursing at her as he wiped her spit from his face. He kicked her hard in the ribs, spitting back at her as he kicked again and again.

Her ribs exploded. It felt like every bone in her body shattered, even though she knew she was made of harder stuff than that. When the booted feet stopped, she didn't even care. Let them touch her. Let them do whatever they wanted but get it over quick because she just wanted to be alone.

The first man knelt behind her, apparently having won against the ties that bound him. She didn't even flinch when his hands came to her ankle, cutting through the cords there and tugging her closer. It didn't matter. She was numb. She wasn't even here. She was shaking in fear, but that was natural… Wait… She wasn't shaking.

The cave was.

The ground trembled underneath them, rocked with a movement that she'd never felt in her life. It was like the stones in the cave were rattling with the force of something deep beneath them.

A shout echoed through the cave, and then suddenly they were all moving. One of the Horde members grabbed onto her arm, her socket screaming yet again as he yanked her after him. The stones dug into her legs, but it didn't matter. She was already a giant ball of pain.

The moment they hit the sands, however, the entire world exploded. Sand kicked up into her face and the Horde member who had held onto her arm vanished. She hit the ground hard on her face. Varya couldn't see anything that was happening, but she could hear the yells. The screams.

The Horde leader was shouting for the men to get their mounts. "Run!" he shouted over and over again. "Move your asses and run!"

What were they running from, though?

Someone needed to help her. She needed someone to push her upright, or at least roll her over. But then the sand beneath her moved. Again. Like the waves of the sea, it rolled beneath her body and shoved her to the side. Her face pressed against something moving in the sands, something warm and smooth and... scaled?

She rolled, unable to stop herself until she was lying on her back. Almost seated, but that gave her the opportunity she needed to move.

Her legs ached. Her lungs screamed that she couldn't run while her heart thundered in fear and her ribs screamed in protest. No part of her body wanted to run, but she didn't have a choice.

The Horde continued to shout. Their cries echoed through the air along with the faint, terrifying sound of a hiss starting deep in the belly of a monster she refused to look at.

She'd felt the scales press against her body. She'd felt the muscles moving underneath her cheek as it easily powered through the sand toward the group of men and horses that were likely to be the beast's meal.

And that terror kicked her upright. That terror kept her legs moving even when she felt like she was going to fall over.

Varya ran.

Chapter 17

This was stupid. He should have gone after her himself rather than wait for anyone else to bring her back.

Yes, there was now the added nonsense of his brother coming to his castle. Gluttony had cut too many ties with all the other kingdoms, and that was the only reason he was coming here. Greed was certain of that.

Of course, Gluttony and Greed did have their shared gripes with their counterparts. The others lived in rather easy kingdoms. No one else had been tricked into taking on a jungle kingdom that was slowly degrading into a desert. And Gluttony's kingdom was a swamp that rarely saw the light of day.

Greed didn't even know what he was going to do with him. He could keep him in the back of the castle, he supposed. He needed to make sure that all his servants understood they were never to be alone with the visiting demon king. Likely, he'd want to put Ivo or Morag in charge of keeping them safe. But that also put them far too close to his sibling who would notice that they weren't human.

Gluttony had a big mouth. His brother would be the first to tell the others that Greed had broken the covenant they had all taken when they first took to mortal form.

No other spirit could join them. Not until they were certain what their existence would do to the world, and how it would affect the kingdoms that they ran.

But... It had been a thousand years since they'd taken these forms and he didn't believe they'd changed that much. The mortals looked up to them as gods, however, and he supposed Pride recognized the inherent problem.

No one needed an abundance of demons or gods running amuck about the kingdoms.

Sighing, he ran his fingers through his hair until it stood up in all directions. He had so much to manage inside these walls, and all he wanted to do was to be outside of them. He wished the sands were blowing in his face, cutting at his cheeks, whispering that he needed to find more hidden treasure. Treasure that he now found in the heart of a woman.

"You're obsessed," he muttered as he followed a stream that ran through his oasis. "Obsession is never good."

He knew this about himself. He'd find something that he wanted and then he couldn't think until he had it. Not even his mind could focus until he could put it on a shelf, looked at it every day, and then eventually grew bored with it.

The woman would bore him. Varya might be a strange mortal who had argued and slapped at him, but she was still the same as all the others. Someday he would look at her and she would have lost her shine. Her newness.

But that day was not anytime soon, and he wanted to keep her for as long as he could. He wanted that thrill in his chest that he had caught something impossible.

And oh, there was nothing like adding something to his collection.

Her golden hair would look so lovely spread out on his dark green pillows. Her tanned skin would lighten each day that she wasn't subjected to the sun for long hours of the day. Soon her muscular body would round with luxury and all the food he would ply her with. He'd watch those changes knowing that he was the one who had bid her to change.

Having a mortal treasure might not be so bad after all. If he could only find her.

Tilting his head back in the air that was cool with mist, he filled his lungs. He could almost smell her on the wind. Her lovely, spicy scent that always smelled like the wilds and the tombs that she haunted.

She was still in his nose. After days of missing her, she was still in every one of his senses.

Until the scent mingled with blood.

A low growl rumbled in his chest and his eyes narrowed on the entrance to his home. The low wall would provide no protection against anyone who wanted to attack the castle, but no one had been so foolish in centuries. Who would want to directly anger the demon king who ruled them all? They had a death wish.

Or they wanted to draw him out.

Again, he filled his lungs with her scent and the acrid bite of blood. It wasn't possible. Whoever had taken her wasn't so stupid that they would drag her to his front door? They would know he would tear them apart limb from limb for the insult.

But maybe she hadn't been kidnapped. Maybe she had been running all this time, waiting for him to find her. Though it was an unlikely thought, he still sprinted to the front door without calling for his guards. Without calling for anyone.

If she was injured in another man's arms, Greed would kill him.

With a single jerk, he flung open the doors. He'd already prepared himself for a wall of men and women, armed to the teeth, ready to battle with him. He was looking forward to the blood he'd splatter across the sands, feeding the very desert itself.

He hadn't expected to just see her. Varya. His little thief and treasure, weaving where she stood.

Alone. She looked so small as she stared up at him with those wide blue eyes. Well, one of them. The other had swollen shut. There were so many bruises over her lovely face that he almost didn't recognize her. Her arms were tied behind her back, every breath was labored, and her clothing was beyond ripped and torn.

His heart wrenched, and he felt his eyes burn with tears at the sight of her. "Varya?" he whispered, as though a loud noise might scare her away.

"I didn't know where else to go."

She staggered forward, and that was all he had been waiting for. Greed opened his arms and gently caught her long before she hit the ground. He cushioned her head against his chest and swung her up into his arms as though she weighed nothing. Light as a feather in his arms, she curled toward him. Trusting him.

He'd never felt this heat in his chest before, but he knew that he never wanted to let this feeling go.

Spinning, he raced into his home once again. Calling out for his guards, he shouted, "Ivo! Morag! Get a healer now!"

His two guards appeared as if summoned by magic, one of them racing out of the gardens and the other appearing high over his head at the edge of one of the glass domes. Morag darted down the stairs toward them, while Ivo leapt from one platform to another, quickly making his way down until they both met him at the entrance to the healing dome.

The healers were... somewhere. He didn't know where they spent most of their day, but he knew they'd come at his call. No one denied him anything in this castle, and he refused to lose her.

Varya had gone limp in his arms, and he could only hope that she'd passed out. Considering the amount of injuries all over her body, he didn't want her awake. That amount of pain was too much for even a demon like him. Let alone someone so fragile.

He looked down at her slack features, at the bruises that turned her lovely skin shades of purple and red, and he found his arms shaking with rage. He would kill them all for touching her. For touching what was his. He would rip their tongues out of their mouths and serve them to her on a golden platter. If she wished for him to paint her with their blood, he would. If she wanted their eyes in a goblet and their heads on pikes, he would gladly tear them to pieces.

"Greed?" Ivo quietly said, his voice pitched low and worried. "Is this her?"

He couldn't answer for fear of what he would say.

Instead, it was Morag who replied. "Yes, that's the woman I saw with him the first time. Hard to recognize her in this state, but..."

She stopped the moment she saw the anger in his eyes. She toed a line, and she knew it. No one would say another word about Varya's injuries until the healers were in the room. She needed their silence, help, and attention. Not their judgement on how ruined her body was.

And it was ruined. He could hardly look at her without a lump forming in his throat and that damned heat burning in his eyes again.

This room for healing was one of the prettiest in his home. Tall windows let in the sunlight that fractured off the warm terracotta walls and floor. Plants decorated the corners, and low beds with cream-colored sheets were placed three to each wall. Not many, but there weren't many people to heal in this castle. The entire room smelled like lavender and chamomile. Shelves on each wall contained items needed to heal. Thread, needles, jars of green healing plants and pastes that would encourage the body to mend itself.

"Greed?" Ivo said again as Morag sprinted out of the room to find the healers. "We need to release her hands."

"Her hands?" he rasped, and then set her down on the bed. "What do you mean, her hands?"

Then he saw them. Her arms were tied behind her back. He'd thought she was just holding them strangely. He hadn't thought they were still tied up. Rage made his vision skew. He knew he was already getting too close to changing into his battle form, incapable of stopping himself as he wondered about all the nightmares that she'd endured and what they had done to her.

They'd tied up his treasure. They'd beaten her and who knows what else. Greed would chew on their bones and anchor their souls to this realm so he could kill them again and again. He would rip out their spines. He would shred their bodies to the last sinew and then stitch it all back together so he could rip it apart again.

Ivo moved behind her, his features carefully arranged into a semblance of calm. "I will remove them."

"I'll do it," Greed snarled, his voice a little too deep and a little too rough.

He reached behind her and sliced through the cord with a single claw. Her free arm fell forward, the wrong way. All limp and stretched while her shoulder looked too bulbous. Swollen underneath her leather armor.

Greed swallowed hard as his eyes trailed down that limp arm to her swollen fingers. Wrong. This was all wrong. He wasn't supposed to get a broken treasure back when she was meant to be alive and well and golden.

He was supposed to decorate her with jewels. Hand feed her and pour wine through those plush lips until she whispered sweet nothings to him and instead, he'd been given this broken doll. Someone else had played with her too hard, and he feared she'd never be the same.

A woman rushed into the room with Morag right behind her. He vaguely remembered this healer had been the woman to put his tail back into place. Her ivory curls billowed around her head, perhaps showing her age, although he hadn't ever paid enough attention to humans to know if that was correct. She wore a white coat around her silk clothing, almost as though she'd still been asleep when Morag had retrieved her.

The healer sucked in a breath as she saw the state of her new patient. "What happened?"

"I do not know," Greed snarled. "She showed up at our front doors in this state. Or are you suggesting otherwise?"

Ivo put his hand on Greed's chest, gently pushing him away from the healer who ignored the snarling demon who stood on the opposite side of her patient. The woman had no fear as she started trailing her hands over Varya's limp body and then shifted her onto her back.

"Careful," Greed hissed.

Again, Ivo moved him farther back. "We have to let her work."

"If she keeps moving her like that, she'll do more damage."

"She won't." Ivo stood in front of him, forcing Greed to meet his gaze. "The healer will do her best. Your treasure is weak and we do not know how long she's been like this. We cannot interfere or we will be the ones hurting her. Yes?"

He couldn't stand to leave her. Not like this. Not when the healer was already cutting her out of the leather armor, and what if she cut through Varya's delicate skin? He refused to see more holes in that skin that haunted his dreams, not when the thought made his throat close up and panic claw in his chest.

He'd never felt like this before, and Greed hated it. He didn't know what to do with empty hands and eyes that had seen too much.

"I can't leave her here on her own," he said, wide gaze locking onto Ivo's. "If she wakes in a strange place... She'll be terrified."

"Humans are often terrified."

"She won't know where she is."

"She will." Ivo gave him a little shove. "She came to you, Greed. She knew where we were and she knew to come here after what happened to her. We will leave her here. This is where she needs to be."

He couldn't breathe. He couldn't suck in enough air because what if she woke up and needed him? What if she required a familiar face in a place that surely wasn't what she had expected?

Breathing like he'd sprinted for hours, he stared into Ivo's calm expression. "She's never been here before, Ivo. She'll wake up and have no idea where she is or who is around her. I can't put her through that after everything that's happened to her."

Ivo's gaze softened, but before he could say a word his sister blurted, "We don't even know if she'll live, Greed."

And oh, he wanted to take out all his rage and aggression on her. He wanted to scream at her to say that again. To suggest that Varya wouldn't make it because that wasn't an option. His treasure would live. He demanded it.

Because he couldn't think of a life where he wouldn't see her mischievous expression in the middle of a tomb. Or the sound of her laughter as she raced away from him in the desert. He didn't want to know what life would be like without her little grunts of frustration as they sparred, or the catch of her breath in her throat when he kissed her.

He couldn't let her go without seeing happiness in her eyes. And not just a smile, but true happiness as she saw the kingdom change because she'd asked him to do it.

He would give her all of that. All of it.

Pushing past Ivo, he moved the healer away so he could lean down and press a soft kiss to her bruised and bloody forehead. "Live for me," he whispered against her skin. "And I will give you the world."

The sun played across her closed eyelids. She'd never seen that pattern before, all spotted and moving across her face. She could feel the warmth, but it wasn't overwhelming like it usually was in the desert.

Varya didn't want to wake up. She'd been having the most lovely dream. A soft bed, a cool hand that touched her forehead and a quiet voice asking if she needed anything.

When was the last time someone had taken care of her? It had been ages. She was the person who took care of others, and that meant she had to stand on her own two feet. Probably more than anyone else she knew. But that was all right. It helped Varya to know that her family and friends were well. Still... Maybe it was okay for someone to take care of her for a little while longer.

Blinking her eyes open, she frowned up at the greenery above her.

She'd only seen plants a few times in her life, and they were always either spiky cactus or the long, thick triangles of aloe vera. Otherwise, she'd only seen a few leaves here and there when someone spent their life savings for tea or healing herbs.

But these were actual plants. Green and bright and thriving above her head as they leaned closer to the sunlight. Pushing up onto her elbow, Varya glanced around the room with wide eyes.

The glass windows were so perfectly made that they almost didn't look like they were there at all. Tall and over three stories, they stretched above her head and warped into a circle at the top. There were two empty beds on the same side of the wall where she was. Three empty on the other side. None of them had anyone in them. The clean, cream-colored sheets were pulled so tight they looked almost fake.

And all the plants. There were so many of them. She didn't know what they were, but some of the leaves were larger than she was tall. They were massive, and the air smelled so good, like herbs and spices and dirt. When was the last time she'd smelled dirt?

Maybe when she was just a child. She'd stuck her nose into a small pot where someone had kept an aloe plant and she'd inhaled just to know what the earth smelled like without it being covered by sand.

Her ribs twinged, and she winced, pressing a hand to the bandages that covered her body. Her arms were wrapped in white, her chest, and she felt something sticky on her face. Wiggling the muscles there, she tried to dislodge it but couldn't.

Whatever it was, she wanted it off.

Varya reached for her head, only to freeze when someone's voice interrupted her.

"Leave it," the deep tones said. "You need that to remain so you can heal."

Stilted words, not quite comfortable speaking to other people, she'd guess. But she recognized the voice. She never forgot a single person she came across.

One of Greed's guards sat in a chair beside her bed, so still she hadn't noticed him. He was the bigger of the two, although she remembered them both being larger than life. He sat on a rickety chair with one ankle propped up on his knee, a book spread out across those massive thighs, and glasses perched on his nose. His light brown hair was streaked by the sun and he was rather handsome, although his muscles made him seem particularly bulky.

His gaze watched her, flicking over the bandages that were slightly red with her blood, before he grunted and stood. "I'll get Greed."

"Where am I?"

"The oasis," he replied. "You're in Greed's castle."

"I am?" She didn't remember coming here. Varya pressed a hand to her forehead, feeling dizzy. "How did I get here?"

"You walked." He tried to smile, but the expression was horrible. Just a baring of teeth rather than a genuine smile. "I'll get Greed."

"Wait," she said, reaching out for him to stop. She didn't know why she wanted him to freeze, she just... "Thank you for sitting with me. You're very kind."

"I am not kind." His shoulders and spine stiffened. "I am loyal."

"I think you are both." Varya tried to smile, but the expression pulled on what she suspected were cuts on her cheek. "Not everyone would sit with a stranger for hours, even if they were ordered to do so."

"Days," he replied.

"Days?" That was horrible. She'd been out for that long? She reached for his hand and gave it a gentle squeeze, even though leaning forward hurt. "Thank you, all the same. What is your name?"

"Ivo."

"Then thank you, Ivo, for your kindness."

He seemed disturbed by her thanks, and she didn't know if that was because of her looks or what she'd said. She was just being kind in return. What harm was there in that?

But he strode out of the room with his shoulders up against his ears. Leaving her alone in this glass dome of a room with so many plants that her lungs felt... lighter. As though just being near them made it easier for her to breathe.

She barely had time to wonder how long it would take for Greed to come see her. She'd expected at least half a day. He was a very busy man, after all, and he had a lot of things to see to in a castle like this. At least, she assumed.

It was a matter of minutes before the doors to the room slammed open so hard she feared they might crack the glass walls. Greed raced into the room, eyes wild and a little too wide. He wore a white billowing shirt that was opened to the center of his chest, revealing all that tanned and freckled skin. Glittering rings dusted across almost every knuckle, a broad necklace clanged against his chest, and there were earrings in his ears. His pants were a little too tight, and she was thankful for it. His tree trunk legs were rather nice to look at.

His panicked expression, on the other hand, was not very nice. She didn't know what had gotten him so riled up, but she had the wayward thought that it might be her. Maybe he didn't like seeing her so injured. Maybe he had been worried about her health.

That was a silly thought, though. He was a demon looking for a plaything. She had no question about that. Varya was his newest obsession, and even though she fully intended to enjoy being so, she knew this wasn't forever.

Neither of them were the forever sort. Now, why did that hurt so badly to think?

He didn't say a word. He just approached her bed and then scooped his arms underneath her. One thick forearm underneath her knees, and a broad bicep against her back. Lifting her blanket and all, he turned away from the healing beds and strode out of the room.

"Shouldn't we ask a healer?" she tried, before stopping when he growled in response.

She hadn't seen his eyes like this since he was in a cage. Golden and gleaming like chips of gold, molten and so hot with rage that it made her shiver in fear.

Was he angry at her? Was she not supposed to come here after all?

She hadn't thought it would mean that much. He could put her in the gardens for all she cared. Varya needed little more than a sleeping pad and a blanket at night. She'd be out of his hair in just a few days once she could stand up on her own without her lungs heaving.

He didn't seem interested in talking. So she turned her attention to the wild jungle that surrounded them. Tall trees stretched up toward the sky, their leaves swaying in the breeze. So many plants. All that she couldn't name or had even dreamed of. A giant pink flower the size of her head hovered above them as he ducked underneath a wall of ivy and then drew her deeper into the jungle.

She caught a few glimpses of more glass domes. Some on the same level as them, some much higher up. And all of them were connected by walkways of stone that were carved out of the desert itself. Naturally made, and Greed's people had built around them so they didn't harm the natural environment.

This place was so beautiful it made her eyes hurt. Until Greed strode toward one of those glass domes, although more of this one was paneling. She couldn't even see inside it, she'd have to be even taller than Greed to get a glimpse. At least the roof was still glass.

He kicked the door open, and she flinched back against him in the wake of his anger. "Are you mad at me?" she asked, her words a little testy and angry as well.

"I am not."

"You could have fooled me."

He looked down at her then and she saw it wasn't anger. It was fear. He was practically shaking with it, and why? They didn't know each other. They had a very explosive and steamy reaction whenever they were alone, but that didn't mean he cared about her. He cared about his newest toy, perhaps, but why would he have such an emotional reaction to her being hurt?

Stunned, Varya remained silent as they strode inside the room covered with streaks of emerald silk that hung from the ceiling in billowing waves as the sun filtered through them. A massive bed in the corner caught her attention, but she didn't have time to see much more before he strode into another room filled with water. So much water.

She'd never seen so much all pooled in the center of the room. Tiny crystals decorated the bottom, chips of rainbow colors that reflected the sunlight and cast rays of waves on the walls. There were a few mirrors and so many more plants. Even a few water lilies dancing on the surface of the still waters, and she'd only heard about them in stories that the elders told.

Greed walked them right up to the edge of the pool and then looked down at her. "Can you stand?"

"I haven't gotten the chance to try."

"Ah." Did he just... blush?

Varya watched him with perhaps far too avid attention as he let her legs slip down his body and then continued to hold on to her waist. He touched her as though she was some frail, fragile creature that he had to take care of. And she didn't like it.

But she was a little wobbly, so maybe it wasn't that awful of a thing for him to help.

He cleared his throat and then swallowed hard. "Take off your clothes."

"I'm not wearing much." She looked down at herself as the blanket slithered off her body. She still had her pants on, although they had been cut up the side of each leg to reveal her skin underneath. Her shirt was gone though, and it was just the band of white fabric around her chest. "And I don't want to remove more."

"I will beg," he rasped. "If I must."

Her lips parted, and she stared at him with confusion. Why was he like this? Why was he insisting that she allow him to take care of her?

"I can clean myself," she said, although the words were hesitant and slow.

Greed leaned closer and pressed their foreheads together. He breathed in before she heard the click of another dry swallow. "Let me take care of you, treasure. I need to know you are all right."

"I'm alive, aren't I?"

"You almost weren't. You showed up on my doorstep bloody and broken and it tore me apart."

Her heart fractured with those words. He wanted to help her. He wanted to piece her back together. When was the last time someone had wanted that?

Taking a deep breath, she stepped away from him and started to unwind the binding around her chest. Then she slid the remnants of her pants down her legs. She had to grab his arm to even do that, but he didn't seem to mind. A small scrap of fabric served as her underwear, and even that was covered in blood.

He was a thousand years old. He'd seen countless female bodies and she shouldn't be embarrassed, but she still felt her chest flush bright red as she pushed down her underwear as well.

Glancing up, she saw his eyes turn that molten gold again. But all he did was gently lift her by the waist and carry her into the water. He strode into the pool, clothes and all, uncaring that the wet, white fabric clung to the muscles of his chest as he set her on a small bench underneath the slight waves.

The water licked at her sides, and she winced as the wounds dotting all over her body ached. But her muscles relaxed for the first time in years and it felt so good to be so cool.

Greed said nothing. He leaned over her and then he had a washcloth in his hands that looked like more silk and a small bottle of clear liquid.

He moved her without asking. His hands tugging and pulling until her back was pressed against his chest. She floated in the water as he unraveled the remaining bandages that covered her wounds. Each one that was revealed made him tense more and more behind her, but his hands were gentle as he passed the cloth over each and every one.

The clear liquid turned out to be lovely smelling soap that reminded her of mint and lemon. He poured it onto his hands after cleaning out her wounds and then started washing her body. The blood and sand sank into the pool of water, running into a small drain or filter on the other side. The pool remained clear, other than the streaks of her blood disappearing from her body.

He took his time washing her. Saying nothing other than small growls of anger every time he found a new wound or bruise. And it made her eyes sting with unshed tears because no one had ever taken care of her like this.

Greed even put his attention underneath her nails. Somehow producing a small brush that he vigorously scrubbed underneath her fingernails as though he wanted to remove the Horde's skin and blood from every inch of her body.

Varya must have made some noise. He looked up at her and that angry expression on his face softened into something that hurt to look at.

He paused in his task and cupped her cheek with his palm. "What is it, treasure?"

"Why are you being so kind to me?"

She knew he probably didn't understand it, either. His expression was one of complete and utter shock, as though he had never expected this reaction from himself either.

Greed's thumb skated over her right eye, and she remembered getting punched in the face and the pain of that bone aching. How could she see out of it? How had she forgotten that so quickly?

His eyes darkened for a moment before he drew her attention back to the present. "You're safe now."

And those words. Oh, how they ran right through her as though he'd stuck a blade into her chest.

A single tear spilled out of that eye that had nearly been broken for good. Greed caught it on his thumb and brought the tear to his mouth. She watched with rapt attention as he licked that thick thumb clean and then scooped her back into his arms. Leaving puddles of water in their wake, he strode into the bedroom and set her down on her feet.

With careful attention, always so careful, he wrapped a silk blanket around her as though that was the best way to dry her. And then he pushed her down onto the bed, so soft and cushioned it felt like a cloud, before he sat down on the edge with her.

Greed took his time arranging her hair on the pillow. His attention was so heady and so focused on her that Varya felt herself squirm.

"We'll wash your hair tomorrow when you're feeling better," he murmured. "For now, you need more rest."

"Here?"

"There is no safer place in this kingdom than in my bed." Greed pressed a kiss to her forehead, his lips lingering on her skin. "Rest now, treasure. I will tend to your wounds and watch over you while you sleep."

She shouldn't need more rest after days of resting, but she was tired. The bath had taken every ounce of her energy, even though she'd done nothing, and...

Sighing, she turned her head into the smooth, cool, soft pillow and felt herself drift as Greed lifted her arm and started to cover each scrape and cut with a sweet smelling salve.

Chapter 19

He was in so far over his head. Greed had brought her to his own bedroom, by all the seven kingdoms! What stupid thought had made him bring her here?

He had quarters for when his women visited. He knew where to bring them, and it wasn't his own private chambers. He made their skin soft with oils that he kept in that other room. He fed them the most exquisite of meals and indulged in every one of his senses with them. He could be greedy there, wanting all of their desire for himself.

But here? This was his sanctuary. It was his own place of safety where no one but himself and his guards came. And now she was in this space. Her golden hair spilling over his pillows and her scent already filling his sheets. He wouldn't be able to sleep in that bed without smelling her for months on end.

And he liked that. He wanted to smell her, even when she was no longer within his grasp. That thought scared him more than anything else this far.

Greed didn't want her for any reason other than her beauty and her addition to his collection. He couldn't afford to want more. He wasn't Lust, and he certainly didn't have a personality that many people would want to stay around.

He was alone. For a reason. And that had to stay that way.

With an entire kingdom to run, Greed had more important things to do than look after a little human who had gotten herself in trouble. She could have stayed with the healers and he could have continued his work uncovering all the lying advisors who had made it seem as though their cities were doing well enough. Instead, here he was again. Checking in on Varya.

He shifted a strand of hair away from her face so it didn't tickle her awake. She'd been sleeping a lot, but the healers insisted she had to. Her body was already healing very well on its own, and the potions they gave her would aid her own body's abilities. That black eye was nearly gone, and most of the bruises all over her had paled to a sickly yellow. The cuts were all sealed, and he'd even taken her bandages off yesterday. But she was still so weak.

Years ago, even months ago, her weakness would have disgusted him. Humans were so fragile and so incapable of keeping up with him and his brothers. He enjoyed them for what they could provide and then tossed them aside. He always held himself back from truly enjoying their company, in case he broke one of them.

Some of his brothers had no such qualms. Gluttony and Sloth were the worst of the lot, but he tried not to think about them when he stared down at her lovely, pale face. It made his heart squeeze to see her like this. She wasn't meant to be lying in a bed helpless. She must hate it as much as he did.

Still, she would not get up anytime soon, and he needed to be sure that his advisors were punished. If not only because they lied to him, but because they hadn't warned him about the Horde.

And now he would hunt down every member who aligned with those fools, every person who had given them information, and every single madman who thought they'd get away with buying or selling to the Horde. He would tear them all into pieces for the small part they had played in her injuries.

Death was the only answer that would satisfy him now.

Stalking to the door of his bedroom, he silently slipped out of the room before he did something foolish. Like wake her and try to convince her to stay with him forever. She needed adventure as much as he did.

Right now, he was giving her a safe place to rest. That was all. A woman like her deserved more from a man than just a passing whim.

But the idea of another man touching what was his? Oh, it made his entire body ache.

"Greed?" Ivo stepped out of the shadows near the door, ever watchful. "She cannot stay here much longer."

"She'll stay as long as I wish," he snarled. Anger bloomed in his chest already, wanting to pick a fight with yet another person who wished to take her away from him. "She has been injured. She's healing."

"I know that. But she is not healing fast enough."

"I will not rush her."

"Gluttony will be here in a week's time. You know what will happen if your brother finds a pretty woman here." Ivo flinched, showing emotion for the first time in a very long time. "You know how he likes blondes."

"I do not know what my brother's fetishes are," he snarled, but then realized that Ivo knew more than he was letting on. "But do you know of them?"

"I do."

"How?"

Ivo took a deep breath. "I try to keep up with all the rumors in all the kingdoms, Greed. If you need that information, then I have it to provide. Otherwise, I ignore most of what is said about you and your brothers."

Curious. He hadn't known that about Ivo. "Does Morag do the same?"

"No. She's not all that interested in gossip or... listening."

Greed looked at his guard with a little more interest. Here he had been thinking that Ivo was still struggling to get over his attachment to loyalty, only to realize that maybe his guard had already discovered more emotions. When had that happened?

Strangely, it felt as though pride swelled in his chest. Greed hated that feeling. It reminded him of his least favorite brother.

"So, you've been listening to the rumors around the kingdoms? And now you're worried about what Gluttony will do when he sees Varya?"

Ivo perked up slightly, his eyes opening wider and his shoulders lifting higher. "Varya? Is that her name?"

Oh no. Had his guard developed a little crush?

Greed suddenly found himself upset. Ivo was a handsome man. He never would have put the spirit in anything but a handsome body, but he also didn't want any competition for Varya's attention. Ivo needed to keep his sights on someone else. Like that pretty little servant girl with the bright red hair who obviously needed to be around more often if Ivo was already excited to see Varya.

Gruffly, he replied, "Yes. That's her name."

"Ah, well. I thought to check in on her health and to inform you that Gluttony has already started sending his people ahead of himself." Ivo tucked his hands behind his back, suddenly all business yet again. "I do not know if you wish us to house these servants. We can provide temporary homes for them all, but ten of them have already arrived. If your brother doesn't arrive for another week, I assume..."

"That Gluttony will send even more." Greed rolled his eyes up to the ceiling. "This is a punishment for both of us. Gluttony obviously needs one, but I have no idea why Wrath wishes to punish me. Send all of Gluttony's servants back home. He knows he has to answer to me if he touches one of my servants, but his own, I have no control over. I cannot protect them while they are here and I will not hide any bodies for that moron who's given himself a taste for human flesh."

"Understood."

"Perhaps..." Greed hesitated, wondering what Varya would have told him to do. She'd been the one to mention that his advisors were hiding information about the water. Maybe she would suggest... "Send them with food of their own. We have enough in the storeroom for them, don't we?"

"We have plenty."

"Good." He cleared his throat, suddenly feeling awkward.

It wasn't natural for him to suggest giving anyone anything. Already he regretted it. He wanted to tell Ivo to forget that he'd offered anyone anything. Gluttony had sent them ahead of him, and if they hadn't packed for a good two weeks' journey, then they could starve on their way back.

He didn't care about others. He just cared that Varya would get angry with him. And all of that thought process was wrong, considering he'd only seen the woman a few times before this. Varya didn't matter either. No one did. He only cared about what they could give him. Greed. That's who he was. What could he get out of these newcomers if he sent them packing immediately?

"On second thought, why don't we try to get information about Gluttony out of them before we send them on their way. I wish to know everything we can about my brother before—"

The door to his bedroom creaked open. Turning, he found himself frozen by the sight of her lovely face, tinged bright red with a blush, and all those lovely gold waves tumbling down to her shoulders. She'd wrapped a blanket around her naked body, but his blood heated because he knew what she wore underneath that green silk blanket.

Nothing. Nothing at all.

And he'd tried very hard not to look too much at her while she was sick. But he was a man, and those lovely pink tips of her breasts had made his mouth water. The lean muscles of her stomach and those strong thighs... Ah, it had only made him wonder at the view from between her legs now that he already knew how sweet she tasted.

Varya blushed an even darker red, almost as though she knew the thoughts running through his mind.

"I thought I heard voices," she said, her own voice rough. "I didn't know if something was wrong."

"Everything is fine. Go back to bed." He tried to say the words gently but sharp enough that she couldn't argue with him.

He should have known this particular human had no problem ignoring him.

She leaned to look past him, her hair sliding past her shoulder and revealing all that lovely skin and swan-like neck to his gaze. "Oh! Ivo. I thought I heard you out here. How are you?"

His guard turned bright red as well. "I am fine, Varya. It is you we should all be worried about."

Her expression amused, she glanced back at Greed. "Did you tell him my name?"

"Accidentally."

"Well, that's quite all right. I should have been more polite and told him myself." Varya smiled at the both of them, and then added, "Your guard is quite kind, Greed. I was lucky to have such an attentive shadow while I was healing."

Oh, he hated that. He hated every moment of her talking about another man with that smile on her lips. Greed didn't want to share her attention with anyone, especially not his handsome guard, who couldn't take his eyes off her.

No, this wouldn't do. He refused to share his newest treasure and he wouldn't watch as they made eyes at each other as though they were friends.

They weren't.

He would tell them when they were allowed to be friends, and that was only after he was done with her. End of story. And he would not change his mind for anything or anyone.

"Get back in your room," he snarled.

"I'll do what I want, when I want," she replied. "Ivo, could I be a bother and ask to see the healer again?"

Both he and his guard blinked. Greed felt all his rage sizzle out of existence as fear took its place. "Are you hurting? I thought we had found all your wounds, but if we have not treated them all—"

Varya interrupted him with a raised hand and a small chuckle. "No,

I'm fine. I want them to look at my ribs one last time so I can make sure the bindings can be removed for good. I've healed much faster than normal here, and I don't want to do anything before confirming with them that I'm allowed. I feel much better, Greed. Thank you for allowing me to heal here."

Oh.

If that was all it was.

He preened at the sound of her thanks. He'd been the one to make sure she was healed, and the king who had deigned to keep his subject well cared for while she was injured. Who knew it would feel so good to help someone?

"Go on, then," he told Ivo, narrowing his gaze at the man to let him know that he fully expected Ivo to take a long time. "I'll get my patient back in bed."

"Your patient?" Ivo replied with a lifted brow. "Since when did you become a healer?"

He was going to punch his guard right in that pretty face and then they'd see how women liked him. With a broken nose, Ivo might look too menacing for most women to even think twice about paying attention to. That would serve his guard right for eyeing what was his.

"Greed," Varya said with another laugh. "Would you help me lie down?"

That was enough to direct his attention back to her. He'd help her lie down. He'd settle her back in his bed, where she belonged, and he would see to it that she never left those silken sheets again.

Backing her into his room, he shut the door behind them with a harsh click. She looked more like herself now that she was awake. Her eyes sparkled with mischief and her steps were sure and strong as she made her way to the small seating area in his room, not the bed. And she clearly needed no help from him.

"What game are you playing now?" he asked, crossing his arms over his chest and glaring at her.

"I didn't want you to fight Ivo, that's all."

"Why?"

"Because he's kind, and he doesn't deserve your anger because you aren't getting what you want." She sat down primly on one of his thicker pillows, a long leg revealed from underneath the sheet. "You put your attention on silly things, Greed. Ivo is a wonderful guard and a good man."

"Stop complimenting him," he growled.

"And why should I? Everyone deserves compliments when they're doing a good job."

Something in him snapped. He could almost hear it cracking in half as he stalked across the room. Footsteps silent. He was at her side in an instant with his hand buried in her hair. He tilted her head up to look at him, and a ghost of something horrible moved across her face.

She didn't like that. And he didn't know why.

Greed crouched in front of her, then raked his claws through her hair instead. He paid close attention to her scalp, watching her eyes close in pleasure at his petting.

"You are mine," he growled. "My thief that I found in the desert. The treasure I unearthed in that first cave. And my Varya that I licked and petted in a tomb. You hear me? Every part of you is special to me, and I dislike sharing your attention with anyone else."

"I am no one's but my own," she whispered, but the words didn't seem truthful.

Dragging her forward, he skated his lips over hers. Not a kiss. A claiming.

"Soon you will see," he whispered against her mouth. She chased his movements, begging for his touch. "You are mine and I am yours, treasure. And I will let nothing stand between us."

"You don't even know me."

"I know enough to feel your spell weave around me. I am enraptured by your adventurous spirit and hearty mind." He kissed her then, branding her with his touch. "Soon there will be time to know each other better. For now, I wish you healed."

She sagged as he released her, moving toward him like she couldn't quite stop herself. She wanted to touch him, too.

He gave her a wicked grin as a knock echoed on his door. The healers would see to her. They would take care of his treasure, building her back to perfect health so that he could play with her once again.

Greed stood and made his way to the door, casting one last look at her. Rumpled and wrapped in his sheets.

And, ach, he could not wait to see her like that again.

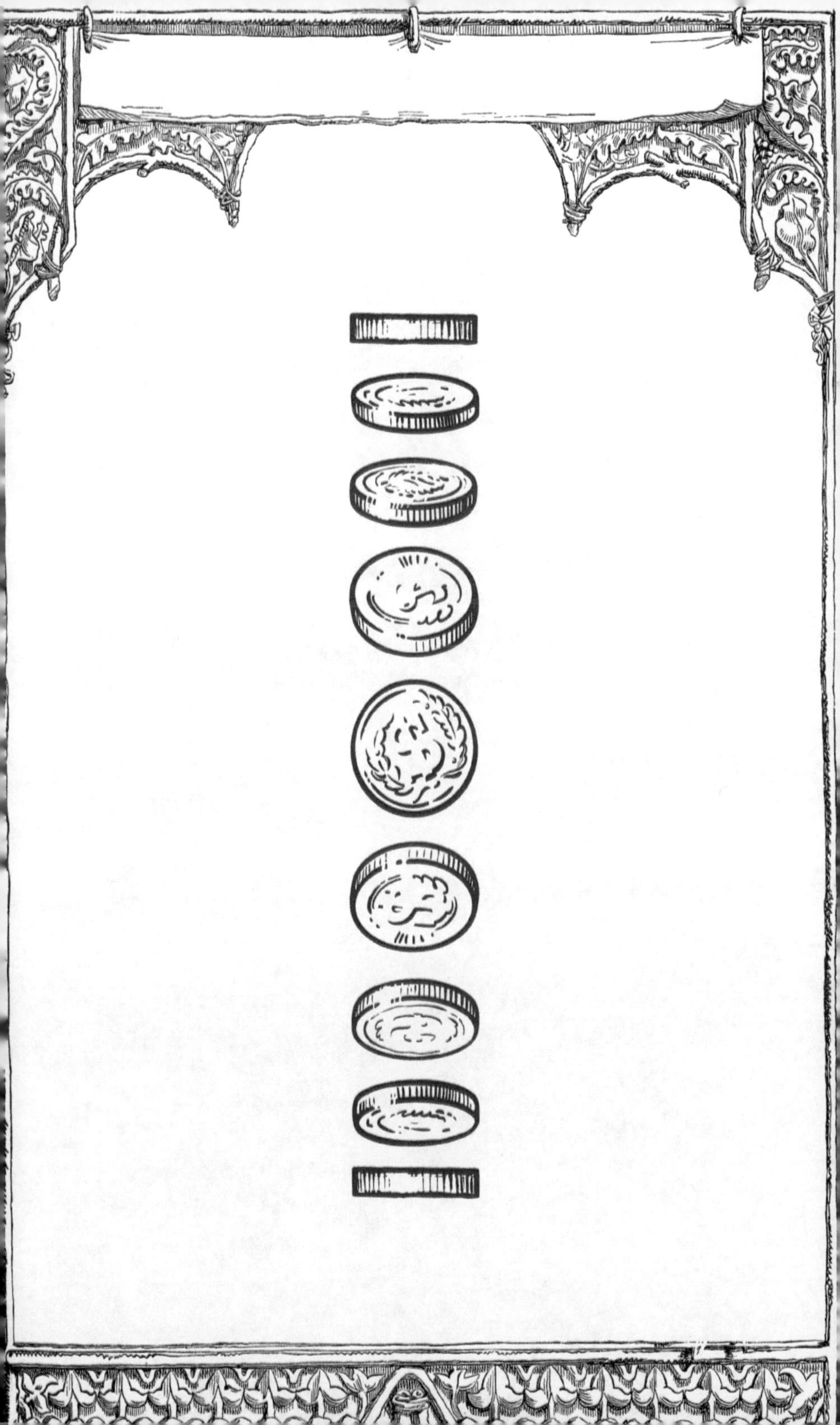

Chapter 20

Varya lost track of how much time she'd been in this place. It was beautiful, and the luxury certainly got to her head. Every morning, she woke up with sunlight playing over her features through the leaves. Cool air caressed her skin, and even cooler silk pooled around her body.

Greed had been more than attentive. And strangely enough, it made her feel a little better to see him so concerned over her wellbeing. He was always close by if she needed him. The moment she sat up, he was there. If she was hungry, he was already bringing food in. And though he hadn't touched her again yet, she knew that he wanted to.

He looked at her with heat in his eyes and plans on his mind. She knew that. She could see it every time he brushed his fingers through her hair or asked if she was feeling better. But he never once touched her as she wanted him to.

Why? She had no idea.

And today she was going to find out.

Rolling out of bed, she searched through the entire room for clothing. Greed had kept her in here to heal, and he insisted that her broken ribs and plentiful cuts required her to stay out of clothing so that his healers could check her over easier. At least he'd stopped dragging those poor healers into the room twice a day. They'd always looked like they were about to fall over from a single push of his finger.

Why was there no clothing in this room? Not a single article. She'd even gone through the trunks that were hidden behind the giant fronds on the opposite side of the room.

Blowing out an exasperated breath, she stared at the bed again. It was a shame to rip up that lovely silk that would have sold for a year's worth of food, but he didn't give her much of a choice.

If she tore the sheets with a little more zeal than she should have, Varya wouldn't tell anyone. It wasn't like there were witnesses to what she did, after all.

"Should have given me some clothes," she muttered as she tore arm holes in the sheet and started weaving it around her body. "What a shame."

But she didn't feel like it was too much of a shame as she strode over to the door, finally clothed for the first time since arriving here. She felt a little proud of herself, and more like the tomb raiding adventurer she had been born to be.

Now, she had no idea what to do. Just that she felt more like herself and less like the shell of a person she'd been while injured. Which meant... what? Should she explore the grounds of the castle? That was ridiculous. She couldn't go get Greed because frankly she'd seen enough of him.

So she just... opened the door.

Her feet would lead her to where she needed to go. They always had. She would walk forward into the unknown and adventure would reveal itself. That was how it had always worked before, at least.

But there was a broad back in front of her door. A tall man who stood at attention as though his life depended on it.

Ivo glanced over his shoulder, looking down. Varya hadn't realized how small she was compared to him. Her head barely came up to his shoulder. Was he as tall as Greed?

No, not quite. But she was much smaller than these men. It should have made her a little afraid but... Ah, she'd lost all ability to be afraid a long time ago.

"You're awake," Ivo said, the words falling a little flat.

"I've been awake for a few days now," she muttered, trying to dodge past him. "I'd like to go, if you don't mind."

"Go where?"

"I don't know." She tried again, but for a big man, he was quick. Huffing out a breath, she crossed her arms over her chest and glared up at him. "Well?"

Was he amused? That was a new expression on his face and she swore he looked down at her like she was a rather adorable kitten he'd found on the street. "Well what?"

"Are you going to get out of my way?"

"No."

"Why not?"

"I'm supposed to watch you." And there it was. His damnable loyalty to Greed that he had shown time and time again.

"Did Greed tell you that?" she asked, even though she already knew the answer.

He gave her a nod and crossed his arms over that massive chest. Eyeing her now with no small amount of worry, he looked her up and down as if he could see her injuries just by staring at her body. Surely he knew she was feeling much better? Taking a deep breath didn't even hurt!

"Well, you can watch me from wherever we go. Didn't Greed say this was the safest place in the kingdom?" Throwing his master's words back in his face seemed to do the trick.

Ivo looked a little confused, as though she'd somehow managed to stump him. That success was all she needed to duck underneath his arm and start down the stone pathway.

"What is this place?" she called out over her shoulder. "I didn't realize there were so many different kinds of plants in this kingdom. I thought it was all cacti."

Nor had she expected to find an actual treasure trove here. There were so many beautiful things surrounding Greed's home, and no one else saw them. She'd barely even seen servants in her time here, but now she saw them. A few people meandered through the leaves, brushing them aside as they moved to the glass domes that bubbled up through the greenery. They were easy to miss, though. All that glass made them almost disappear into the oasis.

Ivo grunted and then she heard his big footsteps trailing along behind her. "This is the oasis, Greed's home."

"Yes, I know that." She turned, walking backward with her arms wide. "But where did all this come from?"

"I do not know."

"Have you ever asked?"

His shoulders rounded in a bit, and Ivo shook his head. "I have not."

"A man of many words," she muttered before turning around. The last thing she needed was to fall off one of these large walkways and injure herself again. Then Greed really wouldn't let her out of the room again. "What's your favorite place in this oasis, then?"

She kept walking even as the wall behind her remained silent. He didn't have to tell her his favorite place if he didn't want to. All of it so far was her favorite.

Varya kept moving, and she poked her head into every glass dome they walked by. Most seemed to be empty rooms, some filled with treasure, others filled with beds. She wondered if servants slept there, but they were far too nice. Maybe they were for guests? One door blasted heat, and she peered into the kitchens that bustled with countless servants and three cooks who were shouting orders.

It was all so domestic. Everywhere she looked, there were people living in this jungle or rooms just waiting for people to join.

Another dome had Ivo's sister sitting in it. She cleaned her blades, sharpening them while she instructed the two others. One of those two was just as tall as Ivo and Morag, but something about the woman made her think that she wasn't the same as the other two guards. The other person in the room was a tiny little woman with spectacles on her nose. Her eyes looked far too large as she blinked up at Varya.

"Come," Ivo said, his hand on her shoulder as he pushed her away from them. "They are busy."

"Your sister and..."

"The large one is another of Greed's personal guards. She's been stationed in Lust's kingdom for a while and only now returned. Perhaps she will remain there for good, I do not know. The other helps with numbers."

"Numbers," Varya repeated, eyebrows raising. "And yet she was in what looked like an armory?"

He grunted again. "She counts things."

"Ah."

Varya didn't care to push more than that. Instead, she tilted her head back to the cool breeze and the sunlight. The air smelled so herbal in this place, and that mixed with florals as they walked by giant flowers the size of her head.

"Go left," Ivo said.

"Left? Why?"

"Left," he repeated.

Who was she to argue? Varya was just happy to stretch her legs. She would have walked right out onto the sands if he asked her to. Instead, she listened to his directions until they stood in front of a massive garden.

Rows upon rows of vegetables grew so large she wondered if they were there by magic. All along the rows were carefully tamped sections where people could walk, and the food. Oh, the food was so impressive. Watermelons larger than her head. Countless peppers and tomatoes and bright green things she couldn't name but looked delicious and made her mouth water.

And it smelled like earth. She inhaled and filled her lungs with the scent of dirt and loam and healthy plants. It made her heart flutter in her chest. She'd wanted to see this at least once in her life, and here she was.

"Oh, Ivo," she whispered. "What a gift to see this."

"Indeed," he replied. "This is my favorite place in the oasis."

"I can see why. Look at all the—" Varya's words froze in her throat.

Because at the very end of the garden was a young woman pulling weeds. She had a smear of dirt across her forehead and the riot of red curls bursting around her head was so lovely that she looked like a rose that had come to life. And as Varya looked up at Ivo, she could see how he couldn't tear his eyes away from the young woman.

"Oh," she said. "I see."

"It is most useful to keep everyone in the Oasis fed."

"Right. Of course, that's why it's your favorite place." She nudged him with her shoulder, forcing him to take a step forward. "Why don't you go talk to her?"

He stared down at her with wide eyes filled with fear. "I cannot."

"Why?"

"Because she…" He swallowed hard and the panic really set in. "She is a servant."

"So are you." Varya shrugged. "Why does that matter?"

"It wouldn't be right. She's human, and I'm…."

He froze, and she realized he wasn't supposed to say that. So Greed's guards weren't human. She'd find out exactly what they were soon enough, but she needed to win his trust. And pointing out his mistake would only make him run.

Varya patted his massive shoulder and shrugged again. "I think nothing matters all that much unless you let it. It's just saying hello, Ivo. You can do that."

"I do not know if I am wanted." He seemed confused by the words, though. As though he'd never thought about whether or not someone might wish to speak with him.

"You'll never know unless you try. Just go say hi."

"I'm supposed to watch you."

"And where am I going to go?" She opened her arms wide and gestured all around them. "I have no idea where I am."

That sealed the deal. He gave her one last stern look before turning his attention to the lovely woman in the dirt. And she was excited to see him. The redhead stood, wiping her hands off on her skirts before loudly saying his name.

It was cute. They seemed so young and so innocent and so unaware that she was going to disappear the first moment she could. What a shame for the guard who would realize that he'd been tricked.

Ah, well. Who was going to get mad at her? Greed?

Sneaking into the undergrowth of the jungle, she slipped into the cool shadows and explored. She didn't want anyone to find her, so she stayed hidden. Servants meandered past her, all of them plump and healthy with jaunty steps as they walked to their next task. They didn't know what it was like to starve.

Did Greed think his entire kingdom was living like they were? That would explain a lot.

She'd gotten lost for about an hour when she found another garden. This one seemed to be more filled with plants that looked... dangerous. Some of them even had teeth that opened and closed toward her, as if they sensed where she was.

Varya lifted a hand, shifting one of the giant fronds in front of her so she could get a better look.

An arm slid around her waist, firm and broad and all too strong for his own good. Maybe she should be embarrassed that she knew exactly whose arm it was the moment it touched her.

"What are you doing spying on my gardens?" Greed growled in her ear. "I thought I'd locked you up."

Shivering, she leaned back against him. She had no other choice. Varya wanted to stay away from him, but even thinking such a thing was impossible. She had her needs, and he was a very handsome man with all those hard muscles all pressed up against her back as though he belonged there.

"Your guards are easily distracted," she replied.

"Did you slip away from Ivo?"

"His attention was more on the pretty redhead in the garden than it was on me."

He cursed, his fingers spreading wide on her belly as he drew her closer. Did he even realize what he was doing? "I'll have to talk with him about that."

"Please don't. I got to explore this beautiful place you call home, and he got to talk to the girl he's very interested in." Varya turned in his arms, wrapping one of her own around his neck. "Besides, you wouldn't have found me all alone like this."

A low groan rumbled in his chest. "You are injured."

"I'm fine."

"I will not tarnish you any more."

Tarnish. Like she had been ruined by what had happened to her. And all of a sudden, she heard their voices in her ears. Whispering words of torment with a weapon only men could wield against women.

She'd thought it hadn't bothered her. That they weren't there anymore in her head because nothing had happened. They'd just threatened. They hadn't actually touched her. And yet...

His thumbs traced underneath her eyes. "What shadows haunt you, treasure?"

"None that you can fight." She tried to pull away from him, but he didn't let her go. Greed held her there, staring into her eyes, forcing her to look at him. And she gave in. "They intended to tarnish me, but I assure you they did not succeed."

His eyes searched hers, and she had the distinct displeasure of watching him understand what her words meant. The rage that poured over him was icy cold, and then it turned into a despair unlike any she'd seen before.

"Ach, my treasure." He drew her tight against his chest, those massive arms holding her close to his heart. "Nothing would ruin or wreck you in my eyes. I do not wish to harm you any more than they already did. You are so very small."

"I am not weak," she muttered against his chest, angry that tears were pricking in her eyes. "I'm fine. I'm healed and I can leave now."

"Not until I show you all my home has to offer. Yes?" He drew back and stared down into her watery eyes with a soft smile. "You will let me show you my home before you go."

She didn't have it in her to say no.

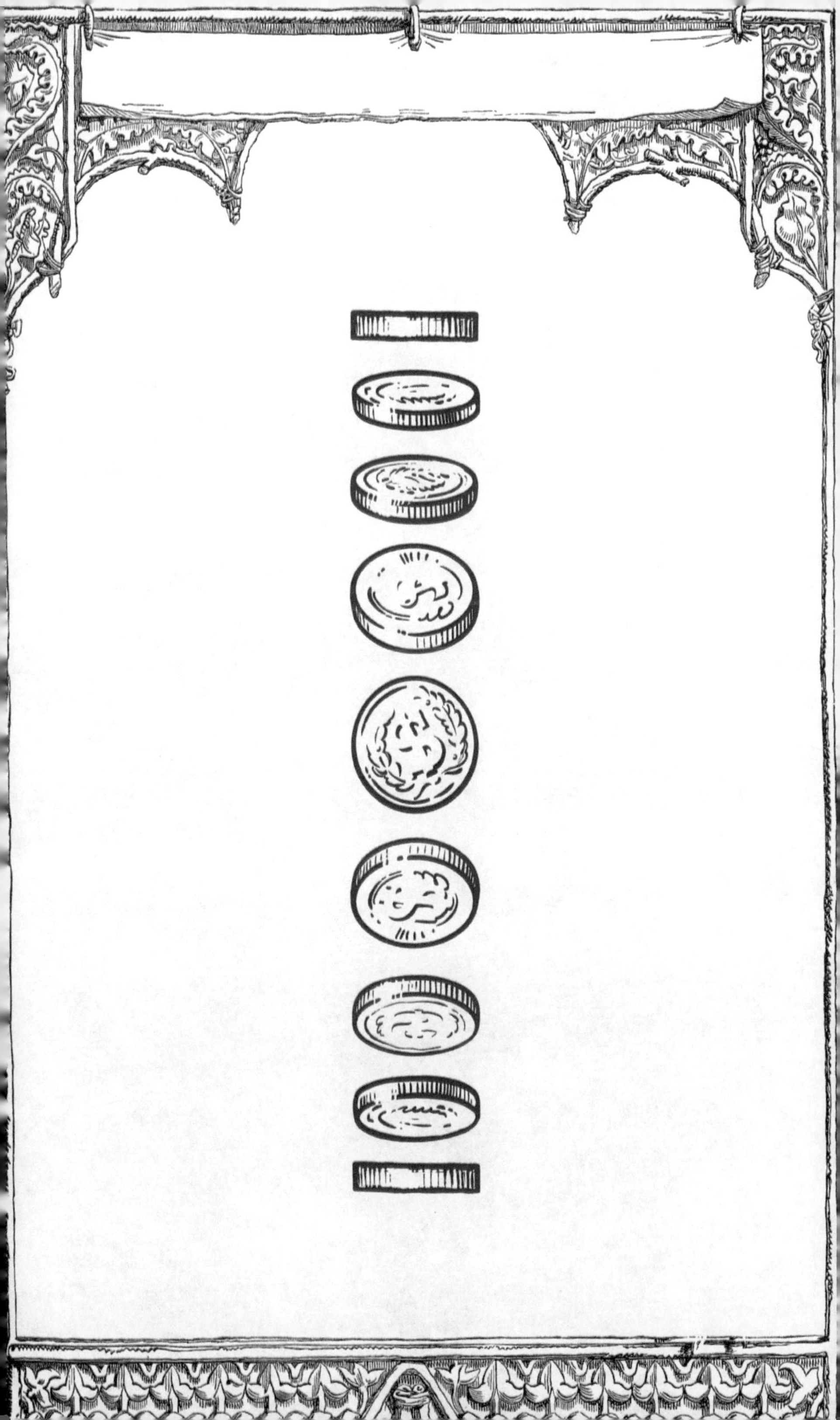

He had one chance. One.

He'd already seen the thought in her eyes. She was a wanderer, just as he'd been when he was first birthed into this world. Greed remembered the desire to see and touch and take, to do as much as he could before the very world bent to his ways. They were kindred spirits in that way.

She'd only give him a single moment to prove to him why she should remain in this oasis while the rest of her people were subjected to the sands. And he intended to tantalize her senses until there was nothing else for her. She'd never return to those tiny villages when she could be here with him. When she could live in luxury and opulence.

So he'd brought her back to his room, ignoring the look of disappointment on her face when she realized where he was bringing her. Because he had plans to make. The entire oasis had to be on the same page as him, and they would give her their best.

He spent most of the morning ordering the kitchens around. Then he turned his attention to his own collection.

Greed had a thousand years' worth of treasures to choose from. So much wealth and beauty that he could lay out at her feet, but he wouldn't. Not yet. She would be terrified of all the gemstones and the beauty that he wanted to give her.

But he knew the dress he would place upon her. The dress that he'd been dying to see her in since the beginning. And perhaps gifts of jewels while he indulged all her senses tonight. That would be enough, he was certain of it.

He arrived back to his private quarters hours later with a dress over his arm and a plan to enact. Ivo was back in front of the door, and he gave the other man a little frown as he approached.

Ivo bowed and started off. Apparently, even his guard understood that he was not to interrupt tonight. Word traveled fast around here.

Clearing his throat, he knocked on the door as though he were a gentleman. As if he was ever a gentleman at all.

Varya opened the door, still wearing her ripped up sheet, and already rolling her eyes at the sight of him. "What is this, Greed?"

"My lady." He bowed low and deep, then glanced up at her with a quirked brow as she laughed. "I am here to dress you for the evening. The Lord of the Oasis has sent you a gown for this evening and bid you to humbly accept his invitation."

"The Lord of the Oasis, huh?" She crossed her arms over her chest and leaned against the door. "So who are you?"

"Your servant for the evening."

"Ah." She nodded, her eyes going over his shoulder as she

exaggerated her attempts to look past him. "Is there a lady servant who can dress me? I'm quite certain that it would be rather... indecent to have a man dressing me."

A flash of jealousy burned through his chest. "Absolutely not."

"No one else touches me but you?"

She'd caught him. Damn it. The woman was too quick for her own good.

His jealousy wasn't a good quality to have. He understood that. And it wasn't quite jealousy, anyway. He just didn't want to share her with anyone else.

Was that so bad?

Pushing her back with his body, he moved into their quarters and ignored her look. He strode into the center of the room and then gave her the gown to put on. "This is for you."

"This is..." She held it out to look, and he knew what she saw.

Molten gold. The entire gown had been made to look like metal poured into a sheet of fabric. It was beyond beautiful, and only three of them had been made. One burned in a horrible fire that had destroyed an entire town. The other he'd gifted to one of Sloth's queens. Greed could safely assume it had been destroyed when Sloth had found something disappointing about the woman.

Turning her back to him, Varya unhooked the gown she'd made of the sheets and let it fall off her body. The silk slithered onto the ground, trailing down her curves like he wished to do. His mouth watered as she revealed the long lines of her body, the muscles in her back that flexed and moved with her, and the round muscles of her ass.

Oh, he wanted her. He wanted her more than anything else in this realm, and he would have her tonight. That's what all of this led up to. One final moment to convince her that he was what she needed.

She stepped into the gown, drawing it up all those lovely curves. Molten gold poured over his treasure, just as she was meant to be seen by all who were lucky enough to bask in her beauty. He stepped closer, his fingers brushing against her spine as he tied it at the back so it would stay on. The dress clung to her ribs, just barely, and hung off her shoulders so her graceful neck and collarbone were bare.

He couldn't resist. Greed skated his lips along that line of warm skin, smiling against her as she let out a little shuddering breath. He trailed the backs of his fingers down her bare sides, tying those strands as well. The fabric covered her front entirely, but the sides were left almost bare other than four strands at her ribs, waist, hips, and just around her thighs.

Sighing, he fell to his knees as he trailed his lips down to each one of those ties until they were all knotted closed. Then he followed the same line on the other side of her body, dressing her as she'd always meant to be dressed.

Staring up at her, he looked up at a goddess who deserved to have an entire kingdom at her feet.

"You are so beautiful," he whispered.

Her cheeks turned bright red. He so adored that color and had the fleeting wonder if this was what Lust had felt like? Maybe it was. He'd never speculated what had captivated his brother the moment he'd seen his new wife Selene, and yet... surely it had to be something like this. It had to be this consuming emotion that made him want to grab onto her and never let her go.

"Greed," she scolded. "It's the dress. It's not me."

"It's absolutely you." He stood and held out his arm for her to take. "Now, would you like to have dinner with me?"

"Am I allowed to leave the room?"

"I had hoped you would."

Greed wondered if he was dressed for the occasion as he walked beside her. He'd put on his best leather pants and a leather vest over his white shirt. His rings always glittered on his fingers, but were they enough? He should have placed more gems on his person, a necklace at least, or maybe one of those rare magical crowns. It wasn't the most gallant of outfits, but he wasn't a very gallant man.

He'd wanted to give her this, though. And so he had tried to make himself look as though he was a little more put together. Because he wanted people to look at him and see that he was the only person who had what they wanted.

Now she was one of those objects that others would desire. And as he walked through his oasis jungle with her on his arm, he knew no one could see them without wanting what he had. They would try to take her from him and he would fight them to the bitter end. Blood would be fed to the desert on her behalf, and he would feed it many times before he was satisfied.

He drew her into the dome where all of his balls and gatherings should have been held. He had been told there were many in this place before he'd taken over the oasis. The floors were made of molten gold, reflecting everything like a mirror. The massive table at the end was full of every food she might desire. Meat, cheese, wine, vegetables, pies, tiny cakes that his chef insisted on placing there. Not to mention the whole roasted pig that took up the center of the table.

Varya hissed out a breath. "This is too much food for so few people, Greed. It's a waste."

"The rest will be given to the staff to eat." And then he froze. Because maybe she'd want something else. Maybe she would desire... "Or a town of your choosing."

"Really?" She frowned up at him. "Why would you do that?"

"Because I already have a treasure that everyone desires." He skated his fingers along her jaw before he could stop himself. "I have no need for food, Varya. Not when you stand beside me."

Again her cheeks flared that bright red color. So lovely, as she seemed to accept that this food would go to those who needed it. Fascinating.

He watched her as she approached the table. Her movements were graceful and so calculated, a true warrior through and through. She had no idea what she did to him moving like that.

Already he was uncomfortably hard. Already his hands burned to touch her, mark her, make her his. But he held himself back because he also wanted to see what she thought of the food.

Varya stood in front of the table, staring down at it, her hands braced on the wood. But she didn't move. She didn't grab anything at all, and it made him wonder if she did not know where to even start. Perhaps she'd never had any of this food before.

And oh, that made his entire body tingle. He'd be the first to feed this to her. He'd be the first to...

Fuck. He could come just from the thought.

Shaking his head, he surveyed the table before making his first choice. A small cracker that his kitchen had been making for years, made of the finest sifted grains. On top, he placed caviar from the fish that they grew in the deepest pools of the oasis. The dark pearls were delicious, and many people would kill to have them.

"Here," he said, holding it out for her to taste. "I think you'll find this interesting."

Obediently, she opened her mouth, her tongue already outstretched for him. He had a flashing image of her doing the same on her knees, and his free hand clenched so hard he could hear the bones creak.

Varya closed her mouth, chewed, and then she moaned.

By all the seven kingdoms, he almost fell onto his knees in front of her again. Her eyes rolled back in her head and he just knew that was the same face she'd make when he brought her to release over and over again. When he'd made her beg him to stop because she couldn't do this anymore, and he made her come one more time.

"That's delicious," she said, her tongue flicking out to lick at her lips. "I don't even have a name for that."

"You don't need to know the name when you'll be eating it for years to come." He turned around before he did something stupid. Like crush their lips together and paw at that expensive dress. "Try this now."

He didn't use a fork to pick up the thinly sliced meat. Instead, he lifted the marbled, shaved beef to her mouth and watched her lips close around his fingers. She licked the juices off his thumb and almost unmanned him that easily. "What is this?"

"A rare beef that can only be grown here in the oasis. They've had this breed of cattle for centuries, only here. They have a specific diet. A very specific way to cut and prepare the meat. And all of it can only be found here, in my home."

"It sounds like you have a lot of secrets, Greed."

"You have no idea."

He took his time feeding her with his own hands. The act was strangely erotic, knowing that she could only get her sustenance from his fingers. They both became more and more adventurous with each other as well.

She'd picked up a saffron dusted roll on her own, but the honey on top had dripped down her chin. Greed used his thumb to chase down the small, sweet drop and then sucked it from his finger.

But it was the chocolate that undid them both. He gave her a small bite of dark chocolate that he'd stolen from Gluttony, and he hadn't been able to stop himself. She bit into it and he leaned forward to lick the smallest hint of that dark magic from her lips.

And then he was lost. She tasted like everything he'd stolen and everything the world desired. She tasted like the finest of wines and he hadn't even poured that into her mouth yet. But she was here, his, and he was the only one with this treasure on his arm.

Snarling against her lips, he backed her away from the table. Greed didn't know where he was going with her, only that he wanted her. Needed her. That he'd shred this mortal form if he didn't get to indulge himself in her for a few moments.

"I want you," she said, her mouth skating down his throat and her tongue leaving little marks of red behind. "I don't care that you think I'm too injured. I want you now, and I will have you."

"Ach, you do not know what you ask."

"I'm not broken." Varya glared up at him, fierce and powerful as the woman he'd always wanted.

A lump formed in his throat and he tried to swallow it down. She was... more than he'd expected. He'd found himself a thief in the desert and suddenly she had become this wild and wicked thing who consumed him every time they met.

For a moment, he feared for his life. He worried about what would happen if he gave in. If he let her devour him, just as she so obviously wanted to do.

But he wanted her as well. He wanted to steal her away, and if that meant giving her a part of himself, then he would. She would rip and tear at all the magic he had, and still he would feed off her greed.

Because that's what she was. A greedy little thing who demanded he attend to her and he would do all of that and more.

Greed bent her back over his arm, just far enough to see her wince. Her ribs might be healing, but they were not entirely where she thought they were. Not yet. "You do not know what you ask."

"I do."

"You think this will be fun evening entertainment and you'll disappear into the night afterward? But I am Greed, Varya. And if we do this, then you are mine."

Though she was clearly uncomfortable, not yet in pain, she still stared into his eyes as though trying to understand him. "What are you asking of me?"

He pressed his mouth to her long neck and inhaled deeply of her scent. "I want your pleasure, and I want your pain. I want every feeling you can give me, my treasure, and I will share it with no one else. If you think you can take that, I promise you that you cannot. No one has yet been able to."

He'd broken so many women. Shattered them from the inside out after they realized this wasn't what they wanted. They'd been enticed by his looks and his fortune, but none of them had wanted him to own them. Body and soul.

But he stared into those wide blue eyes and he wondered if this was the one he'd been searching for.

Chapter 22

Her heart thundered in her chest. Varya knew what his words meant. He was more than just some selfish king who wanted her to bend to his whims. This was Greed himself. A man who would want everything she had to give to him and then still take more because he thought he deserved it.

Could she do this? Could she bend to him completely?

Some part of her hated the idea of it. The same part wanted to stay wild and free, and that was the voice that she listened to. The voice that said she deserved to take what she wanted and not care about anyone else. Fuck whatever he wanted from her, because she was the one with wants and needs and no one had ever listened to those before.

No one had ever put her first until him. No one had healed her wounds after a difficult adventure. She'd never had a single person tell her that she was important to them, or that her life was worth taking care of. Instead, they'd all asked for more.

Her ribs screamed, but even that pain reminded her how alive she was and that this handsome man wanted her.

Greed could never take anything from her that she didn't want to give. And he knew that. He was trying to scare her, and she refused to let him.

Baring her teeth in a snarl that he would understand, she met his heated gaze with one of her own. "I'm not an object to own."

"And yet, you would be mine."

Why did that send a thrill up her spine? She didn't want to be tied down to anyone, nor did she want any man to ever own her, but the thought of him being that person? Well. It made a girl think.

"You think very highly of yourself, Greed. Do you really believe you're such a temptation that I would give up all that I am?"

"Yes, because I want all that you are." He trailed his nose up her neck, the scratchy texture of his beard raising goosebumps up and down her body. "I want your pain, your relief, your happiness, your grief. All of it. I want it and I want to be the only person who gets it."

"And what do I get in return?"

"You get me." He leaned back slightly and licked his lips.

"All of you?" she asked, because she had to know this was an even trade. She wouldn't give him everything if he wouldn't give her the same.

And yet... When had her mind changed to this? She shouldn't even consider saying yes to him!

"There's not much to give." A shadow passed in front of his eyes, one that she recognized very well. A shadow of doubt. The fear that he wasn't good enough and never would be. "But what I have is yours."

"I don't want what you have." Varya leaned up and ghosted her lips over his, so close she could feel his breath and heat. Her abs burned with the movement, but she needed him to understand her. "I just want you."

A low groan echoed in his chest and he kissed her. He kissed like a starving man, trying to devour her whole as if that would somehow satisfy a need he had no name for.

She wanted to claw her way inside him. She wanted to hide from the voices whispering in her ear about what they would do to her and how she was nothing but a sleeve for them to use when they saw fit.

No one took this from her. No one took her right to enjoy using her body as she saw fit and she would not listen to those devious voices of men who had not deserved an ounce of her attention.

Gritting her teeth, she felt the cool wave of fabric part over one of her thighs. Without thought, she swept her bare leg behind his and shoved.

Greed's eyes snapped open in shock as he suddenly tumbled. He was quick on his feet, though. He landed on his bottom rather than his back, bracing himself as he stared up at her with wide eyes and mouth slightly open.

"What was that for—"

He shut up when she followed him down. Varya whisked the long skirts out of her way and straddled him as she sank onto his lap. Control, that was what she needed. He couldn't tell her what to do and he wouldn't order her around. Never.

"I have told you," she said as she palmed his shoulders and shoved him again. "I am no one's object. No one's toy to play with."

"I don't want to make you a toy."

"No, but you want to play," Varya whispered as she lowered him flat. "And I'm afraid you'll never be able to see past that. So do you understand what I'm saying, Greed? I cannot give you all of me. Nor do I want to."

She trailed her own lips down his neck, pressing soft kisses to his overheated skin. He arched into her, his breath already faltering and turning rapid.

"Then we cannot do this," he argued, seemingly with himself more than with her. "I will not have you if I cannot have... have..."

Her fingers danced down his chest as she ground against him. He was already hard and throbbing between her legs, and she knew that this was her choice to make. He wouldn't push her. Greed wasn't those men in the cave.

He'd made it very clear that he wanted her, and he'd also shown he was a man of honor. As much as a demon could have honor, she supposed.

Varya slid down his body, the metal sheen of her dress pooling over his lap as she moved. Flicking her gaze up to him, she waited until he looked down at her. All those freckles stood out against the red tinge of his skin. His cheekbones were blushed with need and his pupils were so dilated his eyes looked entirely black. Like the demon he was.

She smiled, slow and coy. "Are you sure you cannot make an exception? Just this once?"

Varya knew what she asked. She would not beg for him to change his rules just for her, just so she could taste him and know what it felt like to have a demon inside her, but... Some part of her had hope he would agree. That he would let her, for a few moments, indulge herself.

It was almost like he felt the spark in her. The greed that made her even say the words because she wanted to take something for herself right now. Just to see if she still could. To see if those idiots in that cave had broken something inside her.

That hard jaw clenched. The muscles on either side bunching as he ground his teeth and stared at her, watching her eyes as though she could tell him what she was thinking without ever saying a word. That bright gold gaze flashed, and he nodded. The cords of his neck stood out in stark relief as he battled with himself.

"Aye, for you treasure," he finally said, swallowing hard. "I suppose I could."

Oh, that shouldn't give her butterflies. That shouldn't make her mouth water with the plans of what she would do to him. And it certainly shouldn't make her mind whirl with all the possibilities.

Varya knew what she wanted to do most. And that was prove to this demon king, this embodiment of greed, this monster who had ruled her kingdom, that a single mortal woman could bring him to his knees. She wanted him to know that she had more control over him than he'd ever dreamed.

And damn it. She wanted to feel powerful for once in her life. Varya didn't want to feel like the thief who stole for her people and then slipped away with no connections. She wanted to feel like someone gave a shit about what happened to her.

So she would take this moment, and him, in her hands. This would not slip away from her, no matter what shadows or memories clogged her mind.

Focusing her attention on the body in front of her, she unbuttoned his vest and then dragged his shirt out of his waistband. Crouched between his legs now, she couldn't pull her eyes away from the rigid abs that she revealed as she drew the shirt up.

He was a man built for battle. Scars decorated his flesh, and she wondered if he'd let them stay there. She'd seen him like this before, but now he was laid out in front of her like a banquet. Not sick. Not ill. Just staring at her with those gleaming eyes as he waited to see what she would do.

Leaning down, she pressed her lips to his stomach and smiled against the jolting muscles. Tongue and teeth trailed down his side as she reached his waistband and made quick work of the ties.

Then she drew back just enough to pull him out from his leathers and...

"Oh," she whispered.

His smug grin made her want to smack it off his face. "Too much for you?"

A bit. If she was being honest.

The thick, veiny appendage was larger than she'd ever seen in person. And Varya had seen a few in her lifetime. But by the gods, it made her mouth water. She wanted to touch him, taste him, slide her tongue up that throbbing vein and taste the pearly white droplet on the top. More than anything, she wanted to suck him so deep into her mouth that he couldn't talk for just a few damn seconds.

Varya wet her lips before she grasped him. And then she gave him one long lick from base to tip that had him tilting his head back against the floor and groaning.

His back arched again, all those lovely muscles flexing before her eyes. Sliding one of her hands up his stomach, she clawed into his chest. Little pinpricks of pain that made him hiss out a breath and then glare down at her.

He'd said he wanted her pain, hadn't he? She would give him his own if that's what he wanted.

"Bratty little thing," he snarled. "But you know how to suck a cock."

She squeezed the base of him harder, sliding him all the way out of her mouth slowly. Taking her time so he could feel the flat of her tongue against every inch of him before she let him drop out of her mouth. "Are you complaining?"

He arched a brow but remained silent.

Good enough.

Varya circled the tip of him, slow and never quite enough because she liked the idea of punishing him. Making him wait. And she knew what a sight she presented. The short waves of her hair spread across his thighs, her ass in the air, while that dress pooled on either side of her. She made eye contact with a deep pull of him between her lips, nearly touching the back of her throat, and there was still so much of him left.

"Fuck," he hissed. "You look so pretty on your knees."

He'd pushed up onto his elbow so he could watch her better, but suddenly it felt like he was in control again. She moved faster, sucked harder, drawing more and more compliments from him because the man never shut up.

"Yes, Varya. Good girl, now faster. Just like that. Gods, you're so fucking talented with that wicked tongue of yours."

She let him slid out of her mouth with a wet pop before snarling, "For gods' sake, do you ever shut up?"

"Make me." His eyes glittered with challenge, and she knew he expected her to lunge upright. To climb on top of his lap and cover his lips with hers as she sank down onto this massive cock.

She wanted to. Gods, she wanted to.

But Varya knew what that would mean. She knew he would take and she would give and it would never stop.

Besides, she hated being predictable.

In a swift movement, she both shoved him down onto the ground and turned herself around. Knees now planted above his shoulders, she flipped her skirt out of the way so she could glare over his shoulder at his shocked and heated expression. "Can you at least keep yourself busy?"

"Fuck," he growled before planting his hand on the back of her neck and shoving her down where she'd been.

She gripped his cock firmly, holding perhaps a little too tight. And she'd only just started to suck him again when he gave her dripping pussy a long, slow lick.

Lightning.

It sparked through her veins and made her toes curl on either side of his head. And though there were still whispers in the back of her mind, she also recognized who was in control. She was. And if she wanted him to lick harder, she could grind down on him. If she wanted him to stop talking, she could smother him as he worshipped her.

He did it again, his tongue tracing circles around her clit, and she bucked on him. He grasped either side of her hips, forcing her to remain in place while he put that tongue to better use than just hissing out praise.

She didn't want to hear him, and now she didn't have to.

Whimpering around his cock, she swallowed him like it was the last thing she'd ever do. Varya stroked, sucked, and pulled until she felt him tightening underneath her. Until she felt that harsh coil in her belly tightening and tightening.

She couldn't think. Could hardly keep up a regular rhythm, but he was helping with that. Greed lifted his hips, sliding his cock in and out of her mouth as he sucked hard on her clit. And there it was, the pinpoint of pain that burst into a thousand sparks of pleasure. She rode the wave, grinding her pussy against that tongue and lips that brought her down from the shockwave as she pulled her mouth away from him to moan against his inner thigh.

Varya came down slowly, her hand still pumping him and those soft growls echoing against her belly through his chest.

Breathing hard, she slipped him back into her mouth and cupped him. Rolling his balls between her fingers until an actual growl erupted from between her thighs. He pulsed in her hand, spraying his cum into the back of her mouth, both salty and warm and everything she'd wanted it to be.

By the gods, he'd unraveled her. He'd wormed his way into her heart and she didn't even know the man. Couldn't know him. He was a thousand year old demon, and she'd made him cum in her mouth like a regular commoner.

And she'd do it again. A thousand times over.

"Fuck." His voice rang in the room before he let out a little chuckle. "The things you do to me, treasure."

"Oh?" She could barely lift her head from his leather covered thigh. "Like what?"

He slapped her ass so hard the sound echoed through the ballroom. He'd left a handprint with that one, but the slight sting made heat burn through her yet again. She could do this with him all night.

Then she was laughing. Chuckling along with him as they both tried to get their bearings on the floor of the ballroom. What had come over her? What had she even done?

But she couldn't feel guilty about it. She'd taken what she wanted, and Varya felt like she was glowing. She wasn't broken after all.

Fuck the Horde. She could still enjoy herself immensely.

Chapter 23

Greed followed her back to his bedroom in a daze. After piecing themselves back together after the best orgasm of his life, he'd insisted that she eat more. She'd been so injured that food hadn't been her top priority and he wanted her to eat. He wanted her to consume as much as she could, and then he would bring her back to his bedroom and show her what else he could do with his massive cock.

She'd seemed to like that well enough, even if she'd had to stretch her mouth so wide that her lips were still red and puffy from the effort. But gods, he appreciated that effort.

He was still stunned. He'd never had a woman try to murder him with her pussy stealing all his air. He'd thought that would be rather demeaning, but he couldn't get enough of it. Fuck the air. He didn't need to breathe. He was immortal and if that was how he died... What a way to go.

Greed's thoughts turned heated again. He felt like he needed to thank her somehow. That he needed to prove to her that he could do the same. After all, she had thoroughly changed the way he would forever see that ballroom floor.

It would take centuries to wipe away the image of her folds glistening above him, all that gold pouring off her body as if she was a goddess of old and wanted a sacrifice who could survive molten metal.

Ah. He was already uncomfortably hard again.

Trailing behind her through the halls, his eyes couldn't look at anything but the sway of her hips and how lovely her ass looked underneath that fabric. His. All his.

He knew she'd said she was no one's other than her own, but he knew the sound of her crying out in pleasure now. Greed would not stop hunting that sound for the rest of his life. It was the prettiest song he'd ever heard.

They reached the door to his bedroom, and he knew something was wrong. Both Ivo and Morag stood outside the doors, wearing matching expressions of displeasure as the two of them approached.

Apparently, it was time for him to be a king again and not just the man fawning over the young woman he'd found in the middle of the desert.

Sighing, he ushered Varya into the room and caught her chin in his hand. Staring down at those swollen lips, he gently skated his thumb over the lower one. "We'll have to continue this another time."

"Is everything all right?"

"It'll all be fine." Using her chin, he pulled her closer so he could kiss her. Hard. Hard enough to bite and leave a mark for when he came back. "We're not done talking."

"We didn't do much talking."

"We don't ever do much talking," he replied with a wry grin. "But we will talk when I come back. There's much to say."

Why did that make a worried expression cross her features? Varya had to know that wasn't the only thing she would get out of him. She'd wrapped a demon king around her pretty, talented fingers. She wasn't getting away that easily, not with a quick suck on the ballroom floor. No, he wouldn't be satisfied for a long while yet.

Raising an eyebrow, he left her alone with her thoughts as he left the room.

His twin guards were right where he'd left them. Both of them staring at him with no small amount of disapproval, as if he needed their permission to entertain himself with another woman.

"What?" he grunted. "You two aren't usually right in front of my room without something being on fire."

"Gluttony's here," Ivo said, worry already marring his handsome brow. "A day early."

Not just a day early. Greed glanced up to see the red streaks of a sunset already above their head. Gluttony was supposed to be here in a day and a half, in the middle of the afternoon, with an entire entourage warning everyone that another king was coming to visit. He wasn't supposed to sneak into Greed's home with dusk crawling across the sky.

Grumbling, he stalked away from the room. Both of his guards followed him, but he pointed at Ivo with a snarl. "Stay here. No one gets through those doors without my knowledge. Understood?"

"Yes."

"Not even the little thief who has snuck past you enough times."

Ivo's cheeks burned bright red, but his guard stayed where he was.

Morag followed close on his heels, both of them racing across the platforms and stairwells to the front of his home. But apparently, even this spirit couldn't help but jab at him. "You should be more gentle with Ivo."

"He lost her once already."

"Because he was distracted. You can hardly blame him when you're the one who has been teaching us to be more human."

Greed snorted. "More human, Morag. Not for you to both fall head over heels for the first human that gives you any sort of attention. Ivo knows better than to be distracted."

"Is love not the most human emotion we could feel?"

"He's not in love." The mere thought made him chuckle. Ivo didn't know how to love if he didn't know what genuine happiness felt like. Or sadness. Or all the other emotions that humans flipped through on a daily basis and didn't even recognize they were feeling it. "None of us can feel love."

"Lust did."

"Lust is love, now. That's different."

But he'd seen the way his brother had softened around Selene. He'd seen how Lust had fallen under her spell and desired to be a better man for her. Was that what love was? Was that what he himself was feeling?

Surely not. He didn't know how to be anything but greedy, and that was the way it was going to stay.

Before he could answer, they were already at the front gates. They stood wide open to the desert, sand already blowing into his home around the single black horse and tall, dark man standing beside it.

Gluttony hadn't changed at all in the many years since they'd seen each other in person. His brother's dark hair fell below his shoulders, framing an angular and handsome face. Of course, most humans found him unsettling. Red eyes set deep into his skull were perturbing to look at even when he was smiling, like he was now. Though he was the smallest of all the siblings, Gluttony's lithe body was made for speed.

He'd seen his brother gut a man in the blink of an eye and then tug out his entrails in the next. He'd been laughing while he did it, threatening to taste the thick ropes as though that was a normal thing to threaten.

Apparently, Gluttony had gotten a little too close to that threat these days.

"You're early," he snarled.

"And you haven't changed a bit. Ever the warlord, aren't you?" Gluttony eyed the castle behind him with all the glass domes and beautiful trees. "Although this is much better than the tent you used to cart around. Nomadic, isn't that the word? That's what you were the last time I saw you."

He had been nomadic, because this castle hadn't been finished yet, and he had to keep traveling through all the small towns and cities because they were constantly falling apart. He had seen Gluttony before he'd set up the system of his advisors, and why was this all making him feel lesser? Gluttony barely had a kingdom to his name.

"At least I don't eat my subjects," he snarled with bared teeth.

"Oh please." Gluttony waved a hand in the air. "Settle that tail of yours. It was one person, and I hardly ate the woman. She enjoyed herself immensely."

"Until she died."

"Unfortunate, yes." Gluttony's hand twisted, his long nails slicing in front of him as though he was slicing the woman's neck. "I didn't consume her body. Wrath is ever so dramatic."

"Then what did you do?"

"I just drank her blood." Ah, he hated it when Gluttony smiled like that. It revealed those teeth that looked like snake fangs. All together too long and very unnatural. "Like I said, she enjoyed it."

"Until she didn't."

"Until the very end," Gluttony corrected. "She enjoyed every moment because she wished to die, brother. I merely helped her seek the end in a way that was… mutually satisfying."

"I find you disgusting."

"And I find you poor." With a deep inhale, his brother cast his eyes toward Morag. "Now who is this?"

"A guard." Greed moved to stand in front of her. He should have remembered that Gluttony's nose was almost as good as his own. Even though Gluttony wasn't animalistic like some of the brothers, he always seemed to seek out a scent he enjoyed.

"Not a guard at all." Gluttony's smile never moved. "Oh, brother, we all have our secrets, don't we? After all, I have my tastes and you have your games. I'll keep your secrets if you keep mine."

"I will keep none of your secrets." Greed felt his body shaking. He wanted to change into his battle form so badly. All he desired was to rake his nails across that pretty face, even though he knew it would do no good. Gluttony would heal almost instantly.

Perhaps from all the mortal souls he'd consumed.

Gluttony rolled his eyes. "Then send her away before I catch any more of that scent. You could at least hide it better, Greed. Spirits all smell the same, you know."

He flicked his fingers at Morag, who melted into the darkness. Her eyes gleamed for a moment before she was gone. Only then did he round on his brother.

"You will say nothing of this," he hissed.

"Why would I? No spirit is as strong as we were when we changed. Your little pet project doesn't threaten me." Gluttony stepped closer, his hands spread wide and those wicked claws ready to fight if he had to. "Pride might have something to say, of course, but neither of us talk to him all that much. I won't tell him about this if you don't tell him about my new affinity."

"You won't be drinking from anyone here."

"Oh, I don't think you'll have much say in that." Gluttony leaned closer and inhaled. His nose wrinkled in disgust. "You could have at least washed up. You reek of her."

Shit.

He was such an idiot. Greed had forgotten so much about his brother until it was far too late. Now Gluttony knew what Varya smelled like. What his treasure smelled like and if he was correct, Gluttony never forgot a scent.

If his brother knew how much she meant to him, or how tempting Varya had become to his own sanity, he'd...

"Stop it," Gluttony hissed. "You're doing that thing with your face that I hate. I forgot how annoying your existence is."

"I'm not doing anything with my face."

"You're doing a lot with your face and I don't like it." Gluttony waved a hand full of claws right in front of Greed's features before he finally stepped back. And just like that, Greed could breathe again.

Apparently, they weren't going to fight. Maybe the two of them had grown up in the past few hundred years after all.

Gluttony eyed the jungle surrounding them and the glass domes above his head, then he cracked his neck. "You realize you have a problem in this kingdom, don't you?"

"Yes, it's called sand and erosion." Greed rolled his eyes. "This kingdom has seen better lifetimes, I know. Thankfully, the other brothers of ours are more than happy to help. They send food, water, provisions. Helpful men, they are."

Gluttony rolled his eyes at the not-so-subtle jab. "I don't have a lot in my kingdom to give you."

"You have everything in your kingdom, and we both know that."

"Maybe." Gluttony shrugged. "But I'm not the one who doesn't realize there's an entire group of people secretly running my kingdom from the very underbelly of my home. You don't see the problem here? I'd imagine at least your newest plaything would have mentioned it once or twice. It's a real obvious one."

Damn it, Greed was drawing a blank. Who did Gluttony mean?

Of course, Varya had mentioned a few problems. Surely the Horde wasn't that big of an issue, though. They had kidnapped him, yes. They also had some kind of spell or weapon that could knock out a demon. But he'd been attacked many times before in his reign and no one had actually managed to kill him.

Maybe he should have mentioned all this to Wrath.

Eyeing his brother with suspicion, he muttered, "Are you talking about the Horde?"

"Is that what they call themselves? A real nuisance." Gluttony pointed to his horse, his long finger slicing through the darkness. "I was riding that beast through a few towns, looking to have a little fun…" He paused and gave Greed an unimpressed look. "Stop growling. I didn't kill anyone, if that's what you're thinking. Anyway, I stopped to have a little fun and your problem attacked me the moment they got wind that I was another demon king. Not that many people knew who

I was, so I must have told the wrong person."

"And?"

"They threw something at me that spewed out smoke and made me feel downright lightheaded. I happen to be smart enough to hold my breath, but when they tried to collect me, I heard them talking about yet another demon king they'd knocked out with the same weapon." Now Gluttony was glaring at him. "Care to share, brother?"

"Stop trying to make this about me. You're here as a punishment. I'm not the one who messed up."

Gluttony's eyebrows had raised in surprise. "And yet, here I am, accepting my punishment. What do you think Pride or Wrath would do if they found out you were keeping this information from the rest of our family? A weapon that could knock us out for an undetermined amount of time is something the mortals have never created before. And here you are, sitting on that information like it's not that important."

"They haven't killed me yet." He refused to feel an ounce of guilt about this. He was Greed, and he was only proud that people in his kingdom were the ones to create such a weapon.

"But they've clearly tried," Gluttony murmured, watching him with those red eyes that saw far too much. His gaze trailed over Greed's beard, likely where most of the scent still was, and then eyed his hands, his tail with the slightest of kinks still in it. "You seem to need my help more than I need yours, brother. At least if I'm here investigating your little problem, you can keep your attention on whatever has recently made you get all grabby."

"Enough," Greed snarled. "I'll get you settled in your room and then I don't want to hear from you again for at least a month."

"I won't be here that long."

"That's the point."

He stomped through his kingdom, his tail lashing through the air as he desperately tried to get his anger under control. Maybe he wouldn't return to Varya's side tonight.

He wasn't so sure what he'd do now that all this anger and fear coursed through his veins.

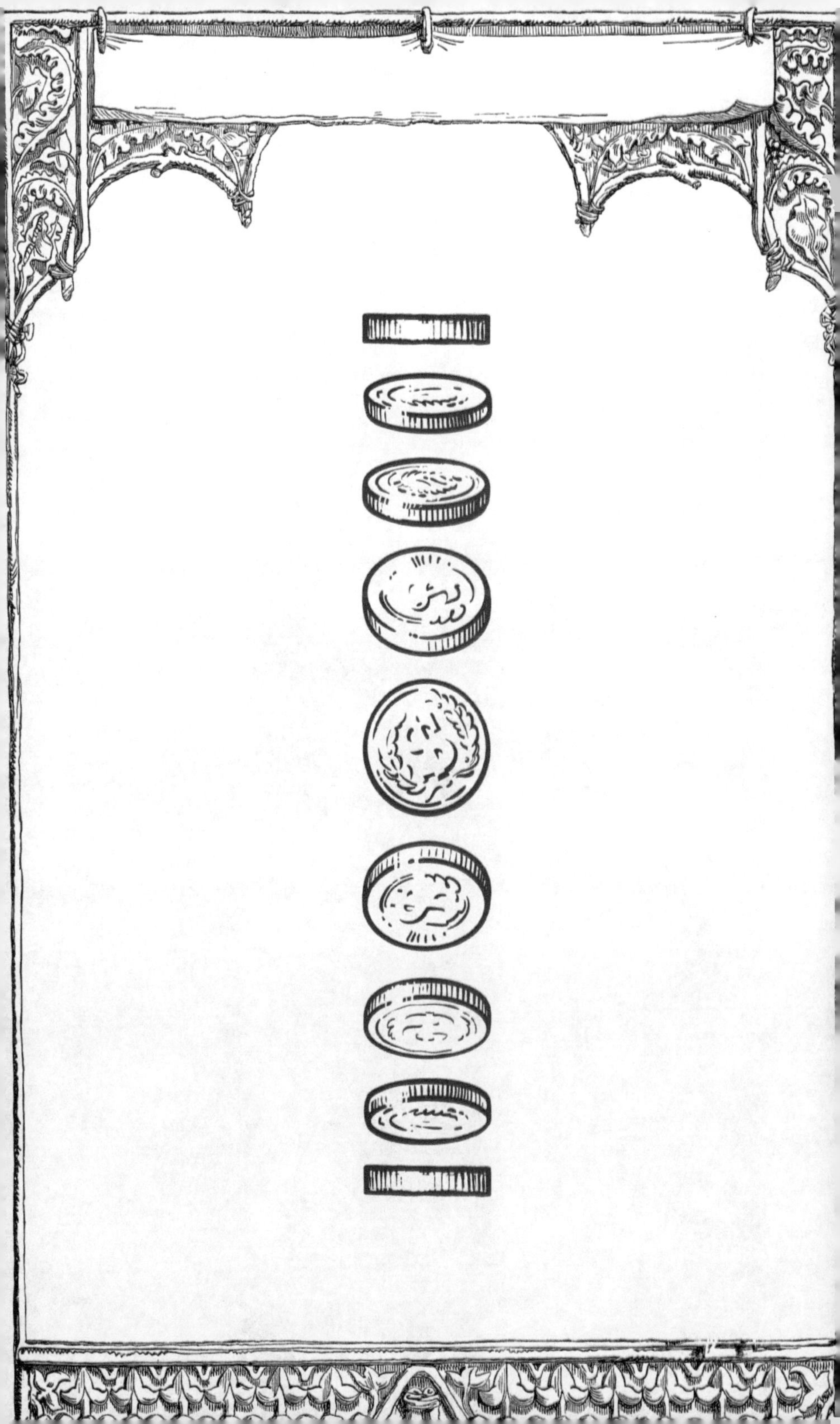

Chapter 24

Varya settled into a kind of routine in the castle. She didn't want to overstay her welcome by any means, but it was easier to be here. And for the first time in her life, she let herself indulge a bit.

One afternoon she'd wandered back to the gardens with Ivo and sat at the edge of the stream with him. She squished her feet in the water, watching as tiny fish surrounded her toes. They plucked at her, golden gems of their scales flashing in the bright sunlight.

"Is anyone worried about you?" Ivo asked, his voice a little deep with concern.

"No."

"Really?" He seemed surprised.

She didn't know how to tell him that she'd never made those

connections before. So she leaned back on her hands and stared up at the clouds. "I'm not sure that I've ever spent enough time around anyone for them to miss me."

"How is that possible?"

"I've traveled my whole life. Adventure is in my blood, I suppose, and I've always been the person to travel across the entire kingdom and take the risky jobs to make sure the rest of my town is safe." And the town before that. The city before that, too.

His brows wrinkled even more before he asked, "Is there no one that you call friend?"

"A few." Altan certainly. He'd been around since they were children on the streets. Maybe a couple of other people, but they'd fallen out of touch in the past few years as her jobs grew increasingly more dangerous and she realized the likelihood of her coming back was getting smaller and smaller. "Not as many as most people might have."

Ivo huffed out a breath and then shook his head. "Well, I would be honored to be called your friend."

"Will you really miss me when I'm gone?" She smiled at him, ready for the punchline of his joke.

But he only solemnly nodded his head. "I will, Varya. You have been a welcome addition to our home."

And those words stuck with her. A little too hard, really. She hated that she'd left a lasting impression on these people. Varya had never and would never be long for this world. Her wandering heart would send her into yet another dangerous job and maybe she wouldn't make it out of that one. Maybe she'd get caught underneath a boulder, or the Horde would catch her again. There were too many variables in her life and making connections like this...

It made her sweaty.

At the time, she'd wiped her slick palms on the fancy fabric that covered her body and laughed at him. She'd nudged his shoulder with hers and muttered something about him being too funny to get his own jokes.

She swore she heard Ivo whisper underneath his breath, "I'm kind and I'm funny."

As if her words had given him permission to be something more than he'd already known. And she didn't know what to do with that.

The days blurred together, but Greed rarely came back to see her. In fact, after that night in the ballroom, he'd made himself rather scarce. She told herself that was a good thing. Neither of them could continue down this rabbit hole of attraction. That's when actual feelings came into play.

Feelings were dangerous for people like them.

He was a demon who had a very dark persona to keep up, and she had to keep thieving from all the people that wanted to kill her. Was there a lasting ability to their relationship? Absolutely not.

What she didn't understand was why he had avoided her. Was he catching feelings? Impossible. People like him weren't capable of falling in love with anyone, so she'd thrown that out the window almost immediately.

But she'd overheard something Ivo and Morag had said while eavesdropping through the door. Something about a brother arriving and that meant there were two demon kings hidden in this oasis. Perhaps therein lay the issue.

Greed didn't want to share her with anyone. Would his brother insist? Would she start a war between kingdoms because two demon kings wanted to fight over her?

She snorted at the thought and shoved a monstera leaf out of her way. That wasn't possible at all. She wasn't some stunning beauty who had fallen into their lives and would tempt even the greatest of kings.

Her inability to understand what was happening was the reason she was out in the middle of the oasis, slapping leaves out of her way as she tried to snoop. Thieves were good at finding themselves in secret places, but Greed made that difficult.

Where was the man?

"Why are we out here?" Ivo asked as he reached above her head to hold the massive leaf out of her way. "I thought you understood that Greed was busy, and that was the only reason he hadn't come to see you."

"Because I don't believe you, liar, and there's something going on here that I want to understand."

"You could just ask me."

She flashed a glare at him over her shoulder. "Really? And I'm supposed to believe you'll tell me the answer to anything I ask?"

"We are friends." He grunted as she let a leaf slap him in the face. "Hey! I said we are friends!"

"I understand that, but you are still very loyal to Greed, a phenomenon I will never understand, which means there are questions you will not answer."

"Try me."

Varya whirled on him, her hands planted firmly on her hips. "Which of Greed's brothers has come to visit?"

"Uh..." Ivo opened and closed his mouth before staring at her helplessly.

"That's exactly what I thought. Now, can we keep moving? I want to see if Greed's put his brother somewhere in here to hide him from me."

"I think Greed understands no one could hide anything from you."

"If he did, then he wouldn't have tried hiding his brother in the first place." She turned around and squared her shoulders. Blowing a hair out of her face, she continued onward through the jungle.

Why he was trying to hide the other man, she'd never understand. Was it because he was dangerous? Obviously he was. She knew that. All demon kings were dangerous. Was it because he wanted to keep her for himself?

That was more likely. The bastard.

Slapping at another leaf, she muttered underneath her breath about men who thought they could control her. "He does realize I have opinions of my own, right? I'm stuck here for the time being, and he wants me to stay here willingly. I'm not immortal, by all the gods! I could die any minute and he's over there acting like I won't do exactly that, just wasting away in that stupid room."

"Varya..."

"You know, I don't know how long I've even been here! Part of it, I was passed out. Injuries make me lose track of time, and for all I know, I've been here for weeks!"

Ivo launched a leaf at her back, nearly toppling her off her feet. "You haven't been here that long. And you said there wasn't anyone wondering where you were."

Ouch. It wasn't all that fair for him to bring that up. "That's not nice."

"What's not nice?"

"Pointing out that there's no one waiting for me if I die doesn't make me feel great," she grumbled. "It's not an easy thing to swallow that I could disappear for a year and it would take that long for people to wonder if I was dead."

"You haven't been here a year. You've only been here sixteen days."

Sixteen days? She had healed so much faster than she'd expected. Her ribs didn't even hurt anymore, and she was certain that had to be because she'd been here at least a month. Sixteen days?

Wait, a minute...

"Oh." She turned around, heading back the way they'd come. "If I've only been here sixteen days..."

She wasn't too late. Varya had anticipated that she'd already missed the Festival of Lights. But because she'd been so quick to heal this time, likely thanks to whatever magic Greed's healers knew, but that meant that she could get back to her people and still partake in the festival.

It was her favorite time of year. Hundreds of people gathered in the middle of the desert. Everyone brought food and water, nothing else because it wasn't about trading or making money. And it was the only time of year that everyone called a truce on the stealing. They gathered together, made paper lanterns they lit, and then let the desert wind take them up into the sky.

It was an honorable night, full of the old ways that had been passed down for generations. Leaping over bonfires. Eating good food and reminding your friends and family that you loved them, even if you didn't all that much anymore. It was beautiful. Everyone was so happy and she could be there this year.

Varya hadn't gone to the festival in six years. Such a long time. But she'd been busy trying to find all those artifacts, and then the Horde had been an issue and she'd been tracking them for ages.

She found the stairs fairly quickly and started up them. Greed had dresses delivered to her room, but those wouldn't suffice. She'd be laughed out of the festival if she showed up in silk and gossamer fabric.

She could just imagine Altan's face now.

Rummaging through the pile of clothes, she couldn't find anything that would work. Sighing, she leaned back on her haunches, hands planted on her knees in frustration.

Maybe Ivo could...

Glancing up, she saw him hovering in the doorway. "What is going on?" he asked.

"Do you know where I can find better clothes?"

"Better?"

"I can't wear any of these around my people. They'll know exactly what happened. They'll think that I've taken up with Greed, and that's just not true."

His eyebrows crept up. "Is it not?"

"No, I'm just here until I'm healed." Which... she supposed was now. "They cut my clothes off me when I was injured, didn't they?"

"They did."

Damn. It had taken her months to get those leathers made for her body. It would take her months to get the same person to make her armor again. The woman had probably gone up in her prices, too.

"Fuck." Varya shook her head. "What's the least flashy garment in here?"

Ivo pointed at her nightgown. It was as thin as moonlight and glided over her body like the cool touch of the wind. She absolutely couldn't wear that out of here, but he was right. The pale nightgown was the only thing that didn't look like she'd pulled it out of a genie's bottle.

Clapping her hands to her thighs, she sighed. "It can't be helped them. To the servants."

"The servants?"

"Yes."

Varya swiftly ran through the halls, racing down the corridors to the rooms where the servants slept. There was no one in the room at this time of day. Why would they be? They had jobs to do and people to take care of. Which meant she could walk right in and pluck the first clothes that would fit her.

The plain dark pants would be a little baggy, but they'd do. The white linen shirt would swallow her form, but she'd roll up the arms and it would be just fine. If she left the top a little untied as well, that would give it a bit more flare. At least no one would think she had been staying in Greed's castle for the past few weeks.

"What are you doing?" Ivo hissed as she started out of the room.

"Stealing."

"Yes, why?"

"Because I don't have access to normal clothes?" Varya arched a brow. He knew where he lived, didn't he?

"That's... But that's..."

"Wrong?" she interjected. "Stealing is a way of life here. If you want to fit in with the rest of us miscreants, then you're probably going to have to learn how to do it."

"Steal?" he spluttered, as though that was the most terrible thing he'd heard in ages.

"Yes." Varya laughed as she started stripping right in front of him. The man had proven he wasn't all that interested in her, and besides, she still had her underthings on.

A choked sound echoed out of his mouth before he spun around like she'd flashed a tit at him. "Now what are you doing?" he groaned. "You can't just take your clothes off in the middle of the city, Varya!"

"I can, actually." He couldn't see her grin, but she was anyway.

This was the first time she'd felt like herself since she'd gotten here. Shimmying the pants up her legs, she buttoned them at the waist and figured out the last bit of her plan.

Honestly, this was the best part of her job. She had to figure out every detail on the fly when she suddenly decided she wanted to do something. Like right now. She knew Greed would not let her go to the Festival of Lights, not unless she snuck out.

Ivo had already heard her talk about the festival, so he knew where she was intending to go. And he'd been around while she stole all her clothes, so he definitely had a clue where she was headed and what her intent was.

What they didn't know was where the festival was, and that was good enough for her.

Greed loved the chase, after all.

"Ivo, why don't you give me a good argument about why I cannot just strip in public?" That ought to get him started. Then she pulled the shirt over her head, leaving it loose and messy, and then slipped down the stairs.

She ran, a wild grin on her face and her heart thundering in her chest. Varya had already found the stables on one of her previous rounds. There were plenty of horses to take, and a few of those leathery beasts with fangs. She eyed one of them that looked paler than the others. That was Greed's mount, wasn't it?

The thought passed through her mind that maybe she could steal that one. But the beast snapped at her, sharp fangs flashing as it tried to bite her and she had second thoughts about that plan.

Instead, she grabbed a big black beast in the back that was already pawing at the door. Bareback, she put a bridle in its mouth and called it good.

She led the horse out of the stables, peered around to see if anyone was looking, and then ran for the front doors. Good enough. No one was here to stop her, and no one was likely to try after she threw open the doors.

Varya swung up onto the horse, her legs spread so wide around its back that it almost hurt. But she wasn't going too far, just a couple hours ride, really. If she couldn't walk when she got to the festival... Well. It wouldn't be the first time, if she couldn't.

"Varya!" A shout rang out in the castle and she turned to see Greed standing on one of the highest platforms. He looked enraged, far more angry than she'd ever seen him before. How had he known?

It didn't matter. Let him be angry for her stealing away. He should be a little.

In leaving, she was taking his most prized possession away from him. Herself.

Giving him a little mock salute, she kicked her heels against the horse's sides. The wind raked her hair back from her face, the sand blasted from the horse's hooves, and the sound of her laugh trailed behind her as she fled.

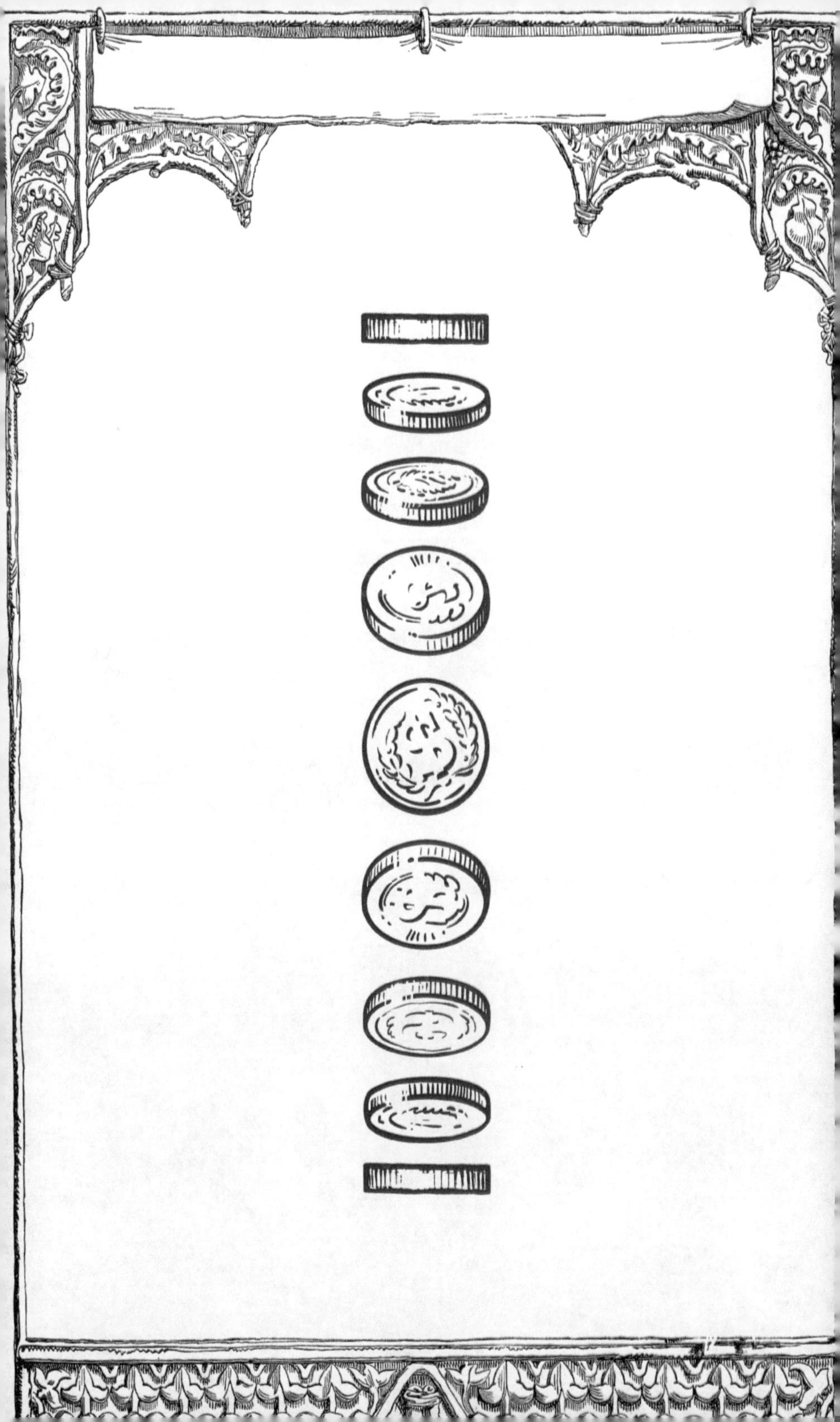

Chapter 25

Damn the woman. She'd run from him. Again.

And he'd let her. Or rather, his guard had left her and Ivo had gotten the shakedown of his life as Greed screamed at him. Though he knew the other man was just as worried about Varya's disappearance as he was, Greed couldn't find it in himself to care that he might be hurting the spirit's feelings.

Varya was gone, and he had no idea where to find her. At least, until Ivo had said she wanted to go to the Festival of Lights.

If the woman had wanted to go there, why hadn't she just told him? He'd have brought her. Maybe. He could have been convinced.

Instead, he had to get off his nuckelavee long before he reached the Festival of Lights. The beast would have to travel home on its own, which was dangerous enough, although he knew very few people that would take his mount on in a fight. Still, it was a risk he now had to take because some foolish woman had run off.

Again!

Taking off the bridle, he slid his hand along the leathery hide, patting it firmly. "Go home, now. I can bring her back on my own."

Even his mount seemed to look at him with disbelief before it wandered off on its own. Clearly, no one believed he could control the wild woman he'd brought home.

Maybe he didn't believe it either. As he turned toward the crowd of people in the distance, he wondered what he'd gotten himself into. It had taken half the day to even find the location this year, and then a few more hours to ride here. She could be anywhere in that crowd.

Greed took his time getting there, and every flash of blonde hair sent his heart skittering in his chest. Every time it wasn't her, he felt the anger boiling hotter in his veins. When he got his hands on her, he was going to wring her pretty neck. He'd drag her back by the hair, kicking and screaming, proving himself to be the warlord that everyone remembered him being.

If anyone tried to stop him, he'd remind them all why they feared him. They thought they could just knock him out with that smoke? He'd survived it twice, and he'd kill many more people along the way. They wouldn't catch him unawares this time.

People flinched away from him, horrified to see their king here when he had never once attended a single festival. Two men's hands shook when they saw him, the tankards of ale spilling onto the sand. A woman hid her child. Likely rumors already had embellished how he'd eaten a child at the last village he'd been seen in. A couple of young women eyed him with interest, though. And their expressions grounded him.

Breathing in the scent of their greed and lust, he steadied himself. She was here. He couldn't seem too angry before he met her or word would spread and then she would run.

So he tried to look like he wanted to be here. He squared his shoulders and forced a smile, nodding at people who wandered past him as though he cared that they were comfortable. He ducked underneath the bright streamers of colorful fabric triangles and meandered past the tables full of food and drink. He even eyed the tents with some form of appreciation. He wasn't all that certain. All he knew was that there were at least a hundred tents in every color, and how the fuck was he going to find her?

He didn't have to look as hard as he thought. The center of all this madness was a crowd of people holding small metal pans. Dots of paint were on each pan, an individual color for each person. It appeared that people were pairing up, already some couples were seated on the sands while they painted each other.

And there, in the heart of it all, was Varya. Her wildly unbound hair had somehow gotten wilder in her ride here. It floated around her head like a dandelion puff of gold. She had a silver plate in her hand, emerald green paint already smeared on it.

A young man stood in front of her, his own silver plate decorated with a pretty shade of purple. They were talking. Varya's mouth spread in a soft, easy smile.

That wouldn't do.

Greed reached for a platter that someone was walking around with, smeared with white paint. The woman holding it smiled up at him, although the expression was a little shaky.

"Shall I get paint for you, my lord?" she asked.

"No need."

He waved a hand over it and the paint turned to gold. He hadn't used that particular spell in centuries—gold was far too easy to find these days—and yet, it felt good to use his powers. The woman's answering gasp almost made him puff up in pride, but he had a job to do.

Treading through the waves of people, he found himself behind the young man. With a palm on his shoulder, he shoved the boy to the side. "Not today, young one."

The young man stumbled, but then righted himself. "Excuse me—"

Greed stared him down, eyes flashing and anger burning in his stomach. "Yes?"

"My lord." With a gulp, the young man looked at the ground. "Apologies."

And then he ran. As everyone should when they saw how angry Greed was.

He turned his attention to the woman who had set this fire in his chest, but she was looking back at him with amusement, not fear. How stupid was she? Varya should tremble at his feet. She should prepare herself to beg for his mercy and then grovel with his cock in her mouth for hours on end. She should...

Varya placed her hand over his heart and he felt all the tension disappear. "You shouldn't scare people like that," she said, her voice shaking with amusement. "They're going to think you're angry."

"I am angry," he snarled, trying to get that emotion to burn in his chest again. "You ran."

"I didn't. You saw where I was going and I distinctly remember telling Ivo that the festival was happening today." She patted his chest as though that settled the argument.

It didn't.

"You can't run off into the desert like that, Varya. Perhaps you have forgotten how you arrived at my castle doors, but I have not." Just the memory of it made him want to put his fist through a wall. Which would be difficult in the middle of the desert.

And then again, all she had to do was smile at him and he couldn't stay mad. Not when she looked at him like that, as if he'd hung the moon in the sky.

Varya smoothed her hand over his chest, her fingers lingering on the planes of muscle before she sighed. "I remember too. But I also remember how to let those memories go, Greed. Right now, I want to celebrate the lights and the coming of the full moon. Will you do that with me?"

"I have never celebrated with your people before," he grumbled. "I don't even know why I'm holding this."

"Do you not?" she gestured all around them. "We paint ourselves before the gods. Our ancestors did the same to honor those who watch over us and gave us the beauty of our world. The paint connects us with every color on each of us. The sky, the sands, the flowers, and the wind."

Humans. They were so fanciful.

Greed eyed the paint in his hand, the gold that would look so lovely on her skin, and he thought perhaps he could play along. If only to see what she looked like with his marks all over her.

"Fine," he relented. "Show me what to do."

Ach, that smile. It would be his undoing.

She took his hand and brought him to a small open part in the sands, right in the middle of the crowd. Sinking down to the ground with him, she ignored all the stares and whispers that burst into life.

Drums started up somewhere. He hadn't seen the musicians before on his walk here, but he had noticed very little. And now, he barely focused on the beat as she dipped her fingers into the paint.

"What symbols are you drawing?" he asked.

"Runes," she replied. "Everyone paints something different. I paint the ones that my mother showed me before she died."

Her finger glided along his cheek, painting a symbol there and then moving to the opposite cheek. Her touch flared something hot inside him, as always. He wanted to tackle her into the sands and push himself inside her warm heat. Crowd be damned, he wanted to hear those little breathless noises she made as he brought her to the highest peak of pleasure.

Instead, he held himself very still as she glided her touch down his neck to his arms.

"You should have worn less," she said with a flirty flick of her eyelashes. "I cannot cover you in as much paint as I'd like."

"You may paint me whenever you wish."

"And anger the gods?" She tsked. "I think not."

He'd had enough of this. Greed palmed her thighs and dragged her into his lap. Legs spread wide over his hips, he looped an arm around her waist as she gasped. Her arms fell over his shoulders, the plate hanging limp from her fingers as their lips barely touched. "Fuck the gods," he whispered against her mouth. "I'm the only god you need to appease."

She shuddered in his arms, but leaned back for him to stare down the length of her body stretched out on top of him. "You're supposed to paint me," she whispered.

Right. He was supposed to do that, wasn't he?

He had gotten so caught up staring at the woman in his lap that he'd forgotten he was still in a crowd of people. Clearing his throat, he shifted his hips, so he wasn't pressing quite so hard against the seam of his pants before he reached for the gold platter.

"Right," he muttered, trying to get his thoughts back to where they needed to go. "Paint."

What would he paint? He wasn't a human. But he wasn't a demon either. No one here knew that.

Eyeing the woman in front of him, he wanted to tell her. He hadn't ever told anyone, but he wanted to spill out all the information and pour it into her, so she was the only person in existence that knew he wasn't some demon lord or god that had fallen from the sky.

Swallowing hard, he dipped his fingers into the paint and trailed one line down her jaw. "When I was young, this kingdom looked very different. There was sand, but also jungle. There were humans, but they were few and far between. Small tribes that followed the herds across the entire kingdom as they migrated."

"I didn't know you were ever young."

He chuckled and trailed twin lines down her throat. "I was never born, if that's what you're hinting at. I came into this form fully grown. But I was not always like this. Once I was young and weak. Merely a spirit who wandered throughout the kingdom feeding upon whatever taste of greed I could find."

Her brows wrinkled. "Why are you telling me this?"

"Because I want someone to know." His fingers danced over her delicate collarbones, skated over her shoulders, as he highlighted every part of her with gold that he thought delicate and beautiful. "I fed, but I still starved. Until I came to this kingdom, where there were so many greedy people who wanted everything they couldn't have. And I grew glutted with their greed, larger and more powerful than any other spirit. That's when I met them."

"Them?"

"My brothers." He trailed his fingers over the globes of her breasts, dipping beneath the low fabric for just a single touch. "They, too, had found kingdoms where they could feed and feast. It was then that we discovered we could take these forms and sustain them. That we would be even more powerful with a physical form on the plane where no one wished to have us."

"So you aren't gods?" she asked, Varya's voice so low he almost didn't hear it. "You're spirits?"

"One and the same," he corrected. "Your gods that you worship are spirits as well. I suspect some of them took physical forms like we did. They were more likely spirits of justice or honor. Perhaps a few spirits of creativity or passion, like Morag."

Varya stiffened in his arms. He dotted a single mark on the tip of her nose to annoy her.

"Morag is a spirit." It wasn't a question that Varya muttered. "So that means… Ivo?"

"Also a spirit." He had to work hard to not grit the words through his teeth. Why was she asking about her guard when his finger was mere inches from her stiffened nipple? "But never in all my years have I felt such greed with a person. I want to devour you, but I also want no one else to ever lay a finger on your pristine skin. I want to take you on adventures and be the only person to feed that ridiculous need of yours to put yourself in danger. I want to destroy everyone who puts a mark on your skin and yet…" He paused, trailing his finger down her long, lean arm. "I want to mark you so everyone knows you are mine."

Her throat bobbed. "All I ask is that you allow me to do the same to you. I will be no one's toy, Greed. If you want to own me, then I will also own you."

He turned his gaze to hers, wondering what she saw in his yellow eyes. "You already own me, Varya. I raced out of my castle after you, taking a precious beast that I left alone in the desert, to wander into what could very easily be another trap. And yet, I do all that because I cannot stay away from you. I cannot get you out of my head."

And then he saw it. He saw the moment she gave in. Greed felt her hips tilting until she'd pressed her core against him, the heat of her searing through his entire body. Rocking against him, she let her arms dangle over his shoulders and slid ever so close to him. Her lips ghosted over his own.

"I own you?" she whispered.

"You do."

"That's fucked up."

He grinned. "I never said I wanted a healthy relationship, treasure. I want you and all our strange desires. Wear my marks, give me yours in return, and let's be fucked up together."

Again, she shuddered in his arms. And he had no idea what she would say to him. He didn't know if she would agree, but by the gods, he hoped she would.

He'd beg if he had to. If she wanted a demon king on his knees before her, begging for her to give him an ounce of her attention, then he would do so. He wanted her in his life and he didn't know any other way to get her there other than this.

She didn't deserve to be anything less than his world. She was... important to him. More than he'd ever felt before, and that was such a strange thing to realize.

"From the moment I first met you," he whispered, brushing a paint smeared hand through her hair. "You captivated me with your indomitable spirit and your heart that beat only for this kingdom. I am less without you."

"You don't even know me." Varya's eyes were wide with shock.

"I know you well enough, treasure. And I will know more every day as I wake up with you next to me and treat every word you say as the treasure it is." He kissed her, lingering only because he knew there were eyes on them. "Stay with me, Varya. Let me treat you like a goddess for the rest of your days."

They both realized the implication of his words at the same time. He saw the sadness in her eyes and felt a pang of regret in his. She was only human. And he was not.

"Come with me," she said, drawing him to standing. "Come dance with my people, and I will consider your words."

Greed could do nothing but follow her siren's call and those sad blue eyes.

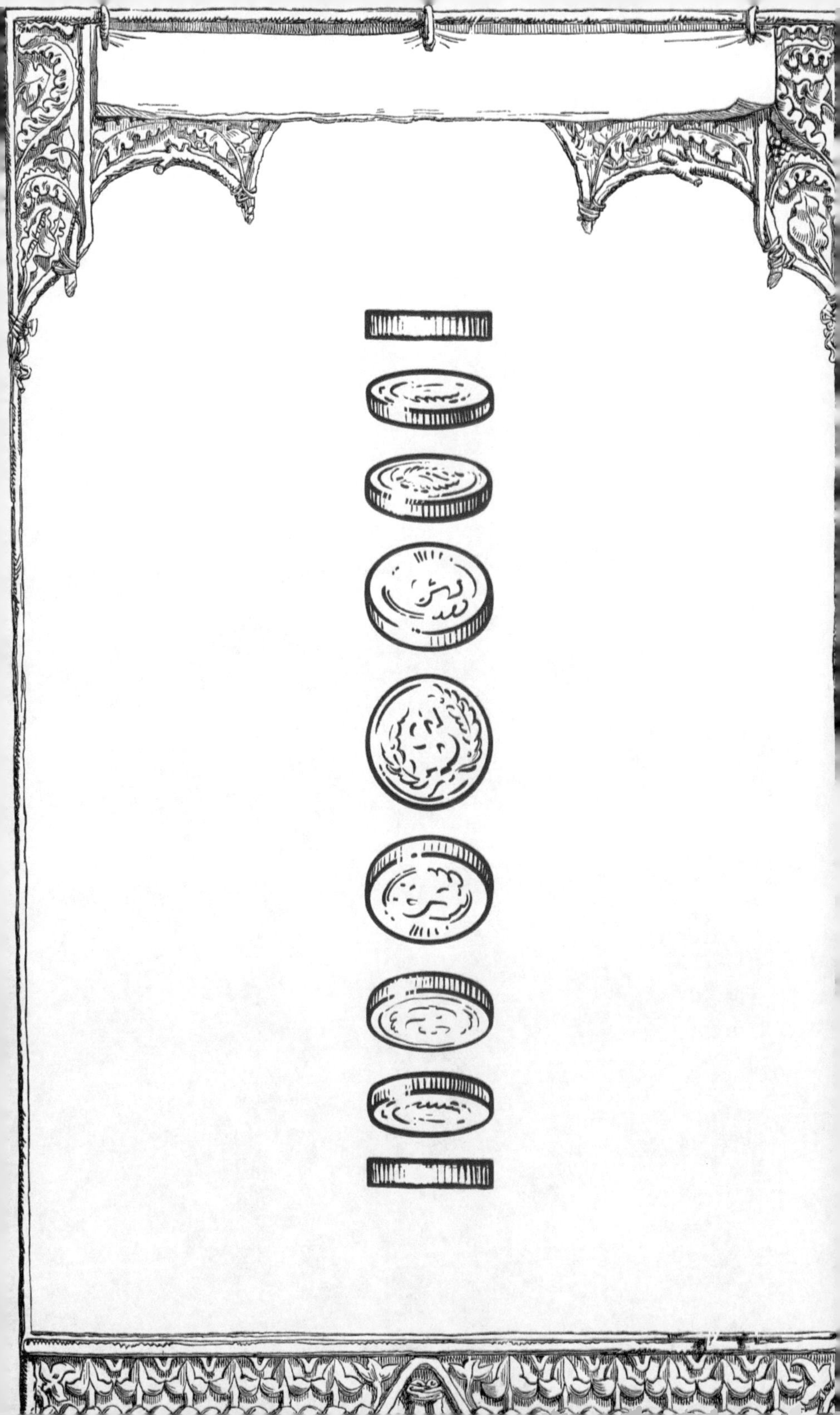

Chapter 26

Watching her was magic. Varya moved to the rhythm of the drums like the goddesses of old. Her body swayed, her muscles flexed, and the innate grace she used to rob tombs proved to make her an impressive dancer who captivated him with every beat.

He'd never felt like this about a woman before. Though, he couldn't be certain if that was simply Varya or if it was because he'd seen Lust with his wife. All Greed knew was that he wanted what Lust had shown him. He wanted to know what it was like to have a woman who loved him, who saw him as the man who hung the very stars in the sky and the man who she would always lie down next to at night.

Greed wanted her. He wanted Varya in his bed and in his arms and to know that she wasn't ever going to disappear again. That she was his, he was hers, and that was how their world would continue forward.

He'd never wanted that before. Leaning against one of the makeshift tables someone had built, he held a mug of ale in his hands and watched as she swayed and leapt with the others who danced all around her.

He didn't dance, but Greed didn't want to. He wanted to watch her with her people—his people—and to see how much they adored her.

This woman had claimed that she was alone. That no one would notice if she disappeared. And yes, he had heard everything she'd said to Ivo. The man was not a closed book when it came to conversations that were private.

Sipping his drink, he saw that she was very wrong.

Varya wasn't alone. She'd never been alone. She helped these people, and they adored her for it. They danced around her, laughing and drawing her into wild, whirling circles where they twirled her until she screamed with happiness.

By the seven kingdoms, she was lovely. Her hair whirling around her head, his paint glittering on her skin, and that stolen clothing barely holding onto her form. Could he love this woman? Absolutely. Would it change him? He hoped to the gods it would.

He'd seen how happy Lust was, and how his brother had felt more than he had in ages, and for the first time, Greed realized he wanted that too. He wanted to fall in love and see what it did to him.

Another person leaned against the table beside him, a mug of ale in his hand as well. The dark-skinned man had eyes that saw everything. Eyes that particularly looked at Varya with far too much comfort.

"Is it true, then?" the man asked. "You're Greed himself?"

There was no hiding it. He was nearly seven feet tall with bright red hair. Who else did they think he was?

Greed nodded. "You found me. Congratulations."

"Never seen you at the Festival of Lights before."

"Never had a reason to come." Greed took a sip of his drink, letting that simmer with the other man before he snorted. "Not much of a reason to come now, if I'm honest. This festival was created before me."

"Most of us still know that." The man turned toward him and held out a hand. "Altan."

"You already know my name."

They shook hands, and he saw a flicker of interest in the other man's eyes. "So your name really is Greed, then? I always thought it was a moniker. Like calling someone King."

Greed chuckled and felt the muscles in his shoulders relax. At least he wasn't about to be grilled. The last thing he needed was a jaded ex-lover of Varya's getting in his way. He'd bury him in the desert, of course. Somewhere no one would find his bones until the dry heat had mummified him. But he didn't think Varya would particularly be happy that he'd done so.

Even if this Altan wanted to protect Varya from the demon king, he didn't think anyone could sway his mind now. He wanted her, and he would have her. No matter what the cost ended up being.

"My name is really Greed," he replied, turning his attention back to the woman who had linked hands with another and was now spinning wildly in a circle. They were going to throw up if they kept that speed up.

"So how did you meet Varya?" Altan asked, his eyes seeing a little too much.

Greed turned the question around on him. "How did you meet

her?"

"We grew up on the streets together. Her parents died when she was very young, so mine took her in. And then they died too." Altan gestured toward her with his mug. "She's like a little sister to me, although I feel more for her than a sibling. She's not blood, but she's the closest I've got."

So there was someone waiting to make sure she had come home. He'd known she must have been wrong about that, but he hadn't guessed the person waiting for her would be such a handsome young man. "Is that so?"

"Her parents left her with one saying in her head, you know? And that's what makes her story about how she met you even more unbelievable. It makes it hard for me to think that she's allowing you to be here, with us... willingly."

Ah, so her parents had hated him. That wasn't all that surprising. Most people in the kingdom blamed him for the state of their lives, and in some way, he was responsible. It had taken hundreds of years to get their people in line. The nomadic tribes were always fighting each other when he'd arrived. No one had wanted to listen to the redheaded man who didn't look like them or sound like them or understand their kingdom in the slightest.

He'd fought. He'd won. Neither of those had won him many supporters.

The people in this kingdom had been searching for someone to blame for years. They didn't want to realize that it was their own folly that had nearly run this kingdom into the ground. So they blamed him. They turned him into a monster who had taken their kingdom by storm, ruined all their good crops and all the people who had once led them.

The rumors about him were terrifying and full of blood. He didn't care. As long as the people in this kingdom feared him enough to listen, that was all that mattered.

But... The other side of that was how lonely it had become.

He watched as Varya and the other woman leapt through a bonfire together. They ran so quickly not a single flame singed either of their clothing, and they fell into a laughing heap on the sands.

"Varya and I are similar in many ways," he replied. "She is not afraid to take what she wants, or to hold a knife to someone's neck and force them to see reason."

"That is not the expression of a man who sees an equal," Altan replied. He stood in front of Greed, blocking his view of the only woman that mattered. "But you don't see anyone as an equal, do you? Demon kings are rare throughout all the kingdoms, and you would be a fool to not realize just how powerful you are compared to the rest of us. Those eyes see her as more than an equal. You see a companion. Why?"

Greed could lie. He could say it was because he'd seen what she looked like with her legs spread wide and her cheeks burned with passion. He could singe the other man's ears as he told him about the sounds she made as his tongue circled that button between her legs that made them shake.

But that wasn't what Altan was looking for. And for a rare moment in his life, Greed was truthful. "She sees what I do not. I came to this kingdom knowing it was broken and that it would be a challenge for me to fix it. I like a challenge. I like a battle. She was the first person to tell me I was doing something wrong. She was the first to show me the lies that have been said in my name and the first to hold me accountable. That woman is not afraid of me, and having someone look at you without fear is addicting."

"Ah," Altan murmured, then spread his arms wide as he stepped back into the crowd. "You will find many here who would have no problem telling you what you've done wrong."

"Is that so?"

"We're all brave, Greed."

He followed the man, curious about what this thief had planned. "Then you are all fools if you think I will accept so many people telling me what they think they know."

"Ah, we have nothing to lose." Altan winked, nearly disappearing into the crowd now. "And everything to give. You are welcome amongst us, Greed, demon king of our homeland. We are not your enemies, just as you are not ours."

Curious. Greed hadn't thought it would be like this. He handed his mug of ale to someone else and stalked the other man with a single question burning in his chest. "Why? This is a kingdom of thieves. I have built this land to grow on lies and manipulation. You think your group of people is different?"

"I do." Altan pointed at the drummers and they sped up their pace. People whirled around them, skirts and jackets flying as they all raced to keep up with the music. "We have nothing to give and nothing to take. Our people live with food and drink and happiness in times like this. Dance with us, Greed. Learn what it is to be part of your people. Not above them."

Greed narrowed his eyes. "What are you getting out of this? No one seeks an audience with me without a desire in their heart."

Altan held up his hands for peace. "Ah, you have caught me! I now have Greed's ear if you dance with us. If you celebrate with my people, then surely you have cast your favor upon our town. We have no advisor to lend you advice. Perhaps if you are kind enough, then you will allow us to have that."

Ah, there it was. And the man likely wanted to vote himself as that advisor.

Yet, it didn't seem like a terrible idea. This man understood his people and their needs. And more than that, he seemed to have a better heart than the others.

Tiny hands slid into his. He stared down at Varya's red cheeks and bright smile. "You came to dance! I can't say I believed that would ever happen."

"I don't know what I'm doing," he replied. His feet didn't know the complicated patterns the others seemed to know. He feared he would bump into a couple and knock them into the sands. He was too large to be in a crowd of people like this. And yet...

He wanted to be. He wanted to be here when she held both his hands in hers and stared down at their feet. "Do this," she said, showing him the movements that weren't all that complicated after all. He leapt from side to side, feeling like an idiot trying to move his bulk as the others were doing.

But she was smiling at him. Grinning so big it must hurt and... there it was. That expression he'd seen Selene wear when she looked at Lust. The expression that whispered of deeper feelings and a heart that ached while looking at another person.

He felt the echo in his own chest. He felt the pulse of something powerful and echoing. He must be the only person in this crowd who looked at her and felt like this. In looking at her, he knew she shared this feeling. She shared the heart thumping desire that burned through him. And not just to fuck her, but to hold, cherish, and keep her.

Strings joined the drums, and he tossed his head up to see the fiddles that three people now played alongside the others. The entire crowd shouted with happiness as the music swelled around them.

He felt himself caught up in all of it. Was this what Altan had meant? That if he danced with these people for an ephemeral moment, he would become part of them?

The crowd surged and Varya tugged on his hand. "Jump!" she shouted, and then leapt into the air. Everyone around him jumped, so their heads were almost at the same height. And he watched them all. Their flashing smiles. Dark skin, light skin, red hair, blonde, dark, all of it. All these people who were joyous in their celebration.

He saw all the colors of their clothing. The freckles that dotted some noses and others who had scars on their eyebrows. Young and old. People from every part of this town that were hungry or thirsty or needy, none of them were turned away. They were all right here, celebrating together, and that joy swelled around them and sank into his skin in a way it never had before.

For all the centuries that he had been their king, he had never seen them like this. And was this greed? No and yes at the same time.

There was no need to steal or take or devour, but these people were greedy, as they gobbled up every ounce of joy they felt this night because it would not come again for another year. They took from each other and they gave. An equal give and take that shared so much emotion it filled him near to brimming.

They leapt again, the swell of people moving around him like a wave, and he stood still in the middle of it all. Watching them and feeling them. For the very first time, he could feel the hearts of his kingdom thudding. He felt their love for each other and he had never wanted to be part of that love until now.

Varya's hands tugged at the waist of his pants, and he looked down at her as a newer version of himself. As the spirit who had spent so many centuries seeking and consuming greed, but who now realized there was so much more that he had never seen.

"Jump!" she shouted again, her words carrying over the drums and the fiddles.

And he did.

He moved less vigorously than the rest of the crowd. Some of them were so small that he could leap over their heads if he wanted and he didn't intend to hurt anyone. But he jumped with them and felt the scream of laughter from all who surrounded him. He felt it in his heart.

More than anything else, though, he felt her smile. Her joy that he was trying. And he wasn't doing it well. He danced like the children who were still at the edges of the crowd. He was too big and too awkward for any of this to look like he had any talent whatsoever.

But she looked at him like he'd done something magical and he felt like he had.

For her. He would do the impossible.

Chapter 27

Her friends were judging her. Varya knew that. She could feel their stares as she sat with Greed on the small sand dune that was far from the crowd. They were surprised she'd even brought him, let alone taken the time to make the lantern with him. But she'd wanted to, and he'd been so fascinated throughout the entire process.

The lanterns were the last part of the festival, and she'd always done this process with her friends. Their gazes had burned as they watched her teach him their ways, but how could she do anything else? Greed was trying more than she'd ever seen him try before, and it called out to something in her heart.

He wanted to make her smile. He wanted to make her laugh. By the gods, he'd walked into a crowd of people he did not know, who mostly disliked him, and he'd tried to dance with her!

It was unheard of. And beautiful. And so giving in a way that she hadn't expected from a man literally named after greed. A man who had claimed to be a spirit of that emotion.

He'd made something in her heart twist and she didn't know what to do with that. So she'd made the lantern with him, and then clambered up the dune where they had some distance from the others. Because maybe she wanted him to herself after sharing him for hours with everyone else.

"So, what do we do now?" Greed asked, his eyes on the lantern.

"We light the candle underneath and wait for everyone else. Then we let it go, and the desert takes her sacrifice."

Others were already lighting their candles, so she reached for her flint only to see that he had snapped his fingers and a small spark danced on the tip of his claws. How? She had no idea. Magic was hard to understand like that. But she hadn't realized he could do more than just change his form.

He flashed her a sheepish grin. "Let me light it."

"Why didn't do that while we were in the caves?"

"Well, I wasn't really myself then, now was I?" He touched his fingers to the candle and then put out the flame on his fingertips. He held the lantern with her, staring into her eyes so deeply her heart raced. "Ready?"

"For what?"

He nodded over his shoulder and she saw everyone else had already released their lanterns. And all the lights that rose into the sky danced behind his head. Those warm eyes made her chest tighten again.

She wanted to kiss him. She wanted to keep riding this feeling of warmth and happiness and joy that came from her people's love of everything that they did. But was it right to want that? He was a demon king and he would only want to take from her and…

"Varya?" he whispered, his voice low and quiet. "Should we let it go?"

She realized she should let a lot of things go. Nodding, a soft smile spread across her face. "Yes. I think so."

They released the lantern together, letting it dance on the wind and rise to all the others that hung in the air, spinning and whirling on the eddies of wind that carried them to whatever desert goddess wanted them this time. All her hopes and dreams. All floating there, waiting for a god to catch wind of what she wanted.

Everyone stood, going back to their tents where they would all spend the night. Then they'd get up at the first sign of sunlight and start packing the entire camp up. They weren't too far from her town, and traveling during the day was still possible.

Now, she didn't know where to go. Was she supposed to head back to Greed's castle? That wasn't home. But the town wasn't her home either. She'd have to sleep on Altan's floor again, and that always made her neck ache in the morning.

A warm hand cupped her jaw, turning her to look at him. "Stay with me for the night," Greed murmured.

"Where?"

He pointed behind them and she realized that someone had set up a tent for them. She hadn't seen anyone arrive with him, yet Greed's guards were likely just off in the distance. They were never far from him, even when he tried to slip away.

Chuckling, she nodded. She could give him one more night. Just one.

They stood together as though in a dream. He held her hand as he drew her toward the dark green tent, slipping inside to light a fire in the round brazier on the ground. He had a table and two chairs on one side of the tent, and thick rugs underneath her feet. The rugs all led up to a mass of sheepskins that served as a bed, soft and cushioned with blankets that would keep them warm during the night.

She hadn't slept through the night with him since the cave. Since she'd curled her body around his big one trying to stay warm.

Sudden nerves clawed at her throat, but she beat them back. This man had tasted her. He'd kissed her within an inch of her life and now was her chance to take what she wanted. Him. She wanted to know what it was like. Just once.

Greed got the fire going and then sat down in the big chair. His legs spread wide, tail flicking at the sand. He had his hands on his thighs, but his eyes watched her with a desire that she knew was only just barely reined in. He wanted her, too. And he wanted her to make this choice.

"Come here," he said, his voice a low grumble.

And who was she to deny him?

Varya walked toward him as if in a dream. Her feet slid along the sands and she refused to let any more nerves get in her way. She gathered up the bottom of her shirt, pulling it over her head. The sharp hiss of his breath made her feel powerful. Just the sight of her made his lungs wheeze, and that was something she'd never done to another man. Not even when she'd indulged herself for the evening.

She stood in front of him, waiting to see what he would do next.

Greed placed his massive hands on either side of her ribcage, feeling her breathing stretch them. Inhale, exhale, as his eyes trailed down from her lips, her neck, to her breasts, like a physical touch.

"You are so beautiful," he murmured, leaning forward to lick at her already stiffened nipple. "Lovely, lovely, lovely."

He wrapped his lips around one, drawing it into his mouth with a slow, sensual pull. She tilted her head back and tried to quiet her moan. Someone might hear them. They would know she wasn't just bringing Greed to their festival, but she was fucking him.

Oh gods, she might be loving him and that was dangerous. That was so dangerous.

Claws gently scraped her skin, and she felt her breath stutter as goosebumps rose down her back. His hands slid down, those big palms dipping into her pants and pushing them down her legs.

"Step out of them," he muttered, then returned his attention to placing open-mouthed kisses along her skin.

She did what she was told. For once.

One of his hands moved, leaving a cold wind in its wake. Varya blinked her eyes open, wondering what he was doing, only to look down and realize he'd freed himself from his pants. That ridiculously large cock, jutting up between his legs and already leaking pre-cum down the veiny side, pointed right at her.

And oh, it was so tempting to just sink down upon him and to finally know what it felt like to have a demon inside her.

But then he cupped her breasts in each hand, thumbing over her nipples as he watched with rapt attention. At the same time, his tail slid up between her legs, gently stroking her folds as he groaned. "You're so fucking wet for me," he rasped. "So perfect."

The sound of his voice saying that did things to her that she didn't know if she liked. A rush of wetness flooded between her legs and her stomach clenched, trying to catch the desire running away from her. She wanted. She needed.

"I think the gods made you for me," he murmured, tugging her forward as if he knew what was in her mind. He palmed her ass, his fingers digging hard into her skin as he urged her to spread her legs wide around him. He held onto her weight as though she were a feather. "They taunt me with the sound of your gasps and memory of your taste."

He held her above him, spread wide above that cock he fisted. Slowly, he drew his hand up and down the velvety hardness that she wanted inside her until she whimpered. Varya watched him, incapable of taking her eyes off that movement.

"I'm going to fuck you," he breathed, his lips pressing against her neck, right over the flutter of her pulse. "I'll be nice this time, because you were such a good girl sucking my cock on the ballroom floor. But this is the only time I'll be so nice, Varya. I told you, I want your pleasure and your pain. And you will give it to me."

Oh, gods, she wanted that, though. She wanted to give him both at the same time. She wanted that knife's edge of pain to make this that much more pleasurable.

As he lowered her, forcing her to spread herself wide around that massive cock, she realized it didn't matter. Her legs trembled as he stroked the head of himself against her entrance. Back, forward, circling her clit, and then just passing over where she wanted him most desperately.

"Tell me," he said, that filthy mouth never stopping. "Tell me what you want, treasure."

"You," she gasped.

His hips bucked. The tip of his cock wedged into her entrance, impossibly large and oh so right. He sank inside, stretching her, filling her, as he pulled her lower and lower on his cock.

Varya arched her back, a moan echoing out of her mouth that

didn't sound like her at all. That was a woman possessed. As he pulled her down again, she wondered if he had already consumed her.

His thumb circled over her clit, slow little movements until she sank all the way down. Hips flushed with his, devouring him whole.

Greed moved his hand from her ribs, trailing up her side, between her breasts, until his hand wrapped around her throat. Not enough to be painful, but just enough so she couldn't get all the air she wanted.

He dragged her forward, the open-mouthed kiss he gave her utterly divine. "Move, Varya. Take what you want from me."

And that sounded delicious.

She lifted her hips, lifting until he almost fell out of her and then sinking back down onto him. She had to stand on her tiptoes just to get that far, but the slow glide of him made both of them groan.

He was too big. Too much. And it was perfect in every way.

Greed dragged her closer, forcing her to arch her back as he caught one of her nipples in his mouth again. He angled her hips so every movement of hers dragged his cock even deeper while his mouth did utterly sinful things to her body.

His hands glided up and down her back, touching everything all at the same time as she chased her pleasure. And it felt like she was using him. But he was right here with her at the same time. His hips rolling against hers, his mouth moving from hers to her breast and back again.

She ground down against him, seeking that almost painful point of pleasure. Wanting to know what it felt like to shatter all around him.

"You want more?" he asked, his lips against hers.

She nodded, incapable of anything else as she tried to force him deeper inside her, but she couldn't quite...

"Ach, greedy little thing. You want to be fucked by a demon?" His cheeks had reddened with desire.

Varya wanted nothing more.

She gave him a small nod, a meek little movement, but she wanted him to show her what he could do. What they could do together.

She didn't expect him to palm her ass and then stand. Still inside her, moving even as he strode toward the bed. And there it was. The faintest bite of pain as he slammed into her once, twice, while standing before he lowered them both to the sheepskins.

He pulled out of her, the movement jarring and harsh even as she felt the loss of him. He spun her around onto all fours, forcing her into the position before she'd even realized what had happened.

Then he grabbed onto her hair, gently wrapping it around his fist before he pulled back. Hard.

His breath trailed down her shoulder and back. "You're going to be a good little thief now, yes? You're mine, Varya. Say it."

"I'm yours," she sobbed out, because she was. Fuck, she was his, and she hadn't expected it to happen, but it had.

He consumed her body and soul and now she wanted him. By the gods, she wanted him.

Greed slammed into her from behind, so hard she could hear his balls slap against her ass as he moved. But there it was. The friction she'd been searching for. The need for him to move faster than she could, so hard that she felt the burn. He tugged harder on her hair, forcing her to arch her back and her neck even further.

She felt like she was going to explode. She could feel that orgasm just out of her reach, so large and consuming that she feared it might break her. Yet she wanted it. Oh, she wanted to chase it for the rest of her life.

"Good girl," he snarled, leaning over and somehow speeding up even more. He drew back and slapped her ass so hard she knew there would be a handprint, then soothed it with his massive palm.

But then he ducked down again, grinding himself against her as his hand wrapped around her throat. Her hair tumbled down her back and his lips pressed against her shoulder. "I'm yours too," he snarled. "You've taken every bit of me I have to give."

Her entire body clenched around him. She stiffened and threw her head back, her mouth falling open as he bit down on the side of her neck and every part of her shattered. She couldn't see, couldn't hear, couldn't think of anything but the orgasm ripping through her and the stilted pattern of his thrusts as he plunged harder and harder, then groaned into her ear.

"Fuck," she whispered, barely breathing even as he lowered them to the furs. "What the fuck was that?"

He slowly pulled out of her, but remained on his knees between her legs. She looked back over her shoulder to see him intensely watching his cum leak out of her, his eyes hot and his cheeks still bright red. With his thumb, he gently pushed it back inside her, slowly rimming her entrance before pressing down hard over her clit.

The sudden spike of pleasure that rocked through her was shocking. She couldn't. Not again. Not so soon.

But his eyes locked on hers and he continued to press firmly, and she couldn't stop it. She came again, the second one rolling through her body as her pussy desperately clenched around nothing.

The feral grin on his face was animalistic. Then he crawled over her, rubbing his cock between her cheeks before he slid back inside her. She was too sensitive, too needy, too everything.

But he growled in her ear, "You will take me again, treasure. And again. I will hear you scream until your voice goes hoarse. Only then will I let you sleep."

And by the gods, he was right. He worked her until she was boneless and every muscle in her body ached.

By the time she slumped across his chest, coated in sweat and cum, she barely knew her own name. But she was happy. Oh, she was happier than she'd ever been.

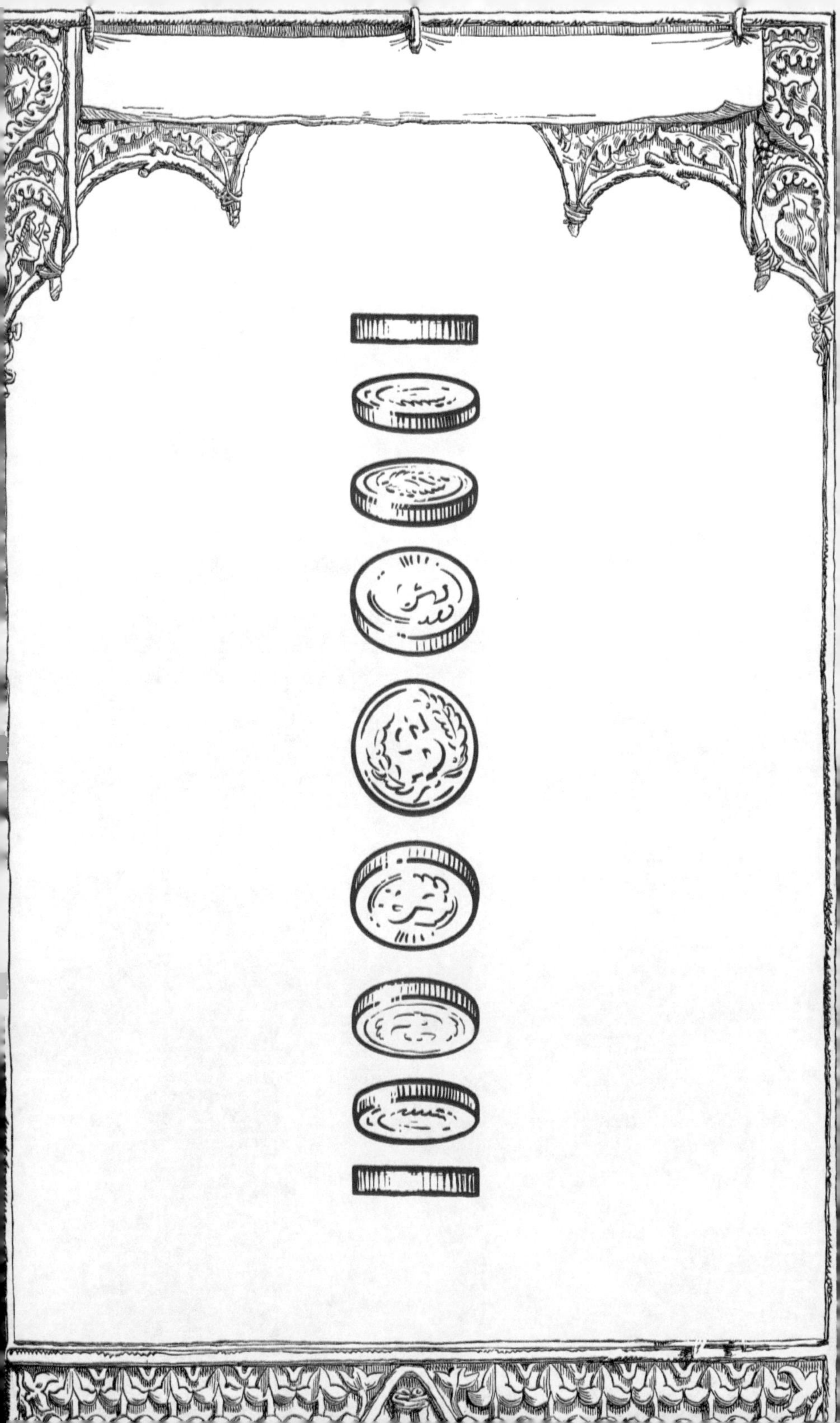

Chapter 28

He awoke to chaos.

Smoke burned his nostrils and tangled into his lungs. Greed rolled, taking Varya with him as he automatically kept her beneath him. But the flames were already licking closer to them, far closer than they should have ever gotten.

Blinking open watery eyes, he tried to see through the thick, black smoke that coiled around them. What the fuck had happened? They'd been fine. Sleeping. He'd woken up before this to pet the long blonde waves off her face where they'd stuck over her eye after their last enjoyable romp and everything had been exactly as he'd left it.

She jolted awake as though he'd slapped her. Varya tried to sit up, but he banded his arm around her chest. Forcing her to stay below the line of smoke.

"Crawl," he growled, turning her onto her stomach and pointing at the back of the tent. "There."

"We can't." But then she looked at the front of the tent, completely engulfed in flames, and nodded. "Right, no other option. Do you—"

Her voice was thick and raspy with smoke, but he lifted a clawed hand and flashed her a rough smile. "Go."

He watched her as she moved, crawling low to the ground and using the sand to her advantage. She grabbed a few skins as she went, placing them over her back to help with the heat.

Smart, his woman. She knew how to take care of herself, and something dark and ugly rose in him. Whoever had given her reason to learn those skills? He would destroy them. He would rip them apart with his hands right after he held the still beating heart of whoever had set his fucking tent on fire.

She reached the edge before him, but not by much. Greed sliced through the thin fabric of the tent and shoved her through first, and the flames roared higher behind them with the introduction of new, fresh air.

His back sizzled as nothing protected his skin from burning. It would heal faster than humans, and all it did was make him even more enraged. He needed to get them out of here. Now. And once the ashes had cooled, he would return here and start his hunt.

Or maybe he would start it now.

Greed rolled into a crouch at the first sound of her hoarse shout. A man stood over Varya, his face covered with the skull of a predator. The massive cat stalked the sands at night, and they were difficult to kill. It was not this man who killed it.

The idiot raised a sword over his head, but he didn't have time to bring it down upon Varya. Greed lunged, his shoulder striking the man in the soft part of his stomach first. A loud exhalation of breath exploded before he hit the ground hard with Greed on top of him. And then all he could see or hear was a blinding red rage.

It was the battle that had always drawn him to this point. He loved the scent of blood in the air, the feeling of it slick on his hands, but most of all, he loved it when they screamed.

He was greedy for it, just as they were greedy for life. For there was no point in a mortal life when they were less greedy as they grasped onto the last moments, struggling and fighting.

He palmed the man's head with both of his hands, grinning down into his face as the man's eyes bulged in fear. Hard fists struck his ribs, over and over again, but he could not escape his fate. Taking in a deep breath of all that greed, the demon inside him whispered for death.

And so he squeezed.

He crushed the man's head between his palms, lip curling in disgust at how easy it was. How quickly the man died and barely even fought as the skull mask cracked and then the next hidden underneath.

Blood coated the sands, soaking into the ground as the desert devoured this life that had been sacrificed to it. It was lovely. It was beautiful. It was...

"Greed," Varya croaked, her voice still raspy. "We have to go."

Ach, he'd gone and done it now. Glancing over his shoulder, he tried to see just how terrified she was of him now. And though there was a look of wariness on her face, she didn't look... frightened? That was good, wasn't it?

He stood, stretching out his long limbs and holding them carefully at his sides. Blood dripped down his claws, and his battle form shimmered underneath his skin. He had a hard time convincing himself to not change right here and right now. He didn't want to frighten her, but he also saw what had happened.

Behind her, the entire encampment burned. Tents everywhere were on fire. Voices lifted in a symphony of screams as a horde of masked warriors descended upon them. Even as he watched, the silhouettes of people fighting appeared. And lost. The masked creatures always seemed to cut down anyone who stood in their way, far faster than the civilians who tried their best to fight. They were unprepared.

And they would lose.

It was a bitter end and one that he knew he couldn't spare them from. Before her, he would have stayed. He would have soaked in all the greed for their lifeblood, and the enemies greed for their death. He would have consumed so much power that he'd be glutted with it for days on end. But now he had her. He had to worry about Varya and her life because if someone ended that... He already felt his muscles tense and his fangs grow even longer in his mouth.

"Come," he snarled, his tail lashing behind him. He grabbed onto her arm and pulled her away from the madness, no matter how tempting it was.

But she dug her little heels into the ground and pulled back against him, surprisingly strong in her fervor to get him to stop. "Wait, where are we going?"

"Home."

"No, we're not going home! We can't. They need us, Greed."

Him, a thief, and likely two guards who were watching in the shadows would make no difference here. Was she blind? She could see the numbers as well as he could. "That's a losing battle, treasure."

Those eyes that had been so full of warmth just moments ago suddenly widened with an emotion that felt a little like... disgust? "I can't just leave them and run."

"Battles are best chosen when one knows that injury will not occur."

"You're a demon king. Surely you can fight a few humans off."

A few, yes. Perhaps even some of them would run if they saw him. But these were the same people he suspected had the spells that could knock him out cold. And then what would any of them do? The rescue would fail. He'd end up back in the clutches of the bastards who broke his tail, and then they would have Varya.

Gods, the things they could make him do if they used her as a threat.

Because she was his treasure, and she had agreed to be that. Just moments ago. Only hours ago, when she had screamed and clenched around his cock. She was his.

And he would protect her. She was more important than a tiny village that no one would realize had disappeared in the middle of festival season.

"No," he growled. "We're leaving. I am sorry to disappoint you, treasure, but there is nothing we can do."

She took a single step back from him and the look in those eyes nearly sent him to his knees. All that work. All that time he'd spent building up her trust and showing her that he was a worthy man to give her energy and time to... it all disappeared.

In that crushing moment, when he felt like the world had ended, she ran from him. Again.

The damn woman was fast. He had known that. But he was a demon king, and he'd been so certain he could catch up with her. The desert worked with her body, though, propelling her forward and rolling her down the hill. Light on her feet. Whereas the sands slowed him down. It was mere seconds, but it was enough for her to disappear, nude, into the fires and the screams.

Bellowing her name, he waded into the chaos with rage simmering underneath his skin. He searched for her, ignoring all the people who ran toward him for protection. He did not care for them. They could defend themselves or run for all that he cared.

Until the first three people turned toward him, their bone white masks gleaming in the firelight. They were not like the other man he'd already killed. That one one had thought he could attack without others. The three of them moved as one.

They were faster than the first, better with their swords and more calculated with their swings. They would die easily enough.

He felt his entire body ripple with his battle form. His hair grew more wild, the claws on his hands lengthening into curved daggers. His tail lashed behind him even as his feet dug more firmly into the ground. Greed became thicker, stronger, more massive than ever before as he let out a roar of rage that shook the desert sands.

The three did not stop to look at this new form, nor did they slow. Their blades whirled, and he caught the first in his hand. It sliced through his skin, but he didn't care. He used the weapon to yank the man forward and tore out his heart with savage glee. The still beating organ hit the ground before his blade did.

One of the others stuck a sword through his chest, but the pain didn't even register. He just used the weapon to drag the warrior forward and then latched onto his throat with his teeth. Shaking the limp body like a dog, he felt the tendons and arteries tear long before the blood sprayed all over his front.

The third? Where was the third? He wanted to taste his blood. He wanted to feel it splatter all over his body as he tore and destroyed and killed.

Then he saw the last man who had dared to attack him, already in the arms of his brother. Gluttony stood in his pretty clothing, not a drop of blood on him. But all ten of his rapier thin claws, straight and narrow like pins, stuck out through the man's chest.

Gluttony tilted his head to the side, watching as the man died before he slowly pulled out his claws. "Interesting when they die, isn't it?"

"Delicious," Greed snarled, his voice hardly recognizable.

"Ah, I forgot you feasted upon them as they died. And you think I am the problem?"

Greed stalked past his brother, blood dripping down his chin as he searched through the crowd for Varya. He felt the shadow of his brother moving beside him, the flames bothering neither of them. "What are you doing here?"

"I heard there may be a fight and why would I not indulge myself in a little fun?" Gluttony gestured with those massive claws, each now about a foot long, as he flicked them free of blood. "Besides, you could use the help finding your little lost bird."

"Treasure."

"Ah, whatever it is you call her." Gluttony pointed at him. "You realize you're naked, yes?"

He didn't care. Greed grunted in response, only to have Gluttony lift a brow.

"If I feast on a little blood, would that really be such a bad thing?"

Right now? Greed didn't care what he did. Another group of warriors ran at them and he felt his mind go blank. Greed did what he was best at. Fighting was no longer as much a part of his life, as he'd promised himself that he would be a better man. He wasn't the warlord who needed to conquer and claim anymore. He had other ways to feed that side of him.

He was wrong.

The rage that coursed through his veins, the greed that he devoured was beautiful and unending. This was who he was. The monster that stalked through the sands, like the great beasts of old. Like the lions and the massive saber-toothed beasts that had haunted these people for generations. He'd taken this desert by force and he would remind them all why they feared him.

His first glimpse of Varya was of her dragging another woman out of a tent. They were both covered in soot and ash, dark streaks over her pale skin that made her look like a banshee. He'd screamed her name, but she hadn't even looked at him before handing the woman off and disappearing into the crowd again.

Then he was back to fighting with his brother. The horrific sight of Gluttony with his fangs sunk into a woman's neck, greedily drinking her dry while he fended off the others with nothing but his claws... It would haunt him for many years to come.

The second time he saw Varya was as she beat out the flames with one of the rugs she'd dragged out with her. Her naked torso gleamed in the firelight with sweat, his visible red marks dotting down her torso where he'd laved her with his tongue and sucked the sensitive flesh.

His roar of rage that anyone would see her in such a state of undress, anyone other than him, had sent her fleeing back into the crowd. And so he spent his evening fighting, seeking her out, and never quite getting close enough.

Until the last of the Horde gathered onto their horses and fled. They let out whooping calls as they ran, clearly still pleased with the damage they had done. A few women were strapped to the back of the horses, but there was nothing they could do. Greed didn't have his nuckelavee. Even he could not run as swift as a stallion across the sands.

Exhaustion ran through him as the fight slowly leaked out. He staggered toward the center of the crowd, his brother in tow looking far too put together for a man who had fought for hours on end. Gluttony only had one single dot of ash on his cheek, where Greed was smeared in blood, mud, and ash. He likely looked like he'd crawled out of a grave.

Staggering, he sat down next to a familiar face and took the water Altan offered him with a grunt.

"Thank you," Altan said, his eyes skating through the much smaller crowd of people who were splayed around them. There was nothing but destruction left.

"Don't thank me for this." Greed gestured to the shambles of what had been a lovely festival. "There is nothing here to be thankful for."

"They are alive," Altan said. "Less of them, but more than there would have been if you were not here. You see that, don't you? Their lives are worth being thankful for."

Ach, he didn't see it. Greed had never understood the mortal obsession with life and living. All he knew was that his people had been attacked, and he had lost Varya. Both of which were harsh blows to his pride that he was unsure he could forgive.

With another grunt, he laid down and threw his blood smeared arm over his face to hide from the rising sun. "Tomorrow, I hunt. You will join us."

Altan hesitated. "I do not know what this hunt is."

Greed didn't even have to respond. He heard Gluttony drag something over to the both of them and then sit upon it, as if he was too good to sit on the ash smeared sand. But then his brother responded, "He means we're going to find who did this and Greed will punish them in the old ways."

"Who are you?" Altan asked.

Curious how his brother would respond, Greed lifted his arm to look up at Gluttony's far too pleased grin. So this brother was not going to follow Wrath's rules, after all.

"Gluttony," his brother replied, holding out a long nailed hand as his red eyes flashed. "A pleasure to meet you, sand walker."

This was all going to shit. With a groan, Greed dropped his head back to the sands and ordered, "Someone find me pants."

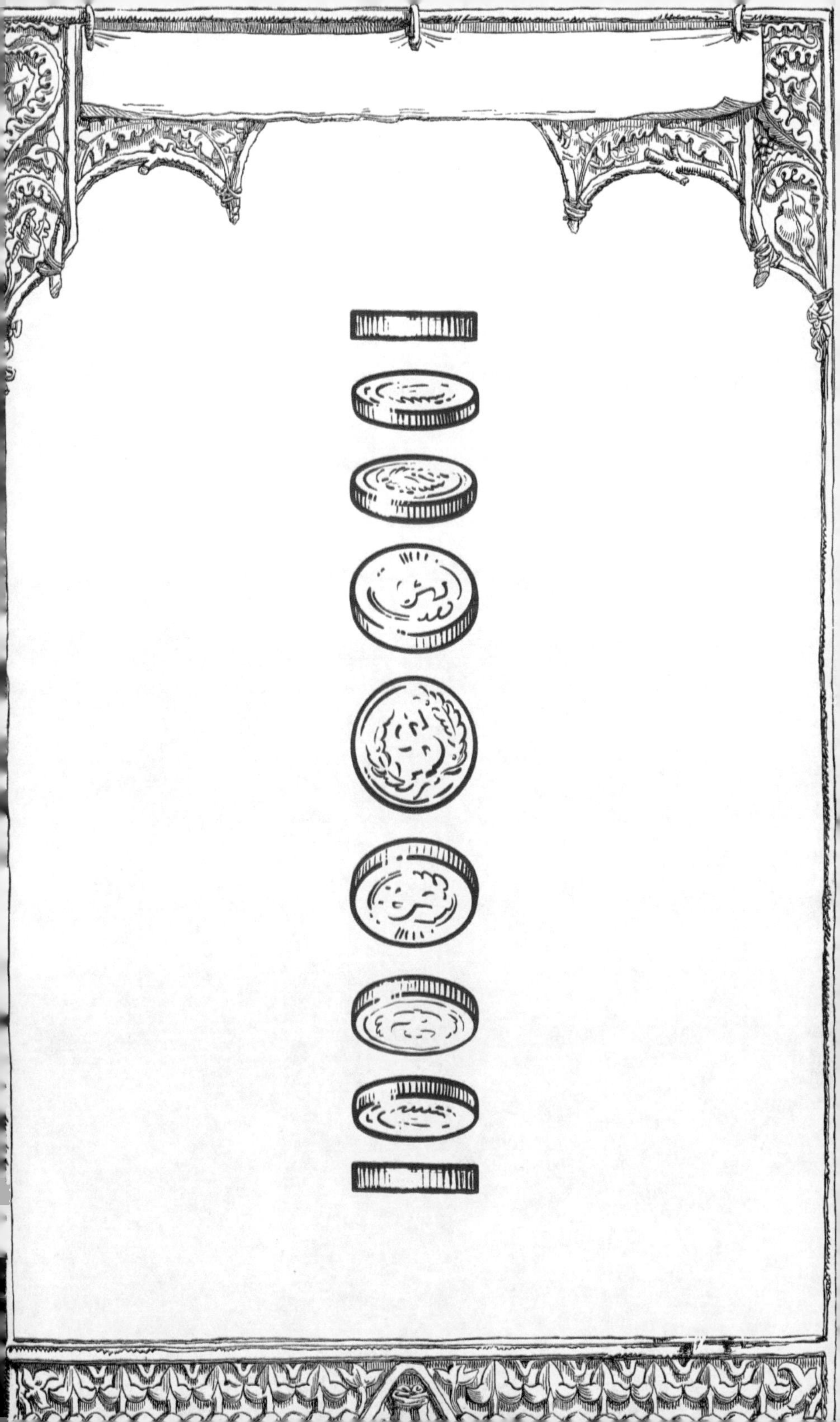

Chapter 29

Varya kept her distance for the better part of the day. She was so angry at him that every time she even thought about him, her hands shook.

How dare he suggest they run? How dare he ignore that their people needed help? His people! Even more so than her own, because he was their damned king! He was the only person who should actually care about their fucking well being and instead, he'd suggested they run because it was a losing battle.

Losing battle, her ass.

And it just made her even more angry because everything had been so good.

She hadn't realized it could be like that with a man she arguably didn't know yet. Every time they started talking about something serious, they always devolved into touching each other and then tongues tangled until her whole mind went blank. She forgot that she wanted to ask about his brother or why he'd given Ivo and Morag bodies. Or were there more spirits wandering around than she had ever realized?

There were a thousand questions she had meant to ask him before she'd fucked him and that had all gone out the window the moment his mouth touched her skin.

And he'd gone and screwed it all up. He'd broken that rose-colored spell that she'd woven through her own mind. Varya had believed maybe he was a good person hidden underneath all that bravado. Maybe this would work if she just put in a little effort and ignored a few key factors.

Of course, that wasn't the truth. Of course he hadn't changed and nothing could be farther from the truth if she thought he was a good person. He was still a demon king. Still the embodiment of greed, and if he didn't get what he wanted, then he would just take it.

There was a reason this kingdom was broken, and he wanted it to be every reason other than himself. Because looking at his own flaws, his own failings, was so much harder than finding someone else to blame.

"There," she whispered, tying a binding tight around a little boy's arm. "Good as new."

It wasn't. She needed to go searching for some magical artifact that still had enough magical juice to heal half a town. There were so many people who were still coughing or still had glistening skin from the burns that would take weeks to heal.

Not enough. She hadn't done enough, and that grated on her. If Varya could just get a horse, then she could start on her journey. That map was probably still in Altan's house, so she could make a quick stop and then she could be on her way. The treasure would be hard to find. Anything related to healing had already been used up. So it might take her a couple of tombs, but she'd find something. She always found what they needed.

But then she saw him. Greed. Stretched out beside Altan while a young man with bright blonde hair and freckles laid a fur over that impressive cock that had done such magical things to her all night. And just like that, something softened in her chest.

He had been a beast protecting her people. Even if he hadn't wanted to fight on their behalf, he had. He'd fought and torn and roared out his rage so all who tried to attack him knew exactly what was coming for them.

He'd been the protector they all wanted, and that hurt more than she expected it would.

Varya's shoulders rounded with exhaustion. She stepped toward them, her eyes catching Altan's warm gaze before she focused on the two demons resting while the town swarmed around them.

His brother stood first. Lean, lithe, and so tall, she wondered if he had a few inches on even Greed. The man held out his hand, long nails not quite drawn completely in. "Gluttony."

"Varya."

"A pleasure." He reached for her hand, bent over it, and pressed his lips against her skin. Ever a gentleman, even though she had the sneaky suspicion he wasn't.

Greed growled from his place on the ground. His arm was still over his eyes, so she had no idea how he knew what his brother was doing. But he still snarled out, "Get your hands off her, Gluttony."

His brother flashed her a dark smile, but he released her hand almost instantly. "My brother has always been territorial about his things."

She bristled at the terminology. She was no one's object, and she certainly wasn't Greed's "thing". But now was not the time nor the place to argue while there were so many eyes on them. Instead, she looked down at Greed and nudged him with her foot. "We can go now."

"I think you can see that I'm resting, Varya."

"Get up." Perhaps the words were harsh, but she had an argument that was already bursting on her lips. If he didn't move, she was going to scream at him with an audience. And it didn't matter to her if he hated her for it. Right now, she wanted to get in a fight and the only person who deserved that was him.

He grumbled, but still rolled onto his feet. The fur someone had laid out over him fell off, and he stood in front of her, completely bare. Though he glared at her like she was the problem, she pointedly stared at his half hard cock and then back at him.

"It doesn't know we're fighting," he grumbled as he strode away from the rest of the people. And it made her even more angry that he clearly expected her to follow him without questioning where they were going.

Stomping after him, she tugged the furs closer to her body and tried to keep the words inside her before they all came spewing out. How dare he? How dare he make that choice and then try to make that choice for her when there were people who needed her help? He knew what she did. He knew she would do anything for her people, no matter the cost.

Nothing would stop her from helping if she could. She would steal and lie and cheat for them. She'd been captured, endured countless beatings, fallen off a cliff, and broken her collarbone in three places before dragging herself home for them. And he thought he could just order her to ignore all that?

The man was insane. He was a selfish, good for nothing prick who had tricked her into fucking him because he thought she was some stupid little girl who would let a dick lead her around on a leash.

Well, that wasn't going to happen.

No sir. She was better than this, and he clearly wasn't.

Once they were far enough away from the tents, she looked back and muttered, "Shouldn't we wait for Gluttony?"

"He made his way here. He'll make his way back." Greed lifted his fingers to his lips and let out an ear-piercing whistle.

The sound of hooves responded almost immediately. His massive, leathery beast had been waiting for its master to call for it, apparently. It appeared in the distance, dunes away from arriving at their side almost lightning fast.

This time, at least, it didn't snap at her. It just calmly waited as its master swung up onto its back. Naked and covered in blood, he looked every inch the warlord the old legends claimed him to be. He held out his hand, and she knew it was an order. There was no denying him when he wore that expression of rage.

She looked at his hand and ground her teeth together. "I'm angry with you."

"Good," he snarled, then grabbed onto her without waiting for her to make a choice. He swung her up onto the back of the leathery beast, his arm a band around her waist. "I'm angry with you, too."

"With me?" she hissed.

He kicked the beast into movement and suddenly they were flying across the desert. It moved like it was barely touching the sands.

Normally, she would have taken a moment to realize how amazing this was. How fast they moved when she hadn't even realized it was possible.

Instead, it just made her even more angry that he'd had a beast like this, which moved so fast, and he hadn't told her. No wonder he found her at that tomb when she had struggled for days to get there. She could have gotten that goblet in a few hours if she had a mount like this. And he'd been hoarding them to himself?

"Yes, I'm mad at you," he snarled in her ear. "You put yourself in unnecessary danger—"

"My people needed my help!"

"—without thinking for a second that you might die. You left my side and then you ran headlong into flames, Varya! There were countless soldiers there who were trying to kill you."

"I fought them off. I can take care of myself, you know."

His arms tightened around her in a punishing grip. "You gave yourself to me last night. You said you were mine, and that means I will protect you above all others. And yet, you seem insistent on risking yourself at every opportunity as though you have no care or regard for your own life!"

"Just because I'm willing to do whatever it takes doesn't mean I'm risking my life!" She tried to twist in his arms, mostly because she wanted to slap him, but he didn't let her move.

"You don't care if you're alive or dead," he argued, his voice low and deep in her ear. Forcing her to hear the words that she knew were true, but they still hurt all the same. "You think it's easier if no one cares about you, no one knows where you disappear, and no one even notices if you get home? You're hiding, Varya. You've been hiding yourself for years. What I cannot understand is why you are so afraid of leaving someone behind!"

This man! How dare he? How dare he strip her bare, all the way down to her rotten core, when he himself was part of the problem? "Because I was left behind!" she snarled. "I know what it feels like to have the person you love die. I know what it is to see friends and family leave you and then never come back. I will not do that to anyone else!"

The beast between her legs slowed, somehow reacting to an order that Greed had given it without using the reins. The much easier glide made the wind die down in her ears, and the sudden echo of her own shouting made acid rise into the back of her mouth.

She'd said too much. As she always did when she was angry. She hadn't wanted to tell him about any of that, because she didn't speak of it. No one needed to carry the burden of her loss or the memories of what it had felt like to be a starving little girl on the streets, hoping that someone would notice her when no one had noticed the bloated body of her parents that had withered as the desert took its price.

Greed tucked a strand of hair behind her ear, his hand shaking and delicate. "Varya—"

"Don't," she hissed. "I'm not asking for your pity. I don't want it. My story is the same as hundreds of others throughout this kingdom. I am not special or unusual. I'm the only one with the skills to get the jobs done. And I do them well. It is all I have, Greed, and I will not give it up for a selfish asshole who only sees me as a sleeve for his cock."

He stiffened behind her, every muscle in his body locking at her words. "Is that what you think I see in you?"

"I don't need to see anything, Greed. You don't see beyond yourself." Why were tears burning in her eyes? Damn it, she was an idiot. She'd seen this coming. She had known what she was getting into. Dashing the tears that rolled down her cheeks away, she shook her head. "This argument is ridiculous. Both of us know who we are. We knew this wasn't..."

He waited for her to finish, but she didn't think she could. Varya stared up at the cloudless sky and silently begged the gods to strike her with lightning, so she didn't have to have this conversation.

Greed slid his finger underneath her chin, forcing her head to turn so she looked at him. She looked at that ash streaked face, those eyes brimming with pain that she had caused, and it broke her heart.

"We knew this wasn't what, Varya?" he quietly asked.

She shrugged, helplessly watching as reality crumbled over his features. "I'm always going to be the woman who doesn't want to tie herself to anyone. And you're always going to be a selfish monster. That either of us forgot it for even a moment was foolhardy. This can and will only end in pain."

"You don't believe that," he replied, shaking his head and frowning. "You gave yourself to me. Every inch of you responded to me, Varya, and I am as much part of you as you are now part of me."

She took a deep breath, steadying herself. This was the right decision. She was doing the right thing, even if it hurt. "It was a fun idea, Greed. We both had our fun for a little while, but that is all that it can be. Fun."

"No," he snarled. "You bound yourself to me."

"I did." She nodded, and her hands shook a little. "But that was before I was reminded of the terrible things you can do. The terrible things that you justify with pretty words that don't match your actions. You will always make the right choice for you, Greed. And I will always make the right choice for them."

Her words distracted him too much to see what came next. Varya hooked her leg over his and twisted. Her hands were on the reins already, but he hadn't seen her move as she'd kept his attention. In one swift movement, she'd unseated him.

It was all too easy to snap the reins and force the beast into movement. She had the fear that perhaps the leathery monster wouldn't listen to her. Or that it would buck her off the moment its master hit the sands. But for once in her life, luck was on her side. Or perhaps the creature was just as disappointed in Greed as she was.

They tore off into the desert. She guided it toward Altan's house where she could get her emergency change of clothes and the map that would help her heal her people. Another treasure. Another life risking adventure.

Tears streaked down her cheeks, probably leaving clean tracks in their wake. Because he was right. She was running headlong toward another injury, or perhaps this time her death, because this was how she coped. This was how she fixed herself.

Proving her worth but letting no one close enough to care if she died. Why did he have to lay it all out for her to see so clearly?

The bastard. He'd wriggled his way into her heart and she hated that now she was afraid to die because she didn't want to leave him alone.

Chapter 30

Greed sat astride Ivo's nuckelavee, glaring at the sands like they were the problem. He certainly wasn't. After all that had happened, he thought he deserved a little time to not believe he was the asshole who had not only ruined this kingdom but also his chance with the most beautiful woman in all the seven realms.

Which was why he was out here. Hunting. Doing everything he could to find the bastards who had attacked the Festival of Lights. The Horde would answer for what they had done, and they would answer in blood.

He knew the desert wanted to feed. The sands underneath his feet already screamed for more blood that would sink deep into the beating heart of this kingdom, igniting it once again. But he also knew therein lay the problem. If he wasn't careful, this kingdom would return to its more... lively habits. He could not, and would not, allow it to return to that state.

No matter how much he wanted revenge. The Horde had taken from him. They'd ruined a night that should have remained precious for the rest of their days. Even the thought of things she'd done, the words she'd whispered, how sweetly she'd bent over his arm and begged for more, even though her thighs were already shaking?

Ach, she'd been perfect. And then he'd had to let her go.

"So, why are we out here again?" Gluttony asked, leaning over the pommel of his saddle. Morag hadn't been pleased about letting his brother take her mount, but there were only so many nuckelavees to go around.

"Because we are hunting down the idiots who thought they could attack my festival and get away with it."

"Oh, your festival is it now?" Gluttony's dark brow raised. His brother had insisted on wearing a wide-brimmed hat, he looked foolish wearing it, but his lily pale skin would have burned by now if he hadn't. "And here I was, believing you hadn't even thought of that festival for hundreds of years. What was it called again?"

"The Festival of Lights," he ground out.

"Right. The Festival of Lights. Where your people send up their lanterns with wishes written on the inside, hoping that the gods themselves would hear their prayers. Isn't that about right?"

"What are you trying to get at, Gluttony?"

"I'm just saying." The creak of leather in Gluttony's hands was the only sound that gave away that he might not be quite as flippant as he pretended. "You were never interested in this before that woman waltzed into your life. And you've never wanted to hunt someone down for burning through a camp. You are the warlord king who took this kingdom and let it burn. Remember?"

Of course, he remembered his own history. Greed couldn't forget it, no matter how hard he wanted to. He'd been here for centuries, had indulged his kingdom in whatever future they wished to carve for themselves. That didn't mean he couldn't change. Or that he didn't want to.

If he didn't look at the desert, casting his gaze out to the wild landscape beyond, he wasn't sure he wouldn't launch himself at his brother and knock him off the horse he'd provided.

Gluttony had always gotten underneath his skin, though. They had never gotten along.

"So we are Horde hunting," Gluttony said as the silence stretched a little too long between them. "Interesting. And why are we Horde hunting?"

"Because they attacked a village of people during what was supposed to be a truce between all the cities. The Festival of Lights is known to not allow stealing, thievery, or murder."

"And that is by your own grace and choices, of course."

"Of course." It wasn't. Greed hadn't ever made those rules, but he would uphold the ones that his own people had made. They wished for peace during this time, and that suited his own needs. He wanted revenge.

Apparently, Gluttony saw right through him and into the thoughts that he tried so desperately to hide. "And this has nothing to do with the woman, then? Or that tent that you two disappeared into? You realize I have exceptional hearing. I know exactly how you were entertaining yourself while the rest of the town continued to celebrate."

"I don't need your approval to do such things. Besides, you weren't even supposed to be there."

"Of course not. But I want to, once again, ask why we are in the middle of the desert hunting the people who are simply doing what you have taught them is acceptable? Burn down villages if you want what they have. Take what is yours and ask for no quarter or apologies." Gluttony lifted his voice to a higher pitch, as though Greed spoke in a tone higher than his own. "They do what you tell them to do."

"And now they will feed my desert with their blood," he growled. He could feel the anger rising. His cheeks burned bright red and his chest felt hot. All at once, that rage coiled in his chest and snapped. "They ruined what could have been the best night of my life. They took from me the treasure that I have always desired and now I will hold their beating hearts in my hands for it! Everything would have been perfect if they hadn't walked into that festival and ruined it!"

"Eh," Gluttony said with a light shrug.

Greed's vision turned white.

"Eh?" he repeated, spitting the word in his brother's direction. "What does that mean? Eh?"

"It means, brother, that you have yet to consider that all of this fuckery might be your fault." Gluttony turned on top of his mount, facing Greed directly while he ticked off his fingers. "You were the one who tried to get her to leave her people when they needed help. You were the one who taught the attackers to do exactly what they were doing. Let's not forget that after you helped save her people, only because she forced you to do so, that you then blamed her for making you feel worried because you thought she might be dead. And then she knocked you off your own horse, and you let her go."

Greed wanted to wrap his fingers around his brother's neck and squeeze. "So you want me to take all the blame for what has happened?"

"I think that's the logical choice, yes."

"You want me to be the villain in this story when there is someone out there that we can actually hunt? Someone we can kill because they have killed so many others?"

"I do not know you to be a man who has any interest in mercy." Gluttony tilted his head to the side, watching him with dark eyes that saw far too much. "This is mercy, brother. You are hunting down the people who harmed innocents. It's unlike you."

But that wasn't why he was doing it. Sure, Greed would take their adoration and their devotion because of what he did.

He was only out here hunting because the Horde had unwittingly stolen from him when they attacked that village. They'd stolen a night of pleasure that he never wanted to forget, and that memory would forever be tainted by their touch now.

He wouldn't stand for it. They would pay for their foolish mistake and he would watch them cry out for mercy. And he would give them none.

Gluttony watched him with those knowing red eyes. Seeing right through to his soul and then snorting. "So it's like that, then. You want to punish them for making a mistake that is actually yours. That's fucked up, Greed. At some point, you're going to have to admit that you make mistakes as well. And sometimes you have to sit in your own punishment."

That was it. His brother had no right to judge his life.

Leaning over his own pommel, he braced himself on the sturdy saddle as his beast shifted between his thighs. "Why are we sitting here talking about me? You're casting judgement, brother, when you are the one here with a babysitter because you couldn't stop eating your own people. Why don't we talk about that?"

Gluttony's face darkened with what Greed could only hope was embarrassment. "We're not talking about me."

"Oh, but we are. You were the one sent away like a misbehaving brat to a kingdom far from your own, because Wrath didn't want mommy to see how badly you had misbehaved." Calling Pride "mommy" was perhaps a bit of a stretch. But their brother in the skies was rather pretty.

Though they both knew it was right, Gluttony would argue. He never failed to rise to a challenge like this. "First, I did not eat any of my followers. I drank her blood dry because she wanted me to. And second, do you really believe Wrath could take me out of my own kingdom if I did not wish to go?"

"Yes." Greed rolled his eyes. "You're a bigger fool than I thought if you believe you could go head to head with Wrath. There's a reason he is where he is. None of us wanted that kingdom, but he looked at the challenge of darkness and monsters and made it his own. You want to fight him? Be my guest. I wouldn't even take a punch from that one."

And that was the truth. Greed would fight anyone and everyone who would give him a chance. He adored fighting. Loved the feeling of a fist meeting his face even if only because that meant he could unleash whatever he wanted on the person. Fighting was a catharsis that so few people ever got to feel. A release of all that pent up aggression in his body.

But fight Wrath? He'd rather lie down and let the sun take him.

Gluttony shook his head, but his red eyes had turned out toward the desert as well. Almost as though he couldn't look Greed in the eyes.

And that was strange on its own. His brother had never backed down from a fight. Not once.

Curiosity burned in his chest, and the feeling was rather welcome considering all he'd been able to feel for a while now was rage and disgust at himself. Latching onto it as though that feeling might save him, Greed pushed. "Well? If you want me to believe Wrath's story, then by all means, stay silent. This is your chance to tell me what happened."

"You are inclined not to believe me."

"You are correct." Greed squeezed the reins a little too tightly in his hands. "But I will do my best to hear you out."

Though Gluttony turned to look at him with suspicion in his eyes, his brother spoke. Halting, shuddering words that revealed he didn't want to tell Greed. Something inside him must feel an ounce of guilt for it. He must know that these dark thoughts and worries needed to be purged.

"She wanted to die," he started, his voice deeper than before. "I didn't want to be the hand that wielded that blade, but there was no other choice. Not for either of us. She had to die, and I had to let her go, so I did. I was the murderer who eased her into the beyond in the only way I know how to, Greed. I'm not a killer, like you."

"I've never killed innocents."

"Of course you have," Gluttony scoffed. "We all have. Every choice we make in our kingdoms kills innocents because none of us were meant to be gods. I have my vices that you judge me for, just as you have your own. I cannot understand your need to take, just as you cannot understand my need to consume. It is who we are."

And that sounded... wrong. Greed urged his mount forward, knowing Gluttony's would follow. "I do not have vices. I encourage people to embrace the part of themselves that keeps them here. We have given the people in each of our kingdoms a safe place for them to feel no guilt for who they are."

"Ach," Gluttony tsked. "You sound like Pride. But you don't actually believe that, do you? We're the problem, brother. We always have been. I know it was our dream to be mortal and that we would take these forms and make a significant difference, but we haven't done that. All we've done is feed in greater volume since we took the thrones. We made the humans worse."

The thought of that didn't sit right.

Had he made this kingdom worse? No. He hadn't. "When I came here, there were hundreds of tribes all over the kingdom, each one vastly different from the one next to them. They fought with each other nonstop. They followed herds of creatures to eat and they were starving. The jungle devoured them day in and day out before I gave them a reason to band together."

"And in doing so, you made them all the same." Gluttony didn't even flinch at the glare Greed sent toward him. Instead, his brother held his gaze with a strength that he hadn't seen in Gluttony for a very long time. "I'm not telling you that you're a bad person, Greed. I'm just saying we're all the villains in their stories, no matter how much they pretend to love us. We're the monsters in the storybook, the ones who fucked up their world and remade it in our own vision. And perhaps it is time for all of us to recognize that about ourselves."

He swallowed hard. "You want us to accept that we are monsters?"

"Yes." Gluttony didn't hide from that. He just agreed with it. "There is power in accepting what you are. The humans call us demons for a reason."

"I don't want to be a demon," Greed muttered, but his brother saw through him, as he always did.

"Don't you?" Gluttony asked, his eyes boring into Greed's profile. "I know I do. I'm not ashamed of it. They call me the demon king and I have become one. I drink blood. I devour their life essence and I consume all that I am given. If that does not make me a demon, then I am unsure of what I am."

Unsettling. Every part of this conversation was unsettling, and most of it was the thought that he didn't want to be the person who others feared. He didn't want to be the reason this kingdom floundered or failed.

But no one had taught them how to be kings. He'd done what he thought was right, and now they were all here. The desert ruled them all in some small part, because his kingdom wasn't like the others. Greed had taken the hardest kingdom because he had felt a kinship to it and that was... it.

The sand rolled underneath him and he sighed. Knowing that his own stupid feelings were getting the better of him. He had to push them back down. To indulge himself in more greed and bloodshed, because that was where he was most comfortable.

If only the desert would let him think. If he didn't have to feel like he was rolling on a lake somewhere or—

"Greed?" Gluttony's voice cut through his thoughts. "Do you have a snake problem?"

"Excuse me?"

Then Greed saw it. The massive snake shifted through the sands, its scales glinting in the sunlight where it poked through the desert before sinking back down. A snake who should have been dead for hundreds of years and yet, apparently, had woken.

"The desert takes what it wants," Greed muttered, the words from an old kingdom that had long fallen underneath the sands. "We feed it blood, and the beasts rise from the deep."

"What are you muttering?"

"This is a problem," he snapped. "Bigger than that fucking Horde who I assume is behind all this. We're following the beast, Gluttony."

"Of course." His brother kicked his nuckelavee's sides and Greed wished once again for his own mount as they raced across the desert after the ancient snake that should be asleep. "Why wouldn't we follow the snake?"

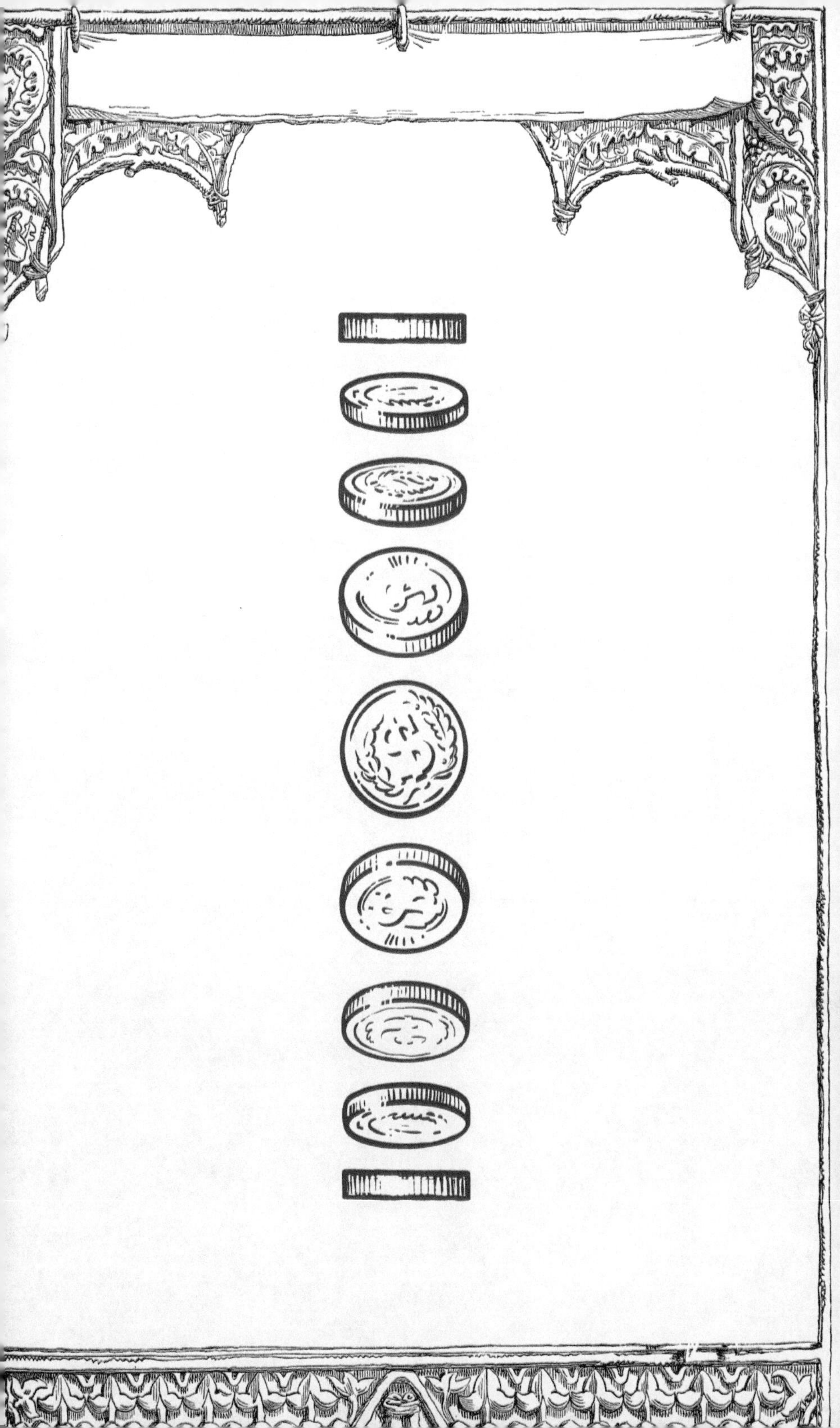

Chapter 31

She'd gotten the damn healing artifact. And she'd done it in the most reckless way possible, almost as though she was trying to make Greed angry at her. But he'd been so pushy with his opinions. So certain he knew exactly who she was and why she did everything that she did.

It was fucking wrong.

She didn't risk her life because she wanted to prove to herself that her life didn't matter. Varya was smarter than that. She risked her life because others needed her and that was the only reason she'd almost fallen multiple times in that ancient tomb. The only reason she'd thrown a rope across a chasm and not tested to see if it would hold her weight.

She was and always would be, a good thief who knew how to

navigate a tomb. Varya didn't need the idiot king who had made her entire kingdom fall to pieces, anyway. Why did he think he was better than her?

Their argument continued to roll over and over in her mind. Greed had been so smug telling her that she didn't care about herself and so someone had to. He hadn't taken a word of her argument as the truth that it was. He'd just dismissed everything she said! Like he had that right. Like he was the only person in the kingdom who didn't have to work on himself.

Not that she had to work on herself. Varya was just fine the way she was, and he'd never convince her otherwise. She wasn't taking risks without realizing the danger. She saw it. Every bit of the danger that she walked into, and she loved it.

She raided tombs every week! By all the seven kingdoms, she'd been just fine before him and now he'd wriggled his way underneath her hard exterior and she was worried about taking risks!

Damn him.

Damn that stupid fucking king who thought he knew her.

"Varya?" Altan asked, drawing her to the present. "Are you so sure this is a good idea?"

No. It was a terrible idea. That's why she'd wanted to come alone. Instead, he had insisted that a small group come with her out into the middle of the desert.

"Not really," she admitted. "The map doesn't tell us what the artifacts are. None of us have ever heard of what the Lamp of Origins does. But I still think its better for us to have it than the Horde. And they'd circled this spot."

Which meant maybe they already had it. And if they did, then they were all risking their necks for nothing. Varya had guided them to the middle of the desert, and their packs were already running low on water.

She stared around her at the few friends who had gotten ancient donkeys and skinny horses, and wondered what she'd dragged them into in her anger at the king. They wore white and tan shrouds over their heads, trying to reflect the heat of the sun as far away from them as possible. They were all hot, though. Sweating right through the shrouds that were supposed to keep them cool and thus wasting even more precious water.

It was cruel to bring them here.

"You should all turn back," she said, returning her gaze to the basin in the sands. "I don't know what this item does. I haven't heard of it before and... well. This is too risky."

"If you can do it, so can we," Altan replied. He sat up a little taller on his horse, but it made her heart race to see him like this.

"You have people back home waiting for you. All of you do." She twisted on her saddle and the nuckelavee beneath her gave a little restless snort. It had been doing that a lot for the past hour. "Don't put your lives at risk for something we don't even know about. It might do nothing. The magic in it might be all used up, or the Horde might have already gotten it. We don't all need to risk our lives."

She knew they'd argue. Because they had argued with her for hours on end before she'd agreed to let them come with her. Each one of them had looked at the leathery beast she'd stolen from Greed, and they had said they'd go. As protection? She had no idea.

Altan nudged his horse closer to the nuckelavee, or as close as he could without the mount trying to bite the other. "One last time, Varya. Is Greed searching for you? We cannot have any trouble in the town."

"I don't think he is." It was a lie. He was definitely looking for her, but she didn't think that was going to be a problem for the town.

It was a problem for her.

Swallowing hard, she stared down into the basin and then got off the nuckelavee. It had been causing her trouble the entire day, but now the beast wished to run. And if that was the way of it, then... She'd let it.

"Off with you," she said before it raced away. Like lightning across the sands, one moment it was there, and in the next, it was gone.

That should have been her first clue that something wasn't right.

Instead, she gave Altan one more steadying look and smiled. "Let's at least keep everyone up here? I'll go down and get it. It's got to be buried right at the base of all this, wouldn't you think?"

"You're the tomb raider, love."

"Then I have a hunch it's right where I think it is." She hoped, at least. Climbing back out of this bowl in the desert was going to be a real pain in the ass.

Sliding on her butt, she let the sand do the work and send her deep into the depression. There were a few skeletons on the way down, large beasts with horns as long as she was tall, a few of the sand cats with tusks the same width as her wrist. Even an ancient-looking beast with a thick plated skull that would have been useful for head butting its enemies. More skeletons than she would see in a regular tomb.

Landing on the bottom, she rolled into a crouch and waited. No traps? Nothing that rumbled with her weight. Strange, yes, but not something she hadn't seen before. Maybe this wouldn't be like the other tombs. Maybe this was just the last known place where people had seen the lamp.

Then she cast her gaze around herself and saw the lamp. Right in the center of the strange hollow was a metal handle. It wasn't large, just about the same size as she'd expect a regular lamp to be. A thin metal circle, likely with a cage beneath it where one would place a candle.

For the first time, she wondered if she should have researched this item a little more. Of course, she hadn't gotten the chance to second guess herself. She'd been so angry that she'd wanted something to work off her tension, and now they were all here. All of them.

Glancing up at the edge of the dunes that surrounded her, she could see her people's worried expressions. This was why she never brought them. They would stare at her like their lives would change forever if something went wrong, and she couldn't take it. Varya didn't want to make them watch her die, just in case she maybe did.

"You have no care or regard for your own life!" His words played in her thoughts before she hissed out an angry breath.

She didn't care what he thought of her. Greed didn't get to live in her head, even if he was an ass who refused to get out.

Creeping over the sands, carefully watching where each foot stepped, she made her way to the lamp. And nothing happened, which only made her heart race even more. This wasn't right. There should be a trap, a fight, a guardian...

The sands rolled around her, the dunes suddenly moving as though something deep inside them had awoken and she realized, "Fuck. A guardian."

Of course, there was something here to protect the magical artifact that hadn't been seen in such a long time that no one even remembered what it did. All around her, the sands moved. The dunes shifted, raining sand down into the deep gully. Something moved in a giant circle and then she saw the flicker of golden scales. Gold, red, orange, and black, all twisting together just like the creature she'd seen before.

The one that had been there when the Horde had thought to take what they assumed was theirs. The one that had made even the Horde scream in fear. It was here.

The massive snake burst its head out from the sands and she stared into its terrifying black eyes. Nothing could be this big. Was she hallucinating? Was there was some kind of poisonous gas down in this maddening pit? But then it opened its mouth and hissed, fangs as long as she was tall, dripping venom that sizzled in the sand and burned so hot it turned the granules to glass.

And she knew this wasn't something her mind had cooked up. The monster was right in front of her, and if she didn't move…

The snake hissed, long and loud, then its hood stood up all around its head. A cobra. A massive fucking cobra that weaved back and forth, staring down at her like she was a mouse someone had thrown into its cage.

Oh, she was dead. She was so dead and all her people were up there, screaming for her to move. Some of them had scattered, racing away while the rest were still there, suddenly off their mounts, on their hands and knees, shouting for her to come to them.

But she couldn't lead the snake to them. She wouldn't be the reason they died, too.

Lunging, she hooked her fingers through the lamp's top and then rolled. The snake hissed again, the sound rumbling through the sand just before it struck. She raced out of the way before those massive fangs dug into the same place she'd been standing. The beast grumbled in anger, then shook its head while sand sprayed out of its mouth.

The lamp swung in her hand, useless, dead weight she should just let go of, but what if it still had power?

"Varya!" Altan shouted. "The dunes!"

Right. She had to get out of this bowl or the snake would eventually catch her. Unfortunately, it had already started descending, more and more of its long mass was revealed as it pushed itself through the sand. And she stared around her, realizing there was almost no way out. Its scales were a giant circle, wrapping around her more than once, twice, perhaps three times.

The snake's hood shook, and it was so large that the sound rolled through the air like thunder. Its scales tightened around her, writhing and moving ever closer and she just... froze.

"Varya!" Altan shouted again, before backing away as the massive cobra turned its attention to him.

She hadn't thought... Well, she supposed she had. Wasn't Greed right, after all? She'd sought death her entire life and now that it had come for her, she didn't want to see it after all. What a fool she'd been.

Damn. She hadn't thought this was how she'd go, but here they were.

The snake hissed, the sound blasting Varya's hair away from her face, and she squeezed her eyes shut. Not quite as brave as she'd thought she would be in facing her end. But then an answering roar screamed out in rage and she knew exactly who had come to collect her.

On the opposite side of the gully, Greed and his brother rode on their lightning fast mounts. The third beast had joined them, its teeth flashing and leathery skin rippling in anger. So it hadn't run away from her after all. It had just been returning to its master.

She shouldn't feel such relief seeing him there. He glared at her attacker as though his eyes alone could slice through the beast. The cobra turned its attention to Greed, those black eyes locking onto him as prey.

He swung off his mount without hesitation and sprinted toward the snake. Though the surrounding scales tightened for a mere moment, the beast seemed to realize that Greed was a greater threat. Casting aside its desire for food, it launched itself at the demon king.

Greed's form changed mid stride. His hair burst out around him in a wild mane, his claws wickedly sharp, his body massive, his tail flicking behind him as he used the snake's body to catapult himself toward the creature. They met in midair, both roaring in rage and shaking with power. She'd never seen anything like it. Because Greed might be smaller, significantly, but he moved faster than the snake could track.

His claws dug beneath scales, shifting before the snake could snap at him. He climbed the long body of the snake as if it wasn't even moving. And all the while, Gluttony sat there on his horse, grinning.

The brother caught her looking at him and then gestured with his hand. Did he want her to come up there? With an enraged demon king who was currently battling a snake as large as his castle, and what? Wait for the demon who was so clearly bloated with rage, like the good little girl she was?

Crossing her arms over her chest, she let the lantern dangle on her right side while staring up at Gluttony. Not moving. Making her point known.

He nodded at the other side, toward Altan, and then lifted a clawed hand to point at the massive writhing tail in her way. Right. Well, maybe he had a point. That didn't mean she had to like it.

Grumbling under her breath, she ducked beneath the massive body that was having to move now to avoid every slash of the demon's claws. It hissed, venom dripping all over the ground, and she kept an eye on the drops that were the size of dinner plates. Varya danced out of the way of each of them, nearly crushing herself in between two mounds of scales before she got herself to the edge of the dune.

And then she started up. Hand over hand, dragging herself through the sand that wanted to drag her back down. She slid a few times, but she'd been born in this environment and knew how to move when she had to.

Crouched on her hands and knees at the top, she dragged in a few lungfuls of air before shakily rising to her feet. Lantern hanging from her fingers, she watched as Greed landed hard on the ground at the same moment the snake let out a long hiss and dove into the sands.

The beast retreated.

Greed himself was slick with sweat, not a wound on him or a bruise that she could see. His hair was plastered back from his face as he spun and advanced on her, so angry that she knew he wasn't quite himself.

"What are you doing here?" he snarled.

She held up the lantern, not trusting herself to answer him without starting yet another argument that would only end in her tossing him onto his back and stealing another mount from him.

He ripped the lantern from her grip, hissing at her. "This? This is why you risked your life? Yet again?"

"It's the Lamp of Origins." As if she knew what that meant.

"And it's been useless for years," he said, before crushing the metal in his grip. The lantern folded in half like paper, then dropped onto the sand and rolled back into the pit. "Get on the horse."

Her knee jerk reaction was to say she didn't see a horse, but Varya knew better than to poke a beast who was quite literally frothing at the mouth in front of her. "Absolutely not."

"Get on the horse, woman!" His voice thundered almost as loud as the snake, and for once, Varya didn't think she should argue.

354

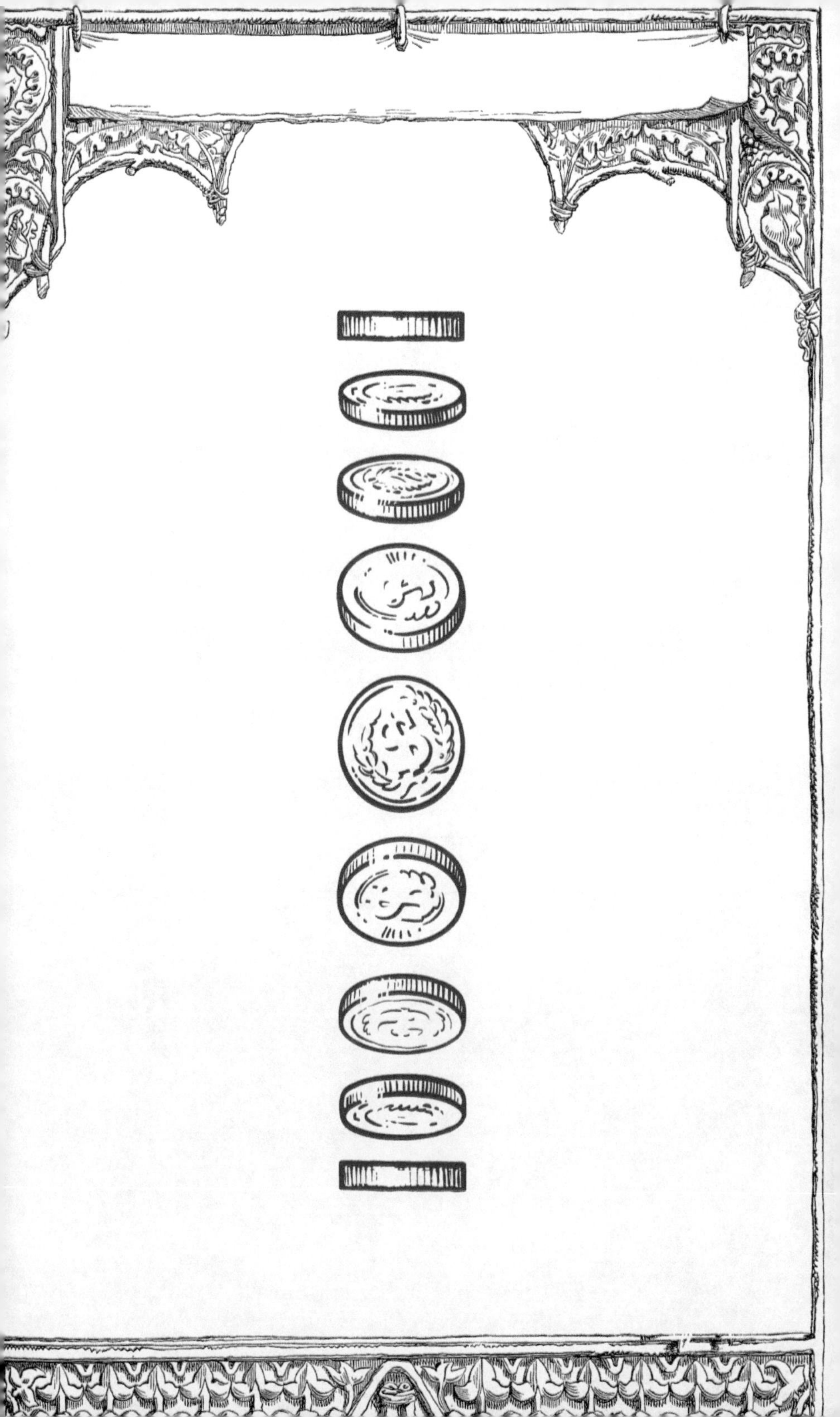

Chapter 32

Greed was so angry he couldn't even speak. What had she been thinking? Not every treasure on this forgotten planet was worth risking her life for and hadn't he just said that she was risking her life for the wrong reasons?

Even now, with his arms barred around her, clutching the reins so tightly they were cutting into his palms, he wanted to argue. He wanted to remind her that she was always risking her life as if she punished herself by doing so. Here she was, claiming to do this for her people, and yet she was trying to gather up the Lamp of Origins, of all things!

That lamp hadn't been useful in years. He'd been there when all the magic had left it. Though it was useful in its time, it was quite literally junk now.

And she'd have known that.

If she had fucking asked him.

Grinding his teeth, he could hear the sounds that his jaw made, but he didn't care that she might be able to hear it as well. She deserved it. She deserved to wonder if he was angry at her, or what she could do to make him less angry.

"Greed," she started, then stopped talking when he answered with a warning growl.

He didn't want to talk right now. He didn't want her to say a word when she'd done the one thing he couldn't forgive. She'd almost killed herself again. If he hadn't been there, that massive snake would have consumed her body. And worse? He was probably the one who had given the desert enough blood to wake the old ones.

That snake wouldn't exist if it wasn't for him. He had been the one to feed the desert all those years ago, waking up those creatures that slumbered deep underneath the sands. They only woke when the scent of blood grew so strong that they could smell it. Miles underneath the sands. That was a lot of blood, and he knew from experience just how much it took to wake them.

Hissing out another angry breath at himself, at her, at the world they lived in, he kicked his mount into movement. Faster. The nuckelavee could move faster and his own personal mount would keep up.

Gluttony's angry shout chased them, but his brother had never been as good at riding the beasts. Let his brother find his way back to the castle on his own. Greed didn't care.

He wasn't supposed to be a babysitter, anyway. If Gluttony got himself in trouble, Wrath could deal with him. Their brother in the underworld should have taken care of this himself.

He needed to have a conversation with a little troublemaker who needed to understand where her place was. And that was beneath him. On top of him. Sideways. Upside down. Whatever position he wanted her to be in.

Now that he'd gotten a taste, he wasn't willing to give it up so easily again. She was his, and she'd admitted it. She didn't get to take that away from him.

Varya had made a vow, and now he would remind her exactly what that meant.

They arrived at his home in record time. The servants and guards had seen him in the distance, so the gate stood open and ready as he thundered into his home. The nuckelavee raced past countless people who had prepared themselves to be useful, but he didn't need them. Not right now.

Greed urged the beast as close to the stairs that led to his private quarters as it could get, and then he leapt from its back.

"Greed," Varya tried again, her eyes wide with shock or fear. He didn't know. He didn't care.

In response, he hooked his arm around her waist and deposited her onto his shoulder. He could barely feel her tiny weight as he turned them from the beast and up the stairs. And perhaps it was dramatic, but he swore the oasis shuddered with his movements, as though it feared what he might do to the lovely pale flower that had wandered through its leaves.

She said nothing. Smart. Just dangled over his shoulder until they reached his rooms, where he placed her on her feet and then stalked past her. His mind was on one thing, and one thing only. He needed to prove to her why she wanted to stay. That she wanted to stay. That all they had discovered together, their pleasure, the blinding ache that had built in his chest with every peak they'd crashed over together. It was worth giving up her life for. She could stay here. Safe. He would keep her safe.

His chest rose and fell with anger, or rage, or… fear. He didn't know. Greed barely even recognized that his breath was too quick, that his tail hadn't stopped flicking since they'd gotten into the room, or that little growls were still rumbling through each of his exhales.

He couldn't get control of himself. He didn't think he wanted to.

"Greed," Varya said a third time, this time with a bit harder tone. "I don't know what's going on, but I cannot help unless you tell me what is running through that mind of yours."

"We have not resolved this." Greed stalked to the back of the room and threw open a standing wardrobe. He'd given her time to indulge herself and explore his body. He knew what she wanted, but now she should know what he wanted.

All of her. Every inch. Every ounce of pleasure and pain and all the emotions she could give him. And he wouldn't rest until he had been gifted all of that.

The wardrobe held sex toys of all shapes and sizes. Gags, bars to hold her legs open, cuffs that would suspend her from his wall or tie her down onto his bed. Soft cushions, bolsters for underneath her hips so he could hold her exactly where he wanted her. His favorite were the floggers, one in particular that was thick, sharp leather straps that left lovely little marks all over the skin. But she wasn't ready for that one. Not yet.

Instead, he chose the one with the strips that had been softened into a buttery texture. They felt lovely to drag over his hands, and the soft scent of leather filled his lungs. The scent provided the slightest moment to settle himself.

He'd never hit her in anger. That he had promised himself years ago when he'd realized just how good it felt to leave a mark on his partner's skin. He would never forget the red handprint that had started it all, or the claw marks above. Tiny pinpricks, not enough to bleed, but they were still there.

Proof that they were his. And Varya had said she was. She'd vowed that she was his and his alone.

He turned to her then, seeing the wariness in her eyes and how she watched him like he was the predator and she the prey. That was right, he supposed. He was going to devour her whole if she let him.

"What do you have there?" she asked, her voice low and calm.

"Need I remind you what you said?" He dragged the flogger over his palm again, letting the little strands play through his fingers. "I said tell me what you want. You said you wanted me. I asked you whose you were, and you said you were mine."

The lovely line of her throat bobbed. "I did."

"Were you lying, treasure?"

Again, a swallow. Perhaps more of a gulp. Her eyes flicked to the door. "I was not."

"So you offered yourself to me for one night only? I told you, I don't do that. Once you are mine, I keep you. Those are the rules, Varya. Rules that you have now ignored."

"Rules I didn't agree to. I will tell you again, Greed. I am my own person, and you cannot control where I go or what I do."

She was right. He knew that. Even Gluttony could see that she was her own person and that he couldn't just expect to order her around and have her follow every damn order.

But that feeling in his chest hadn't gone away. The fear. The tension that, no matter how long she stood alive in front of him, wouldn't go away. All he saw playing in his mind was her risking her life over and over again. Choosing to do so. Ignoring the fact that he'd be so messed up if she died and he wasn't there to at least try to save her.

The tiniest amount of that fear slipped out. His voice hoarse, he met her gaze and said, "You risked everything."

And though he didn't want her pity right now, he could see the thoughts flicker behind her eyes. She understood what she'd done. That in risking her life, she hadn't just threatened her own. She'd threatened him, because his damn heart existed inside hers now and he didn't know how or when or why that had happened, but she was important.

More than anyone else had ever been. And that terrified him.

Her gaze flicked to the flogger in his hands, to his tail, to the set of his shoulders, before returning to look back into his eyes. "What do you want from me, Greed?"

"Everything." He repeated the words as though it could explain what was happening in his chest. He knew it didn't. She couldn't read his mind, and even if she could, it would be nigh impossible to untangle the thoughts in his head.

"You've said that before." She took a step closer to him, another, walking so close he could smell her scent that unraveled some of the fear. She was here. Right in front of him. He'd gotten there in time.

And then his hand tightened around the handle of the flogger again. Because he'd remembered that she'd been in danger. A-fucking-gain.

Her hand joined his, her long fingers still so small against his hand. And he couldn't stand the sight of it because she'd almost...

"What do you need?" she asked, heat back in her voice that he'd thought he would never hear again. "Tell me."

It was the question he'd asked her, in some form. She'd accepted this. Accepted him. Knew that he needed her to give him the only thing that would make him feel calm, to know that she was right fucking here and that no person or monster was taking her from him.

A shudder of pleasure traveled down his spine and he nodded at the chair he'd had custom-built in the corner. It was smoothly cut, cushioned, all comfort and swells that would present her body to him if he wished, and in any position he wished.

"There," he grunted, waiting to see what she would do.

Her eyes skated over the cushioned chair and she seemed to know. As if she was in his head and knew what he needed. And that pressure in his chest that had been building since the moment they stepped into the tent, it got worse. He hadn't thought it could.

But it felt like someone had taken hold of his throat. He couldn't even swallow as she turned her back to him and made her way over to that chair. She stood in front of it, eyeing it for a few moments, before moving in front of the highest peak and then gracefully folded over it.

And oh, the sight she presented made him groan. Ass in the air, like a pretty upside down heart. He wanted to run his hands all over her, mark her as his, make it so no one would ever question who she belonged to, or who protected her.

He wanted the world to know that if they touched her, he would find them. He would kill them. And then he would hunt down their families and kill them, too.

Greed didn't recognize this feral side of him, but he kind of liked it.

Striding behind her, he smoothed his palm down the globe of her ass, squeezing gently while he ran the flogger up her arched back. "Are you going to enjoy this treasure?"

"I don't know." Good, she didn't sound afraid. Only curious.

He pushed her shirt up, revealing long lines of muscle on either side of her spine. The valley between those ridges would look so pretty with his cum running between them, and he intended to paint her long before he ever let her go.

"Ach, I think you will." He leaned over her, blanketing her in his heat and strength as he whispered in her ear, "I want you wet for me, Varya. You will make a mess of yourself before I give you what you want."

And there it was. That pretty little moan that came from the back of her throat. Exactly what he'd wanted.

He rocked against her, letting her feel how hard he was. Sliding his hand down her side, not touching anything that she would beg him to touch soon enough. And then slowly, ever so slowly, he pushed her pants to her thighs. Not taking them off. She hadn't earned that yet. But she would. Soon enough.

Because for all the risks she took when she was in this room with him, she was his good girl.

Greed leaned back, staring at the slick, glistening core of her that was already as wet as he'd hoped. She flattered him, so ready when he had barely even touched her. But she remembered just as well as him how they fit together. How everything was better than it had ever been before.

Testing her, he flicked his wrist, and the flogger struck her with a little smack. Not hard, not even enough to leave a mark. Still, she arched into him so prettily with a little gasp.

"No more risking your life," he snarled, another snap punctuating his words. A little harder this time. "Not without me. You hear me?"

"I hear you."

Snap. Little red stinging lines appeared on her left cheek. Just seeing them settled something deep inside him. "You will not run from me again. No?"

"No," she moaned, her hips already moving against his chair.

"No, what?"

Another snap of the flogger, another gasp that echoed out of her mouth and turned into a moan. "I won't run from you any more."

"No more lies." Again he struck. "No more hiding from me." Again.

She dripped down the inside of her thigh and he had to pause and just stare at her. This woman who met him no matter what he asked. He took, she gave, and then she took it all back from him. He... by the gods, he could love her. So easily.

But love was dangerous. Love made a man do foolish things, like drop to his knees and worship the goddess spread out in front of him when this was supposed to be about punishment. Not reward.

"Do you hear me, Varya?" he asked, his voice hoarse. "Or are all these answers just more pretty lies?"

"I'm not lying."

He dropped the flogger to the floor with a hard thunk. He cut through the laces of his pants with a long claw, then lined himself up with her. Rubbing himself into her wetness, dragging the tip of his cock over her clit. Not hard enough to give her the pleasure she sought, just enough to tease and torment.

"I don't believe you," he snarled, leaning over her again. She could only see, feel, taste, and smell him. Only him. He was her world right now and she would never fucking forget that. "But soon enough it will be the truth. This isn't pleasure, Varya. This is punishment. I won't be sweet. I will be quick and hard and you will like it. Do you hear me?"

He sank into her, just like he'd said he would. A quick thrust, burying himself until their hips were pressed against each other. Core to core. And instead of the grunt he'd expected, or the little whine in the back of her throat that he'd heard before, she moaned as though he had given her everything she'd wanted.

And fuck, he felt the same. He was lost in her. Lost in knowing that he'd gotten her back, that she was alive, that she was well, that he had made it in time.

Greed pounded those emotions into her. His relief. His love.

Ach, even in this, it was only with love.

No claws scratched her skin. No part of her hurt more than she wanted because even as he had her bent over in front of him, he couldn't be too rough. Not with her.

When he was close, he reached between them and pressed where she needed him. Circling and giving her the pressure she'd been seeking. Buried as deep as he could go, he came with her. Together.

Exactly where they were supposed to be.

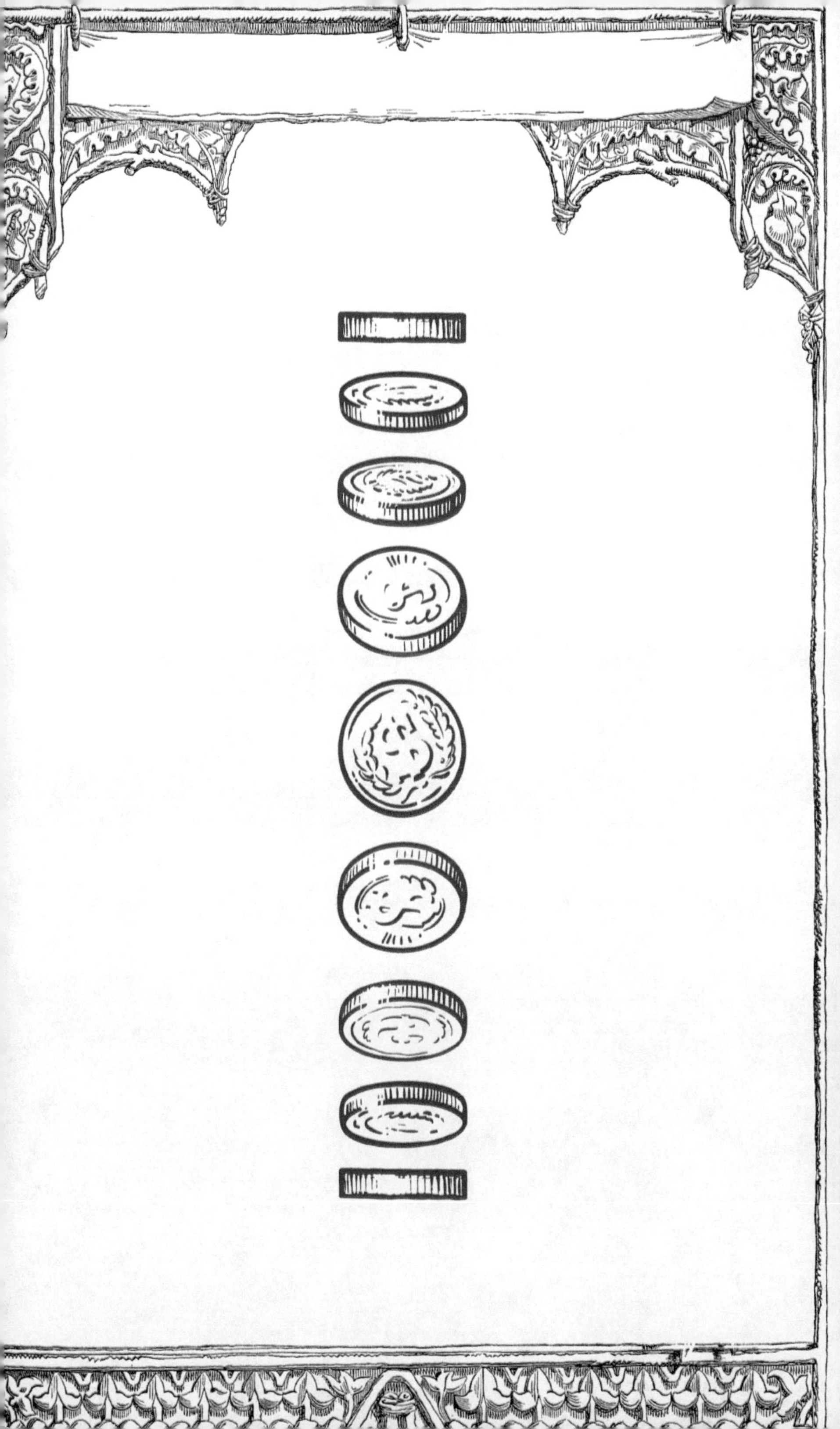

Chapter 33

She wasn't supposed to be here. Varya knew that there were other places for her to be right now. She could be out there, finding more artifacts. Hunting down beasts with Altan and his men. Getting water to the towns that needed it most. There were so many places for her to be right now, that needed her help, that needed someone.

And yet, she couldn't drag herself out of the comfort of Greed's bed. She stared up at the ceiling, watching the sunlight play through the fronds over her head. Every muscle in her body was so relaxed, so comfortable, so at ease. And she just couldn't make herself get up.

Besides, she'd promised him. No more running. No more trying to hide who she was or what she wanted from him. And he'd so deliciously convinced her of that.

Still, there was a part of her that held back. She didn't want to fall in love with him. But she had. Every inch of her wanted every inch of him, in whatever way she could get it. That didn't mean it was right.

Her heart hurt even thinking about him. Because all he'd done, time and time again, was prove that he only thought about himself. Maybe about her now as well, but was that enough?

No. It wasn't. Of course it wasn't. She wanted him to care about this kingdom and the people in it. She wanted him to see that there were so many people he could help, and then she wanted him to choose to do that.

Of course, all of that was hard to see through the haze of pleasure he yanked over her head every time he touched her. And that was fine, too. She didn't mind waking up like this, with her muscles feeling slightly overstretched and tender.

Still. There had to be some way for her to convince him that there was more than this. More out there. More that he could...

The door to the bedroom opened. Ivo stepped inside, a gown draped over his arm that was as yellow as a daffodil, then faded into the pink and lovely violets of a sunset at the hem. It was a beautiful dress, but it was the last thing she wanted to wear.

Without looking at her, he placed the dress over the back of a chair and then laid out the other pieces he'd brought with him. A necklace that had enough jewels to make a kingdom rich, earrings that looked so heavy they'd make her ears ache, and ten bangles that would decorate her wrists.

Too much. It was all too much.

Sighing, she sat up, clutching the emerald blankets to her chest as she looked over the offering Greed thought he had given her. "What is all this, then?"

"A dinner he's requested you to join him at." Ivo looked down at the clothes sadly, then back at her. "He's going about this all wrong, isn't he?"

"He is."

"But you'll stay this time?" He seemed almost hopeful.

"I don't know."

A flicker of hurt in his eyes made her heart sting. "He said you'd promised to stay this time. That you wouldn't run and we wouldn't have to track you down."

Making sure the blanket was tightly wrapped around her waist, Varya padded over to his side and placed a hand on his arm. "I'm not running because I don't like this place or the people in it. You see that, Ivo, don't you? There's just so many other people I can help."

He nodded, but the little furrows between his brows made it seem like he didn't quite understand. "Greed mentioned that you know... that I... Morag and I... That we're..."

"Spirits," she said for the poor, stuttering man. "You were spirits, you mean? You aren't anymore. I look at you and I see so much more than just a spirit of loyalty."

"It is still who I am at my core."

She patted his shoulder one more time and then turned him toward the door. "Then turn your loyalty to more than just Greed. You have an entire kingdom who could use your help, Ivo. You and your sister could make a difference that stretches so much farther than your original master."

A spark lit in him. She could almost feel the magic that glowed at his fingertips as he stood in front of her door, then squared his shoulders. "You think we can do that?"

"I think you can do anything you put your mind to."

Then she closed the door and dressed herself like the good little doll she was. Varya's movements were slightly wooden, aching as though she had been placed back in a prison she didn't wish to be in. Greed had... Oh, he didn't realize that what he was asking of her was wrong. And that was part of the problem, wasn't it?

He wanted to keep her safe. He wanted to keep her, period. Varya had always wanted that, hadn't she?

She'd wanted to be the person who just one man couldn't keep his hands off of. She wanted him to be consumed by need for her, and that he'd do anything to keep her safe. She'd told herself countless times in her life that all she needed was one person. One. That's all.

Now she had him, and it didn't feel right. None of this was perfect, yet. What if it was never perfect? What if she was so broken by all these years of being on her own that she could never get what she wanted?

The dress coiled around her neck, flowing out from her waist like the petals of a flower. The gems sat heavy on her collarbone and chest, while the bangles felt like shackles around her wrists. She just wanted... something.

Damn it, how was she supposed to tell Greed what she wanted if she didn't know the answer to that herself?

She made her way out of the room and down the stairs as Ivo guided her to a new glass bubble she'd never been in before. This wasn't the ballroom. It was a much more intimate setting that was all readied with a small dinner, a much smaller table, and a smug-looking demon king waiting for her.

Just seeing him made her cheeks burn red, but she knew this was the only time she'd be able to pin him down. To tell him what she needed, and how it was going to happen around here.

If she didn't force him to have this conversation, then they never would. She'd drown in his kisses and his touches and their shared needs and then wake up years later to realize that they didn't even know each other. Or worse, that they'd never even tried.

Varya sat down and he poured her a glass of wine. Saying nothing. Just looking at her with those smoldering eyes as he licked his lips. And damn it, her mind had already gone down the same path his had. All it would take was a single movement on her part. Just a slight flick of her fingers and the tie at the back of her neck would crumble. This dress would slither down her body, pooling in her lap until she wore nothing but gems and gold. Just like he wanted.

She could see it in his heavy-lidded eyes and the way his finger carefully stroked the edge of his wine glass. He wanted her. She wanted him. He saw no problem in fucking their way through the years until they grew bored with each other.

Taking a deep breath, she folded her hands in her lap. "How was your day?"

He blinked at her. "My day?"

"Yes. How was your day?"

"I..." Again, he blinked at her, confusion spreading across his features. "Why do you want to know how my day was?"

"It's a question people ask each other. We say what we did, how we felt during the day, who we saw." Varya reached for food to put on her plate, but her mind didn't recognize what it was that she touched. Were her hands shaking? They were, damn it.

Through all of this, Greed hadn't moved. Nothing other than his eyelids. "My day was... fine."

"That's good."

"How was..." He paused when her gaze flicked up at his in surprise, but then he finished the question. "How was your day?"

"It's just starting. I slept in longer than I thought I would."

Gods, this was awkward. They didn't even know how to talk to each other! What was she doing?

Grinding her teeth, Varya tried not to stare down at her fingers twisting in her lap. She tried to look at anything but him. She was so afraid he'd realized she was hoping he would do something when he clearly had no intention of doing anything at all.

"Varya?" he asked, his voice low and quiet. Like he was trying to lure a wild animal closer. "What is all this about?"

She swallowed. "We don't know each other."

"I'd say we know each other quite well."

Ah, there was the flash of anger she needed to get through this. "I don't know anything about you," she countered. "I don't know where you came from, what your favorite food is, who you learned to fight from. Nothing. All I know is your favorite position and that you don't know what's going on in your kingdom at all. Neither of those are lasting qualities."

"Lasting?"

"Yes, lasting." She repeated the word, spitting it at him like that was the answer to all her problems. Hissing out a long breath, she finally looked at him. Angry now. So angry she could throw something at his face. "I don't want to stay here if we don't know each other. This is just using our bodies as a distraction, and that means, at some point, you'll tire of me."

Greed lifted a single brow. "You don't want to stay here?"

"That's not what I'm saying." She'd be an idiot to not want to stay here, but she didn't want to if he wasn't... Oh, her thoughts. They were all so muddled. So she settled on, "I want to know who you are, Greed.

I want you to know me. If we know each other then maybe this will all be a little... easier."

That finger started moving again, stroking up and down the bowl of the glass in his hand. Tempting. Mesmerizing. "You think this is hard so far? I can tell you something that is hard, Varya, and it's not our relationship."

"You don't want to know anything about me?" she asked, her brows furrowing in concentration and her heart already stuttering in her chest. "Do you really not care enough to have questions?"

He looked even more confused before that expression disappeared into heat. "I have questions. If you fear that I will no longer desire you, Varya, I promise that will take a very long time. There is much of you I have yet to taste."

But that...

That wasn't the point.

Her heart clenched so hard it hurt. Everything hurt at the words he used because he just... he didn't understand. And she was suddenly so afraid that he couldn't.

She wanted him to understand. She wanted him to want her and he'd led her to believe that he did. But now she wondered if he just wanted anyone, and she was the only person no one would notice if she disappeared for good.

"I'm not here to answer your boredom," she muttered before standing. "I don't think I'm very hungry."

"Then we will skip to dessert," he replied. That heat flashed in his eyes again, and he reached for her.

But she knew if he touched her, then she would break into a thousand pieces and he'd put her back together exactly how he wanted. She would not break this time. He didn't deserve to touch her when she knew it was only for a few moments.

Because... Fuck. She loved him. And she wanted him to love her back, but that wouldn't happen if he only saw her as a sexual object to please him.

So she flinched back from him. She watched as that anger clouded his expression and he reached for her again. This time she didn't think, she just acted.

Varya grabbed her glass of wine and tossed it in his face. The red liquid dripped down his beard, ruining his lovely shirt, and she refused to feel guilty for it. He'd acted, so she'd done the same.

"Treasure," he said, calm. Too calm. Slowly wiping the wine away from his eyes so he could glare at her. "What is all this about?"

"I'm not a toy," she said, her voice wavering. She was so fragile right now, and she hated every moment of it. "I'm a person, Greed. You cannot lock me up in this castle thinking that you will be the only person to play with me and then degrade me into being less than a human being."

"I'm not doing that."

"You don't care about me!" she shouted, and the words echoed through her mind. "You only want me for my body. Every time I try to ask to know more about you, all you want to do is fuck me. You think that is a way to get out of a conversation or to not talk about hard things. You can't just... Do that!"

And there it was. In a garbled mess of words, there was her problem.

She wanted to talk to him about everything. She wanted a partner who saw the kingdom as a challenge to overcome and who would listen to her concerns. Not a man who every time there was a conversation that was even the slightest bit difficult, he reached for sex as a crutch.

This wasn't right. It wasn't who she wanted to be.

So she stood there, holding herself hostage so that he would hear her.

But he didn't.

He shook his head, taking a step back from her with a stunned expression on his face. "I am not a man of words, Varya. I never have been."

"What is that supposed to mean?" Desperate, she needed him to tell her something that would make this all okay.

But he lifted his hands and held them out to her. "This is how I speak, Varya. With my body. My actions. I cannot... I cannot do what you are asking of me. I need you to see me, just as much as you want me to hear you."

And oh, it made her heart break.

This wouldn't work. This couldn't work, even though they both wanted it to be real. And it was so real. It hurt to look at him and know that he wasn't capable of what she needed. Or wanted. Or...

Her mind was so jumbled. Rambling in her own head because she wanted to make this concession for him. She wanted to forfeit all that she'd dreamed of just so she could have him.

And was that wrong?

Was that the wrong choice?

The future she'd wanted turned to dust in front of her and all she could do was run. She made it to the door before his voice cracked like a whip and she froze with her hand on the door. "Remember, Varya. You vowed you would stay."

She would. She was nothing without her word.

Nodding, still not looking at him, she slipped out of the room.

Ivo jumped in surprise from where he leaned against the wall, blinking as though he'd perhaps been dozing. "Varya! That was quick. Is there anything I can get you?"

She looked up at him with tears in her eyes and saw the big man melt. Without asking a single question, he put his arm around her shoulders and tugged her in close. "It's all right, little one. It's all going to be all right."

The first sob was ugly. It rocked through her body, too loud, loud enough that Greed surely heard her. And she shouldn't feel bad about that, but she did.

Varya forcibly pulled herself together, only taking a few seconds of relief in the hug that Ivo offered before taking a big step back. "I'm sorry. I shouldn't..."

He lifted a hand. "You may do as you wish, Varya. But perhaps I might suggest an evening with my sister instead?"

"I don't want anyone else to touch me."

"Oh, she won't. But her blade might." He smiled at her surprised face before holding out his arm in the direction he wanted her to go. "Fight, Varya. Perhaps that will fix everything."

And that sounded good right about now. Or, if not good, the best she was going to get.

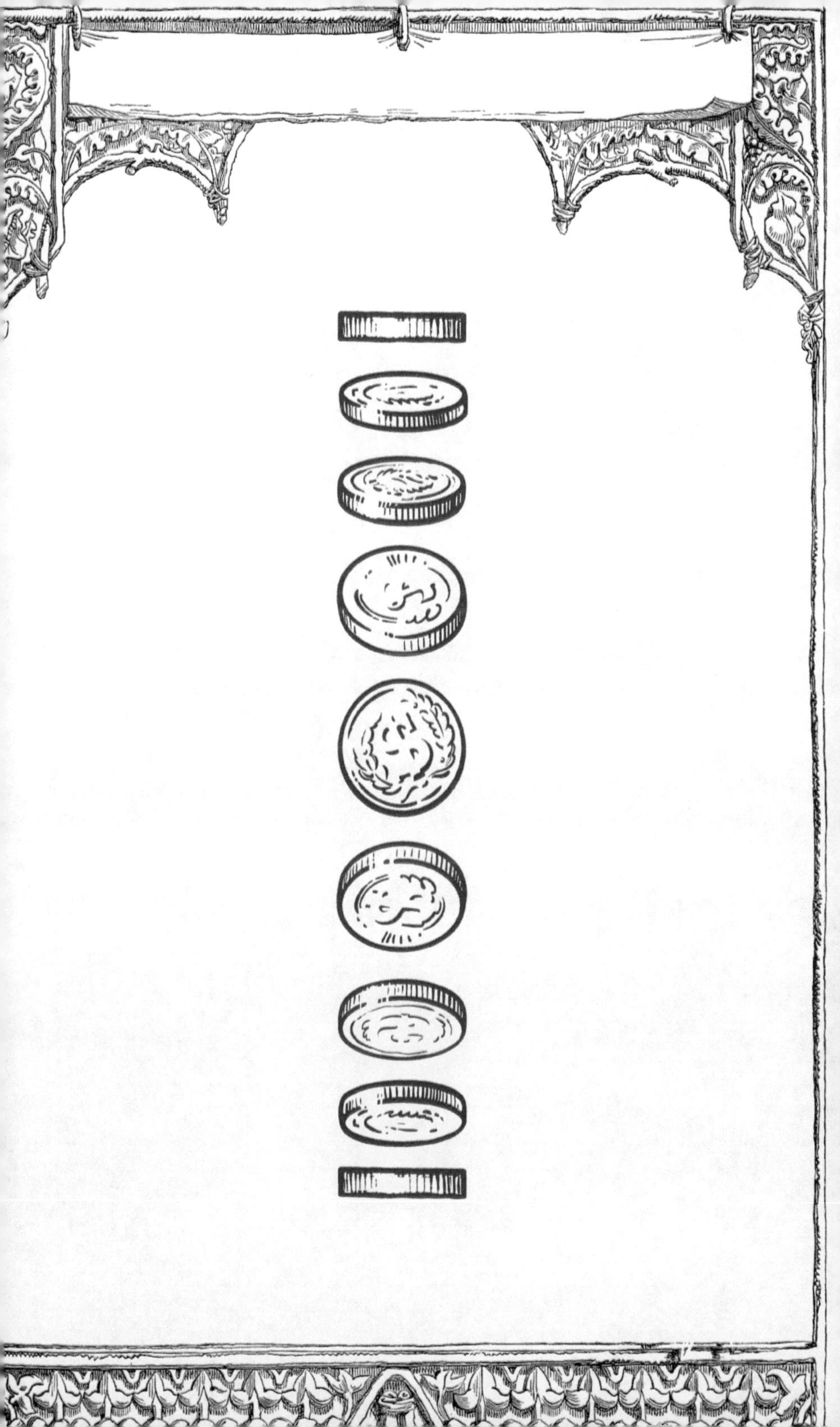

Chapter 34

S o," Gluttony said, shifting on top of his mount to look back over his shoulder. "Here we are again."

Here they were again.

Hunting in the sands like the idiots they were. For two very different reasons, of course. Gluttony was here because he couldn't keep his hands to himself and Wrath had heard he'd been eating people, even here. They'd both heard ringing in their ears for days after that confrontation. It didn't matter that Gluttony was helping Greed, nor did it matter that people had attacked them. He'd fed. That was the problem they were trying to fix.

Whatever. Wrath had bigger problems than Gluttony getting his fill in Greed's kingdom.

Greed was only out here because of a much bigger problem. A

problem who was giving him the silent treatment for the better part of a week because she refused to even unlock his door. He had a key, of course, but what kind of a person would he be to just barge in when a woman said no?

A demon, some dark voice in his mind, whispered. And she expected him to be a demon, didn't she?

No, that wasn't right. Varya needed her time. She needed to come to terms with the realization that she wasn't getting away this time. Not from him. Not from their world. She'd completely and utterly given herself over, and now she had to pay that price.

"Shut up if you aren't going to keep an eye out," Greed snarled.

"An eye out for what? We've come out here every day for five days now and we haven't gotten a single whiff of what you're looking for. Just admit you're asking the impossible and let's go back to your castle." Again, Gluttony shifted on the saddle, wincing slightly. "I'm getting sores."

"Maybe those would remind you to keep your mouth shut around Wrath, then."

"I wasn't the one who told him I'd been feeding."

"No, but you did it." Greed could use a fight right now. He was itching for it. His hands opened and closed in clawed fists, and he stared at his brother with eyes that were already slitted in the sun. "You're the one who can't control your own urges."

"Hilarious." Gluttony looked him up and down, then gestured in the same motion. "Look at you. We're out here, starving, burning up in the sun, and you're quite literally salivating. There's drool on your chin at the mere thought of keeping her forever, and you think I'm the one who can't control my urges?"

Was he drooling?

Greed wiped at his chin. And damn it, there was some foam after all.

What did that mean? Nothing. Only that he couldn't control his urges with her and that was realistically something he shouldn't worry about. There had been other objects he'd wanted just as much. Armor that would protect him from every type of weapon. Magical amulets that made him stronger or allowed him to be as weak as a human if he wished. There were plenty of items here that had been tossed aside by so many kingdoms he could wallow in the power for the rest of his life.

And yet...

Yet, he knew his brother was right. Gluttony saw straight through him. His reality was that he was pleased with the idea of keeping her because it was Varya. Of anyone and anything he'd ever seen in his life, he wanted her. More than magic. More than power. More than his namesake.

He wanted—no, needed—to have her. And he would give up the rest of his collection if it meant she stayed with him for just a little while longer.

Gluttony's eyes widened, watching the emotions flicker across Greed's face. "You're in love with her."

"No." The word wrenched out of him before he could catch it. Greed cleared his throat to get rid of the sudden tension there. "That's our brother's new domain, yeah? Not me."

"You think you cannot be greedy while also being in love?" Gluttony leaned over the pommel of his saddle, turning his eyes out to the sands. "Lust might have been the only one of us who struggled with love. And Pride, I'm not sure that bastard even knows what love is. But none of us are immune to the notion. We can love, Greed. Just as hard as we can fuck and live and conquer."

Ach, it wasn't the right thing. He wasn't in love with Varya. She could barely look at him right now and ... she wouldn't be able to do it after this.

He scrubbed the back of his neck with his palm, an ache blooming in his chest. "And if I do? What do I do with that? She doesn't want this life or anything that I can give her."

"Perhaps all she wants is you." Again, that soft gaze turned to him, seeing right underneath the armor that he'd so carefully built up around himself. "And you're so afraid to show her that ugly underbelly of yours."

"That's all she's seen."

"Then you're afraid to show her the best of you because you do not believe there is anything left of that person." Gluttony shrugged. "There are many reasons to be afraid, brother. Countless reasons to convince yourself that you are unworthy, or that she could never want a man like you. Or you could let go of your fear and dive in. See what she can offer you and what you could offer her."

When had his brother gotten so perceptive?

Eyeing Gluttony, he tried to see past the hard exterior. Or perhaps it was better to call it Gluttony's mask, since no one really knew who his brother was.

Gluttony had left them all very early in the battles for their kingdoms. He'd seen the swamp kingdom and taken it for his own, knowing that none of the others would want the dark and the muck. Since then, Greed hadn't heard from him at all. None of them had. Gluttony had taken to his kingdom like a fish to water and then was gone. From all of them.

So what had his brother been doing? Certainly not becoming this rather insightful version of himself. He refused to believe a man who devoured his own subjects was so able to look within himself and see reason.

"You eat people," he muttered, then shook his head. "I shouldn't take any advice from you."

"You shouldn't believe everything you hear." Gluttony's eyes never once moved from the sands. "Wrath tells whatever story suits himself best."

"You mean suits the kingdom best."

"Sure. Claim that's what it is. Put that mantle of goodness and righteousness on the brother with the greatest anger problem and the background to prove how fucked up he really is." This time, Gluttony met his gaze without hesitation. "Neither of our brothers like me very much. Have you ever asked why? Does Pride see fault in me? Does Wrath wish to punish me? Or is it because I seem to be the only other brother who sees fault in them, and they do not like feeling inferior to anyone else?"

This opened up way too many doorways that he wasn't all that certain he wanted to walk through. Greed had never cared that two of his brothers seemed to think they ruled all the other kingdoms. He didn't care as long as they didn't meddle, and they didn't. They took whatever they wanted as far as respect, and then they left him alone.

He was fine with that. Greed rarely left this kingdom anyway. It was large enough for him to spend a thousand years exploring, and that was enough.

But... What if Gluttony was right?

He wasn't so certain he wanted to understand what was going on with the rest of his brothers. And he certainly didn't want to agree and be the reason they were all at war. It was too much for him to consider. Too much for him to uncover when there were already problems in his own house.

"Brother," he started, not sure what he was going to say. "I don't—"

Gluttony interrupted him, pointing ahead. "There's a spirit, if that's what you've been looking for."

Greed didn't have to be told twice. He kicked the sides of his nuckelavee, and launched into action. It took him a second to see what his eagle eyed brother had seen, but the spirit wasn't trying to hide. It rolled across the sands, a faint greenish color of mist that stood out all too much. The little thing had no idea that it was going to die today, and that was unfortunate.

There weren't a lot of them already. And if it wasn't the right kind of spirit, he wasn't certain what he'd do with it. After all, they needed the spirits of emotions so that humans could truly feel them.

But his temper had already simmered underneath the surface for far too long. If the spirit wasn't the right one...

Greed leaned over the edge of his mount, holding onto the saddle with his thighs, powerful body nearly skimming the sands as he leaned low. Lower... lower still until he scooped the spirit up with his clawed hand.

It let out a little shriek of anger, a good sign to be certain, and struggled to get free. While its form might be mostly mist, he was a demon king. He'd been what this little spirit had been before, and he knew how to contain it. Struggling to continue scooping it back between his hands, he juggled the damned thing as Gluttony took his sweet time to join them.

His brother's amused smile only served to make Greed want to smack him, but at least he held out the glass jar quickly enough. Only then did Greed let the mist fall between his fingers, then he capped it.

The greenish light turned darker with anger. It didn't even have eyes, or the ability to speak, apparently.

"How long have you been wandering the desert?" he asked, lifting it up so the spirit could see his face.

It glowed sporadically, apparently trying to get some message across that he didn't understand. A long time, he'd guess. Considering how weak the spirit was, it had likely not seen a single human in at least a few years.

"You'll need to feed before I use you," he muttered, shaking the jar so he could see the spirit from all angles. "This won't suit. But don't you worry, you'll live on if you're the right sort. What are you?"

Of course, it couldn't answer, and he barely remembered the times when they lacked this physical form. They'd all been like this. A glowing light, weak and struggling to even stay illuminated. Then they'd found the better way to feed. They'd glutted themselves on the mortals that they found growing stronger and fighting off all the other spirits who might take their food.

But that was all he remembered. Nothing specific. Only the story that they'd told a thousand times over to explain how and what they were.

Sighing, he looked at Gluttony to see his brother had turned ashen, even his lips lacking all color.

"What?" he asked.

"Nothing."

"Do you recognize it?" He shook the jar again, tumbling the little spirit around in a circle. "I can't remember this color, to be honest. It's a little like pea soup."

"It should be a spirit of adventure," Gluttony replied. His brother's voice was quiet and breathy. "But it's changing."

"Into what?"

"Loss." And that choked noise didn't sound like Gluttony at all. "What would make a spirit of adventure turn into loss?"

Greed looked around them at the desolate landscape, at all the adventures that might have been had which were now buried underneath the mounds of sand. He knew what had made this spirit start to change. And he knew the struggle that made it weaker.

Adventure required hope and excitement and all the other spirits that should have accompanied it. Emotions that were so rare in his kingdom, it was no surprise that they had died out.

He tucked the jar against his chest, holding it tightly as he'd wished someone would have done for him. "Adventure," he muttered underneath his breath. "Perhaps we should visit a few of Varya's friends before we go back."

"And bring the Horde right to their homes?" Gluttony shook his head, still far too pale for Greed's liking. "It's folly you seek, brother. You wish her to love you in return? Stop risking her people."

That would be the logical thing to do. And a voice in his head whispered that it was the right thing to do as well. Risking others was a stupid idea. He could go back to his castle and seek the servants that might give this little spirit a feast. Not to mention it would grow very strong inside Varya's adventurous body. But he didn't want to take any risks.

She was his. Varya was his to protect, and he intended to make sure she lived a long, healthy life. Longer than any human before him.

"I was there when Lust's bride almost died," he said quietly. Even the spirit in the jar stilled, looking up at him as though it knew the importance of this moment. "I saw her withering away. I felt her soul detaching from her body. But it was a spirit of affection that saved her. A single spirit who had grown strong and healthy and could have even taken physical form if it wished. But instead, that spirit gave itself up. It joined with her, possessed her, allowed her to remain in control over herself even though it knew that meant a life almost like death."

Gluttony hissed out a long breath. "I'd always wondered how he managed that."

"It made her immortal," he continued. "It made her stronger. It healed her, every battered part of her body. Like magic. Better than magic. It was a gift that this spirit gave a woman who had fed it beyond any other. I will not lose her, Gluttony. I will not see Varya age or die because I was not willing to risk a few mortals."

And there it was.

The ugly underbelly that Gluttony had mentioned. The darkness inside him that whispered for him to tear this entire kingdom apart if it meant she would stay alive and well.

He'd take whatever she could give him. He was greedy for it. He wanted her hatred, her love, her passion, her pain, all of it. It was all sweeter than any nectar or honey he'd drank in his life and he didn't care how fucked up that was.

If he had to endure her hatred for a hundred years, just for a taste of her love, then so be it.

He lifted the jar to the sunlight, watching the golden rays play through the green spirit. "You are going to be her salvation, little one. I will feed you now, and then you will join with my queen."

It shuddered in the jar, but then seemed to still. Almost as though the spirit was considering what he said, even if it was frightened.

"You will be her savior," he breathed. "Or I will return you to the desert and you can seek out the end of your life here."

In the end, it was no question what the spirit would choose.

Chapter 35

Wiping sweat off her brow, Varya let her sword drop toward the ground. She could keep going—she swore she could—but they'd been going at it since this morning and her shoulders were screaming.

It felt better than wallowing in that damned room, though. At least she was out in the training yards with the sun on her back and sweat drenching her clothing. Morag didn't care about sweat. Neither did anyone else who had gathered to watch them fight.

She'd thought she was quite good at fighting. Varya spent a lot of her life learning how to be scrappy, how to fight when she needed to, and how to convince others to fear her. She knew how to crawl her way out of the dirt, how to take a punch, and how to punch back. All of that was as deeply ingrained in her as breathing.

She'd been so wrong.

Morag fought like a dream. Her entire body was lithe and quiet, moving and looping through stances as though the muscle memory alone guided her. And she was damn hard to pin down. The other woman moved like an eel in her arms and made it almost impossible to hold her.

Varya had managed for only two full seconds before Morag and thrown her clear across the arena and then slapped her hard across the back with their wooden swords.

But even though she should have been angry, or perhaps embarrassed that she'd been bested so thoroughly, Varya could only stare at the other woman in awe. She could learn a lot from a warrior like this. More than any other person had ever taught her.

Clearing her throat, Varya coughed a few more times to clear the dust out of her lungs before reaching out her hand. "Again, tomorrow? Same time?"

"I have guard duties, you know," Morag said, but the grin on her face revealed she'd be here. "But, I suppose, we do have to entertain all those who couldn't fight with us if they tried."

Varya clasped the other woman's forearm, telling herself not to look too starry-eyed as she met Morag's grin with one of her own. "I'll get you in the dirt tomorrow."

"Unlikely, thief."

"I'm learning. Every time you throw me, I hope you know I'm going back to the room and practicing the same move. Soon enough, I'll know everything you plan to do before you even know it."

Morag tilted her head back and laughed. The strong muscles of her throat worked, and the slight sheen on her skin glistened in the sunlight. A goddess of war, Varya thought, that was who stood in front of her.

"Ah, human." Morag shook her head, her laughter still bubbling up every now and then. "Your courage is admirable but foolish, isn't it? We aren't the same, you and I. I believe you've already been told that."

Of course she had. Ivo had sat her down and told her everything. That they were spirits. Poured into bodies just like Greed. She'd known all of it already, but hearing it from him helped.

The more she understood about him and his sister, the better. The more accepted she felt because they were kind and welcoming and everything that Greed wasn't.

She'd thought perhaps the problem had been that he was a spirit. He'd made it very clear that he wasn't like her, or anyone else, for that matter. He and his brothers were something else entirely. Not demons. Not men. Creatures unlike what she'd ever experienced before.

Her sword hit the dirt with frustration as she spun toward the opposite side of the arena. Stomping away from Morag, she tried her best to get out of her head. Again.

"What is it, little human?" Morag asked, her voice more than a little amused. "Have your demons returned so soon?"

"He's your demon too, you know."

"Him? Nah. He's no demon to me. But he certainly haunts your steps if it takes battle to get him out of your mind. It's been a week, thief. How long are you going to torture yourself?"

"As long as it takes," Varya muttered as she ducked underneath the wooden guard rail.

"As long as it takes for what?" Morag was laughing again, that mocking tone trailing along behind her. "Until one of you snaps? Until you discover that, without a doubt, you cannot live without him? Or perhaps it will be when you greet death again. You two are old friends now, aren't you?"

A shadow loomed in front of her, dark and too large to be anyone but her guard. The only person who rivaled Ivo in size was Greed himself, and she'd know him anywhere. The sensation of him danced over her skin every time he was inside the castle. She knew where he was. Always. And yes, it was a torment to know that he was right there and she could have him if she only reached out and grabbed him.

"Enough, sister." Ivo handed over a rag for the sweat on her face. "Humans feel more deeply than you or I."

Morag leaned against the railing, watching as Varya cleaned herself up. "I'm sure she likes to think that. She's all bark though, and no bite. If she didn't want him, she'd have left by now."

"I promised to stay." Varya covered her face with the cloth, slowly breathing in and out so she didn't challenge the woman to another fight. "I will not go back on my word."

"And why not? Humans do all the time."

"Because I am nothing if I do not stand by my word."

"That sounds ridiculous." The sound of crunching footsteps approached, so Morag must have jumped the fence. Strong hands gripped hers, forcing the cloth to lower, so she had to look Morag in the eyes. But that gaze had softened, ever so slightly. More so than normal, at least. "If you want him, claim him. He is yours for the taking."

Was that the problem, though? He wasn't hers to take. Greed wanted to take from her, and that was it. He wanted her to submit, to be his, to be all right with his faults and not call him out on them.

Or maybe she was just... making it all up in her head. Maybe she couldn't change him because he didn't want to change. Maybe he would look at her one day and see an old woman. Therefore it was all a waste of time, anyway. She just wanted everything to work out on its own and instead, it felt like she had to fight tooth and nail to get anywhere at all.

Sighing, she pulled out of Morag's grip and shook the damp towel at her. "If it was that easy, don't you think I'd have already done that?"

"I think if it was that easy, you wouldn't even notice." Morag crossed her arms over her chest. "What is so wrong with Greed?"

"Everything!" Her shout carried across the arena and everyone who had been standing around scattered.

They raced away from the conversation they weren't supposed to hear. No one dared insult Greed himself. No one even dared overhear another insulting him.

Just their actions made her angry. Uncontrollably angry.

She flung her arms wide, gesturing at them as they all ran. "That! That's what I'm talking about. The servants won't even listen to someone speak ill of him, let alone hold him accountable for his actions. He's an ass, Morag. A selfish ass who only thinks of himself and what he wants and how he can keep what he wants because he can't fucking share."

"He thinks of you." Ivo leaned against the fence next to his sister, both of them watching her with all too knowing eyes. "He thinks of you every day and every night. You know you're the first thing he asks me about every morning? He has an entire kingdom to run, advisors who are all trying to stab him in the back, quite literally for some. And the first thing he wants to hear is how you are doing. The last thing he wants to hear? What you did during the day. All the things he missed."

Her chest hurt. Right over her heart that was supposed to avoid all these feelings and emotions and soft sounding words. Rubbing her chest, she shook her head. "He wants to collect me. That's what he wants."

"So what?" Ivo shrugged. "He worships everything that is his. And don't you want to collect him as well?"

"I don't collect people."

"So the idea of someone else touching him, lying in the same bed, commanding his attention as much as you do, is fine?" Ivo lifted a brow. "If you don't mind sharing him, I'm certain there are plenty of women willing to take your place. They'd flock to this castle as they always have done. I just have to let them know when."

That rage boiled over. She could feel it flushing through her cheeks, across her chest. It made her want to hit something. Not because he was hers. It couldn't be that. But because she was... was...

"Damn it," she muttered, glaring at Ivo, who looked all too proud of himself. "That isn't fair, and you know it."

"Is it not?"

"I can play dirty too, you know." She gestured between the two of them. "I'm the one who helped you with your little redheaded friend, remember? You be careful, Ivo, or I'll invite my friends and tell them about the pretty little gardener who doesn't have a single attachment in this castle."

The smug expression fell from his face, replaced with a scowl that would have seared the flesh from her bones if he had any magic to put with it.

Morag rolled her eyes. "The two of you are ridiculous. Jealousy has no place in either of your positions. Ivo, she's absolutely obsessed with you. The poor thing has been waiting for you to make a move for nigh on a year now, so would you grow a pair and just kiss the girl? Varya, you're a selfish little brat as well, so stop calling the kettle black when you're sitting on the same stove. Greed adores you. Probably loves you, even. He's waiting for you to forgive him and once you do, then all of us can go back to normal."

And with that, the sister walked away from them with a spring in her step and a jaunty whistle that echoed through the jungle leaves surrounding them.

She stood there, awkwardly, trying to look anywhere but Ivo considering they'd both thrown their own version of punches. She hadn't meant to threaten the gardener. Not really. Besides, none of her friends would be interested in someone who worked for the castle. Altan certainly would not be leaving his tiny desert town any time soon.

Damn it, she had to let go of her pride. Blowing out a long breath, she rolled her eyes up to the sky and tried her best. "I shouldn't have said anything about the gardener. I know you..."

"Her name is Bella," he muttered. "No one calls her by her name, but it's the most beautiful word I've ever heard."

It was strange, hearing a declaration like that from a man his size. He was massive. Taller than any person she'd ever seen, and yet he had no fear using words that were so soft they rivaled the down of a duckling.

"Ivo," she whispered, waiting until he looked back at her. "Can't you see what I want? You talk about Bella like she's the only person in the world that exists. You tell everyone who will listen about her beauty, grace, talent in the gardens, her kindness, how her smiles make you feel like you're made of liquid gold. All those words are so lovely and that is what I wish to hear about myself."

His face paled.

"No," she muttered, waving her hand at him. "Not like that. I don't want you to say them to me. I want Greed to say them to me. He's not a man of words, and he's said that to me already. But I need to hear those words. I need to hear him say that I'm important or that he even cares!"

The problem was laid out before her, and she hated it. She hated that she was weak enough to need those words. Everyone had a certain way to show the people they loved that they were loved, and Greed was a man of action. It was her own insecurities and weakness that made her need more from him.

It wasn't fair to Greed, she knew that. She understood that he only knew how to love in certain ways and that she couldn't expect anything else from him but...

She did.

She wanted more. Needed more. And he couldn't give her that.

Ivo ran a hand through his dark hair, the locks sticking up in all directions. "I don't think he can do that for you, Varya. Though I always thought he was quite good at talking to you. I'm on the other side of the door all the time, you know. So I hear more than I should."

Her face flamed. "That's not exactly when I need to hear him talk."

"Ah." Ivo nodded, his brows furrowed in concentration. "So that's why you tell him to shut up so often. I'd wondered. I thought women liked it when men told them they were a good girl and to—"

She had never moved so fast. One moment she was standing in front of him, and the next, she'd slapped her hand down over his mouth so hard it must have hurt.

Ivo's wide-eyed gaze met hers, obviously wondering what had just happened.

"Don't say that stuff in public," she hissed. "Private words for private times. If you want to tell Bella that, I'm sure she'll appreciate it, but people don't just talk about what should be said only in the bedroom where anyone could overhear them."

Laughter erupted at her words, coming from behind her at the same moment she felt warmth flood over her entire body. Greed. He was the only one who made her blush from head to toe just by being near.

After the laughter came the sound of clapping. She spun around to see both Greed and Gluttony stride into the arena. They both wore travel clothes, tighter pants than normal and a white billowing shirt. Matching, but oh so different. Where Gluttony was dark and tightly laced, Greed already looked as though he was halfway through taking his clothes off.

Rings glittered on his fingers, a heavy necklace hung around his neck. And she'd never wanted to snap a chain that badly. Just to see what he would do if she ruined another one of his precious gems.

"I'm glad to hear you aren't entertaining his words," Greed said, his mouth twisted in that handsome smile. "I'd have to take his tongue if he said any more to you."

"Greed," she hissed. "He's your friend."

"And you are mine."

He said the word so simply. As if there was no argument she could utter that would convince him otherwise. She was his. That was all. Nothing else could be added to that statement and it sent her heart racing.

"I suppose I am," she whispered, releasing Ivo, who straightened.

He ran a hand down his chest, seemed to think better of saying anything else, and then promptly left. Along with Gluttony, who was already asking some asinine question that Varya didn't care to listen to.

Her eyes were only for the demon standing too far away from her. The man who had sent her entire world upside down, inside out, and all wrong. But all right at the same time.

Perhaps some of her thoughts had shown on her face, because his expression flickered into something like pain before he reached out his hand for her to take. "Come with me, treasure. We have a lot to talk about."

By all the gods, she couldn't argue with him. Not like this.

So she slipped her hand into his, and let him lead her into the dark.

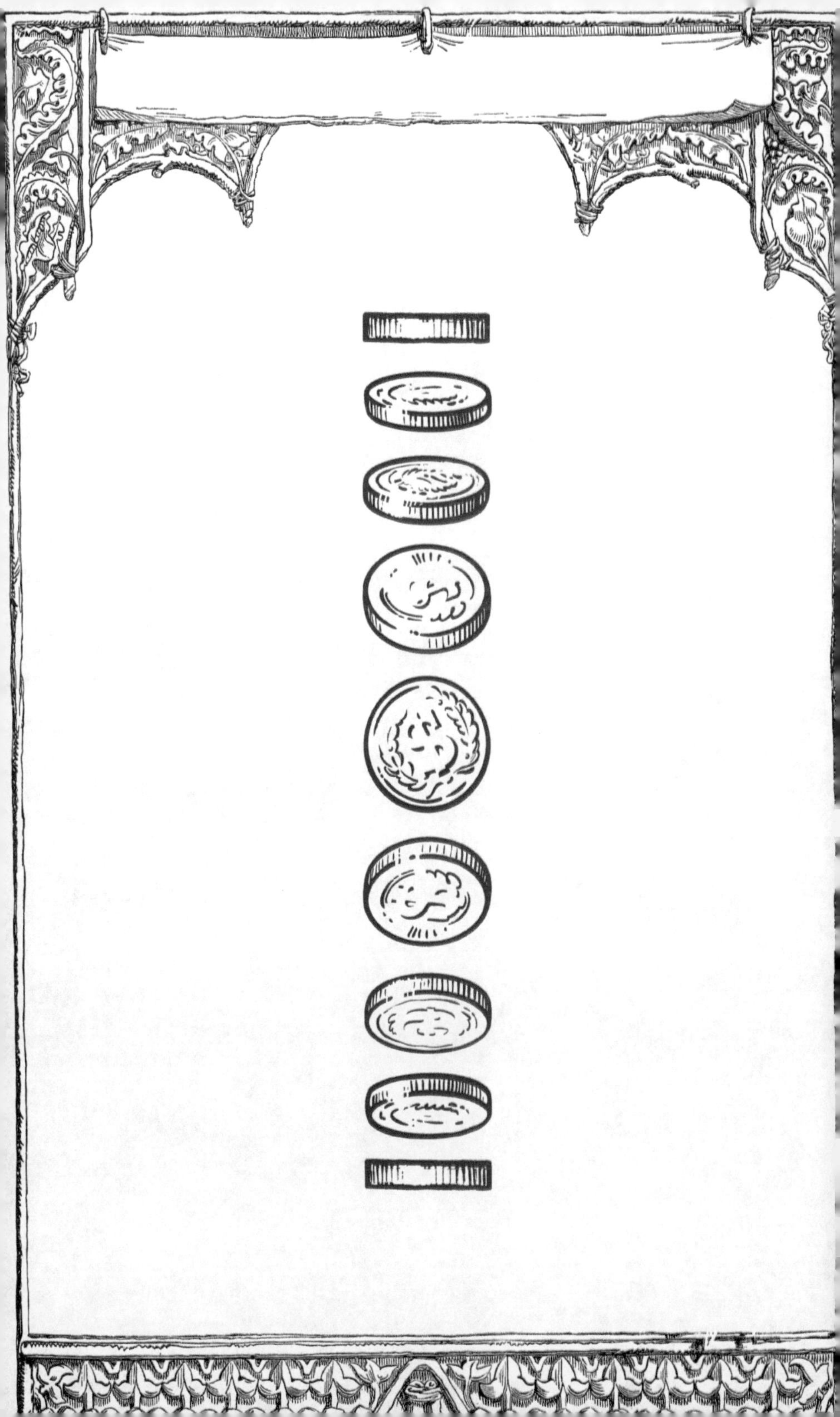

Chapter 36

Greed curved his much larger hand around hers, drawing her closer to his chest like he was in a dream. And maybe he was. This was the moment when he had to prove to himself and to her. They hadn't wasted their time. She would stay here with him, because she wanted to. Because she needed to. Because he provided for her as no one else had ever done in her life.

And that was the gift he was giving her. A gift that was as self serving as any other gift he'd given, perhaps even worse in the long run. He would make her immortal, and he couldn't do it without her permission.

He'd thought about it. On the ride back home, he'd let it play through his mind after allowing the spirit to feast on the people in her village.

Gluttony could hold her down for him. His brother wasn't squeamish about actions that were questionable, at best. And Gluttony would do it if Greed asked him. Together, they would hold her down, forcing her jaw open while Greed had to sit on her chest to keep her still. Then he would pour the soul down her throat, explain away that it would not be that bad. That she would live forever and the spirit wouldn't affect her.

But she'd be so angry with him. His Varya had always been the woman to make her own choices. She'd only lived for herself this entire life, and he couldn't take that away from her now. He had to let her know why he was doing this. The reason for all of it.

And that would be the hardest part. Greed hadn't lied, instead he'd just said nothing.

He drew her away from the arena, toward the massive leaves and jungle beyond. If she only gave him the chance to explain, maybe he could get the words past the knot in his throat. Maybe he could tell her how he adored her more than life itself and he wanted to give her the world on a platter if she'd take him.

"What did you want to talk about?" she asked as they ducked deeper into the oasis.

He didn't say a word until he'd drawn her to his favorite spot in his entire kingdom. A smaller waterfall, much smaller than it used to be, but the cascading water was a few feet taller than he was. He used to come out here and bathe every single day. Now, he gifted the secret of its existence to her.

Turning around, he caught her other hand in his and held them both against his rapidly beating heart. "Have I ever told you about my brother?"

Varya arched a brow. "You have told me very little about anything,

Greed."

Right. He hadn't been particularly good about sharing details of his life. She was right in their last argument. He used sex as a shield so he didn't have to tell her about the darker parts of himself. So he didn't have to admit that he was a flawed man and she shouldn't waste her time trying to get to know him. He was afraid of what she'd think if she knew who he was.

None of that came out of his mouth. Instead, he started talking about Lust.

"I went to visit Lust a while ago. The bridge between our kingdoms needed repairs, and I thought it was a good chance to snoop on his life. He had a new... we'll call her a distraction. At the time. And I'd never seen him quite so riled up. I thought I'd make it more difficult for him, because he'd never been all that interested in women. He used them, tossed them aside, found someone else to please. It was his way."

He looked up, staring into her eyes that were so confused. And he wondered how he was already fucking this up.

Taking a deep breath, Greed continued. "But then I saw him with her. And I'd never seen him like that before. He watched the way she moved, smiled when she talked, softened when she looked at him. This one was different. I didn't know why. She wasn't all that different from the countless other women he'd entertained himself with. And then... then she almost died."

He could still remember it. The metallic scent of blood on the air, the fear that rolled off Lust in waves. It had been a terrible few weeks while he watched his brother waste away to nothing. Lust hadn't been himself, and that had terrified Greed.

Varya stared at him like he'd lost his mind, and maybe he had. Though her brow at least wrinkled when she heard Lust's bride had almost died.

He licked his lips. "I saw what that did to him. I saw how it almost made him crumble. This impossibly strong demon king, nearly brought to the very end of his power because of a woman. At the time, I didn't understand it. I couldn't. He had fought so hard to be powerful, just as I had, and to throw that all away? All because this woman had been injured... It..."

He didn't know how to say the next part. Releasing her hands, he drew his fingers through his hair, which likely sent it rioting in all directions.

He must look like an idiot. Standing in front of her, fighting for words, incapable of just saying how he felt, but he couldn't do it. The words stuck in his throat, knotting up around his collarbone. Greed had spent his entire life becoming more impressive, more terrifying, everything that a warlord should be. He was the raging king who had destroyed this kingdom and then built it back in the image he most desired.

And this woman... right in front of him...

His body moved, pacing before her while his hands moved with his words. "I thought perhaps it was a weakness in him that I simply hadn't seen, and then the Horde captured me on my way home. I was ready to kill them all. There was plenty of rage left in me after dealing with Lust and seeing that gentle relationship between him and Selene. It made me want to hit something. And it made this awful feeling grow in my stomach that I still haven't named yet, but..."

He took a deep breath, stopped moving, and froze in front of her. "I met you."

The words stuck, harder to get out than anything he'd said before. "And I..."

She stared up at him, her eyes growing wider with every word he said. Each one, ripping out of his chest, tearing free from his body.

"Feel the same way."

He finally blurted the words out. He let them tear from his very soul and land at her feet like he'd torn out his own heart. It wasn't likely what she wanted to hear. It wasn't the pretty words he'd heard Ivo wax on about his lovely redheaded gardener, or the words that Lust had said to his bride. But they were words.

Words that she'd asked for. And damn it, he was trying.

Though she clearly had no idea where this came from—honestly, he didn't either—Varya kept her gaze on his face. He couldn't read the expression that flickered across her features, or understand why she reached out her hand and placed it softly on his forearm. She held her hand there, her thumb smoothing over his arm.

And her eyes softened, the same way Lust's always did, as she asked, "What happened to her?"

"To who?"

"The woman that Lust fell in love with."

Ah, of course. The woman who had almost died and torn his brother's heart from his chest. This was the harder part than admitting his feelings to her.

Greed swallowed hard. "He gave her a spirit to keep her alive. A spirit of affection, a good fit for her, though some might argue otherwise. It sacrificed itself, possessing her body but allowing her full control over their shared form. That act of sacrifice saved her life, and she is still alive today. Immortal and with him for the rest of their days."

Did she understand what he was trying to tell her? Could she understand that he needed her to be here, uninjured and not in pain, no matter where he was or how far she strayed from him?

This wasn't a gift, he realized. It was a desperate attempt at self preservation because if she said no to him, he feared he would implode.

Reaching into the bag around his waist, he drew out the jar where the adventure spirit still remained. It had gotten stronger, although not by much. Her old village wasn't quite as full of adventurous spirits as he'd thought. Still, it was better than it had been when they'd first found it. And the little thing was pulsing with excitement at having a body.

"This is for you," he breathed, handing the jar over to her.

His body vibrated as she lifted it up to the sun and stared into the green mist.

"What is it?" Varya asked.

"A spirit of adventure. A weak one, unfortunately, but I think it's a good match. For a woman who travels across the sands, seeking out magical artifacts in ancient tombs, I believe the two of you will get along quite well." He could only hope, at least. Otherwise, he'd need to find her another, and this one had been hard enough to find.

"Why did you bring me a spirit?" Apparently, he hadn't been as explicit as he thought he had.

Greed took a deep, steadying breath. "You are dying. All humans are. Every day brings you closer and closer to death. Perhaps I am a selfish ass, as you've pointed out before. But I cannot let you die, Varya. Not when you mean so much to me. Not when I have the ability to help."

With a slow sigh, she lowered the jar and held it closer to her chest. The spirit was already knocking against the glass, struggling to get a little closer to her. "Greed. I can't take this."

"I will not give you a choice if it comes to that. I want you to choose this, Varya, but..." He couldn't. He couldn't force her. That would be the stupidest thing he'd ever done. She'd hate him for the rest of his days, but maybe he would take that. It was better than nothing from her at all.

Her expression hardened. "You want me to kill a spirit?"

"It will not die. They live on in you. They see through your eyes, experience through your actions. It will still feed off of your emotions, but it will be safer than it was rolling around in that desert with no food at all." He took the risk. Greed stepped closer to her, cupping her cheek in his hand as though just that touch might anchor them together. "Please, Varya. I cannot lose you."

He saw her break. The resolve in her to not harm the spirit crumbled at his begging. And he would do so if she required him to get onto his knees because, for the first time in his life, he realized that he was terrified of losing someone else. Not just an object, but a person.

Greed pulled her closer to him, wrapping an arm around her waist and cupping the back of her head with his free hand. The jar pressed against his ribs, the pain anchoring him to this moment. "You are so fragile. So delicate. And I know you don't want to hear that because you are one of the strongest women I have ever met, but you are just human, Varya. A plague could kill you in an instant. A wound that goes sour. A fall from a cliff edge or a tomb that outwits you. The fear for your life has consumed me and I cannot endure the pain any longer. I need you here with me."

"Why?" she whispered, her eyes glimmering with what he hoped weren't tears. "Why do you need me here?"

He pressed their foreheads together, soaking in the feel of her. It had been too long since he'd been able to touch her. To feel the power of her body rolling against his own. "I just do. I cannot explain it, Varya, but I do."

Perhaps it wasn't enough. Perhaps she needed to hear him say the words that he feared weren't the truth. He was Greed. A demon king. He couldn't love anyone but himself, unless loving her could change him. Just as it had changed Lust.

She took a deep, steadying breath, and then he felt her nod against him. "All right."

"All right?" He leaned back to be sure. "You'll do it?"

"Yes." Again she nodded, staring down at the jar still clutched in her hands. "I don't know how, though."

"I do." Thankfully.

It was a little different than bringing Ivo and Morag to life. Those had been spirits he fed on his own until they were strong enough to conjure an image that was powerful and strong, just like himself. This was a possession. A little different, but he'd seen Affection and Selene do it. Surely he could replicate that.

Honestly, the adventure spirit likely knew what to do.

Greed reached between them and uncapped the jar. The sickly spirit slithered out of its container, barely able to drag its body over the lip of the glass. And a small spark of worry skittered down his spine. What would happen if he allowed a weak spirit to possess her? Would she need to feed the spirit first? What would that do to the both of them?

He didn't have time to question this choice, though. The spirit made its way up her arm, gathering itself up as though this was the most arduous battle of its life. When it reached her neck, the exhausted spirit paused, hanging off her collarbone as though it had no more fight left in it.

"What now?" she asked, her eyes flicking back and forth between him and the green mist on the shoulder.

"I thought…" Affection had melted into Selene, but it had been a significantly stronger than this one.

With gentle hands, he cupped the tiny spirit in his palms and drew it closer to Varya's mouth. He didn't know where the knowledge came from, perhaps some age old feeling from when he'd been the same as this little one. He remembered what it felt like to be so weak that he could barely move. He remembered lying in a gutter and waiting for his existence to end until someone had walked by after pick pocketing a man.

"Consume it," he whispered, pouring the spirit toward her mouth as though it were an elixir of immortality.

Because it was. It had to be. For her, he would do anything.

Varya trusted him. She opened her mouth, and the spirit slithered past her lips. Pouring into her body and then disappearing.

They waited. Heartbeats drumming in his ears with every passing second. Maybe he'd been wrong. Maybe this spirit was strong enough to exist inside her without feeding too much, after all.

"What—" Varya's eyes widened for a moment before they drifted shut.

Greed caught her in his arms, a low grumble of fear rocking through him. "I'll take care of you, love," he said, swinging her up into his arms. "You'll be fine, Varya. I promise."

Chapter 37

Her awareness came in fits. Mostly she was lost in the darkness of a deep, dreamless sleep that should have been terrifying. Was this death, she found herself wondering a few times. Was this what it felt like to slip into that bitter darkness that never allowed her to wake?

Hissing out a breath, she sat straight up in bed. Clinging to the sheets, she held them against her chest as she tried to get her bearings. Where was she?

She couldn't quite remember what was happening. She'd been... in the jungle? No, there were no jungles in this kingdom. Only sand. Dust. The overheated sun that made her sweat, just like she was doing now. Dripping with all the emotion that she couldn't shake off her body because this was wrong. She was wrong. Something was very,

very wrong.

"Shh." A voice. The same voice that had soothed her time and time again. "Stop fighting it, treasure."

Stop fighting what? The fever? The heat that billowed off her body and slicked her skin with so much sweat she couldn't think or breathe through it? She had to fight it. It would kill her. Didn't he know fevers were deadly to humans?

She needed to get out of this bed. A bath. Water would cool her off, and maybe then she could think or remember what had happened.

Cool hands skimmed down her shoulders, sliding over her bare skin with a little too much ease. "It's all right," he said, his voice deep and low and oh so soothing. "You are well. It is the spirit inside you, remember? You are giving it a chance at life, Varya, and it will make you immortal in return."

"I didn't want to do this," she whispered. "I don't want to be immortal."

"Ach, my love." She felt his lips against her shoulder now, pressing so delicately that it made tears prick in her eyes. "It's not something you can take back."

His love.

She'd always known she was his love, hadn't she? She had just wanted to hear it from his lips and then everything would be all right. Well, she'd heard it now. And everything would be all right. He'd watch over her and make sure that nothing happened, no matter how hard it was to keep her eyes open.

She drifted again. Back into that dreamless place that frightened her as much as it was a comfort. At least here she didn't have to think about anything. She just floated in the darkness. Nothing and everything all at once.

The next time she woke, she felt a bit more like herself. Varya could remember the choice she'd made, how she had ended up in this familiar bed, covered in silken sheets that clung to her sticky body. Stretching out her arm, she searched for him.

And then she remembered that he'd never been too far. How many times had she woken in a panic? The illness that spread through her body had consumed her mind, as well as heating her from the very core. He'd explained with so much patience countless times, telling her that she was all right, he was with her, he wouldn't let any harm come to her.

By the gods, he'd been amazing. And she'd been... less than amazing.

Sitting up, her long hair a tangle around her face, she held the blankets against her chest and tried to still the rolling nausea from the movement. She wasn't entirely herself, it seemed, but this was significantly better than before.

Bathing would be a good option first, then food, then water. Oh, she needed something to drink. Her mouth was so dry, her tongue stuck to the roof of her mouth.

The door to the room opened and Greed slipped inside. He had a tray balanced in one hand, clearly trying to not make a single sound. He even exaggerated his steps as he closed the door so slowly that it didn't make a sound as it clicked shut.

Was he... tip-toeing? He was! Just gliding across the floor as he stared at the tray with so much concentration. Like he didn't want the single cup to touch the single plate. As though making no sound at all was life or death, and if he did, then everything would crumble down around his ears.

This darling, dear, ridiculous man who wanted nothing more than to take care of her. He wanted to treat her like a queen. Like the most precious item he owned and for once in her life, Varya couldn't decide if that was a good thing or a bad thing.

He had done so much wrong. She was mad at him for so much.

And yet he looked like a complete idiot trying to be quiet when his big body already thudded hard against the floor. He was a bull, rushing into the room but trying his best to be quiet as a mouse.

"I'm awake," she said, her voice filled with wry amusement.

Greed almost dropped the tray. But he got ahold of it before it toppled over, balancing everything in a wobble that should have sent the glass to the floor. Somehow, he recovered.

She might have laughed if his eyes hadn't found hers. And the relief she saw there, the hope that burned through him like a fire... Ah, it made her burn too.

"Varya," he said, his voice strained. He rushed to her side, setting the tray on the table beside the bed before sitting down at the edge.

She'd thought he would be gentle. He certainly had been the entire time she'd been fighting with the spirit. And he still was. But he didn't ask permission to reach out and run his hand down her bare back. And he didn't ask if he could skim his lips down her shoulder, sending goosebumps scattering across her body.

"You're awake," he whispered against her skin.

And how did she respond to the reverence in those words?

Varya leaned closer to him, wincing as soon as she smelled herself. "And I haven't bathed in how long?"

"A week." He pressed another kiss closer to her neck. "A week of utter torment."

"I thought you said the spirit would heal me."

"It will now. It was too weak to stay inside your body, so it had to feed upon you or be expelled." His voice deepened, a little gruff and angry if she heard it right. "I should have guessed it would do that. I should have known."

Maybe he should have. She couldn't have guessed it.

But Varya felt... stronger. More powerful. More capable than she had in a very long time. As she stretched out her arm, staring at the muscle as though she'd never seen it before, she could almost feel the little spirit inside of her.

"Should I be able to know it's there?" she asked, her voice low and quiet.

"No." He moved her tangled hair out of his way, his lips skimming over the long column of her throat. "It will be as if it is not there at all."

But she could feel it. The heat that burned through her before was much less than the fever she'd been suffering from, but it was still there. And it wasn't her. She could almost sense the strangeness that moved through her body at its own whim. First in her arms and hands, then into her belly, where it coiled up. A life, inside her. Not a baby, but a spirit that lived deep inside her very being.

"Come on," Greed said, his hand petting through her hair. "Let's get you clean. If you feel well enough?"

She did. She thought. Maybe she shouldn't move, but a bath sounded lovely. Almost enough to distract her from the strange spirit deep inside her body that already seemed to stir again at her thoughts.

At her nod, Greed scooped her up in his arms. Gentle, oh so gentle. Didn't he know she was stronger now? He didn't have to treat her like she was made of glass, even though it felt rather nice to have him holding her.

Again, like the last time they'd bathed together, he didn't remove his clothing. He just strode into the water of the pool with her. Greed held her tightly against himself, almost as though he didn't quite trust himself to let her go.

And that was ridiculous, wasn't it?

That power stretched inside her again, unfurling like a bloom with soft petals dancing in her mind.

"What an adventure it would be to test him," it said. "Perhaps we should push. Just a bit. How deep do you think that well of patience goes?"

It was wrong. So wrong. She shouldn't push him when he seemed so focused on making sure that she was well.

He poured soap into his palms, lathering it between his hands before he started on her shoulders. His fingers dug into her muscles and she couldn't help herself. A low moan erupted from between her lips.

He stilled behind her, shifting ever so slightly back before he cleared his throat and continued.

"Again," the voice whispered in her mind. "What a thrill."

She shouldn't. The temptation, though... It was too hard to ignore. Varya arched her back, lifting her arms over her head in a stretch that displayed her body for him to stare at. One more light twist of her hips and she pressed up against him, his hardness sliding between her cheeks.

Rocking against him only flared that need inside her a little brighter. It wasn't much of an adventure, it was no tomb to raid or endless dunes to gallop across. But she had no idea what he would do next. And that little thrill was enough to satisfy.

A low growl rumbled in her ear. "Careful, treasure."

"Why?"

"You are still not well."

"I'm well enough."

Well enough for this, at least. He was touching her too carefully, with too much intent. She wanted his hands, hot and hard, on her hips as he held her in place. She wanted to hear him panting, grunting, straining against her as he worked himself into a frenzy. She wanted… Wanted…

Another rumble against her back distracted her from those thoughts, even as his soapy hand slid over her belly. "Something is different about you. I cannot tell what it is."

She could. The spirit he'd given her was running the show right now. Though, she was still very aware that she had a choice in this matter. But she didn't want to choose. They both agreed on what they wanted to do.

The man they adored, probably loved, was right behind them. They were both slippery and alive.

What an adventure it would be to try this in the pool, as well. What a wonderful, thrilling, exciting time to be had.

Some thought in her mind blared with anxiety. This wasn't like her at all, and Varya had never been one to actively seek out the most dangerous parts of her life. She'd always had some knowledge of when she needed to be careful. But right now? That wasn't there at all. The natural ability to realize when something was going to be dangerous had flung itself out of her body.

Turning in his arms, she plastered herself against his chest. Her hands made quick work at the belt of his pants, tugging it free and letting it sink to the bottom of the pool around their feet.

"I'm alive," she said, moving him through the water until his back hit the edge of the pool. "I'm alive and you're alive and I don't want to waste a single second of that."

His throat bobbed in a swallow. "Varya."

"Greed." She hummed low in her throat, her lips going to his neck as he had just teased her before. He smelled like man and musk and bright, glorious sunlight.

She wanted to bite him.

"Bite him," the thought echoed in her mind. "Mark him. Claim him. He's yours for the taking, isn't that why he gave me to you?"

With a little moan, she let the spirit make the choice. She didn't bite him hard, just a light nip against the vein in his neck that thrummed against her lips. His heart beat pounded and her teeth closed down on him.

It was like she'd struck him with lightning.

He wrapped an arm around her waist, flipping them so her front was pressed against the cool stones and his hot body lined up perfectly with hers. The warm head of his cock slid through her folds, stroking and teasing, mimicking what she wanted him to do.

His hand coiled in her tangled hair, tugging her neck back so she was forced to arch, pressing herself harder against him.

"Is this what you want?" he growled in her ear. "You're supposed to be healing, and this is what you beg for?"

"Yes," she hissed. Varya ground her hips against him, trying to coax him to slip inside her.

Greed was not so kind. He used her hair as reins, holding her in place for his touch as his free hand slid between them. He touched her, his thick fingers sliding inside, stroking her inner walls in a tempo that wasn't enough. Would never be enough.

His thumb slid over the puckered hole that no one else had ever touched. "This is mine," he snarled, his cock pressing against her entrance, but never quite pushing all the way inside. "You are mine, all of you, every moan, every gasp, every whimper."

Anger rose in her chest. Defiance against his words as she rolled her hips, tempting him, showing him who owned who. "Tell yourself whatever you need to hear," she hissed. "We both know who belongs to who."

With a grunt, he pushed inside her. One powerful thrust that shoved a wave over the stones near her hands and spilling out onto the floor. But the feel of him... Oh, she'd missed him. Too big, too much, and yet never quite enough.

He was everywhere. His hand now holding one of her breasts, her hair tumbling free as he grabbed onto her hip, anchoring her to him as he rutted against her like a beast possessed.

She was the one possessed. She was the one who wanted to consume him, brand him, mark him so that he knew no matter how many times he said he owned her, he didn't. He was hers. He'd been the one to find her a spirit, so she was immortal. No one else would ever worship her the way he did, and she claimed that here and now.

And as he worshiped at the altar of her body, his grunts echoed in her ears. She hissed out words that sounded like, "Faster, harder. Fuck me, damn it." It all made sense.

He wanted to claim her, but she wanted him to worship her.

They'd both been fighting for the same thing. Wanting the same thing.

And as his fingers pinched her nipple hard, forcing her mind back into this moment, with him and no one else, Varya realized this was right. Together. They were meant to be doing this even as the waves rose higher with each of his powerful thrusts.

She was his. He was hers. They owned each other, body, mind, and soul.

With a gasp, she coiled tighter around him. Clenching, squeezing, hearing the curse as he felt her react.

"That's it, treasure," he grunted, somehow pushing inside her even harder. "Give it to me."

And together they spiraled out of control. She felt herself sinking, that spirit inside her appeased by the madness of their frantic fucking. And she felt the heat of him spurting inside her, his thrusts slowing as he leaned over her.

His panting breaths brushed against the back of her neck even as he slid his hand up her bare back. There were no words in this moment. Nothing they could say.

Only the knowledge that everything had changed.

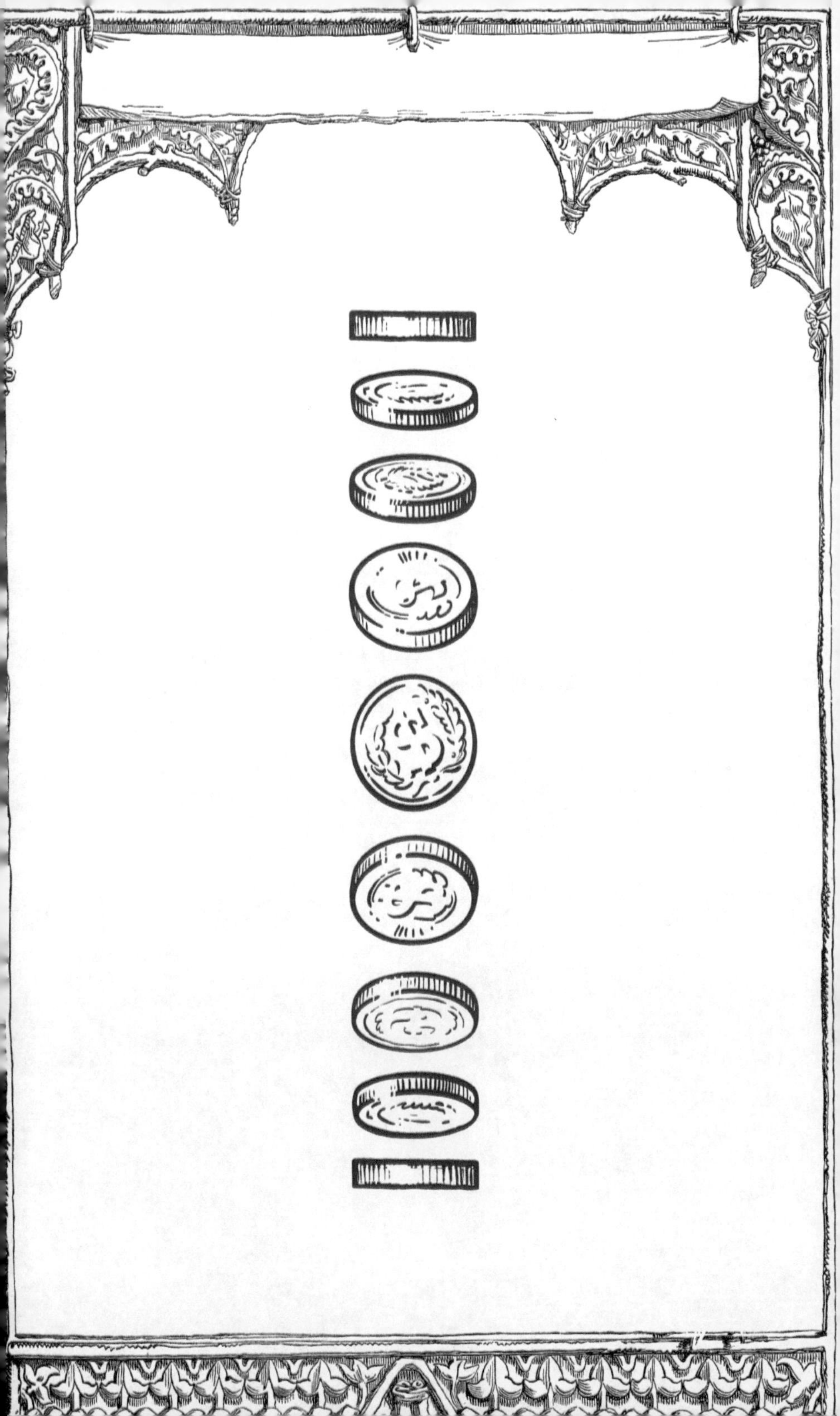

Chapter 38

He hated to admit it, but he lost himself in her for a while. Varya reacted to him like she couldn't get enough of his touch, his taste, anything that she could get her hands on. He made sure she was fed and hydrated, and then he fucked her into oblivion.

He'd never once thought that he would meet a woman with a passion as deep as his. Greed was always the partner who asked for too much. Who had to wait while the other person recovered, while his skin itched for more.

With Varya? For the first time in his life, he'd had to leave a bedchamber before he hurt himself. His cock actually ached. There were bruises all down his ribs and hips where she'd held onto him a little too hard, and scratch marks down his back that had long ago started to bleed.

It was... Perfect.

And of course, he'd told her a few more details about himself in the short breaks they took. He told her stories about visiting Lust's kingdom, about how he'd cornered Selene and made her realize that she actually wanted his brother more than she could admit.

In return, she told him stories about growing up in his kingdom. Troubling stories where she recounted spending hours upon hours searching for food and water. Living on the streets after her parents died, while Altan kept her safe. She'd been the runt of the pack of children that roamed those streets.

Though he hated the man for having claim to what was Greed's, he could also see that he owed Altan his thanks. Without the desert stranger, Varya very well might not be here.

He closed the door carefully behind him, trying his best to not wake up the sleeping beauty who had proven herself almost too ravenous for him. Though Greed could admit that might be the spirit he'd poured inside of her.

She wasn't acting like the same woman he knew so well. And potentially lo—

He stopped himself before the thought even came to life. He didn't love her, he couldn't love her, and nothing had changed for him. Unlike his brother, Greed was so deeply rooted in his own emotion that he would remain this way forever.

Varya would be all right with that. She didn't expect or want him to change, and there was beauty in that. She loved him for who he was, and he was certain that she loved him. He'd asked for every emotion from her, and the woman was a giver.

A shudder ran down his spine and buried itself in his tailbone.

Just the thought of how good she "gave" made him want to turn back around and wake her up.

Fuck waiting. Who cared if he rubbed himself raw? This was worth it.

He'd already turned before his brain caught up with him. If he was sore, then she was as well. And he had to take care of her. His most precious treasure could not be harmed or dented by anyone. Not even himself.

So he dragged his exhausted body to the kitchens, preparing to at least get some food into himself before he keeled over. Thankfully, it was still nighttime and none of the servants would see his staggering pace or the scratches down his chest. And there were plenty of those.

He shouldered the door open, staring down at the marks with a soft smile on his face. He'd found himself a lioness. Even though she'd made it clear she wanted to know more about him, that hadn't dulled her need. In fact, the more he told her about himself, the more she wanted him.

He hadn't thought... Well. How could he think at all when she was on her knees, staring up at him with hollowed cheeks and a moan vibrating her throat?

"Fuck," he muttered, running a hand through his hair as he steered his body toward the back room where they kept the food.

"It does seem like you've been doing that, yes." His brother's amused tone did not amuse him.

Greed spun around, his tongue already sharpening to lash out at his brother, only to realize that Gluttony was eating with both Ivo and Morag. The three of them blinked at him, not tired at all, and his hackles rose.

"What are all of you doing here?" he grumbled, grabbing for the nearest item of food, which happened to be a rather large head of lettuce.

"Greed," Ivo said, his voice pitched low, as though he didn't want to startle the confused demon in front of him. "Perhaps you should put that down and maybe have a glass of water."

"I've had water."

Gluttony snorted into his cup as he lifted it. "Clearly you haven't been drinking anything other than what comes from between your lady's legs."

There was a moment of stunned silence before all the idiots burst into riotous laughter. Their entire bodies shook, the table squeaked against the floor, and he thought Morag was going to break the cup in her hand. None of them had any food, and he could smell the alcohol in the air, so he supposed he couldn't blame them for their laughter.

"Yes, yes," he muttered, turning around to find actual food. "Laugh all you want. At least I've spent time between my lady's legs, while the rest of you lot have been wallowing here."

Morag snorted. "Maybe those two have. I've been busy myself."

Since when? He hadn't ever heard her say she had any interest in anyone.

Frowning, Greed grabbed a loaf of bread, jam, and thinly sliced meat before joining them at the table in the center of the kitchen. "So these two sad saps are the only ones not finding their little death?"

Morag gave him a feral nod. "Indeed."

"For once, you and I are the favored ones." He grabbed Gluttony's mug and clinked it with hers before draining the burning liquid inside.

They'd gotten into his barrels of whiskey, he realized. Those barrels were hard for anyone to find, so obviously his two most trusted guards had given him up.

Assholes.

Digging into his food, he ignored their ribbing as he tried to fuel his body once more. His stomach clenched at the scent of food and a wave of dizziness nearly unseated him. Greed wasn't certain he even breathed as he dug into the meat and bread like an animal, not pausing until his stomach was finally satisfied and the shakes left his legs.

Sighing, he leaned back in his chair and gestured for a mug of his own. "The least you can do is give me a drink to get through your incessant chatter."

"Incessant!" Gluttony repeated, but he slid over a clean mug that was brimming with whiskey. "It's like you didn't care if anyone knew you were fucking her into oblivion."

"We weren't gone that long," he grumbled.

"Three days, actually. Three days the entire castle had to listen to the echoing sounds of your grunts, her moans, and a lot of—" Gluttony smacked his hands together over and over.

The two other idiots at the table dissolved into laughter once again. Ivo flopped down on the table, his cheek pressed against the cool wood as mirth shook through his massive frame. It took a while for them all to gather themselves, and for the burning in Greed's cheeks to ease.

"All of you shut up," he grumbled when they could all breathe. "At least you know I'm doing my job right."

"Ah, and was it the job you wanted?" Gluttony's grin hadn't moved from his face. "You were the one saying you weren't certain if you loved the girl just a week ago, brother. What changed?"

And all the mirth disappeared. Because realistically, nothing had changed. He was fighting against whatever emotion this was, but he also knew damn well that there was nothing he could do about it.

Greed wasn't Lust. He hadn't found the woman of his dreams and then fixed himself, or whatever it was that was the problem.

Jerking his chin at Ivo and Morag, he pointed them to the door. "Go on. There are better things for my guards to be doing."

"Is there?" Morag asked, her brow raising. "We are supposed to watch over you."

"And some conversations are for demon kings alone." Then he pointedly stared at Ivo, who had yet to lift his head from the table. "And you've drunk your brother into a stupor. He needs sleep, Morag."

His guard grumbled, but she hauled her brother up by the armpits and helped him out of the room. Though his ankles kept twisting over each other, she did eventually close the door behind them.

If she was listening at the door, he didn't care. He just wasn't able to look her in the eyes while he admitted this to his brother.

Gluttony leaned forward, hands laced around his mug, those red eyes seeing far too much. "You're troubled. Are you regretting finding that spirit and putting it inside her?"

He swallowed another gulp of whiskey to steel himself for the truth. "No. I don't regret that in the slightest."

"Then what's the problem? You've spent the past couple of days in nirvana, so I don't know why you're upset." Gluttony tilted his head to the side, clearly trying to see underneath his skin and get into the meat of the issue.

Greed hated that his brother always did that. Even when they were spirits, Gluttony hadn't been picky about his food sources. At least Greed wanted to steal and take only objects. Gluttony? He would feed off whatever he could. Information, people, a gluttony for punishment or knowledge or power, no matter what he did.

Sighing, he rolled his eyes up to the ceiling and let the worries spill out of him. "I didn't change."

Only silence was his brother's response.

"Lust did," Greed ground out. "He's off, defeating his own demons, becoming the better version of himself because he poured that spirit into his love, and now he's something that none of us have ever achieved."

"Which is?"

"You were the one that put this thought into my mind!" Greed slammed his fist down on the table, shaking the mugs and plates. "You were the one who said we were the demons, the monsters, the ones with something wrong with them. And here I was, believing everything was fine until you wriggled your way into my head, you fucking asshole!"

Gluttony leaned back against his chair, looking far too pleased with himself. "I just wanted one of my brothers to agree with me. I wanted you to see that there is something wrong with our lives. I never said we could change."

"Lust proved that we can."

Gluttony rolled his eyes. "Lust was always the fickle one. He was more likely to change than any of us. He never really wanted to be Lust, yeah? He wanted people to love him, to adore him, to follow him to his bed blindly. What better for a spirit like that than to turn to love?"

He wasn't following. And apparently, the furrows on his brow gave him away.

Blowing out a long breath, Gluttony took another deep drink before he explained. "Lust and love go hand in hand. How many humans have you seen that spent time in each other's bed, only to realize later on that they were rather destined for it? You and I aren't like him. We aren't Lust. It's hard to fix Greed or Gluttony, or Envy for that matter. Lust can easily change. The rest of us? That's a work in progress that might never be fixed."

He didn't want to hear that, though. Maybe he didn't want to be the demon king who couldn't control himself. Maybe he wanted to be a better person. For her. Because she wanted him to be someone else, and that wasn't fair to him when he knew it would be almost impossible for him to change at all.

"Greed," Gluttony said, leaning forward and shaking Greed's almost empty mug. "Let go of this dream. You won't change for her, because people don't change for others. That's not how it happens. We change for ourselves, and you are still yourself. Still greedy. Still putting a spirit inside her because that will keep her cleaved to you for all eternity. Still fucking her within an inch of her life while ignoring your kingdom because you want to. That is your vice, just as mine is to consume and devour and… Kill."

He hissed the last word, muttering it underneath his breath with a darker tone than Greed had ever heard from his brother. Almost as though Gluttony didn't want to do what he had done. Or continued to do.

"I suppose you're right," he muttered. "We all have our vices."

"Indeed we do. And fixing those takes a lot more than a lucky woman who thinks it's smart to waste her life with us." Gluttony lifted his mug, waiting for Greed to cheers him. "What more could we ask for, brother, but a willing woman and a kingdom at our feet?"

Greed could ask for people who didn't run from him in fear. He could ask for that woman to look at him with wide, prideful eyes. He could ask for once, just once in his life, to feel like a good person when all he'd done was take for himself.

Instead of saying any of that, Greed clinked their mugs together. Because he knew that Gluttony felt the same. The darkness that gathered in his brother was very similar to his own.

They both hated themselves. They both lived in that cesspool of their mind, berating their own actions as they became the monsters they claimed they weren't.

Neither of them believed in themselves. And worse? Neither of them really wanted to.

They'd accepted the darkness a long time ago. And that meant that they were here, alone with each other. Still just as bitter and exhausted as ever.

Sighing into his cup, he slumped in the chair and stared at the table. Gluttony mimicked his posture, just as morose as he felt.

Greed wanted to be more for her. By all the kingdoms, he'd thought this would work. He'd thought they would awaken soon enough and he would feel different. That he would have changed into something newer, better, more for her. Because she made him want to be a better man.

But apparently, just as his brother had said, it didn't work like that. He would not change for her, he had to change for himself.

Damn. He didn't think he could do that. And deep in his heart, he feared he didn't want to.

Chapter 39

S he had woken when he left, but Varya hadn't wanted him to know. Even though her entire body was slick with sweat and other fluid she didn't want to think about, she was still ready for him. She'd wanted him to come back, slide underneath the covers, and give her all the attention that she so desperately wanted.

It had never been enough. No matter how many times he made her clench around that beautiful, thick cock, it wasn't enough. And not because her body wanted more. No, she was more sore between her legs than she'd ever been in her life. She wanted more because the spirit inside her wanted to push a little harder.

Just what would happen if she did this? What if she arched her back like so? What would happen if she used a little teeth, even though he'd hissed at her not to do it?

Varya wasn't complaining. The spirit had very interesting ideas that she agreed with. What she couldn't understand was why it was in her head, talking as though it was another person existing inside her body.

Once the door closed, she sat straight up in bed. "Are you listening to me?"

"Yes."

"How long are you gong to be able to listen to me?" She tilted her head to the side, wondering if this was just the beginning stages of the bond and if it would fade away.

"Forever if you wish." The spirit seemed to hesitate before adding, "Unless you wish me to go."

Did she want the little spirit to be gone? It was rather unnerving to have someone else talking to her inside her head. Varya hadn't been quite so aware of her own thoughts in a very long time. It had always just been her own voice and now it was two people, and that was rather disorienting.

But she didn't mind the thoughts that it gave her, and she didn't mind the suggestions it liked to give so... Well, maybe they could try it a little while?

"How long do I have to make a choice before we're stuck with each other?" she asked.

"We're already stuck with each other. I live inside you."

Right. Well.

How strange was it that she was talking to thin air? Varya wasn't certain that she'd get over this.

Running a hand through her hair, she stood up and went to get dressed. Of course, her clothes were everywhere, and it took a rather long time to even find them. Why were her pants hanging up there on that leaf?

A flash of memory had a vision of Greed in her mind, his eyes flashing yellow and slitted like a cat while he peeled these pants off her the last time she'd tried to put them on. He'd thrown them over his shoulder before diving between her thighs with a growl that still made a shudder dance down her spine.

Ah, but that man did make her quiver. Even the spirit inside her did a little shake, shuddering underneath her ribcage in a rather concerning movement before its attention turned to something else.

"You're still thinking about your family," it whispered in her mind. "You think they are in danger."

Of course she did.

The Horde hadn't disappeared just because she wasn't there. They would continue to fight and claw and tear away at the world until they got what they wanted. And therein lay the problem.

She was here. Safe and sound and well taken care of. Well fucked, as well, if she were being honest with herself. While the rest of her people stayed in their homes, terrified and uncertain of their future.

"Wouldn't it be an adventure to sneak out?" The little spirit said, vibrating so hard that she could feel the hairs on her arms rise. "We could leave right now, he wouldn't know. He's with his brother. You've already stolen one of his mounts before, and then we'd disappear into the sands too quickly for him to catch. The dunes will hide us, and then we can find your people. We could gather them into an army! We could—"

She had to stop the spirit before it started making more sense than it already did. "I promised I wouldn't do that."

The door creaked open and her eyes flew to Greed, standing in the doorway. Though she'd expected him to be angry, that perhaps his eyes would flash with more anger than ever before, he only looked tired.

"Promised you wouldn't do what, treasure?"

She should lie.

She should tell him something that would make him forget this ever happened. Or fall to her knees again and draw him into her mouth, since she knew he loved that so much.

But she couldn't lie. Not now. Not when her heart thudded hard in her chest at the sight of him, and when her entire body clenched to be nearer to him.

They didn't really know each other. Or maybe they did. Maybe her heart knew his, and she was the only one holding them back.

So instead of lying, she chose a better path. "The spirit you gave me isn't quiet, Greed. I'd argue that it's quite loud."

He tilted his head to the side, nostrils flaring with some unnamed emotion before he cleared his throat. "What did you say?"

"I said, it talks. A lot. Most of the time I don't even realize that it's talking, but it's gotten better at speaking in my head and, to be honest, the ideas that it tells me are rather good ideas. I was just telling it we will not be sneaking out the window and stealing another mount, even though it's quite convinced that the last time we did it was an adventure. And I'll be honest, since you gave it to me, I have been more likely to seek out adventure in a much less... careful manner than I'm used to."

Oh gods, he was turning rather sickly pale. His normally sun-tanned and freckled face approached the color of parchment, and that wasn't right at all.

Even though she still wore nothing but her skin, she darted forward and grabbed his elbow. He listed to the side before she caught him up, wedging herself under his arm and drawing him closer to the bed. "Come on. Easy, now. You're a big man to fall that far, and don't expect me to catch you."

He grunted before landing hard on the bed. She sat down next to him, skating her hand over his back as he seemed to struggle to piece these thoughts together.

"The spirit—" he started, then stopped, staring at her hand when she placed it on his leg.

She felt it too. The strange desire to pick up where they had left off. Like they hadn't gotten their fill when they'd been so deep in each other's bodies that she knew every wrinkle, every scar, and every hidden place like it was her own. She wanted to touch more of him, to hold him tighter inside her body for just a few more moments.

Maybe because it felt like things were going to shatter into a million piece at any point. Like everything was going to break and they would get none of it back.

"The spirit is talking, yes." She turned her hand over, pressing the back of it to his leg while she waited for him to take her hand. "I know it's not what you expected, but it's happening and we will move forward from here."

His fingers laced through hers. "And you do not mind this new... situation?"

"I don't think so," Varya chuckled. "I don't know what to think. This all has been so strange. First you tell me I'm immortal, then you give me a spirit who talks in my head. I have moments where I wonder if this was all some fever dream and I'm going to wake up any second realizing I've been in this bed the whole time and that you've been trying to heal me."

Even though she knew that couldn't be the case, she still had that vague thought in the back of her mind. What if she'd conjured all this up? What if she had made it up in her head that he had spent so much time making sure she felt loved, honored, and cherished?

He lifted her hand and pressed it to his lips. "You are here, Varya. This is not a dream, though it is my honor to hear that you believe it is a dream to be with me."

She felt her cheeks burn. "Stop that."

"Stop what?" His tongue slipped out, tracing between her fingers before he pressed one more kiss there. "I cannot get enough of you, woman. That should tell you all you need to know about how I feel."

Did it? Not really. She wanted to hear the words as well, but they'd get there. She had to believe that.

"It wants me to save my people." She traced her fingers over his, keeping her touch gentle and soothing. "I want to do that as well. Perhaps the spirit only amplifies the feelings that are deep inside me."

"You want to run?"

"I don't know." No, that wasn't quite right. She knew the answer to that. "I don't want to run from you. I don't want you to be angry at me again, or to feel like I've betrayed you somehow. But I cannot linger here in this luxury as you do."

Varya looked at him, then. At the fine cloth that clung to his body, the loose pants made of silk, even though her own people wore scratchy cotton and wool. At the rings that always decorated his fingers and the gold clips in his hair that swung from tiny braids.

"You are Greed," she whispered. "I know that means you will take whatever you can and make no apologies for it. But I am not you."

"I know we are very different. But I…" He paused at the thought, perhaps trying to figure out a better way to tell her no. And she knew he was going to say it, long before he did. "I cannot risk you again, Varya. The idea of losing you tears me apart. And I have no wish to see you harmed."

"That's why you gave me this spirit, didn't you? So it could heal me if I did get harmed."

"You can still lose your head. We are immortal, not deathless."

And she was willing to risk that, if that's what it came to. If her people were alive and better off without the Horde? Then she would gladly lose her head.

But he would not turn into a different man, not for her, and Varya still loved him. She felt that knowledge settle in her mind. For all his folly, for all his faults, she loved him.

And damn it, that meant she had to come at this in a different way. A way that would make him see the reasoning behind it.

Varya slid off the bed onto her knees in front of him. She moved so his thighs were on either side of her, the same position she'd found herself in many times throughout the past few days. His eyes flashed briefly, that heat she knew so well returning before he leaned back on his palms.

Smoothing her hands up his thighs, she pressed her kiss to the inner right one. "The Horde attacked us both, Greed. I'm sure you remember that. They took from both of us. They broke your tail, your ribs, made it so that you had to run from them."

He grunted, obviously ignoring that he'd ever been injured at all.

She flicked her tongue against his skin, drawing his attention back to her. "They hurt me, Greed. I showed up on your doorstep broken and bleeding. Remember how that felt? Do you remember what it was like to see me like that?"

The flash of rage in his eyes was her only warning. Claws curled in her hair, pushing it away from her face as though he had never seen anything more lovely. His voice deepened to a low growl. "Careful, treasure. You don't want to remind me what they did to you."

"I want to remind you." She tilted her head back, letting his claws play along her throat. "I want you to get angry at them, my king. I want you to punish them for what they did to me and to your kingdom."

Oh, those were the words to say. Though he didn't mind worshipping at her feet, she thought perhaps these were his favorite moments. When she begged.

Perhaps it was because seeing her like this was so rare. She got on her knees for no one other than him, and if this could convince him...

"You will stay here," he said, his fingers picking through the knots in her hair. "You will be safe where I will not worry about you."

"Greed, you don't know how to find the Horde," she replied. "You've never been able to find them, but I am good bait. You know they want me. You know they will do anything for the map that I stole from them."

"Perhaps that is true, but I will not risk you." His eyes had changed again, golden coins that flashed with more greed with each passing moment. "They do not get to touch you again."

"And if they do?" She'd grown tired of being on her knees. Because Varya knew she wasn't going to listen to him. She would fight by his side, just as his woman should. And if he had an issue with that, then he could fight with her later. In the bedroom, as all their fights should take place, tangled in his sheets.

"I will remove their hands." Greed palmed her hips, dragging her a little closer. His mouth found her sternum, just underneath her breasts, where he lingered. "And then I will take their heads."

"Mm," she hummed underneath her breath.

Never in her life had she thought she would find it so attractive to have someone threaten another person's life for her. The mere thought of murder had always enraged her. She'd seen it happen enough times in her life that it had always been senseless. Life wasn't meant to be dealt with so casually.

And yet...

"I like it when you're possessive," she said, straddling him. "I like it when you want to kill for me."

"Do you?" His claws dug into her sides as he drew her with him so he was laying down on the bed with her on top of him. Greed trailed his nose up her neck, inhaling deeply. "You smell like me."

"I'm surprised I don't reek."

"You do." Again he inhaled her, then flashed her a feral grin. "I love it."

She wanted to hear him say that one more time. She wanted to hear him say that he loved her, and those words would carry along with her for the rest of her days, but...

This had to be good enough.

Reaching between them, she grasped his cock in her hand and lined him up where she wanted him. And as she sank down onto his massive length, feeling the burn and the stretch and her body telling her that they needed to rest, she let out a sigh of happiness.

Perhaps a little pain with her pleasure wasn't all that bad.

Chapter 40

When he rolled over the next morning, his nose buried deep in her freshly washed hair, Greed felt a sense of happiness that he'd never experienced before in his life. He'd always had moments of peace, certainly, but that need to steal, take, and keep always crept back in.

Not now.

Not with her.

He tightened his arm around her waist, drawing her deeper into him just so he could hold her a little tighter. She was the peace he'd been searching for. The energy that he'd been missing when he'd been trying to satisfy his urges in a thousand different ways. She wanted to be around him. She wanted him. And just knowing that eased some dark part of his soul.

By all the gods, he was a lucky man. Waking up with the sun filtering through the glass above their heads, the leaves of their jungle leaving pretty shadow patterns on her bare skin. Blonde hair draped over his bicep where she rested against him.

He would never get over the marvel it was to have a woman trust him so much that she would fall asleep in his arms. All the others had either not stayed at all, or they had woken at the slightest sound. He'd spent a thousand years knowing that he had given no other person enough peace of mind to sleep in his presence.

But this one did. Her chest rose and fell with each deep, even breath. The graceful length of her neck all stretched out. She'd have a crick in her neck if he let her keep sleeping like that.

How was he supposed to wake her, though? When she looked so perfect, all curled up like that? Her legs tucked in, one of his own in between hers. She was... his. Completely. And this time, he didn't question the thought as it crossed his mind because he knew how right it was.

She'd given in to him, and that was the sweetest success he'd ever accomplished in his life.

"You're staring at me," she muttered.

"It's hard not to." He pressed a kiss to her warm skin, watching as the leaf shadows fluttered over her pulse. Or was that her? Was she excited to wake next to him as well?

"It's creepy."

"I'm not creepy." He rolled over her, his own shadow now encompassing her as he braced himself above her head.

Whatever else he'd wanted to say fluttered out of his mind as she stretched underneath him. All that lithe muscle working, her body waking up and meeting his with that innate grace that he wasn't all that certain she knew she had. And gods... She was so stunning.

"Stop looking at me like that," she whispered, looping an arm around his neck and drawing him down closer. Her lips played with his, barely a kiss and more of an exploration. "I can't be responsible when you look at me like that."

"And are those emotions you or the spirit inside you?"

"Both." She nipped at his lip, the little sting making a zing of lightning dance down his spine. "But we really need to get going. You promised."

"Ah."

He had promised. He would find the Horde and he would destroy them for her. Because if his queen asked him to do anything at all, then he would do it. Especially if that request came with the promise of blood.

He'd rend this entire kingdom to dust if that's what she wanted. Greed had no question that he would become the destroyer of all kingdoms if she gave him the order, and that should have terrified him. Instead, it made him want her to ask him to do it. It made him want to beg her to tell him to bring all her enemies' heads on a platter, so he had an excuse to be so truly feral.

Growling low underneath his breath, he reached between them and traced a finger through her pretty folds. Wet. Always so wet for him, and he loved that about her.

He sucked on the finger as he rolled out of bed and gave her a wink as she moaned in response. "You said I needed to get ready, didn't you?"

His queen was anything but lady-like. She was sprawled out on his bed, the sheets tangled around her naked hips, and she never once tried to hide herself from him. Instead, she wantonly stared, licked her lips, and then shook her head. "We need to go. You're distracting me."

"We?" He arched a brow and started toward his wardrobe behind the walls of monstera. "I thought I made it very clear last night, treasure. You're not going anywhere. You want them dead? I'll gladly bathe the desert in their blood for you, but I will not have you in the midst of the battle."

But he wouldn't let her leave this castle. He couldn't see her in danger again. The fear that already lanced through his chest was a horrible feeling. It zinged through his entire body, arced across his chest, pushed through his very heart as though reminding him that he was weak and she was weaker, and that was terrifying.

What would he do if she died on that battlefield? No, she couldn't. The spirit. He'd put that in her so he wouldn't have to fear that he'd lose her at every corner, but... he was consumed by the what ifs.

He heard her padding feet approach, but he could only see the image of her pale body flung across the sand, blood splattering across every surface that he'd so thoroughly loved.

Varya spread her hands across his chest, her hands anchoring him in place. Her fingers dug into the muscles of his chest and he had nowhere to look but her. But those big blue eyes, staring up at him with so much worry that it made his heart ache.

"I'm a fighter," she said. "I've been a fighter my entire life. You cannot cast me aside and put me in a box to keep me safe, Greed. These are my people just as much as they are yours."

"I don't care that they're your people," he growled. And because he needed to, he pulled her against him, wrapping both his arms around her waist and holding her just a little more securely. "You are going nowhere, treasure. You will be safe, because I command it."

"When have I ever followed commands?" Her words were garbled against his pecs, though, and he pretended he didn't understand her.

He set her back on her feet and clapped his hands to her shoulders, squeezing perhaps a little too tight. "Let me do this for you. Stay safe, where you will not distract me with worrying about where you are or how I need to protect you. Yes?"

She frowned. "They still have that cursed object that makes you fall asleep, Greed. Who will protect you if I'm not there?"

"Ivo."

He hated even saying that, though. Really, he'd feel better with Gluttony watching over her, but his brother had absolutely no interest in helping. He wanted to hunt and Greed couldn't think of a reason why he shouldn't.

Though his brother's heart wasn't in the right place, at the very least, it gave Gluttony the right time to use that need of his to their advantage. He could already see the Horde running as they realized his brother had a taste for human flesh.

Shuddering, he flashed a grin at Varya and then kissed her forehead. "We're hunting today. I'll probably be gone for at least a week before we return to get what all the other groups have found."

"You're leaving?" she asked, appearing a little dumbfounded. "Right now?"

"You told me you wanted this taken care of. I told Ivo last night to summon the hunt. We leave the castle today and then we will cover the entire kingdom with my scouts. Soon, we will find the Horde. And even if they move, once I have their scent they cannot get far." He tapped his nose as though that explained everything.

In truth, he expected to spend most of his week in his battle form like the animal he was. Tracking was part of the fun, after all. He liked to chase his prey for days on end until they were too weak to run from him. Then they understood the true meaning of fear.

A little growl escaped before he drew her in for one more heart melting kiss. He pressed all his worries and fears into her lips, hoping that she understood him. That she wouldn't betray him. That she stayed right where she was supposed to be because, for gods sake, he was going to lose his mind if she didn't.

And when he withdrew to put his pants on, she seemed to stay. Varya watched him with a wary gaze, apparently seeing right through his hope that she wouldn't see why he was so nervous.

She stayed in the room, though, and that had to count for something.

Greed had to tear himself away from her because all he wanted was to stay right here. He wanted to crawl back into that bed with her and spend the next few days lost to the world and all its responsibilities.

Being with her made him feel whole.

Ivo stood outside the door, leaning against the wall with his eyes focused on the wall before him. The poor bastard had to listen to them for hours on end, and his ears were probably still ringing.

Greed almost felt embarrassed about that. Rubbing the back of his hot neck, he asked, "Are they all ready?"

"Have been for a few hours now."

"It's still early enough to start."

Ivo pointedly stared up at the sky before looking back at Greed, his lips twitching. "It's almost noon."

"And that is the perfect time to start a journey!" It wasn't, and he knew it just as well as the rest of them. Greed shook his head and stalked forward, knowing that Ivo would come with him. "Gluttony is ready?"

"Your brother has complained for hours that we dragged him out of bed, only to wait for you."

"Good."

"And he also complained that none of the beds here are anywhere near as comfortable than his own, that your nuckelavee are terribly trained, and that if your bride was going to keep you in bed all day, could you at least provide the men and women waiting for you a distraction." Ivo's eyes darkened with the last bit. "I threatened to take him aside for my own kind of entertainment, but he said he wasn't interested in men like me. I think he missed the point."

As they started down the stairwell that led to the courtyard, Greed snorted. "I think he got the point, Ivo. He was trying to get underneath your skin."

"Well he did." Ivo's hands flexed. "He's been looking at my beauty a little too long, if you ask me. Said he's got a thing for redheads and I don't like it."

Greed looked at his friend, realizing in that moment that Ivo had gotten even more human in the past few months. Ever since meeting Varya, really. His dearest friend, the man who was probably more of a son to him than any other person, had done what Greed did not think was possible.

A spirit, fully grown in a mortal form, battling his natural instincts, stood before him changed. Not just a spirit anymore, but a real life mortal who had thoughts and feelings and desires. It was more than Greed had ever hoped to see.

He wrapped an arm around Ivo's neck, forcing the other man to bend as he dragged him toward the others. "I'm proud of you, Loyalty. You've come a long way since those first days when you could barely walk."

"You gave me a massive body," Ivo grumbled.

"And one you've put to good use." They paused before the others, and Greed released him. He eyed the other man, taking in all the bulk that stood before him until he nodded. "Take care of our women, Ivo. Make sure nothing takes them from us."

"I will."

And it wasn't loyalty that made him say that. It was true love for the woman he had fallen madly into that pit for, and respect for the woman that Greed likely loved just as much.

Nodding, he swung up onto the back of his nuckelavee and looked at the crowd of men and women before him. They were all decked out for a hunt. Their faces painted with broad, black strokes that would keep the sun out of their eyes. Their mounts twitched beneath them, just as prepared for a long, hard ride as his own people. These were the men and women he would give his life for, time and time again.

Lifting his arm over his head, Greed waited until silence fell through the crowd of a hundred. "We ride for the Horde. They have attacked me, bested me, and then they attacked my brother. But worse, they attacked and harmed my woman! I will not keep her hidden away in this castle for the rest of her long life. I will deliver her their heads on a platter and feast upon their hearts with all of you!"

The roar that erupted from the crowd shook the very sands beneath him. He felt the hunger for the hunt roll through them all, and knew that he'd gotten larger, that his claws came out of his hands and his eyes must flash gold in the sunlight. They would see a beast before them and they would ride at his side.

They did not fear him. The Horde, however, should.

Gluttony nudged his beast beside Greed and watched the crowd of hungry warriors before them. "You've amassed quite an army, brother."

"This is not my army." His voice had deepened into a low growl.

"These are just the scouts."

And as he turned to look at Gluttony, he had the distinct pleasure of seeing his brother's face pale. Perhaps this was the first moment that Gluttony realized just how powerful Greed had become. If there were a war between the kingdoms, Greed did not fear for his own. He would not attack any other kingdom, but he would protect his own.

These people would fight beside him. Each one more mad than the next, desiring blood and looting at the end of it all.

He tilted back his head and let out a roar that could be heard even over the thunderous cries of his scouts. "I promise you wealth!" he shouted. "I promise you glory! I promise you all the looting and maiming you desire! Whatever you find is yours. Take it and make your king proud!"

Reaching into his pack, where they always were, he drew out the twin daggers that had always been his preference for fighting. Lifting them crossed over his head, he squeezed his thighs around his mount and rode forward through the crowd.

A stream of a hundred men and women followed him across the desert, their thirst for blood fueling him.

Chapter 41

If he found her, Greed was going to kill her. Well, not really. Varya didn't worry that he'd ever hurt her. The man didn't have it in him to raise a hand, but he'd roll her up in a blanket and then lock her in a closet for a while.

But she would not stand by and let his army fight on behalf of a people they'd forgotten a long time ago. The castle folk weren't the same as the rest of those in his kingdom. They saw the world through rose-colored glasses and the protection of their king. And so few of them were lucky enough to even get to work there.

The warriors of Greed were impressive, with years and years of training under their belts. And still they didn't help her people if they saw them in need. No one did.

The desert people of this kingdom had to survive on their own, with no one willing to help them. And if that meant that Varya had to sneak herself onto a horse and clamber over a few stone stairwells to get here, then that was fine.

She'd covered her face with her old mask. Greed didn't even know she still had it, and considering how out of it he'd been when he first saw her, she wasn't too worried. Her hair was hidden underneath a pale yellow hood that would hopefully not roast her alive while they spent hours underneath the desert sun.

They'd find the Horde. She would make sure of it.

Initially, Varya had hoped to get in with a group of the scouts that were headed in the opposite direction of Greed, but she knew one of the Horde's hideouts, and that was a good place to start. Unfortunately, that meant joining the group right next to Greed.

She kept her head down, making sure that her eyes never lifted to his. Instead, she watched the horizon. Someone would think she was doing her job if they saw her. They'd think she was a damn good scout, ready to find her king's most hated enemy. This was good. She was a fantastic actress.

"Varya," the word echoed from beside her, buttery smooth, like silk sliding over her skin.

Damn it.

"Gluttony," she whispered under her breath, turning away from Greed to look at his brother. Somehow, he'd snuck up on her. "Don't give me away."

"Are you trying to give me an order?"

"I will cut off all your hair in your sleep and glue it to your arms," she hissed. "Don't try me. I'm going to hunt because I'm the only one who knows where the Horde usually is."

"Maybe I will join your group, then." He adjusted himself in the saddle, looking very much like he was uncomfortable. "One knows I don't wish to be in the sun any longer than required. Did you know that my kingdom rarely has sunny days? It's always slightly overcast and misty. Absolutely beautiful."

It sounded horrible to her.

Varya made a face, wrinkling her nose and shaking her head before she replied. "You're trying to distract me. Are you going to tell Greed?"

"Of course not. But he's going to find out sooner rather than later."

"Not if you don't tell him."

"He's already halfway into his battle form, little thief. Do you think he won't smell you?" Gluttony tapped his nose, then pointed a clawed finger behind her. "You'd best get a move on. He's already in a hunting mood, and I hate to think what he'll do when he realizes you aren't safely tucked into your bed."

Shit, she was in so much trouble.

Varya cast a glance over her shoulder and she swore she saw Greed's nostrils flare. Like he had scented her on the wind. Maybe it was time for her to get going.

Kicking the sides of her horse, she sped away from the others, forcing her beast to run faster until she was at the head of her scouting party. Perhaps that gave her away, but she knew the direction to go. Anyone who tried to tell her otherwise was an idiot. None of them knew this kingdom like she did. Not a single one.

The scouting party veered to follow her, and the only time she looked back, she saw Gluttony had joined their group as well. The idiot. He was going to give her away far more than her own actions.

Why would Greed's brother join a random party if there wasn't something interesting going on? He wasn't the type to just randomly do what he wanted, and what he wanted was to not be here at all.

Which meant she had very little time. She had to get them on the right track, and so she did.

Varya led them across the dunes for half a day. She charged through the sands, the hooves of her horse beating in time with her heart. She could do this. She could remember.

And she did.

Varya brought them right to the heart of where she had first found the Horde. Where she herself had picked up on their trail to bring her to where she'd met Greed.

And though they were no longer there, signs of life remained. Fires that had recently been extinguished. Food that hadn't quite gone rotten yet, and footprints. Hoof prints. Items of belongings that proved they would return.

She'd known she was right. But this victorious feeling, this thunderous pride in her chest that only bolstered the spirit inside her? This was what she lived for.

"Adventure," it whispered in her mind. "Oh, it's so glorious."

And it was.

Oh, it so very much was.

Varya picked through the Horde's belongings with the other scouts, trying to find some hint that would tell them where they had disappeared this time. But quickly, there was another presence following along behind her. A presence that made her stomach twist and roll.

"Varya," Gluttony said, standing behind her like a wall of fucking ice. "You know he's going to show up soon. If you want to remain anonymous, then you need to go."

"What I need to do is find out where they are going," she snarled.

"There are other scouts for that."

"And they've never been as good at my job as I am. I will find out where they are and I will be the one to hunt them down." She whirled on him, her heart in her throat as the words poured out. "They hurt me, Gluttony. They hunted me down like I was an animal and they threatened to rape me. They almost would have, too, if it wasn't for that stupid snake that Greed fought off. The same snake that saved me and I don't... I don't know how to get through these memories without being the one to hunt them down."

And there it was. The thoughts she'd tried her best to bury so deep inside her that she wouldn't ever remember them.

But their voices still came up in her mind. They still slithered into her thoughts, even when she was lying in Greed's arms. Words of other men who wanted to take, just like Greed wanted to take.

Perhaps he saw how wild her eyes were, or perhaps he felt more for her than she'd ever thought. But Gluttony approached her like he might a wild animal, his palms raised for her to see, every movement slow and calculated. "You know I didn't know that."

"I don't care that you don't know." How many women had suffered the same fate? Or worse?

"And you don't have to. But I need you to hear me when I say this, lovely thief, that was not your fault. They did not leave a stain on your skin when they did it, nor do they likely even remember their transgression."

They were the same words that Greed had said when she'd glossed over what had happened to her. She hated that the Horde probably didn't remember her. But she wanted the leader of the Horde to never forget her face.

"I want them dead," she snarled again, her teeth bared in a snarling grimace. "I want them to know what it feels like to be so afraid, even if they don't have to suffer like I did. I want to see it in their faces when they realize I was the one who returned. Even if they don't recognize my face, they will know my rage."

She saw something twist on his expression, a wild look that mirrored her own as though he, too, wanted to know what that would be like. "Does Greed know this?"

"I glossed over it and we moved on," she hissed. "I didn't tell him the details, nor does he know how much it has affected me. Don't you think I realize what he would do if he heard the truth? If he knew their voices were still in my head even while lying with him? He would tear this entire kingdom down until there wasn't even a grain of sand left. He cannot know, Gluttony."

"He should."

"He won't."

But Varya's wild thoughts stilled as Gluttony stood right in front of her, his hand outstretched for her to take. "But he should, Varya. You need to tell him so that he truly understands why you have to be here."

And with that, she broke. Snapped like a string that had been held far too tight.

She couldn't keep the emotions in her chest, the ones she hadn't really felt since it had happened. They bubbled up inside her, pressing against her lips and tongue until they poured out of her body in a great heaving sob.

She reached for him, wrapping her arms around his waist and holding onto the only person who could hold her. To his credit, Gluttony didn't touch her back. Perhaps he feared she would tense up, or be thrown back into those dark memories. But she didn't think he would make her feel like that. Not really.

Instead, she grabbed his arms and wrapped them around her shoulders. He wasn't touching her in any dangerous way, and she knew who he was. No dark memories could even come up, anyway. They hadn't raped her, they'd just threatened it and somehow that had still cut through her mind. The fear of what they could have done plagued her. The dreams of what they might have finished if she hadn't slipped away after that snake interrupted them... It consumed her.

A god of the desert had saved her life, and she didn't even know how to thank it.

Gluttony sighed, his cheek resting on top of her head for a brief moment before he pulled back to stare down at her. "You have to tell him."

"You're not supposed to be nice." She wiped her cheeks with her hands, annoyed at the raw feeling beneath them. She was probably red-faced and snotty. This was not the way she wanted to face Greed. "You're a demon king. All of you are supposed to be terrible people."

"Ah." He nodded, then flashed her his fangs. "Would it make you feel better if I bit you?"

A choked laugh rumbled out of her mouth. "No, not really."

Another voice interrupted them, one which made all the muscles in her body go slack. "If you'd said anything else, treasure, I'd have to kill my own brother."

Shit.

Shit, shit, shit.

Greed had found them. Of course, it only took a few moments for him to get to this section of the desert when he should have been half a day's ride away from them all. He would have come right away as soon as he heard there was even an inkling of the Horde.

And now he'd caught her in his brother's arms, teary-eyed and joking.

Just great.

Gluttony's arms tightened for a mere moment and he hissed in her ear, "Tell him everything, Varya, or I will."

She saw the tension that rode on Greed's shoulders. He hated that his brother was touching her at all, let alone holding her so intimately. And she knew she had to tell him. But here? Right now? She couldn't.

But the demon king who had his arms around her had different plans. He shoved her toward Greed, a little too hard, so she stumbled toward the man who would always be her undoing.

"Varya needs to speak with you, brother." He gave them both a meaningful stare. "Now."

Rounding her shoulders, Varya turned toward Greed and resolved herself to a long, terrible conversation that wasn't... right. It didn't feel good. But she had to tell him, and he needed to know. "Can we talk?"

Some of the aggression leaked out of his body and he wrapped an arm around her shoulders, drawing her against himself with a watchful eye on the man behind her. "Of course, treasure. Anything for you."

He might not want to say that after she told him everything. But that was her own fear to get over.

Varya followed him to a more private part of the encampment in the sands. She sat him down and then let the words pour out of her mouth. Reminding him of how they had captured her, how injured she'd been. And when she got to the words they said, the words that continued to echo in her mind, Greed had stood.

He prowled in front of her, tail lashing, hands curving in and out of claws. "I will kill them all," he snarled. "I will rip out their hearts and mount their skulls in our castle."

"Greed."

"They dared? In my kingdom? They know what I will do to them. Death will be a mercy by the time I'm finished. They will greet death a hundred times before I let them fall into that dark oblivion."

"Greed," she tried again.

His hands flexed into dark claws. Was he somehow larger? Again?

"I will tear into them." His voice deepened in a low growl that brushed along her spine. "I will rend flesh from bone and then I will feast upon their blood. I will bathe in it before I return to you, queen of my heart."

Queen of his heart?

All the worry and concern bled out of her body. Varya walked up to him, not caring that his claws slashed through the air around her in anger. She walked right up to his chest and buried herself in it.

His arm came around her without thought, even as he continued to snarl and growl and mutter about death. But his arm around her shoulders and his hand on her waist were infinitely gentle, as though she were the only thing he cared about.

And she wondered if maybe she could get used to this. Being the center of someone's world, and loved so much that even in anger, he didn't hurt her.

"Thank you," she whispered against his chest. "For believing me. For wanting to fight for me."

He froze in her grip. "You're welcome."

"I'm not the first woman they've done that to. I'm just one of the lucky few who escaped." She shuddered. "It could have been so much worse, Greed. But for the sake of all those other women who didn't get away, I want to be there with you. To fight. To kill a few of those fuckers, and I need you to let me go with you."

She felt him melt in her arms. He curved around her even tighter, drawing her ever closer as his sigh brushed through her hair. "My treasure, if it will make you happy to kill them, I will present you their throats and hold them as they bleed."

She'd never heard a more romantic declaration of love.

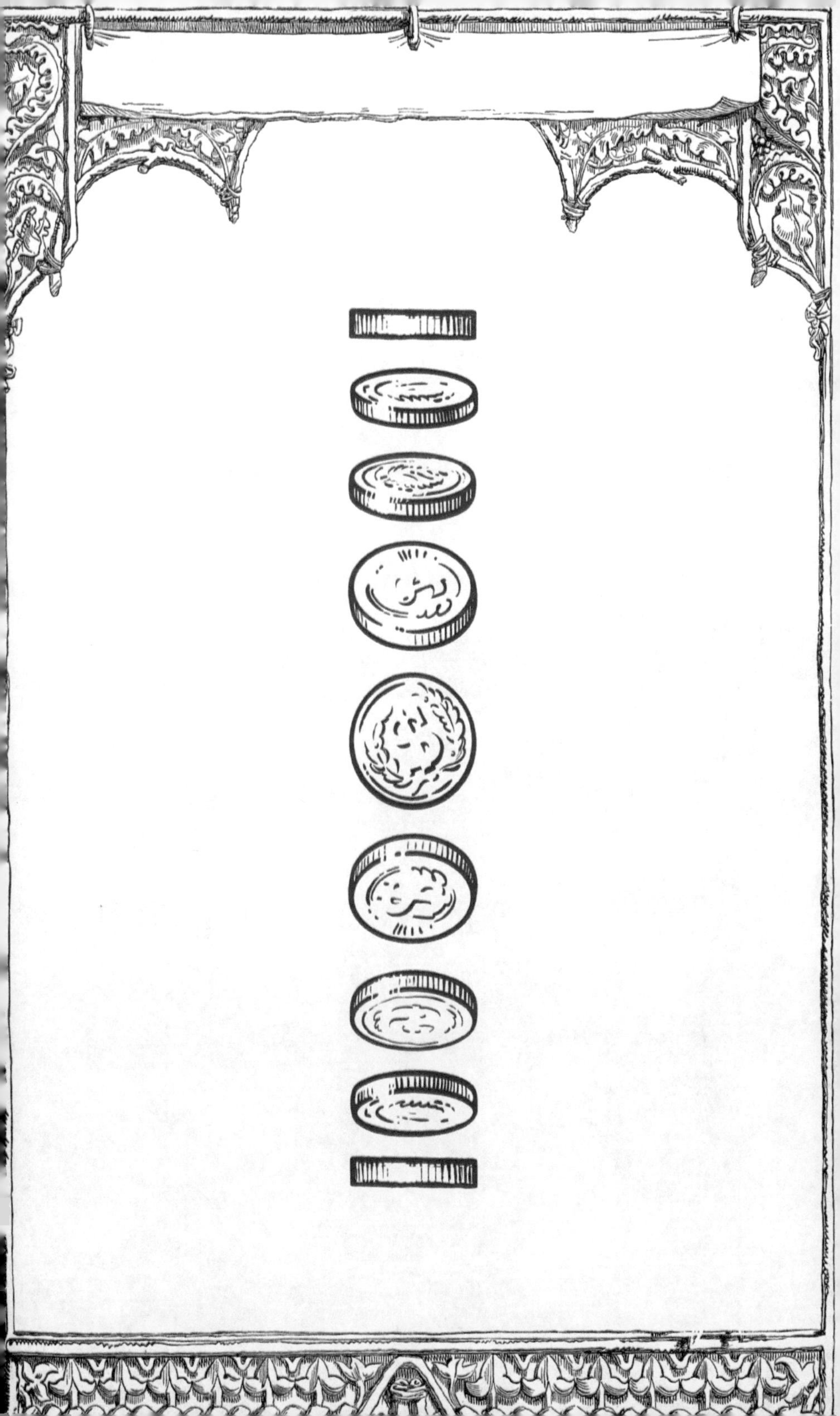

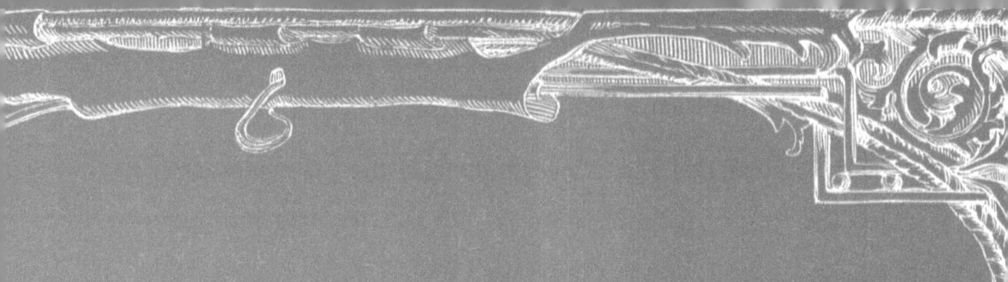

Chapter 42

They rode together on the hunt, Greed and his bride, with the sands kicking up behind them as they charged toward their mutual enemy. His mind told him to be frightened. That she would soon find herself in a predicament that neither of them could fix. What if he lost her? What if she was attacked?

But his heart knew that she could handle this. His heart crowed with glee that he'd found someone just as feral as him. Someone he could fight beside rather than hide away like the treasure she was. She was both a hauntingly beautiful gemstone and a sharpened blade. A weapon as much as she was a safe haven for his mind.

By the gods, he was a lucky man.

She rode like she'd been born on the back of a horse. And though her mount could not keep up with his, they still rode together regardless. He watched her strong thighs grip the beast beneath her, watched the look of determination on her face warping into one of pure malice as they followed the Horde's trail.

The last time they watered their mounts, he grabbed her by the waist and drew her closer to him. Whispering so no one could overhear them, he asked, "What do you think?"

"I think we're hunting the hunters," she muttered in response. "They seek to do damage. To draw us both out of hiding, but I do not know why."

"I think I do. Your Horde leader seemed fixated on me, yes?"

He'd been thinking about it on their ride. The Horde wanted to take over the kingdom, and they knew they couldn't as long as he was standing in their way. Which meant they needed to take care of the king first.

The attack. The fog. The magic. Wounding Varya. It all made sense for them to be attempting to draw him somewhere they could capture him for good. Exactly what Wrath was terrified of happening and spreading out to the other kingdoms.

Gluttony appeared beside them. His brother's eavesdropping really needed to stop. But at least Gluttony had decided to be helpful.

His brother pensively stared at the scouts around them. "So you think Wrath was right."

"I do."

Varya looked between them, confused. "Right about what?"

"He thinks that there are groups throughout the kingdoms trying to spread the idea of trapping us all. People who wish to put us in cages for the rest of eternity so that others can rule our kingdoms. And now I'm thinking perhaps that is exactly what they are doing." Greed rubbed the back of his neck. "Unless it is all about you."

"I doubt that. They didn't care in the slightest who I was or where I came from." She frowned at him, and he took the time to adore how expressive her face was. Her thoughts played across her features long before she said them. "If they're trying to take over the kingdom, you would be the first person they'd need to fight. You're right in that."

He sensed she wasn't entirely on board with his thought process, though.

And, of course, his treasure pointed out something that neither of them had considered. "Why are they going toward a town, then? They know you won't stop them. You never have before."

Greed looked at Gluttony, who just shrugged. "Don't know. Why don't we ask?"

He loved the feral grin that crossed Varya's face at the thought. Who would have ever guessed that he would find a bloodthirsty woman so damned attractive?

He had. Of course, he'd always hoped he would find someone who was as bloodthirsty as he was. He'd just assumed that he would never find someone like her. Women didn't exist who wanted to tear apart the world like he did, and then this one had fallen into his lap.

As they gathered their mounts, ready to make the last stretch toward the town as the sun dipped to the horizon, he watched her swing up onto her horse and pull out one of his blades. It was one of the twin blades that he always carried with him, and here she was, somehow having stolen it from him.

He loved her. It hit him as hard as the hammer had when all of this started.

He loved her so much that it was like she'd crawled inside him and become a part of his very soul. He wanted to hold her all the time. He wanted to hunt with her just like this for the rest of eternity. But mostly he wanted to kiss her, because she had ruined him for anyone else.

The light in his soul affixed on her. She was the guiding star in his night sky that drew him toward good and better and best.

What he wouldn't do to offer her a life that she deserved. A partner who was better than Greed, more than just a demon who only knew how to satisfy himself. He wanted her to see him and to light up just like he was now.

And that was the thought that spurred him forward. The thought had consumed him as they raced into a blood red sky, toward a town that might very well be destroyed by the time they got there.

They made it in time. Or at least in the midst of what the Horde had planned to do.

The buildings in her hometown were made of stone, which was good. The fires that consumed the town only raged through the thatch roofs and the wooden pillars holding up the stalls in the center of the street. But the Horde had brought a new weapon with them, one that he had not seen in ages.

The gauntlet used to be used by the miners deep in the ground. They had carved out entire kingdoms beneath the sands with that powerful metal, but then it had been used much in the same way the Horde was using it. The man who wore it was not the leader of the Horde, but an equally large beast who pounded through the stone of a home until he could stand aside for other members to rush in. Women and children screamed. Men fought back, their wives brandished pans behind them as they tried to remove the Horde from their homes.

Fires burned hotter, the screams rose to a crescendo, and Greed knew what they had to do.

He leapt from the back of his horse and landed on the ground, his hands already curving in massive claws. They were hunting, and now he got to track his prey.

Though he only had his scouts, he already knew there were a few who had headed back to his oasis. The rest of his army would arrive soon enough, but they would likely find the battle already complete.

Varya strode up beside him, both of them standing on the top of a dune that looked over what had once been her home. "Don't underestimate them. They were looking for that map so they could gather more magical artifacts, but that means they have at least a few of them in their grasp. Almost no one even knew that map existed."

"Magic won't stop me."

"But that gas will." She cupped his cheeks, forcing him to look at her when he would have just run off into the fray.

And he paused. Allowing her to touch him, to stroke her fingers over his cheekbones as though she were memorizing every angle of his face. She took her time, though perhaps they should have been rushing.

Greed smiled. "I will see you again, Varya. You don't have to worry about me."

Though she must know it was the truth, Varya still sighed and shook her head. "This isn't about me, Greed. You aren't going to fight against the Horde for me. Do you understand? If you go into that town, it's to save the people there."

He did not understand, nor was that the truth. He wanted to rush into that madness because he loved the sound of flesh squelching beneath his claws. The screams of his dying enemies lulled him to sleep at night. Nothing inside him wanted to save, he just wanted to punish because that was what he was good at.

Except...

He turned his gaze to the town, and he saw all the people there. People who had accepted him during the Festival of Lights. Who had seemed surprised he was there at all, but still wanted to make sure he knew how to put a lantern together and showed him the right steps for the dance.

These were the people he was supposed to protect. Varya had reminded him of that, and it hurt to know that he had forgotten it after so many years of serving them.

They were the reason he'd taken this throne. He'd remembered that at some point, and he'd been greedy for their love and devotion at the time. Now? He just wanted them to be happy. He didn't need them to worship him like a god, only that they live their lives in a better way than before. And perhaps that he was the reason they were living better lives.

He would save them now. All it would take was a bitter battle, and that was really no cost at all. They had been kind to him. They deserved this.

With a curt nod, he pressed a firm kiss to her lips before saying, "So be it."

"You'll do whatever it takes to save them?"

"I promise, treasure. And I don't make promises I won't keep."

He stalked toward the city, shaking out his arms and feeling the battle form rolling over him. He could sense how dangerous he was becoming. The claws, the hardening of his skin, the way his muscles and body swelled in preparation for a fight that would live throughout the ages as the most terrifying battle his kingdom had endured.

Because he was going to bathe in their blood. He would coat his skin with it, dousing his entire body in every bit of their life force until no one could tell who or what he was.

The Horde wanted a demon king? They would have one.

He waded into the madness, all claws and gleaming blades. And then his thoughts faded out of his head. Gone. All he thought about was the bloodbath and the death that came at the ends of his claws. He saw their faces blinking in and out. Men and women wearing the skulls of animals, each of them believing they could fight the famed demon king and all of them failing.

He barely registered the pain of blades slashing across his flesh. That was the beauty of this form. He did not feel pain. He did not feel fear. All that remained was the brief intelligence to let him know when there was a person in front of him who did not need to die.

He came close, once. A little boy stood in front of him, skidding to a halt as Greed's claws slashed down. But he froze before he ever touched the young man. Only a drop of blood splattered from his claws and touched the boy's cheek.

He let the young one run. He had no intention of killing any of the villagers and even in this form, he knew that. He was their protector. They would run and hide from him later, but right now they used his massive body as a shield and begged him to help.

So help he did. Over and over, death came from his hands. So many of the Horde fell, screaming and crying out for a mercy he did not know how to give them.

He remembered seeing his brother. Greed had charged down an alleyway at the sound of screams, only to find Gluttony with his back pressed against a wall and his fangs dug deep into a man's neck. His brother sawed his teeth through tendon, all the way to bone, gulping at the blood that gushed out from a severed artery in the man's neck.

They'd locked eyes. Two monsters who were likely more plague on their kingdom than they were saviors. And yet... This was their moment. Their chance to prove that they were more than just nightmarish creatures from the depths. They were men who would stop at nothing to save their people.

He'd left Gluttony in the shadows and returned to the fight with renewed vigor. He hadn't seen Varya, but he already knew why that was. She was helping to get the survivors out to his waiting scouts that would bring them to the castle where it was safe. Where his army already had fortified the walls and stood at the ready to battle any and all who thought to attack Greed's home.

One by one, he would get these people safe. He would.

Greed didn't know how long he'd been fighting when he first came across the Horde leader. The man stood in the center of so many dead bodies, surrounding him in piles where they had tried their best and failed. His massive chest heaved, those gigantic arms somehow seemingly even larger from the use. And he held a hammer in his hands. A hammer that looked rather familiar.

"You," Greed snarled.

The Horde leader turned with a grin on his face that was full of malice. "So we finally meet, Greed."

The screams swirled around them, a breeze kicking them up along with a massive amount of sand that coiled around the man's legs like a snake. Greed wasn't afraid of him. But he was afraid of the bright light that appeared behind the Horde leader. One who smelled of spice and who had illuminated his future.

Varya stood behind the Horde leader with her blade already raised. She locked eyes with him, and he knew what she wanted. She wanted him to let her take on this behemoth of a man and to continue getting her people out.

He wouldn't. Not when it was such a risk for her.

But she took the choice from him. Varya let out a scream of rage, a battle cry like the warrior goddesses of old as she charged at the Horde leader. The man barely even turned. He reached out with his hand and caught her by the throat, watching for Greed's reaction.

"Make your choice, demon king."

There was no choice. He would murder this man and he would feed his heart to his bride. The battle form he was so comfortable in grew even more powerful, stronger, larger, throbbing with the need to kill.

But then he heard her. "No!" Varya screamed. "Get them out!"

And he saw the rest of them in that moment. All of his people who were still failing to beat back the Horde. And he knew... Damn it. He knew he had to keep his promise.

Gluttony drew up behind him as the Horde leader backed away from them, using Varya as a human shield. She watched him with eyes that glimmered with rage. Not for him, but for the man behind her.

Greed pointed at Varya, his claw curled and warped. "Stay alive, woman," he snarled. "I'm coming for you."

And then he turned this attention to the people who needed him more. Even if it broke his heart to let her go.

Chapter 43

She wasn't afraid. Varya thought maybe she should be. She knew what to expect in the clutches of the Horde, and worse, she knew this time she wasn't getting away. They knew she had led Greed to them, and they would want reparations for that.

The Horde leader threw her into the arms of the big man who had been punching through the walls of people's homes. He gave her a far too pleased grin before wrapping her up in his arms and tossing her onto his horse.

The town burned behind them, but she quickly realized she wasn't the only one who had been captured. Other men and women sat before the Horde members on their mounts. Most of them were listing to the sides, their bodies limp and unaware. She wondered how they'd knocked them out when she couldn't see any blood on their heads.

The man holding her leaned forward, looming his entire body over hers and dragging her tightly against him. She felt his hand curving around her ribs, cupping her breast in one hand with a satisfied growl.

"Do you want to be awake for this?" he growled in her ear. "Or do you want to be the like the others?"

She knocked her head back so fast she caught him off guard. The back of her skull connected with his nose, and she heard a satisfying crack before his roar of rage.

The Horde leader rode up beside them, laughing at her antics. "I should have warned you, that one bites."

Though she could still hear the man behind her swearing, he kicked his horse forward. She rode away from her home, though she knew she wouldn't be gone for too long. Greed wouldn't leave her behind for much longer than he had to, and she wasn't all that worried about him finding her. He had their scent, after all, and she'd long ago learned to not question her demon king.

So she bided her time as they raced across the sands. She found all the markers that would let her lead them back home if some of the other prisoners happened to awaken fast enough for them all to make an escape attempt. And in between those thoughts, she planned how to stay alive.

She could use the map to her advantage. She knew where it was, so it wasn't all that much of a stretch for them to believe her. They wouldn't keep her alive for that alone, though.

The man behind her didn't grope her again, perhaps fearing what other parts of his body she would harm. But she wouldn't put it past him to try the moment they stopped.

What she didn't understand was why they were kidnapping townspeople. The Horde only had members who willingly joined, at least that was what she had assumed.

Glancing around herself, she found it hard to believe anyone in this party didn't want to be here. The Horde members enjoyed killing and thieving far too much. So what did they want these people for?

She was jumping too far ahead of herself. Right now, she needed to focus on creating a distraction until Greed could find her. And then they would kill them all together.

The Horde moved quickly. One moment they were in a familiar part of the desert and the next, she wasn't really sure where they were. The moon was just a sliver in the sky, and without its silvery light, the entire desert started to look the same. The deeper they went, the less she recognized.

Eventually, though, they reached an encampment much like the others she'd seen that the Horde had left behind. Tattered leather tents dotted the horizon, each one a little more dingy than the first. And when had she missed that the Horde wasn't... prepared? It wasn't ready for almost anything at all. They'd always seemed to have quality tents, but now that she'd lived in Greed's home, she realized they were just as poor off as the rest of them.

The only difference was that the Horde had better fighters, and they were hard to find.

It was the Horde leader himself who came to yank her off the horse. He pulled too hard, and she ended up on her knees in the dirt. Spitting out a mouthful of sand, she glared up at him as he hauled her upright.

"Oh, yes. Glare all you want, little girl," he snarled as he hauled her toward another tent. "I'm getting what I'm owed from you, one way or another."

Did she owe him the map? Or did he have worse, more devious

plans?

Letting out a snarl of her own, she only allowed him to push her toward the tent for show. But once inside, she whirled on him with her fists raised and her body much more prepared than it had been before. She'd spent hours training with the best, and she'd become a better fighter for it. Morag had shown her how to take down a man much larger, and how to fight against someone who couldn't move as swift.

She would not go down without a fight, and he would have to learn the hard way. If he wanted to take her, then she'd have him spitting out his own teeth before he managed.

"Put away your claws," he said, blocking the exit to the door with his body. "We're going to have a little fun."

The tight quarters of the tent would make it harder, yes. And she needed him to talk a bit longer so the other Horde members would think he was succeeding in what he intended to do.

He wasn't a talker like Greed, but this would have to do.

"You will not touch me," she warned. "Not after everything you put me through. If you think I'm going to just lie down and take it, you are sorely wrong."

"I think you'll do exactly that, after you tell me everything you know about Greed's castle." His thick beard twitched as though he smiled underneath all that fur. "You're going to tell me how to get in. How to get out. How many people he has and the easiest ones to pick off. You're going to draw me a detailed map, exactly where I can find all the places best suited for an explosion, the kind this kingdom has never seen."

Her mouth fell open as she realized the Horde hadn't been baiting Greed at all.

They'd been trying to capture her.

"How did you know I was even there?" she hissed, dodging him when he tried to grab her. She slipped between his legs and rolled upright on the other side, not even looking at the exit of the tent.

Out there, there were a hundred people waiting to fight her. In here? There was only one.

He turned with a growl, realizing far too quickly that she wanted to deal with him herself. He grinned again, this time with a flash of yellow teeth. "I'm no fool. I know that Greed is too powerful for me to fight on my own, which is why I plan to take him out at the knees. Destroy his army, his home, and there will be nothing left for him. Not even his pretty new toy, who will be ruined by the time I give her back to him."

"You've trapped me twice before and it didn't stick."

"No, but this time I'm prepared with chains. I have people on all sides of this tent, so you aren't getting out." He reached for her again, but it was like trying to capture an eel with his bare hands. He caught the back of her shirt, but she slipped out of it before he could reel her in.

It worked to her advantage. The sight of her barely clothed torso was enough to make him freeze for the briefest second. The salacious grin on his face made her skin feel like she was covered in ants.

But it was enough.

"I refuse to tell you anything," she said, making sure her words were loud. "You will have to torture me first."

"I can make that happen."

He lunged and this time she used his own weight against him. Varya wrapped an arm around his neck and flung her legs up. It gave her a small amount of purchase on his own body as she wheeled him around, wrapping her legs firmly around his throat and squeezing tight as both of them thudded hard into the sand.

He grappled with her, his powerful hands grabbing her thighs and trying to wrench them open. But she had the better angle, seated upon his shoulders on the ground with his head awkwardly at an angle. He tried to roll them. She twisted against him, using the momentum and fear that he must feel against him. She rolled if he wanted, like a snake she'd trapped against her limbs. But she never let up. Squeezing tighter, harder, until his face turned a deep purple and his eyes bulged as he stared up at her.

"I don't like people who try to take what is not freely given," she hissed. "Now you're going to make a noise for your men to hear. You're going to think you're letting them know that you're in danger, but all they'll hear is a man in the midst of passion. Yes?"

She let him have the smallest amount of air. Not nearly enough to keep him alive, but enough for him to let out a garbled groan.

"Perfect," she murmured.

There were even a few chuckles from outside the walls of the tent. She made a whimpering noise, then added in a breathy moan, just to make it more believable. The man between her thighs choked again, but then she squeezed harder than before.

Baring her teeth, she murmured, "They're out there thinking that you've turned me over. Probably making some jokes about the size of your cock and how no woman, willing or otherwise, wouldn't want it. And all the while, I'm sitting here suffocating you between those thighs you so desperately wanted. How is it? Is it what you expected?"

That shade of purple was not one she'd ever seen on a person before.

"I suppose it's terrible." She leaned just slightly, using her back muscles as well as her thighs to put even more pressure on him. "I want you to know it was the haven you sought in the bodies of women that killed you. You might never have tasted this pussy, but I hope you can smell it while you die."

And then she laid back in the sand and waited. She never loosened the hard clench of her muscles, not even when he stopped moving. Not even when he stopped breathing.

She laid there, her legs shaking, muscles quaking, lungs burning, and she kept squeezing until tears burned in her eyes. She counted to a thousand and then back down.

Varya wanted to let up a hundred times. She wanted to just give up and if he wasn't dead then she could maybe wrench his neck to the side, but she wasn't sure she was strong enough to do that. All of her strength was in her legs.

So she kept going. For all the women who came before her who hadn't gotten so lucky. For all the women that would certainly come after if she failed in doing this. It didn't matter that his hand slid to the sand, limp and curled. It didn't matter that the chuckles from outside the walls of these tents continued, jabbing at their captain for never lasting long enough. That they bet she'd passed out because no one could take a tent pole like that.

And she vowed deep in her heart that she would murder them all.

Greed would come for her. He always did. Even when she didn't want him to find her, he was there. At the end.

Finally, she couldn't hold on any longer. And it felt like her hips had snapped into this new position. She had to forcibly remove her legs from around the beastly man's neck. And even then, she wasn't sure. She couldn't be sure unless she touched him and she didn't want to.

But she did.

Varya leaned down, wincing at the pain of the bruises covering her legs as she felt for a pulse. There was none. Thank all the gods.

He was still a behemoth in his death. Far too large for her to move, so he would have to stay in the center of the tent. Finally, she looked around, searching for anything she could use as a weapon. Unfortunately, there was nothing at all. Just sand and more sand that had been kicked up in their struggle. She could see the patterns where they had rolled, struggling for purchase.

Shit, how long had she been quiet?

This time, her whimper sounded much more real. Because it was. Because she was going to do something that she had never even thought of in her life. But she crept around his body and removed the belt from around his waist. Lifting it over her head, she cracked it down upon him.

It felt a bit like she was massacring the dead, but he deserved it.

Another whimper, another crack. Then the voices outside the tent started up again, commending their leader for his stamina after all. Let the girl have it, they said. Teach her what it means to hold secrets that the Horde wants.

She hated them. She hated them all.

And then she remembered that Greed had said the desert needs blood. It feasts upon the souls of the wicked and that likely all the death in their kingdom had raised the snake. It had sunk through the sands, awakening the creature.

One body wasn't likely to do the same thing. She wouldn't summon the snake here, though it had likely already reached her small stone town. But it still felt right, like she was honoring the gods, to pull the Horde leader's knife out and then slice it across his throat.

Huddling in the back corner of the tent, she held the knife against her chest and stared at the door.

If she was wrong, then one of the Horde members would come through that entrance first. They would likely try to kill her. She would kill them and run. But she wouldn't get far because there were a lot of them and only one of her.

But if she was right, then Greed would come through that entrance first. And the sight of him doused in their blood would soothe the tremors that ran through her body.

Chapter 44

Greed hated this. Every second of it. He hated that he didn't know where she was, what was happening to her, or how he was going to get her back. He hated how she could be anywhere right now, waiting for him to come and find her. Or maybe she'd already escaped. Maybe he would ride across the desert to save her, only to find nothing waiting for him.

Fear of the unknown churned in his belly and his heart told him to leave everything here. The villagers would find their own way. Everyone knew where his castle was. They weren't being attacked by the Horde any longer, and if they couldn't figure out how to save themselves now, then they didn't deserve his help.

But then his gaze would find one of the younglings. The little girls and boys who stood beside their parents with fear in their eyes.

And his heart whispered that he couldn't leave them. Not yet. Not when they were so frightened and their homes were destroyed and none of them knew where they were going to go.

He was their king. He was meant to protect them, and so far he'd done a rather shitty job of it. None of them felt protected when the world had fallen down around their shoulders.

And he would fix this. He would.

So he'd left their stone town behind and rode with them. He helped carry many of their things, strapping down his nuckelavee with so many bags that the animal nipped at his arm when he brought the last one. But he patted its back and whispered that he wouldn't be riding.

Because he wasn't going to.

He walked among them. Greed hadn't ever done this in all the years that he'd been ruling this kingdom. Never once had he thought to spend time with his people unless they were actively training for war. And even then, it was less because he wanted to be around them and more because he wanted to make sure they didn't embarrass him.

They were afraid. So many of them had no idea what they would do next, and somehow, they turned to him for answers.

He didn't know how to respond. Greed barely knew how to take care of himself. But when they looked at him, like he was the hero they'd been waiting all their lives for, he found himself discovering those answers.

He'd house them in the castle while they rebuilt their village. The Horde would not be around for long; he would see to that himself. He'd fix what had been broken, and he swore that time and time again. In the meantime, they needed to band together and get a group of leaders for him to speak with. When he returned from finding Varya, then he would need some of their own people to help him with the plans.

And the people responded in kind. They told him about all the things they'd been lacking. They explained how they needed him to give them more food and water, and if it wouldn't be too much of a burden, perhaps he could open trade with the other kingdoms. There wasn't enough here for them to grow good food or even create good clothing.

The guilt that gnawed through his chest after he realized most of his people were wearing rags... Ach, he knew Varya would be so pleased to know how much it hurt.

It took them too long to reach the castle, and even then he knew he wasn't going inside. He trusted his own people to get them settled. There was plenty of room in the oasis, even though it would be a little tight.

Greed didn't care if they emptied his food supply or destroyed the remaining plants in his kingdom. He'd fix this. He had to. And the only person he trusted to tell him how to do any of it was the woman the Horde had taken.

Simmering rage still burned deep in his belly. The moment he found those murderous tyrants, he would unleash a rage unlike anything they'd seen before. They thought they could play with a god? They were about to learn how stupid that really was.

Gluttony remained behind with him, leaning on the pommel of the saddle with a feral grin already spreading across his face. "So we are not done hunting?"

"Did you think we were?" Greed wheeled his mount around, turning it to the blasting wind of the desert and the icy night that spread out before them.

Her scent was still in the air. He didn't have to go back to the town to smell her. Likely, his brother could scent the same. Gluttony had spent enough time with her, although he doubted his bloodthirsty sibling could smell her hair or the fine scent that always lingered on her clothes. No, worst case scenario, he'd ask Gluttony to track her by the scent of her blood alone.

The rage that suddenly burned through him... He inhaled it. Allowed it to spread throughout his body and into his fingertips that curved into claws. If he wasn't careful, it would consume him. Override all thought and reason until he had her back in his arms.

A low growl rumbled through his chest, but then he realized the sound was also coupled by the heavy hoofbeats of horses joining them. How dare anyone try to stop him now? He'd gotten them here, hadn't he? He'd brought them to safety and now they would leave him alone.

He turned toward the newcomers, a snarl on his lips that should have frightened them off. But it was Varya's friends. Altan and the others who had been there when the snake had attacked her. The men and women who were supposed to have protected her.

Some vicious part of himself whispered that Altan would never be able to protect her like Greed could. Even though he knew the other man had never wanted her like that. Or at least, so he continued to say.

"Let us ride with you," the dark man said, pulling his horse up right next to Greed's. "This fight is all of ours, not just yours."

It was just his. He'd made it almost impossible for anyone else to fight with him. Mostly because he intended to plow through the Horde members like they were blades of grass and he a scythe that had come to cut them close to the ground. They would not exist after he was finished.

They would beg for his mercy. He would not give it. Someday

soon, they would talk of this day. How the Demon King of Greed had taken to the war path all on his own, with his bloodthirsty brother at his side. They'd nearly destroy the entire kingdom together, but wasn't that the reason everyone had always feared him? The Horde thought to test his legends.

They would die screaming for that foolishness.

He opened his mouth to tell them all just that, but his brother beat him to it first.

Gluttony sounded like an actual king as he imperiously said, "You may join us, but remember, you are all mortals. A battle is significantly more dangerous for you to join than it is for us to start. Stay out of our way."

"We know how to fight," Altan replied.

"Not like us," Greed growled. And he knew he didn't sound like a person at that moment. He sounded like an animal, and he wanted them to see him as such. Because he was.

He was a terrifying beast, and they needed to see him as that. He wasn't just their savior. By the gods, he wasn't even remotely a savior for anyone. He did what he wanted for himself.

Except... His gaze skated to the castle, and he felt a deep-seated satisfaction knowing that everyone had gotten through the walls. They were safe. He'd done that. He'd made sure that they were taken care of, at least for the time being.

Surely that counted for something? Perhaps that even proved he could be more than just a demon.

And if he could be more than that, then perhaps he deserved the woman he was rushing to save.

Casting his gaze over the men and women before him, all covered in ash and sand, he wondered if they were thinking a similar thing.

That if they saved her, then they were proving they were worthy. Perhaps not of her attention, but worthy of whatever else it was that they were afraid of.

By the gods, he was proud of them. They were here when no one else had thought to do so. They were here, risking their lives, ready to perhaps die not just for the woman who had helped them all, but for their kingdom. These were the true warriors. Not those that he'd trained for years and years, but the people who actually cared if this kingdom prospered.

They wanted their own vengeance. He could see it in their eyes.

They wanted to watch the Horde burn not because he had ordered it, but because they had seen their own homes go up in flames. They had lived in terror of this group for too long, not knowing how to stop them and all the while praying that someone else would.

How could he not let them fight? How could he not give them the chance to take back their kingdom in the only way any of them knew how?

Through blood and thievery.

That was the kingdom he'd created. And here were the people he had nurtured for centuries. They were perfect.

Emotions stuck in his throat, he tried to clear it before saying, "You will fight beside us. You will be careful, because I will not suffer through her wrath if a single one of you is stupid enough to get killed. Do you understand me?"

Altan flashed him a bright grin. "I think you'll be surprised to see how well we fight, demon king. You don't have to worry about losing any of us in this mad dash toward the end."

He very much had to worry about that. Not only because Varya valued them, but also because... well. He supposed he did, too.

Stupid thoughts. Stupid feelings. He hadn't wanted any of this in his life and then that ridiculous woman had stomped all over his heart and forced blood back into the dead organ.

"Come on, then," he grumbled, turning his attention to the sands and the darkness beyond. "We have a queen to save."

They all let out a cry of rage and hope that they would find her in one piece, and then they were thundering across the desert. He tried to still his mind. To make sure that he wasn't overthinking anything by the time they got to wherever the Horde had hidden themselves this time.

Greed needed to think clearly. He needed a brain that was geared toward battle and battle alone. He could not afford to lose his temper because someone had taken his bride. He loved her, she loved him, and he knew just how dangerous his love was.

And then, when he had her back in his arms, he would tell her how much he loved her. He would whisper those words into the lovely crook of her neck. That spot was his favorite place in the entire world. He would tell her everything and that he'd been a fool who had waited too long in the first place.

Varya would forgive him for that. She'd forgiven him for worse.

And so, with her scent in his lungs and his heart racing in his chest, he drove them hard throughout the night. The sand gave to him, almost as though the desert knew he was going to feed her with so much blood that she had no reason to even try to stop him. She eased their journey, giving them no tempests or dust devils to slow them.

The Horde's encampment blinked to life on the horizon. A tiny dot of shimmering fire was all that glowed in the distance, but he knew exactly what it was. No other nomadic tribe would dare to be so foolish as to leave their fires burning.

Especially when they knew who hunted them.

A part of him wanted to rush into the camp and start the bloodbath. He wanted to hear them screaming out his name in fear, as he gave them no mercy.

But there was too much at risk. If he rushed in with his blades out, they would know he was here. They would hide Varya, or worse, they would kill her just to spite him. He didn't want to take that risk. He couldn't.

Greed would get his revenge and his blood, though. He would bathe in it before this night was done.

He lowered himself from the horse and quietly dropped onto the sands. He crawled forward, making sure no one would see him as the others followed suit.

Surprisingly, this group of ragtag soldiers was just as intuitive as his own people. It was strange how wonderful that felt to know there were people behind him, willing to care for him, who wanted blood just as much as he did.

He pointed to the tents. "Use your blades to cut through the leather hides. As quiet as possible. And then slit their throats in their sleep."

Altan looked at him with surprise, playing across his features. "You want us to do this quietly?"

"For now." Greed shrugged. "Someone will scream. A gurgle will be too loud and they'll figure out we're here. There are too few of us and too many of them for this to remain entirely silent. But I want to get eyes on her before I unleash everything upon these people. I want them dead. I want them gone. And I want her back."

Everyone nodded and started down the dunes, slithering on their bellies until they reached the tents. In the distance, he could see there were still a few Horde members standing around the central fire. They were all drunk, though he suspected there were scouts out here somewhere that were not.

He came across his first one as he started cutting through the first tent. He smelled the woman before he saw her. Greed whirled, blades ready to silence her before she could make a noise, only to hear a wet sound as her eyes opened wide.

Gluttony was attached to her neck, drinking deeply as his own eyes rolled back in his head.

His brother disappeared into the darkness, dragging the woman's heels through the sands, and he couldn't find it in him to care at all.

They would all die. No matter how innocent they were.

He finished cutting through the tent and then slipped into the firelight inside. No one was awake. Three Horde members, all men. He bared his teeth in disgust at what he was going to do. No one deserved to die without at least trying to fight. Unfortunately, these people would not end up in the afterlife they hoped for.

He sliced two of their throats with a ferocity that was unnecessary. The knife slid through their flesh all the way to the bone, not giving them even a moment to wake up before he'd nearly beheaded them. But the third one? Ah, he had plans for that one.

Landing hard on the man's chest, he put his hand over the man's mouth and the knife to his throat. As the Horde member woke with a start, eyes wide and then filled with terror as he realized who had him pinned, Greed said, "You're going to tell me where she is, my friend."

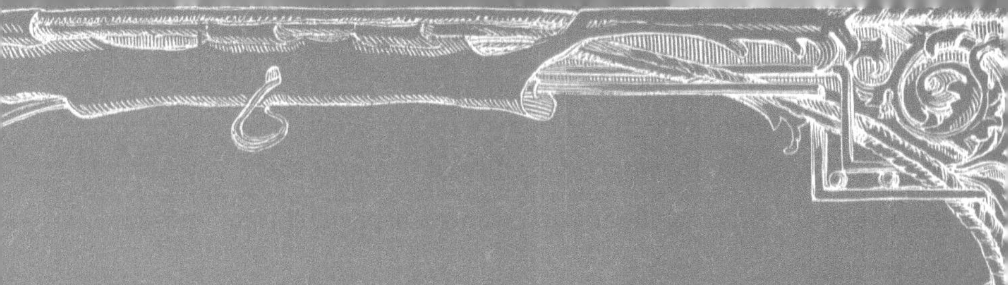

Chapter 45

The little spirit inside her was working hard. Though there wasn't as much for her to heal, it continued whispering in her mind, "We need to run! Disappear into the darkness. They're going to find us, and that's not the adventure either of us wants."

No, it most certainly wasn't. But she also had no intent on running because she knew that if she stayed put, Greed would find her faster.

Besides, there were so many other people who needed their help here, too. The other prisoners needed her help, so the moment she was free, she had to focus on them.

No matter what the Horde planned to do, that would all change once they realized she'd killed their leader. And the timing of that realization would happen more quickly than she wanted.

He'd had guards outside his tent, making sure no one interrupted them, and probably looking out for Greed. Unfortunately, that also meant she was privy to all the conversations happening right outside the tent walls.

At first, the words were all pretty easy going. After the lashing she'd given the dead body beside her, they'd snickered about his tastes in bed, and how so many of their own women had tried to go head to head with him and very soon realized they would only fail.

It made her sick to her stomach, wondering what that meant. Was he known for harming women in bed? Was that supposed to be normal for the people here?

And then their conversation had gotten quiet. They were clearly whispering, so they didn't disturb their leader, where he must have fallen asleep on top of his new toy. But then... then they started to wonder.

"Should we check on him?" one of them muttered, the words sending lightning up her spine.

"He'll be mad if we walk in there and wake him. And then he'll probably start the whole process over again. You know how his mind works."

"Yeah, but what if something happened?"

"That little slip of a woman? She didn't kill him, that's for sure. And if she had tried to escape, don't you think one of us would have seen her? We don't even have our backs to the tent." The sound of a smack echoed after that. "Keep your greedy eyes to yourself. He'll have your head sooner than allow you to see him bare assed."

So, she had a little more time before they got suspicious again, but not for a very long time. Soon enough, that meddling prat who thought he knew everything would say again that they should check in on the couple who were making no noise.

Should she speak again? She could throw out some "no, please, no" and maybe that would put their mind at ease. But the Horde leader hadn't been a quiet man. Everything about him was loud, from his footsteps to his voice. And if she was guessing right, he was probably just as loud when he was...

Ugh. Her stomach lurched in her body and bile threatened to spew from her mouth at the very thought. Whatever it was they called it when he brought a woman into his tent, that was a good enough explanation for her rioting mind.

Just a little while longer. She could wait a bit more.

"Why wait?" came the little voice inside her head. "We're capable of escaping ourselves."

She didn't want to point out that the guards admitted to staring directly at the tent. No matter where or what she did, they'd see her move. And if the tent was even so much as lifted on any of the walls, they'd know that something was wrong.

Varya knew she had to just sit here. And wait for something to happen.

Whether that was Greed arriving and tearing everyone apart, or them discovering that she'd killed their leader long before he got here. Those were the only options she had.

The shakes started a few hours later. Varya shivered so hard her teeth clacked together. She tried to fold in on herself so she wouldn't make more noise, but she wasn't exactly quiet. They would know that at least someone in the tent was awake. They'd come in and...

Rustling came from outside the tent. Not the sound of someone approaching, but of the guards turning.

"Did you hear that?" someone asked on the opposite side of her tent.

"I heard something."

"I thought the sentries were already at their posts?" The sound of a sword being drawn followed the question. "They were supposed to send out the signal if they saw anyone."

A third person answered from her right. "Then there must be nothing out there. We're skittish. It's not unusual when we all know who's hunting us. Keep your ears and eyes open."

"Someone should tell the captain."

Damn it. One of them was going to walk into the tent and realize that their leader had been dead for a very long time. And unfortunately, that meant she had only a few minutes to scramble beside the tent flap and clutch the knife close to her chest. Varya would murder them if she had to. She could do it. She'd killed before and would likely have to do it again, even if it made her want to scratch out her own eyes.

The tent flap lifted. A guard stuck his head into the space and before he could so much as open their eyes wider at the scene laid out before them, she palmed the back of his neck and threw him onto the sand.

He shouted in anger, and that's when the entire world seemed to explode around her. The guards swarmed, all of them slicing through the tent with their blades, and there was nowhere for her to go.

So instead of running, she grabbed onto the unfortunate guard who had volunteered to look, and used him as a human shield. He spluttered in terror, his shouts slowly degrading into nothing as the swords and knives sliced through him.

He fell onto the sand, right on top of her. Varya grunted, but that worked in her favor as well. Though the knives and swords were no longer right around her, she might need to use his body as a shield for a little while longer. She wrapped an arm around his waist and held him in place, ignoring the wince of pain from across her forearm.

Had she gotten cut? Maybe. And then the knives descended lower.

Unfortunately, they also cut into their Horde leader a few times. But maybe since he wasn't shouting, they thought he had left? She had no idea what was going through their head.

Until the knives stopped and she heard the growl that rumbled across the desert like thunder. And then she realized why they had been cutting so quickly and frantically.

They were afraid.

They were terrified because what stood on the other side of the tent was likely more threatening than their Horde leader or any other evil creature they had faced. Because Greed would show them no mercy. And if they killed her, that was their last bid at defiance before he hurt them very, very much.

She heard the screams first. The cries that were garbled and messy. The sound of flesh being parted and the horrible stench of fear. Maybe that was the man who'd fallen on top of her, though. He was still alive, but only barely.

The sounds outside died down. Getting quieter and quieter until there was just... nothing. Not a single thing.

The sound of the desert was the only thing she could hear. The faint hum of wind as it brushed through the sand grains, and the whisper of a breeze through the holes in the tent. Just complete and utter silence.

Was that a good thing?

It had to be Greed outside the tent, right? She couldn't imagine it was anyone else fighting the Horde. Unless another town had gotten it in their head that they were going to help. But she had heard the growl. She knew that sound anywhere, so surely...

Another growl rippled through the night air, and then she heard his voice. "Keep them all back."

Gluttony responded with a snort. "Won't be too hard."

"Don't make too much of a scene. We don't need any of this getting back to Wrath about how I unleashed you on an entire encampment of my people."

There was a strange sound, like fabric rustling, and she wondered if Gluttony had just saluted Greed. "You know I'm more careful than that. I'll drain them, and they won't scream. Besides, no one is going to make it out of here alive tonight."

"Get the others, then. Make sure they're all together when they attack the Horde. Everyone's waking up now."

"Understood."

Quiet from outside the tent made her muscles tense up. What if he continued on? She didn't want to yell and draw more people to the tent. They were clearly at least trying to be as quiet as possible.

But she wanted him to find her. She wanted him to know she was here, and that she had waited. She was doing her best for him, and she was so close to breaking down.

Then his voice broke through the silence. "If you're alive in that tent, anyone other than my queen, then you will die. I'm giving you this chance to run, but know that I will hunt you. I will chase you. And I will devour you the moment I find you. Do not stand between me and my woman, or I will cut you down and gut you."

Oh, if that wasn't the most romantic thing he'd ever said.

With a broad slash of twin blades, his daggers cleared a new entrance to the tent from where he stood. He stepped over the carnage of a body on the other side, and she felt the man laying on top of her take a deep breath.

Was he going to scream? That wouldn't do.

Varya wiggled her arm out from between them and drew her own blade up as she went. It cut through both his flesh and hers, but she didn't care. He needed to be quiet. So Greed could rescue her.

So she could rescue the others.

She was so afraid he would leave the rest of the townsfolk here. It was just like him to barrel toward her without a single thought to his own safety, but also for the safety of others. And already she was trying to figure out her argument so that he would stay and help. There was more to do. They were both exhausted, but surely —

He leaned over the shoulder of the dying man and wrenched the man's head back by his hair. Varya only had a brief moment to gasp before he snapped the man's neck and tossed his body off her.

"Varya," he said, and his voice shook with some emotion she couldn't name. It didn't matter. Greed was here. He was right in front of her and she was covered in blood and... and...

He gathered her up in his arms, yanking her against his chest even though she winced in pain. He held her tightly, his arms banded around her while radiating heat and power. Greed wouldn't let her go. Varya could break down for the few moments this would take and then she could piece herself back together so no one knew she'd been crying.

An ugly sob wrenched out of her. She bent into his arms, pressing her face against his shoulder as he buried his head in her neck and sank down into the sands with her. Away from the bodies. Away from everyone.

He cradled her in his lap as though she was made of glass and in that moment, she felt like she was.

"You're okay," he whispered into her hair, brushing his shaking hands over her back and hips. "You're okay, treasure. I'm here. You don't have to be afraid anymore."

A part of her wanted to scold him and say that she wasn't afraid at all. She hadn't been the entire time. But this newfound softness in her chest whispered he was right. She didn't have to be afraid anymore and she could lean on his strong shoulders for a few more minutes.

Varya knew she couldn't sob for too long, though. There were people here who wanted to kill her. Men who wanted to hunt her down. Others that they needed to save. And she couldn't let them linger for too long while she had her breakdown.

Sucking in a shuddering, deep breath, she leaned away from him to scrape her palms over her cheeks. "I'm all right. I wasn't even gone very long this time. I wasn't."

"I know you weren't." He looked at her so soft, so kind, and it made something deep inside her flutter. Greed smoothed his thumbs across her cheeks, chasing the tears that she'd missed. "I'm a fool, Varya. A fool who let you slip through my fingers without ever telling you the truth."

"The truth?"

His brows wrinkled, and she had a momentary spike of fear before he whispered, "I love you, treasure. More than any of the objects I've collected, more than the sun in the sky and the sands on the desert. I love you more than anything I have ever stolen in my life, so much so that I didn't recognize the emotion until it was almost too late. With you, I am a better man. Without you, I am not a man at all."

Oh.

Oh, those were the words she'd been waiting for. She'd wanted to hear them for such a long time and now that he'd said them...

More tears raced down her cheeks and her knee jerk reaction was to say, "You had to say this when I am covered in blood?"

He tilted his head back and chuckled, the muscles of his throat working so beautifully until he looked at her again. "Yes, my love, my treasure, my life. I had to say it now, because you beat me to the blood bath. You've never looked more beautiful."

She wrinkled her nose and looked down at all the blood and sand, but then she shrugged. "Well, if you don't mind it, then I suppose I can say I love you, too. I have for a long time, you know."

"I know."

"You do?"

He leaned forward and pressed a kiss to her bloody nose. "I always have, treasure. From the first moment you yanked me into a cave and wiggled your butt against my spine. You are mine, and I am yours. Forever more."

Oh, and what poetry that was to hear. She might have said more if someone didn't step between the moon's light and them.

Hissing, she lifted a blade only to lower it immediately when she realized it was Gluttony peering down at them, amusement on his features.

"What?" she asked, maybe a little too aggressively.

"You look positively lickable," Gluttony replied. He laughed when Greed growled, then held out his hand for both of them. "Come on, there's still some fight left. You know there's other prisoners, Varya?"

She didn't take his hand. Instead, she let Greed pick her up and stand for the both of them. Curled against his chest, hidden in his arms, she felt like this was the only place where she could find a little peace.

"Ready?" he murmured in her ear, gently nudging her hair to the side.

"Always."

Chapter 46

They hunted together, both him and his queen, cutting through the Horde with her family at their side and his behind them. Gluttony was more of a help than the humans, of course. He was much quicker. Just a blur between them and the Horde members as he picked them off one by one.

Greed, in comparison, was a sledgehammer. Just as they'd used against him before, just as they had tried to destroy him, he took them all out. Though Varya showed a few moments of hesitation, he did not. He was more than happy to kill whomever he could.

Though he'd never tell her, it stung a bit that she'd gotten to kill the Horde leader before he did. He wanted to see the man laid out and bleeding at his feet, yes, but he'd wanted to use his blade to saw through tendon and bone. Instead, she had protected herself.

And with that thought came the pride.

His woman was no wildflower to protect. She was the thorn and the arrow, a weapon all on her own that she could throw at anyone who tried to stand before her and her freedom.

He'd never been prouder.

Never been more turned on.

The sight of her covered in blood, fulfilling every fantasy he'd never known he had, was a memory that would never fade from his mind. Not easily, at least.

He wanted her now. He'd want her in a hundred years. And together, with that spirit of adventure bursting with power in her chest, they would rule this kingdom with a little more caution and a significant amount more patience.

Breathing hard, he stood in the carnage and watched as the last members of the Horde fled. His soldiers dragged a few of them off their horses, swiftly delivering their end rather than the salvation they'd hoped to see.

But when Altan and his people readied themselves to get onto those same horses and chase down the others, he called out, "That's enough."

They all looked at him in surprise, but he was tired. He had his woman. And the Horde wouldn't regroup any time soon. A handful of people running for their lives would not affect his kingdom very much.

And he'd send out more scouts to find and kill anyone who admitted to being involved in that Horde. They would find their end one way or another, but it didn't have to be right now.

Varya staggered over to him, her breath sawing in and out of her lungs as she slumped against his side. She wrapped her arm around him, and that was when he knew what bliss felt like. "You're letting them go?"

"For a good reason." He pressed a kiss to her bloody temple. "They're going to find all the others who weren't here tonight. They will lead us to the last members of the Horde, the wounded or the old. Perhaps the masterminds of all this."

"No, that was definitely the man I killed."

"Then his second in command. Or his third. Anyone who might want to continue this madness when they know damn well I will hunt them for the rest of their days." He twirled her stiffening hair around his finger. "Let's go home, treasure. Your people are waiting for you and we have a lot to do."

"You really don't want to hunt them?" she asked, leaning back to stare up at him with a pretty little frown on her face. "It seems unlike you to not want to race across the desert to remind them why they should fear you."

It was. But he'd felt something shift inside him halfway through the battle, and a voice he didn't recognize had whispered for him to go home. He'd done enough. He'd protected his people, his family, the love of his life. They were together, and he didn't have to fight anymore if he didn't want to. There would be another day for battle.

But there were only so many days to see the people who waited for them at the castle.

He sighed, filling his lungs with the fresh desert air, and then nodded again. "Yes, I'm sure I don't want to hunt them. We'll need entertainment later. Why would we ever wish our lives to get boring, my love?"

"My love?" she repeated, and her eyes went a little glassy. "Now there are a few words I like to hear."

And because he couldn't stop himself, Greed gathered her up in his arms and carried her to his nuckelavee. The beast even seemed rather happy to see her, nipping slightly at the air around her feet as they got on, then mouthing her pant leg as though it wished to taste blood.

Dangerous, monstrous beast. He'd never been happier with the gift he'd gotten from his brother.

Speaking of, Gluttony walked over to them before they could leave. "Go get your castle situated, demon king. I'll stay here with the others and journey back with those who were also stolen. Some of them are injured, and it will take a while."

"You're staying?" Greed said with an arched brow.

"Yes. I think your people could use a demon to watch over them." Gluttony winked. "And I'm not done with all the bodies here yet."

A slither of revulsion quaked through Greed's body before he nodded. "Do nothing to make Wrath more mad at us, yes? I have no interest in turning this into a battle between myself and the Underlord."

"Underlord," Gluttony repeated with a chuckle and a shake of his head. "I like that one. Maybe that'll stick."

He watched his brother waltz away, and he wondered yet again if they were all wrong about Gluttony. The man was dangerous, but they all were. Perhaps Greed was the most bloodthirsty brother after all, considering he held a woman in his arms completely doused in blood and he'd never wanted to fuck her more.

Varya turned in his arms and cupped his cheek. "You have the whole town in the castle?"

"Eating me out of house and home, I'm sure. They're probably stomping through the gardens right now and stealing all my treasures." He turned his face into her palm and kissed the center of it.

"And that doesn't bother you?"

"I have the only treasure I need right here." He tightened his arms around her and pressed a kiss to her lips before urging the nuckelavee forward into a speed that battled the wind.

They didn't stop for anything, although Varya fell asleep in his arms a few times. And he took the opportunity to bury his head in the crevice between her neck and shoulder, breathing her in. Even though she smelled like metal and death, there was still her scent underneath it all. Still his queen, his bride, his reason for life now.

Ach, he'd almost lost her. Again.

Greed promised himself he would never let her go like that again. But that new voice in his head whispered that he would. If he had to let her go for the good of the kingdom, yet again, then he would do it. And then he would battle to have her back at his side.

This was proven the moment they arrived back at his castle. Hands helped Varya get off his mount and then the people swarmed him. More people than just the town he'd saved. Some of his own workers from the castle, and somehow more. Women and men who commended him for doing what needed to be done. They wanted to know if he'd succeeded, if he'd driven off the Horde for good.

"The Horde is gone!" he shouted, his words carrying through the courtyard and Varya's blue eyes matching the vivid sky above them as the sun came out. "The Horde will no longer torment you. But hear me now. I have neglected my kingdom for too long. When I first came here, I thought the only way to indulge your needs was to turn this into a warring kingdom full of thieves, bandits, and murderers. I see my folly now. I see that my kingdom is full of good people who, yes, will steal from others, but mostly those who see the light. You honor your gods. You honor me. And for that, I will never again forget that you are here, and that you are mine."

The cheer that rose settled everything into place in his chest. And all that he'd been missing and searching for, all that suddenly appeared in front of him. All within reach.

Varya smiled and grabbed onto his neck, drawing him down so she could whisper in his ear, "Celebrate with your people. I need to bathe, eat, and sleep. But join me when you can, my king."

The old him would have said fuck the rest of them. And a part of him wanted to throw anyone aside that dared stand between him and Varya when she looked like that.

But another part of him wanted to enjoy the energy that filled the oasis with these people in it. They were alive and well and so damned thankful for it that he couldn't deny them a day with him. Neither did he wish to.

He reeled her in for a searing kiss that would likely plague the both of them for the rest of the day, and then he sent her on her way.

Greed indulged himself. His people. He fed them and gave them all the stores of alcohol in this place, but it didn't matter. Their lives were what he treasured now. Each individual person gave him a reason to be who he was, and to keep his kingdom flourishing as only he could. He'd make more trades, with more kingdoms, to bring food and wine to this place. He could replenish it.

Just a single one of his magical artifacts alone would have been enough for a full year of food to feed his kingdom. And now? He wasn't as afraid to part with it.

He did not know how long they celebrated because soon they were all so swept up in the celebration it was almost impossible to know what the time was. He knew his brother returned with the missing villagers and that started the festivities all over again, even though most of his people were barely able to walk in a straight line.

But he watched them with a sense of peace and happiness, grinning at Gluttony as his polished brother joined him.

"You look almost sweaty," Greed said, handing over a mug of ale that they'd found deep underneath his castle.

"Shut up," Gluttony muttered before downing the entire mug. "You have no idea how much of a pain in the ass it was to drag all those wounded people through the desert. And here you are, looking like you haven't bathed or done anything at all since you got back. Are you the king of this kingdom, Greed? At all?"

"I am." He gestured toward the people surrounding them. "This is my proof."

Gluttony snorted, rolled his eyes, and then stilled as he stared at Greed. "You're... different."

"Exhausted."

"Different." Gluttony frowned at him, his eyes skating over Greed's entire form before he snorted again. "Was this what it felt like when you'd seen Lust had changed? Here I was, thinking that both of you were idiots and yet I'm the one feeling jealous. You've got a new calling in life, brother. After a thousand years, I suspect that's a rather welcome change."

Had he?

He brushed a hand down his chest, not quite certain he had changed that much. But then he thought back to the voice in his head, the one that had urged him to come here and the one that had told him to stay while Varya went to bathe. The same voice that had told him he couldn't leave quite yet, not when there was more he could feed them and more drink to be had.

"Well, damn," he muttered before finishing his mug. "Here I was thinking it was love that had made Lust change. That he'd gone and found himself a woman who made him want to be better and I was the idiot for it."

"So what was it?"

A part of him didn't want to tell Gluttony. He wanted his brother to go through it all himself, just like Greed and Lust had. But the other part, ach, it saw Gluttony in a different light. "I needed to find a new use for myself. Stop being a greedy bastard who thought only about himself and I suppose..." He gestured to the crowd again. "They did it for me."

"That's disgusting."

"Probably." Greed clapped him on the back. "Enjoy your own merriment, brother. I have a woman to find."

"And to fuck if I know you well enough."

"You know me very well."

With a wink that felt like a promise, Greed started off to find his bride.

He had to wade through crowds of people, but thankfully they disappeared as he reached their more private areas. Even his guards had been aware that he'd want time alone with Varya.

Ivo and Morag stood in front of the stairwell that led to his private chambers. Their arms over their chests, their eyes slashing toward every single movement. He'd never been more grateful for either of them.

Walking almost in between them, he clapped his hands on their shoulders. "You both deserve a little time to enjoy yourselves as well. Run off with you."

"One of us should stay," Morag replied. "Just in case."

"No one is going to find us. Besides, you have a bed mate to find." He cast a glance toward Ivo and grinned. "And you have another one to chase, I imagine. Still fighting against every ounce of yourself to get her?"

Ivo tried so hard not to grin, but he gave it away immediately. "Ach, she's a pretty little thing with a heart of fire. I suspect it'll take quite a while before she bends to me."

"Enjoy the hunt, my brother."

And then he walked away from them, allowing them to make their own choice of what they wanted to do. Namely because he had a woman waiting for him. A woman with a heart of gold and beauty that stole his breath away.

She stood waiting for him in the doorway. She'd changed into a lovely, sheer nightgown that hid nothing from his view in the slightest. Leaning against the doorframe with the afternoon sun pouring over her body, he forgot how to speak at the sight of her.

"Are you finally here for me?" she asked, clearly amused that he'd gotten so distracted. "I've been waiting for hours, demon king."

He could have dropped to his knees then and there. She was so beautiful and so perfect for him that it was a distraction.

He wanted... Her. Just her.

And so he would have her.

Chapter 47

She didn't recognize the look in his eyes as he stalked into the room. Though it was still her Greed in front of her, she also thought perhaps this was someone else. This was... more.

He looked at her like a man possessed. Like she was the most important thing in his life, and right now? His attention was only on her. She wasn't sure if she wanted to be the only one that he was focused on, though. All of a sudden, it seemed like a lot of pressure.

"Greed," she said, walking backward as he followed her. "Can we talk for a moment?"

"There will be time for talking. That time is not right now."

"Ah." A thrill of pleasure zinged through her body. Those eyes watched every single move she made. From the deep breath that she pulled in to the flutter of her pulse at the base of her neck.

She felt so beautiful when he looked at her like that.

And suddenly she wasn't sure she could do this right now. She'd been covered in blood the last time he'd seen her, and they had both murdered an entire group of people. She'd almost been... she couldn't even think the word still, and what if that made him want her less?

What if everything was different between the two of them because she'd revealed everything to him? Not just assumed he understood when she vaguely hinted at their actions. She'd admitted everything and he might very well feel it made her lesser. Or tainted. Or...

"Varya," he murmured, his voice deep and soothing.

"Greed?"

"You're going to lie down on that bed, belly on the thicker pillow. You're going to hike that pretty little skirt up, and then you're going to lie there and take whatever I give like the good girl you are. Understood?"

Oh.

Yes. Very much so.

She found her tongue a little tied after that, so she spun around and made her way to the plush bed. She knew the exact pillow he was talking about. The one that would hold her hips up so high that there was no way to hide from him. Not from his gaze, not from his desires, nothing at all.

And yet, even though nerves still ran rampant through her mind, she found her hands gathering up the material of her nightgown. She tugged it up higher, pulling it over her hips and then lying down onto the pillow that was so soft it almost made her nerves go away. The silk slid over her cheek as she arranged herself exactly like he'd asked.

He let out a low groan that went straight between her legs. Wetness pooled there, and she could feel her thighs sliding over each other so easily it was almost embarrassing.

"You look so pretty." His hand came down hard, spanking her right side. She knew there would be a handprint left there and wasn't that what she'd come to expect from Greed?

He wanted to mark her now even though he'd already seen his handprint on her countless times before.

He gathered her hair up in one hand, arching her back so he could slide his lips along her cheek and down to her neck. "Did they succeed in touching you this time?"

She shuddered at the thought. "No. I killed him before he could do anything."

Another low growl that did things to her insides like no other sound. "Good girl. Then, if you're still interested, I plan on marking you everywhere on this tight little body so that I can feel like you're really here. Alive, in my arms, and mine."

Varya moaned. "Yes, Greed."

That was all he needed to hear, apparently. He let her drop a little hard, but she loved it all the same. Spread out on his bed, breathless, so turned on she could barely think straight. He went to that wall, oh the wall, where his hidden toys were and she already wasn't sure what he would bring back.

But it was the sight of the flogger that almost made her delirious with lust. That beautiful instrument that had already given her so much inspiration for what she wanted from him.

And she wanted. She wanted him so much it hurt.

He walked behind her, his eyes on her the whole time as he trailed the leather straps up her back. "We'll start slow, my treasure. I wouldn't want to break you."

Varya didn't even try to stop the snarl that came out of her mouth.

"I am not some weakling, Greed. Hit me. Fuck me. Make me yours."

The sharp crack of the flogger across her cheeks made her arch, but the pain was so delicious, so right. It made her heart race in her chest and her thighs clench together.

"I didn't say you could speak," he said quietly, tracing the end of the flogger along her spine.

"I'll speak when I wish."

"You'll speak when you're spoken to and no more than that." Again, another crack. This time a little harder and surely leaving red lines down the backs of her thighs. But it was perfect.

It was them.

Everything about this was them. The mild brutality of it, the push and pull for dominance. The desire to build up all this passion, need, and...

"Greed," she whispered against the sheets, already wanting him so much that she would beg. "I almost died. I thought I lost you and I fucking need you. Now. Inside me."

He only barely relented. "Here?"

His fingers traced along her slick folds. Those thick fingers had her rocking back against them, but he never let her impale herself on him. Instead, he played. Toyed. Driving her mad with need, until he asked, "What do you want?"

"Hit me," she replied. "And fuck me at the same time or I'll do it myself."

"Ach, love. We're not there yet."

And then she heard twin thuds hit the ground behind her. She had just enough time to send up a prayer to the gods that he did what she wanted, and then she shrieked as his tongue replaced his fingers.

That wicked mouth did things to her that no mouth should. She shook and shivered against his touch and then arched up with a curse as he slid the handle of the flogger inside her. He worked her with gentle strokes, bringing her up to a frenzy with his lips, hands, and tongue. He pushed her further and further to the very edge of madness, not nearly giving her what she wanted, but close... close...

He wrenched the flogger out of her and stood. Varya whimpered. She'd been so close and he was the one who had stopped.

But then he slid inside her, that massive cock spreading her wide and forcing her to take him. He slammed into her, forcing her body to stretch around him, and then she was screaming. Coming hard around his cock because that was what she had wanted for so many nights now, and finally he was inside her.

He stayed perfectly still while she came, surrounded by her and buried to the very root. He let her have her moment and endured it with her until she was shaking and limp beneath him.

Then he leaned down, wrenched up her head, and whispered, "You said to hit you while I fucked you, Varya, and I intend to do just that."

He let her go and then the crack of the flogger came again. Spreading over her ass cheeks and sending hot fire up her spine. He slammed into her again, crack, then pulled out and slammed again. Each time harder, more furious, more unstoppable than the time before, and she couldn't even think.

They existed in this bubble of pleasure and pain and torment and she wanted to tell him that he was an asshole, but she also didn't want him to stop for even a second. He was devouring her body and soul and it was so perfect that she couldn't think past the slide of his cock inside her, the slap of flesh on flesh, and the blistering orgasm that surprised her again.

Her entire body clenched hard around his. She hissed out a long breath, incapable of even making a noise as he slammed home, harder than ever before, buried so deep it almost hurt.

Then she felt him coming inside her and spraying her with everything she'd wanted.

Both of them were breathing hard by the time they were finished. She was probably decorated in red stripes and didn't care in the slightest. He was still dirty from the journey, likely still covered in blood, and she had never felt more like the treasure he'd called her.

Because in this moment, she was the gift for the avenging warlord who had protected his people. She was his reward and damn if she didn't love every second of this moment.

"Greed," she whispered, tilting her head to accept his kiss. "That was…"

"Exactly how it should always be between us," he filled in as he slumped to her side. He slid out of her and she hated the sudden emptiness of it.

If she could keep him inside her forever, she would.

Breathing hard, she stared up at the ceiling and tried to get her bearings. She'd wanted to talk to him about something, hadn't she? Wasn't there something they needed to talk about?

Ah. Right.

She rolled onto her side so she could look at him, watching his face as though she had never seen it before.

He wore an expression of peace that made her so happy to see. Like he was finally at ease, with no worries or fears or desires.

"Everything's different now, isn't it?" she whispered.

"Did that feel any different?"

"Well, no." She rolled her eyes at his grin. "Greed."

"What?"

"That's the only thing that doesn't feel different. You're here with the rest of my town, and somehow not angry that they are taking so much from you. Food, time, likely stealing from you as well. I don't understand it, and I think you do." Varya watched him to see if there was any flicker of truth in his eyes after she said that. "Right?"

He palmed her hip, gently rubbing the red marks he'd left that had curled around to her front. "Do you remember what I told you about my brother? The one who had found his new bride?"

"Yes." She hadn't forgotten the story of the poor woman who had nearly died. That was why she had a spirit inside her as well.

"Good. The whole point of that story was for me to tell you that a demon king changed who he was because of a woman. And I had thought…" He stared into her eyes and she saw something else in them. "I had thought that falling in love with a woman would be the answer. But then I fell in love with you and I was still the greedy fucker that I'd always been."

"And still are," she added with a grin.

"Mildly." He shrugged. "It's part of who I am. However, I realized I am not like Lust. I didn't need you to change, nor did Lust need Selene. We both had to be realistic about who we were and want to change for ourselves."

She frowned. "Are you saying you changed?"

"I did." Greed nodded and then slid his hand all the way up her body to cup her jaw. "Partly for you. And partly for me."

"What… changed?" She could already sense it, though. There was something about him that wasn't her Greed. It was more.

"I don't want you to call me anything else. But a spirit, when exposed to certain circumstances, to differences in their lives or sometimes horrible things, they change. Just like people and emotions."

He swallowed hard, and she saw a shadow of doubt in his gaze. Almost as though he didn't quite want to tell her. "I think I might be Benevolence now."

"Benevolence?" she whispered. "Really?"

"It doesn't mean I cannot feel the original part of me. I will still be just as greedy for every part of you, pain, pleasure, love..." He stroked his fingers through her hair and tugged her closer with a low growl. "And I also know, without a doubt, that I will waste far too much time between those thighs, treasure. Because I want you to be happy here. With me and our people."

Varya licked her lips and then grinned. "I think I can be happy with you forever, Greed. No matter what kind of spirit you are."

And as she sank into his kiss, she thought... yes. This was perfect.

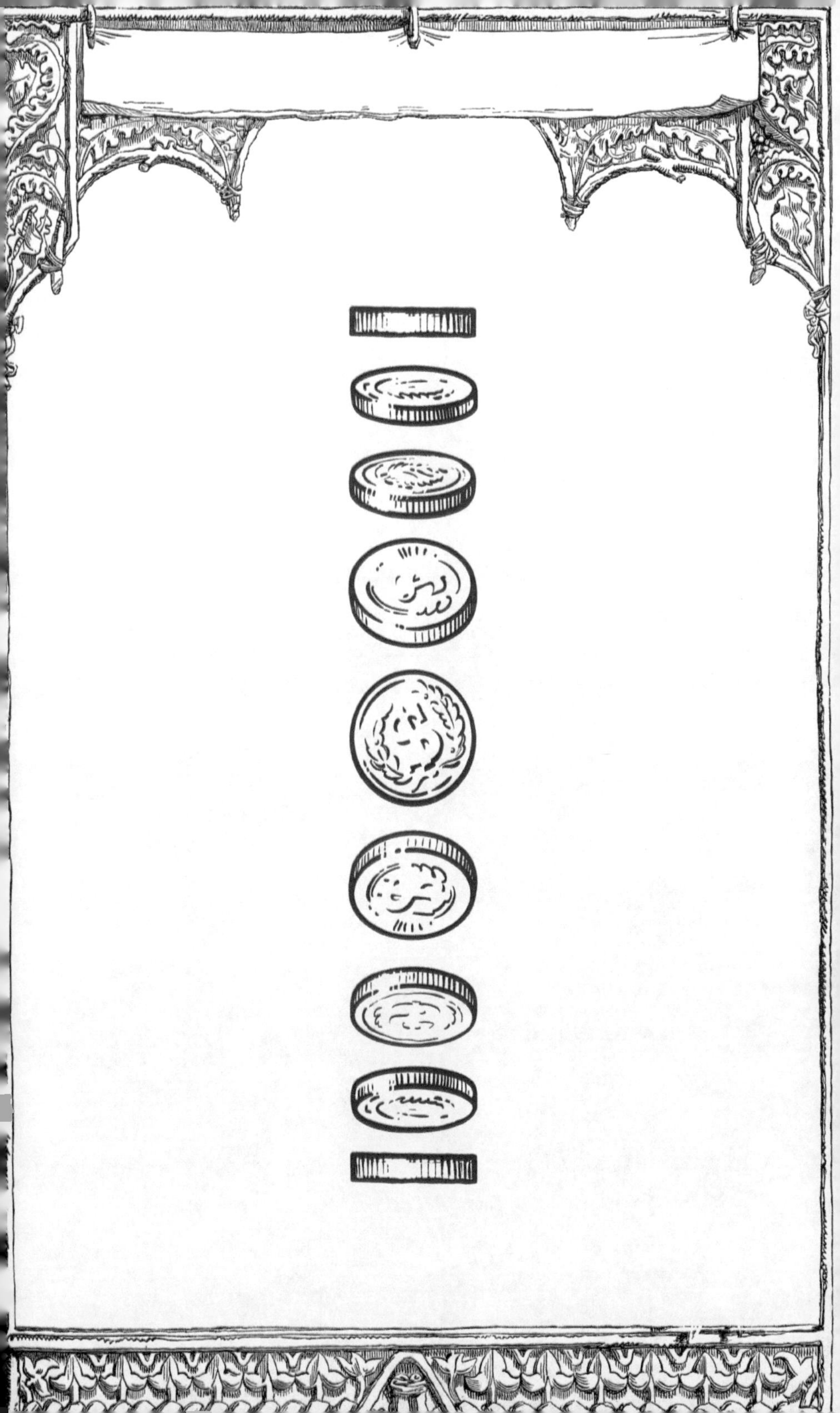

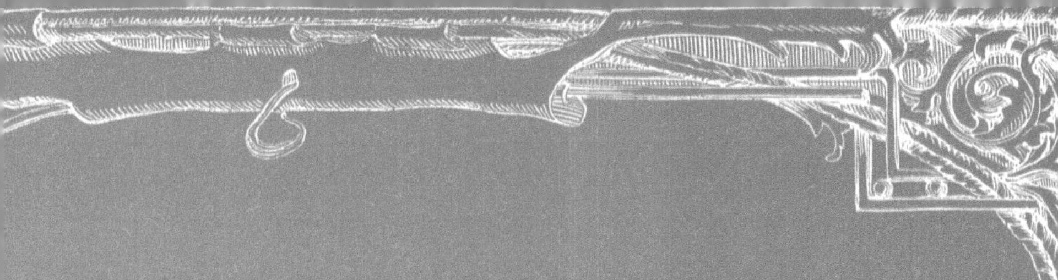

Chapter 48

Greed leaned on the fence that surrounded his training yard, watching the flashing of blades. The lithe bodies whirled in front of him, two warriors at battle not with play swords but the real thing.

Normally he wouldn't let any of his soldiers practice with real blades, but these two? He trusted they were capable of avoiding each other. And if they weren't, then they'd be annoyed enough with themselves that he wouldn't have to warn them again.

Footsteps approached, light and far too easy to be any of his people. And then his brother leaned against the railing with him.

Gluttony looked a little better, with a slight burn on his cheeks. His skin hadn't darkened with all the sun exposure, but at least he appeared a little more alive these days. Less like a corpse. More like an actual person, at least.

"Spoke with Wrath," his brother said, eyes on the two warriors in the ring. "He said it's all right for me to head home now. Apparently, it's all died down enough that I don't have to worry too much."

"What did he do to make it all die down?"

Gluttony shrugged. "I never know what Wrath does. It's a waste of time to question his methods."

Or to question the man himself.

Grunting, he shook his head. "I don't like it. Seems strange that Wrath would go through all that trouble just to leave you on your own afterward."

"I don't think he was trying to steal from me," Gluttony murmured, but his eyes said otherwise. "I don't think there's anything in my kingdom that he particularly wants, but... I'm not sure. I don't think there's anyway for any of us to be sure. Part of me wonders if he's more interested in the spell your Horde had devised. You're sure you're all right with me taking it home?"

"I don't know what to do with it. You've always been more magically inclined than me," Greed replied, then ran a hand through his hair. "I don't know what the right answer is here. All I know is that I have to focus on my own kingdom and my own people for a little while. I've neglected them for long enough."

"Indeed." Gluttony straightened and then clapped a hand to Greed's shoulder. "Keep an eye on that woman of yours. I think she's more likely to stab you in the heart than she is to let you leave her room alive."

A blade soared through the air, but at the last second, Gluttony grabbed it. Red stained his palm as he squeezed the metal a little too hard, but the blood dripping on the sand was only more payment for the desert looking out for them.

Greed crossed his arms over his chest and raised a brow. "I don't think she liked you saying that, brother."

The two women in the arena had stopped their fighting. Even Morag was drenched in sweat, and she said his queen had gotten much better in her fighting skills than before. Varya enjoyed practicing every single day with the other spirit influenced person, and she'd gotten even closer to both Morag and Ivo.

Well, when they even saw Ivo now.

Greed had released him to go live with his redheaded beloved. Far away from Gluttony's wandering eyes and in one of the few places where she could grow food.

"Go away, Gluttony!" Varya called out as she sauntered toward them.

His eyes trailed over the lovely muscles that rippled across her entire body. He lingered on the drops of sweat that slid underneath her shirt and between her breasts. The long length of her legs made his mouth water and the sway of her hips had him seeing stars. Ach, but he loved this woman.

Would it ever end? The wanting her?

Probably not. Because she was looking at him with the same eyes right now. Those eyes that said, I need you, I want you, and I will never let you go.

The feeling was mutual, even though their world had gotten a little bigger as of late.

Gluttony grumbled under his breath, "I intend to leave if there wasn't always a crowd of people here. I preferred it when it was just servants and Greed."

"Yes, well, you haven't learned how to temper yourself yet,"

Greed scolded. Then he ducked underneath the railing and strode up to his wife. "Go away, Gluttony."

If he noticed that Varya gave a wild grin to his brother over his shoulder, he pretended he hadn't. Because once he had her in his arms, his lips on her neck and her hips grinding against his, nothing else mattered.

He'd found home in the arms of this woman, and he would never let her go.

531

Follow me on socials or Amazon to keep your eye out for the next book. And for all you vampire lovers, I'm just saying, Gluttony has a... taste for the extreme.

ACKNOWLEDGEMENTS

This book would not be what it is without my team of wonderful beta readers, and all the people who gave their thoughts/advice/opinions along the way. Your help is and always will be absolutely invaluable.

So from my heart to yours, I hope you enjoyed this new series and are getting excited for Gluttony ;)

ABOUT THE AUTHOR

Emma Hamm is a small town girl on a blueberry field in Maine. She writes stories that remind her of home, of fairytales, and of myths and legends that make her mind wander.

She can be found by the fireplace with a cup of tea and her two Maine Coon cats dipping their paws into the water without her knowing.

For more updates, join my newsletter!
www.emmahamm.com